Fantastic tales of Nothing

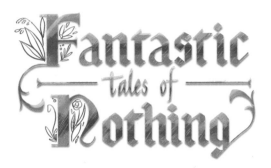

Katherine Tegen Books is an imprint of HarperCollins Publishers.

Fantastic Tales of Nothing

For the endless hours of silly role-playing
games, growing friendship, bad jokes, and
ongoing inspiration. This book wouldn't
exist without you and your annoying
perfectionism. Thanks for Nothing.

—Ale

To my best friend, who told me not to
dedicate it to her, then pulled the reverse
Uno card on me. May we wander into
more worlds beyond Nothing together.

—Fanny

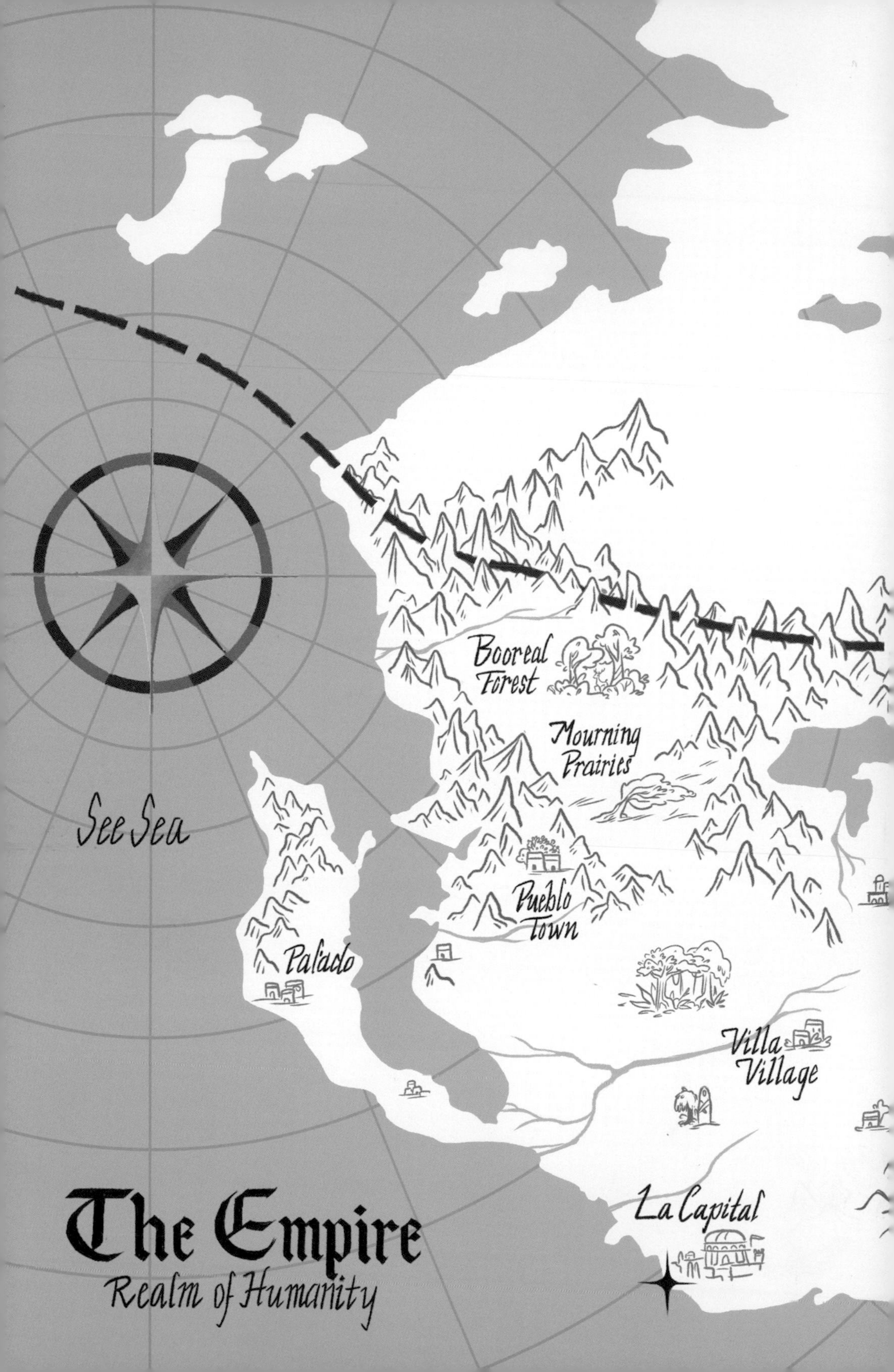
Booreal Forest
Mourning Prairies
See Sea
Pueblo Town
Palado
Villa Village
La Capital
The Empire
Realm of Humanity

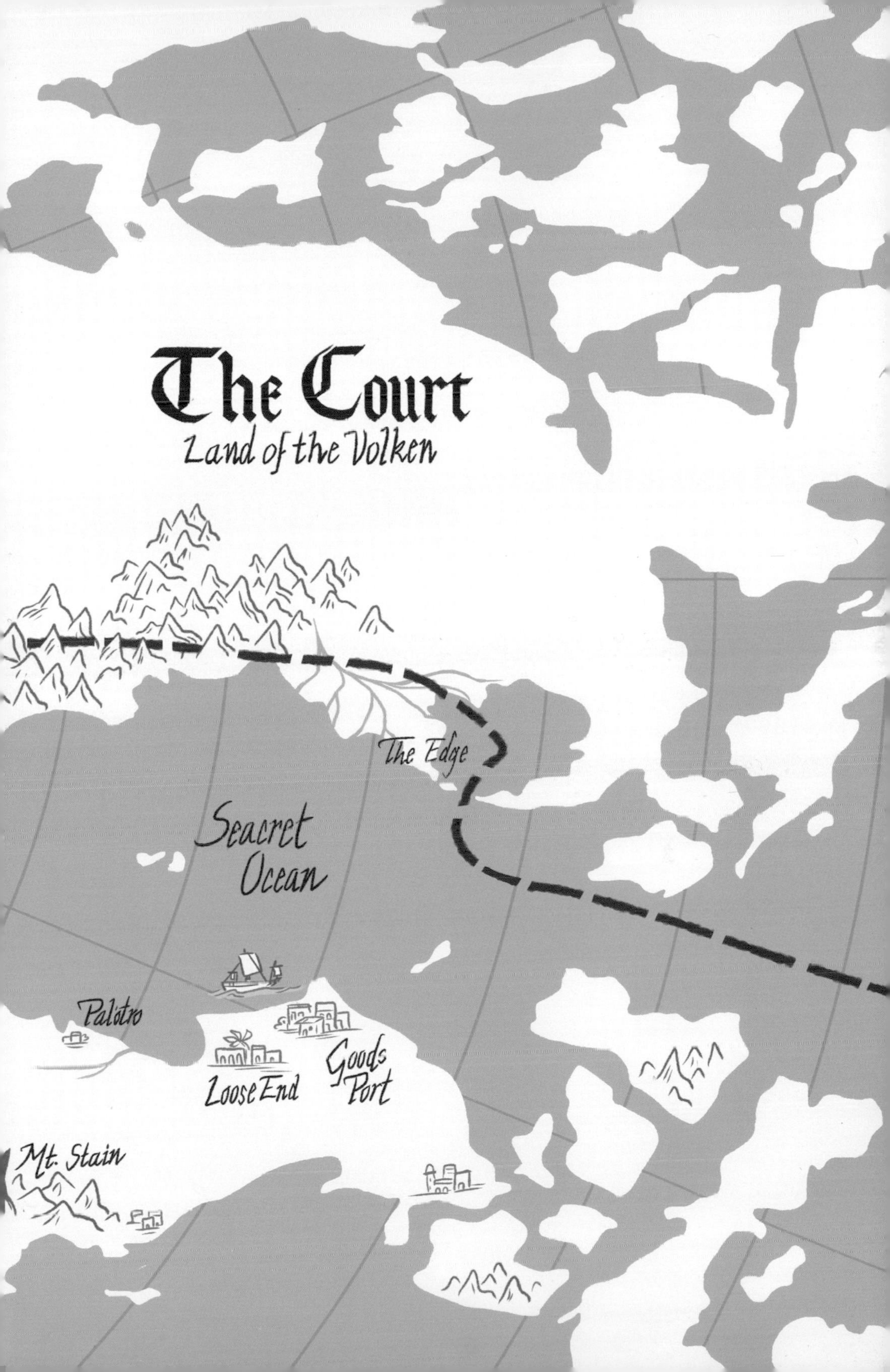
The Court
Land of the Volken
The Edge
Seacret
Ocean
Palótro
Loose End
Goods
Port
Mt. Stain

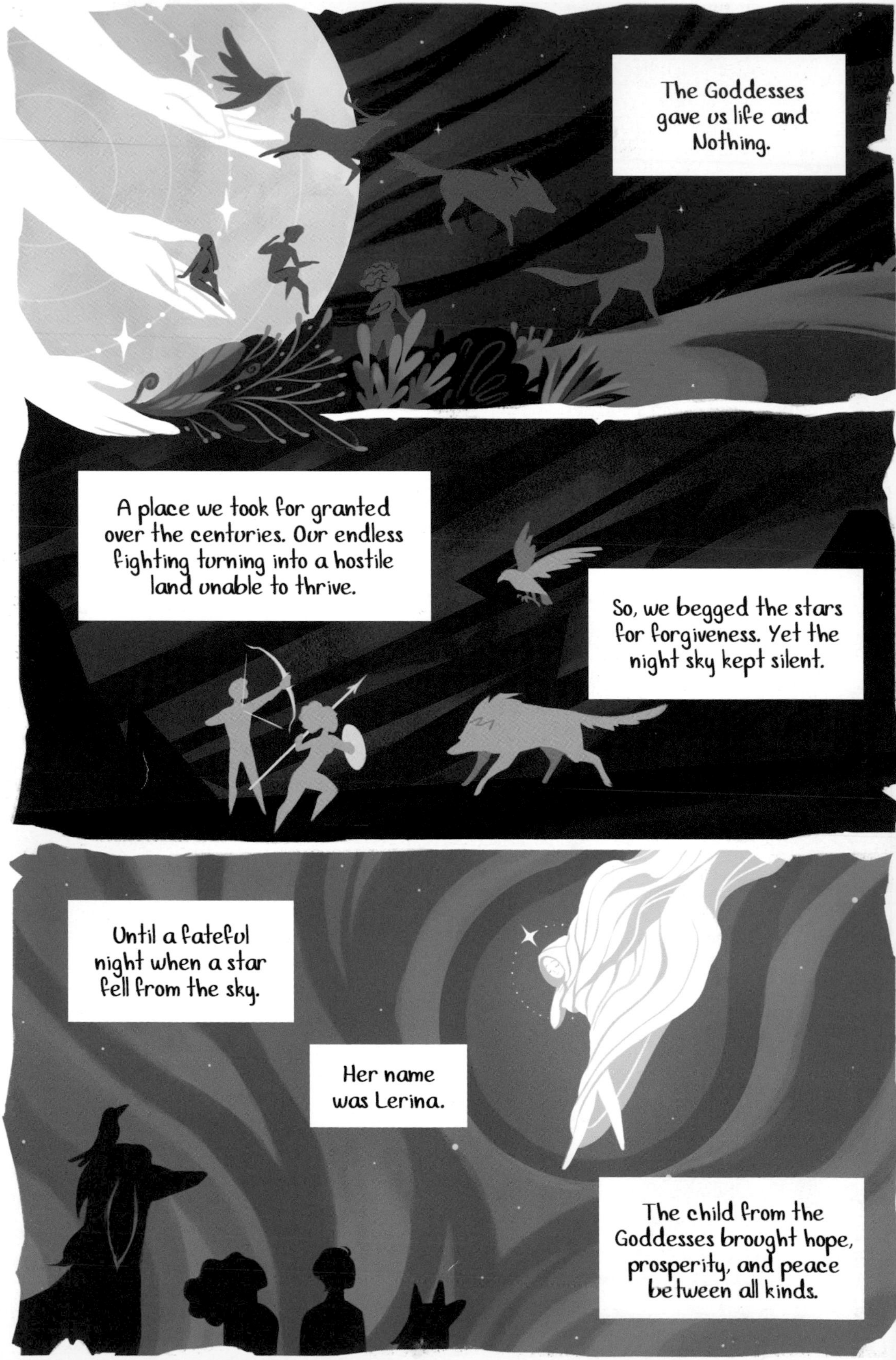
The Goddesses gave us life and Nothing.
A place we took for granted over the centuries. Our endless fighting turning into a hostile land unable to thrive.
So, we begged the stars for forgiveness. Yet the night sky kept silent.
Until a fateful night when a star fell from the sky.
Her name was Lerina.
The child from the Goddesses brought hope, prosperity, and peace between all kinds.

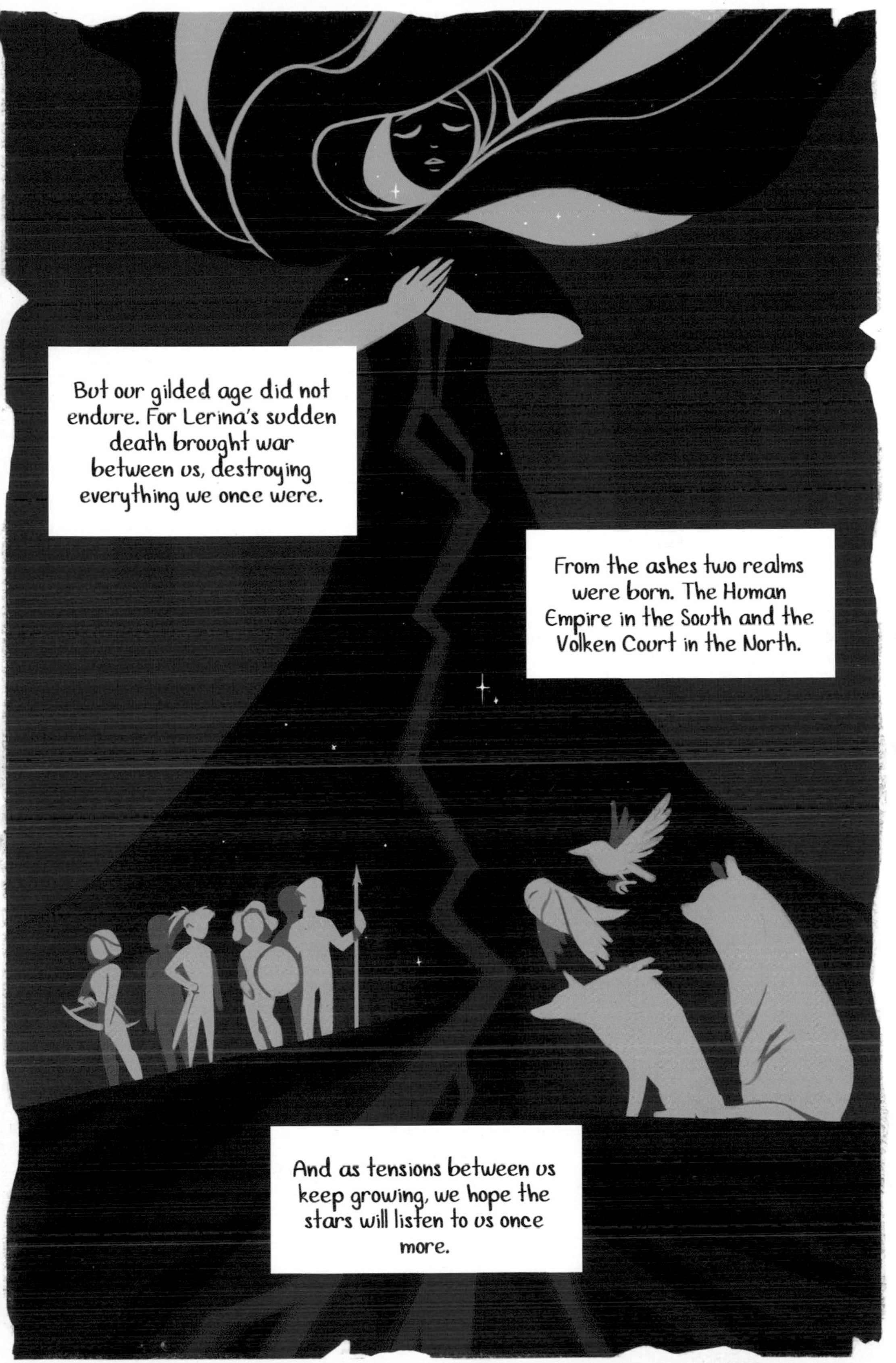
But our gilded age did not endure. For Lerina's sudden death brought war between us, destroying everything we once were.
From the ashes two realms were born. The Human Empire in the South and the Volken Court in the North.
And as tensions between us keep growing, we hope the stars will listen to us once more.

Alejandra Green & Fanny Rodriguez

Fantastic tales of Nothing

KATHERINE TEGEN BOOKS
An Imprint of HarperCollins Publishers

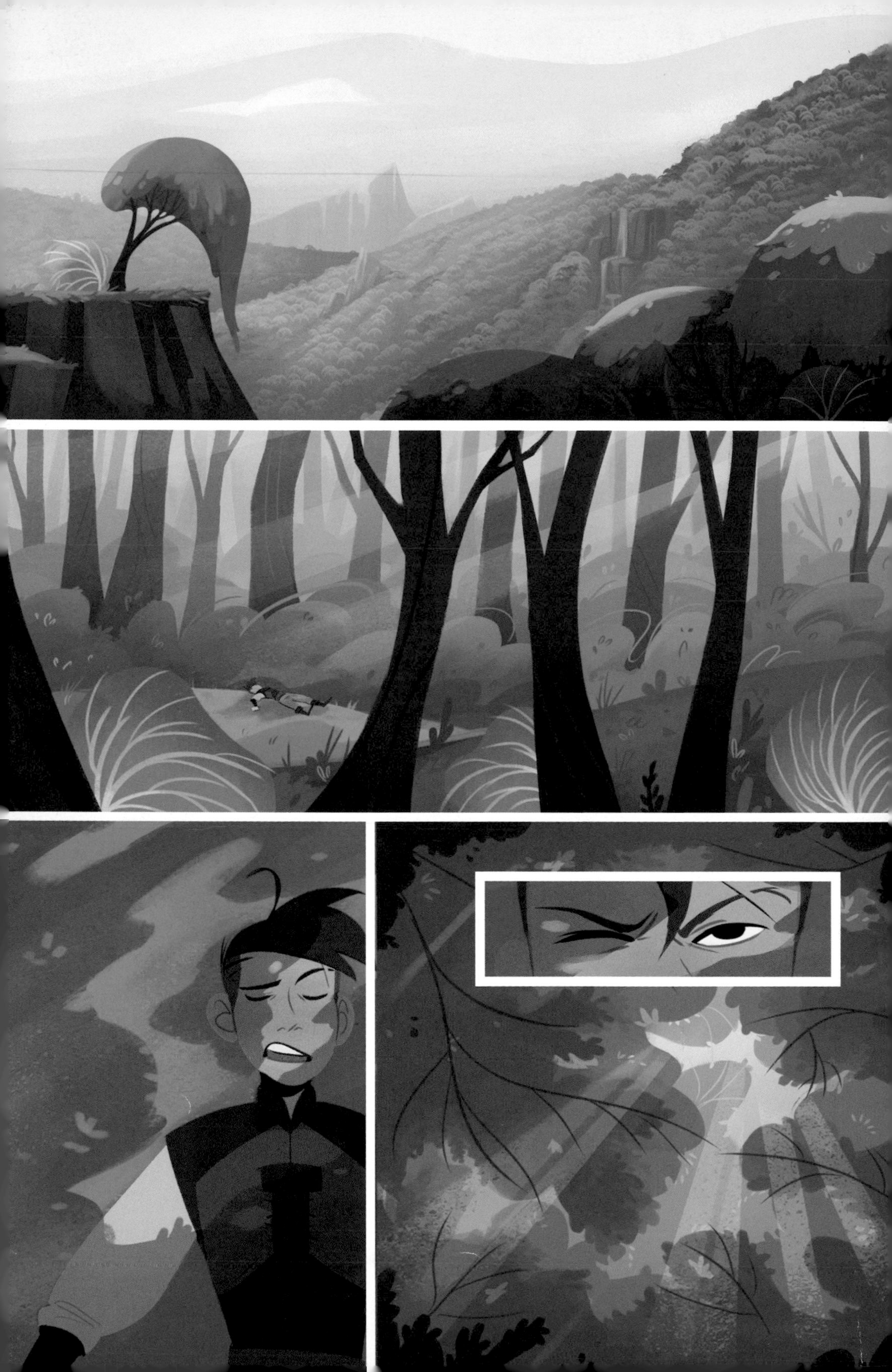

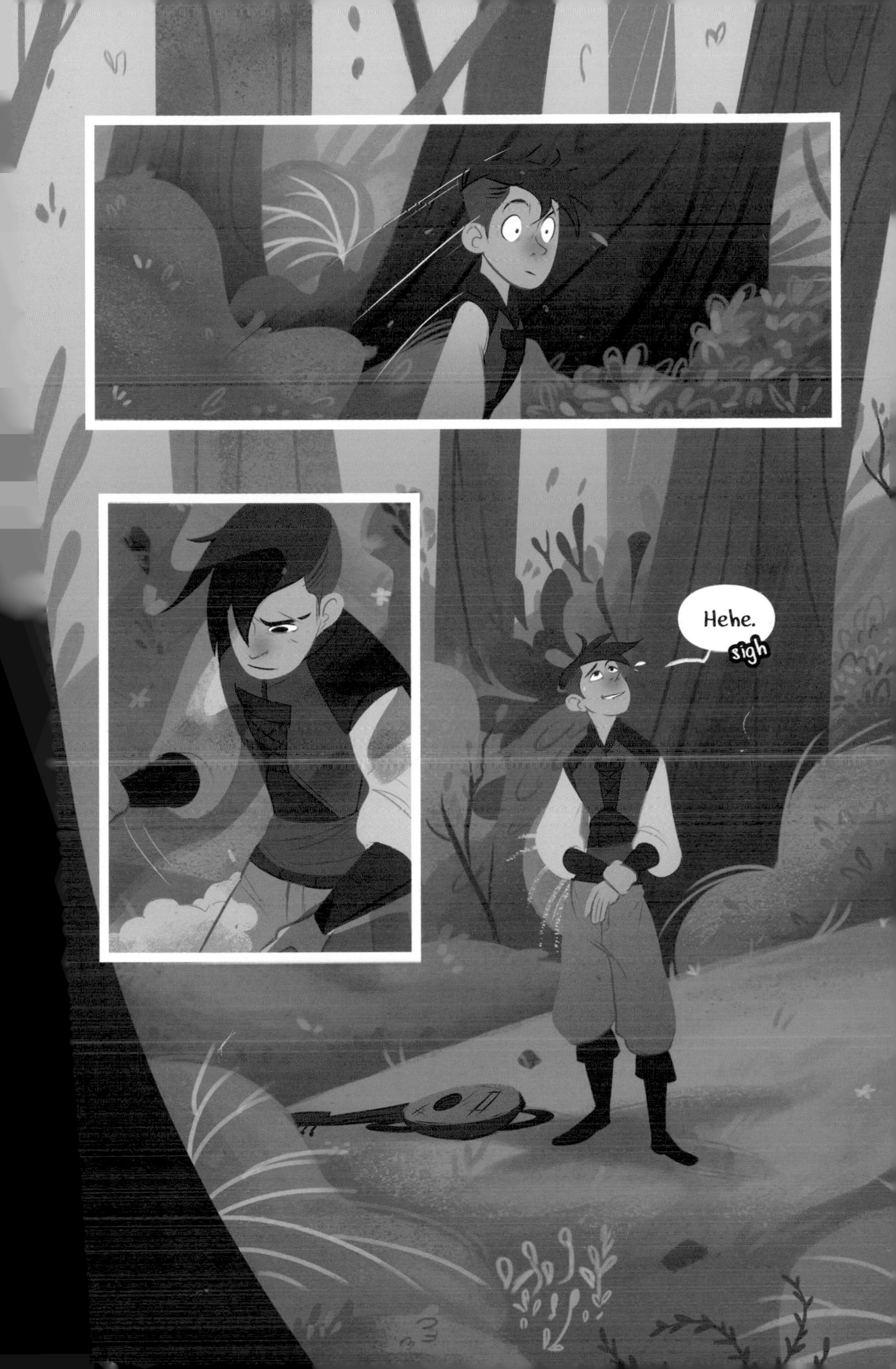
Hehe.
sigh

Chapter 1
Is This the Everafter?

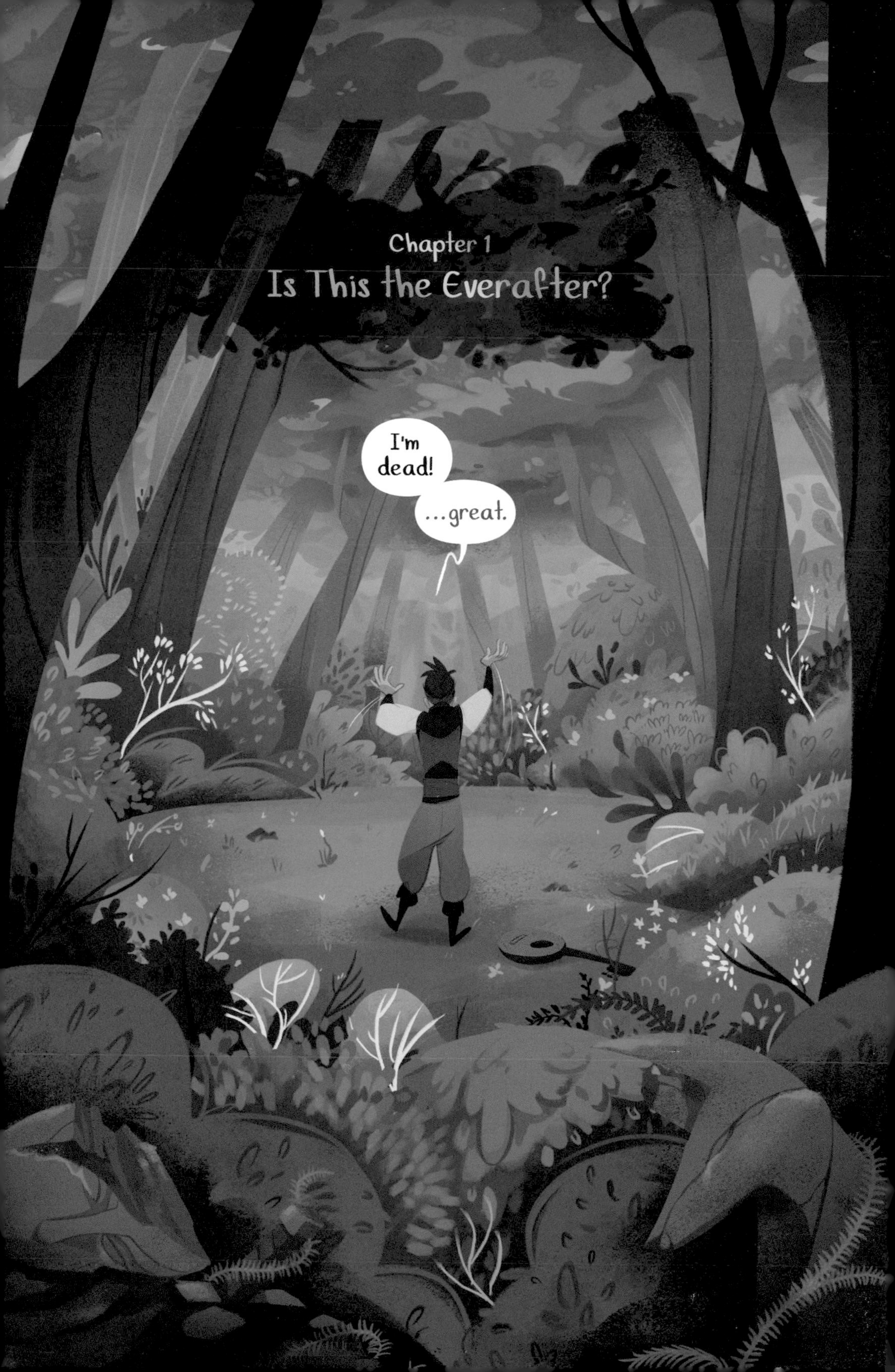
I'm dead!
...great.

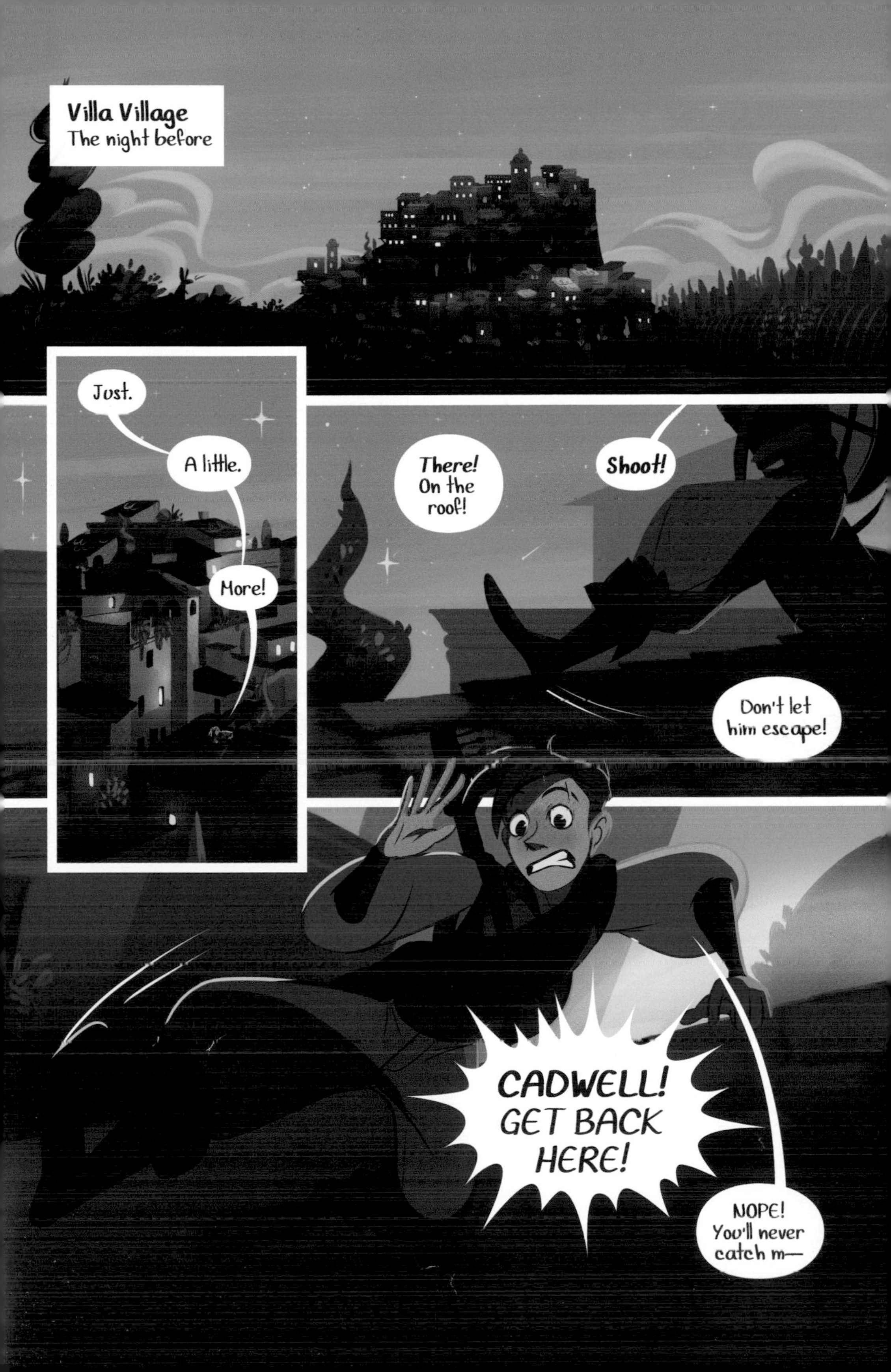
Villa Village
The night before
Just.
A little.
More!
There! On the roof!
Shoot!
Don't let him escape!
CADWELL! GET BACK HERE!
NOPE! You'll never catch m—

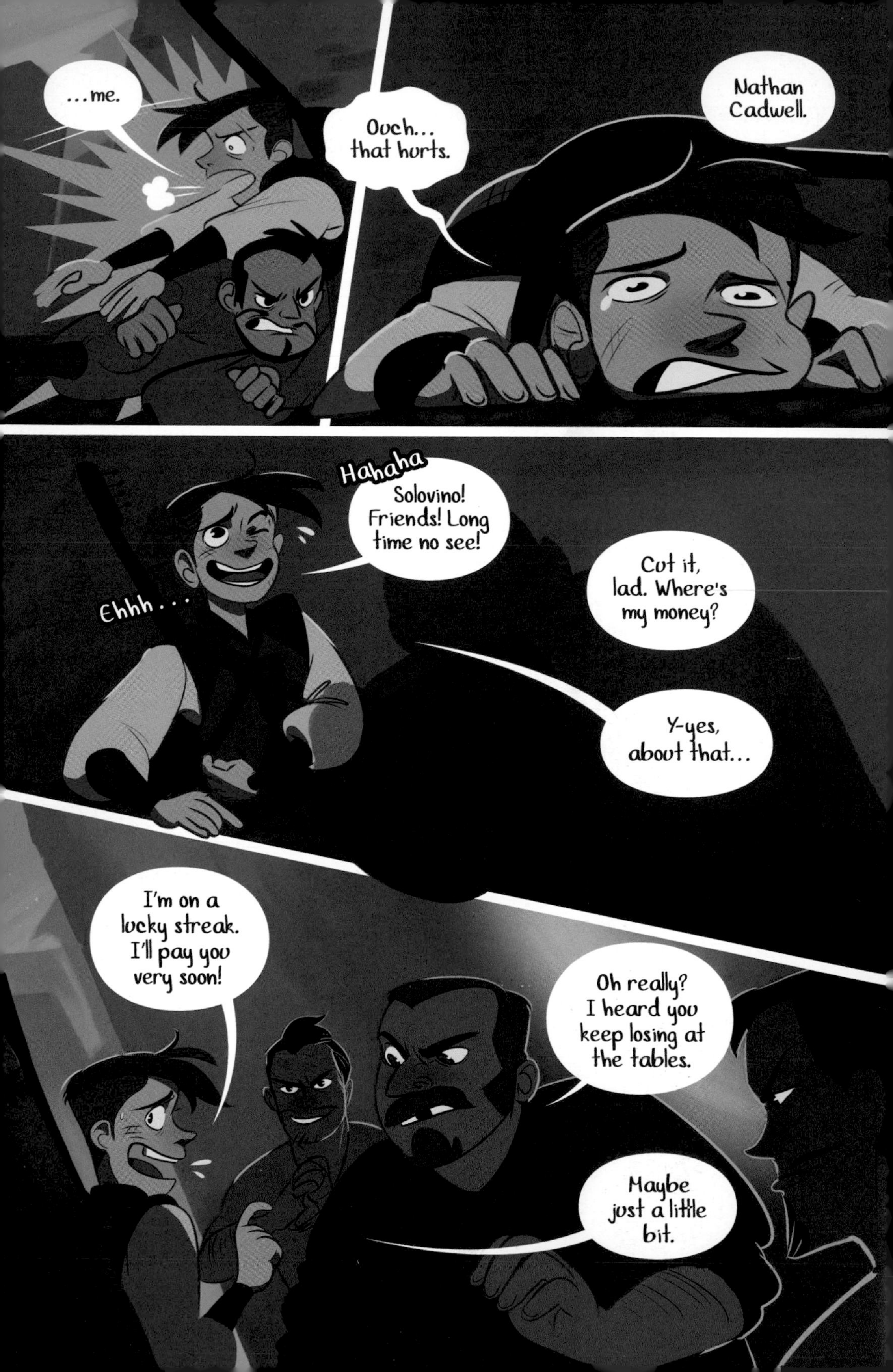

...me.
Ouch... that hurts.
Nathan Cadwell.
Hahaha
Solovino! Friends! Long time no see!
Ehhh...
Cut it, lad. Where's my money?
Y-yes, about that...
I'm on a lucky streak. I'll pay you very soon!
Oh really? I heard you keep losing at the tables.
Maybe just a little bit.

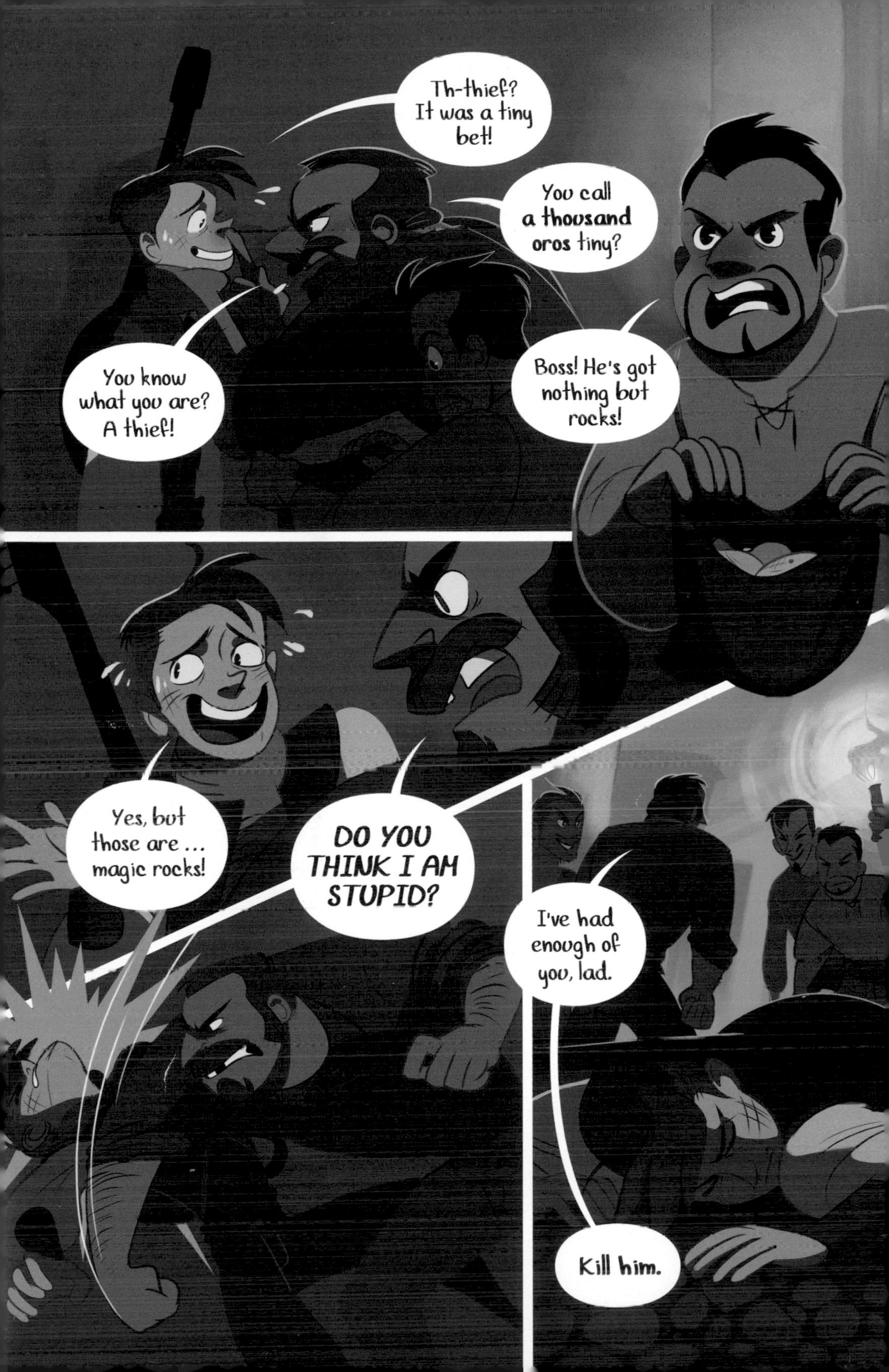
Th-thief? It was a tiny bet!
You call a thousand oros tiny?
You know what you are? A thief!
Boss! He's got nothing but rocks!
Yes, but those are ... magic rocks!
DO YOU THINK I AM STUPID?
I've had enough of you, lad.
Kill him.

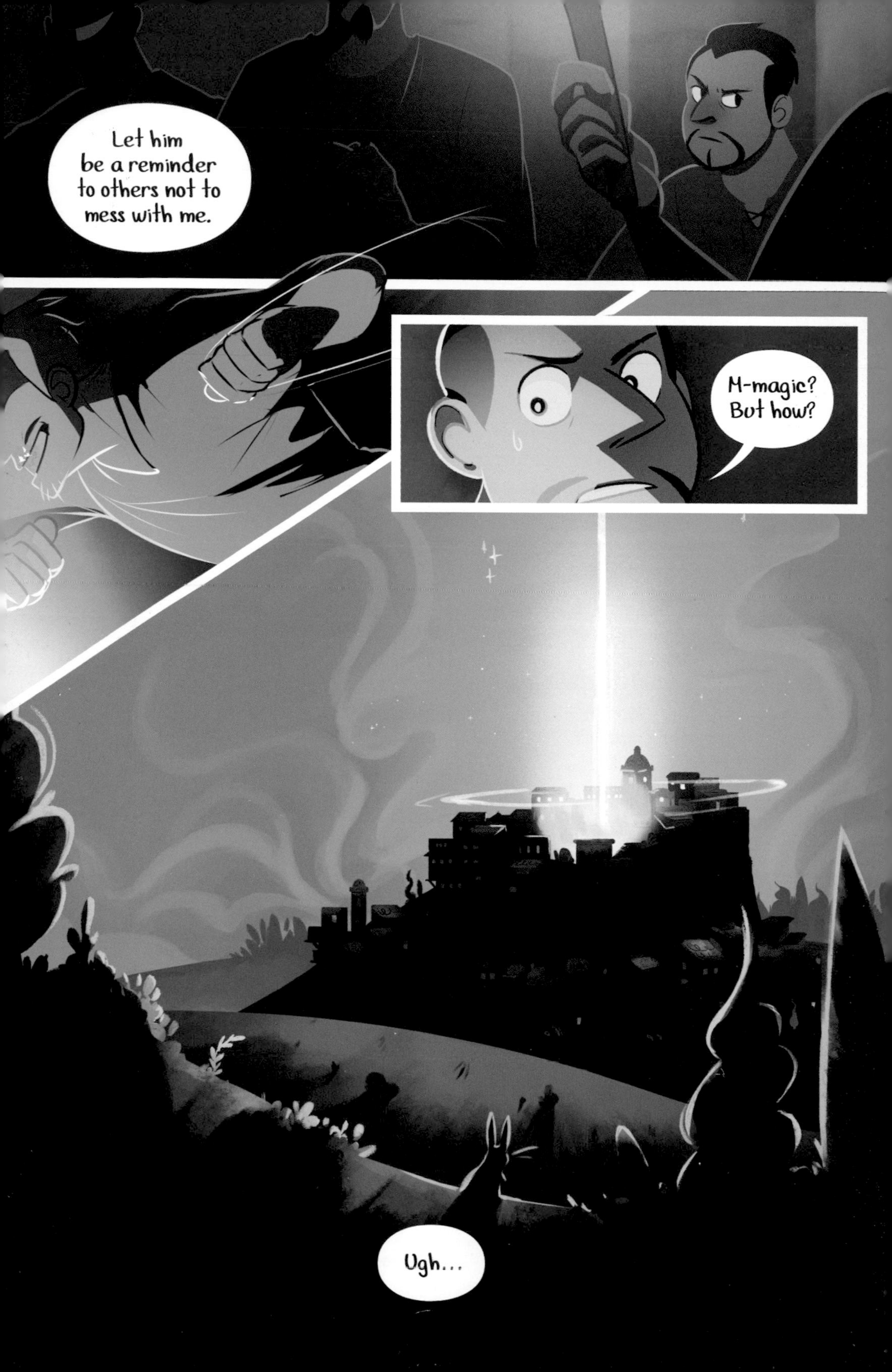
Let him be a reminder to others not to mess with me.
M-magic? But how?
Ugh...

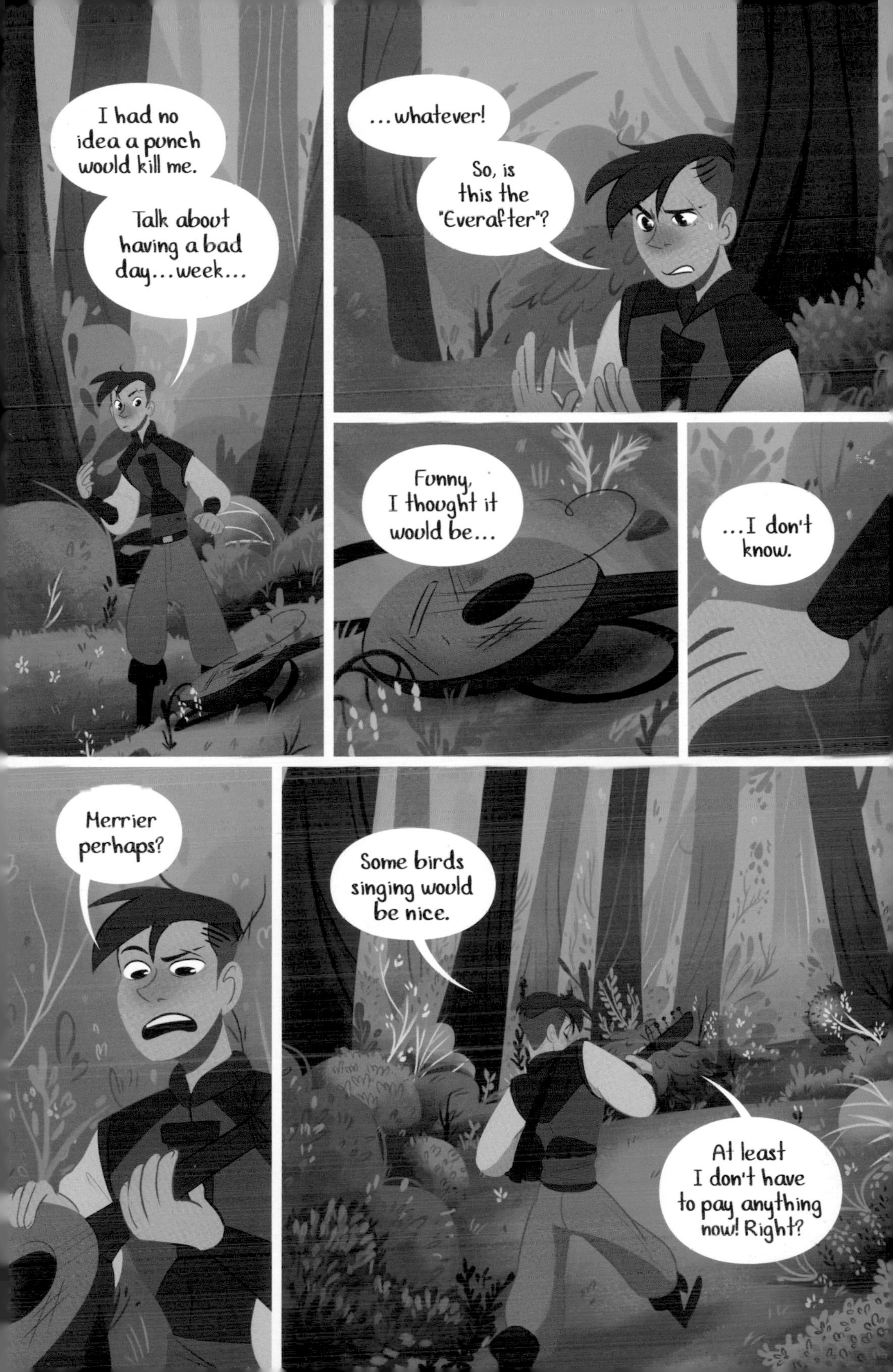
I had no idea a punch would kill me.
Talk about having a bad day...week...
...whatever!
So, is this the "Everafter"?
Funny, I thought it would be...
...I don't know.
Merrier perhaps?
Some birds singing would be nice.
At least I don't have to pay anything now! Right?

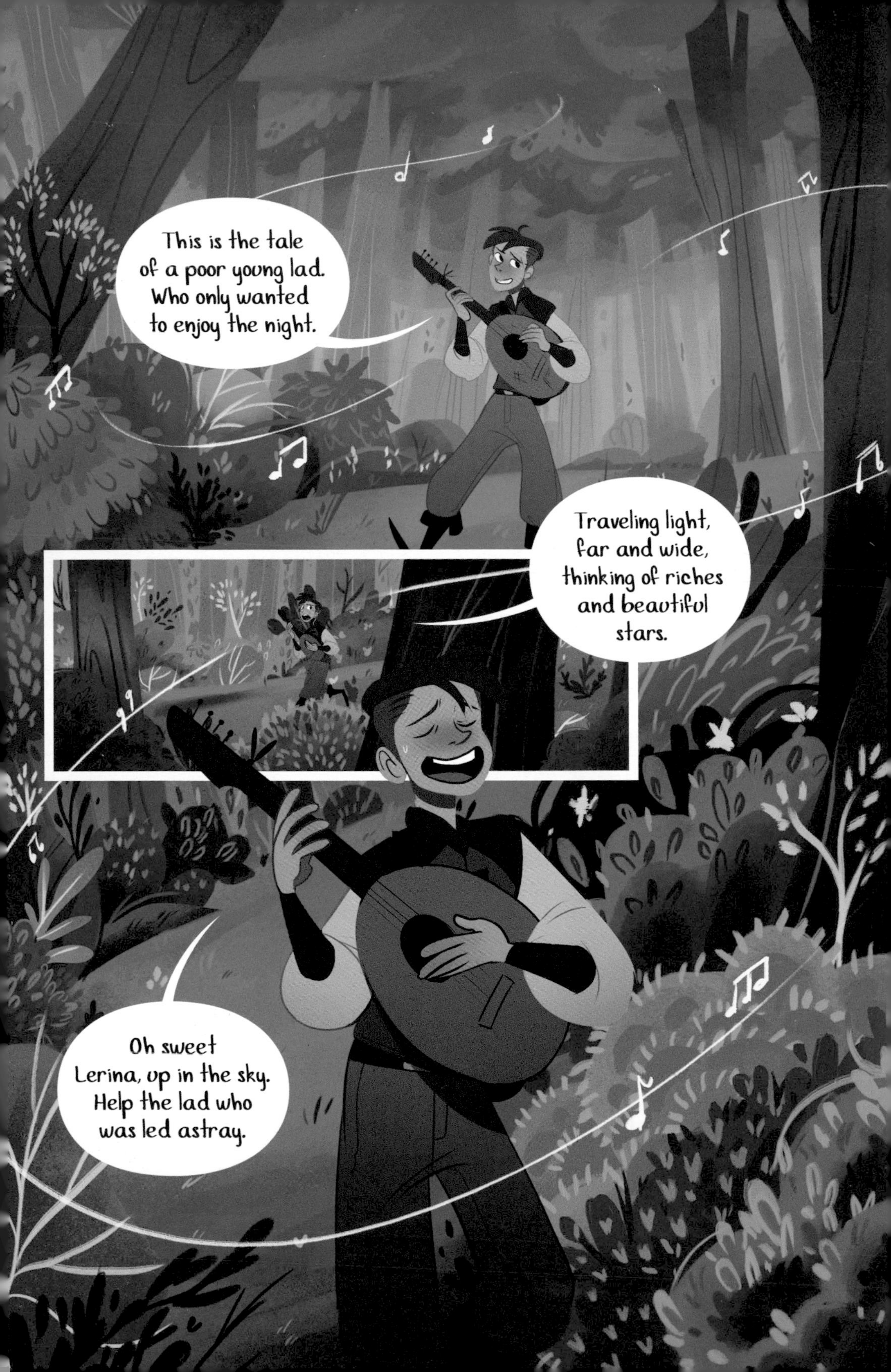
This is the tale of a poor young lad. Who only wanted to enjoy the night.
Traveling light, far and wide, thinking of riches and beautiful stars.
Oh sweet Lerina, up in the sky. Help the lad who was led astray.

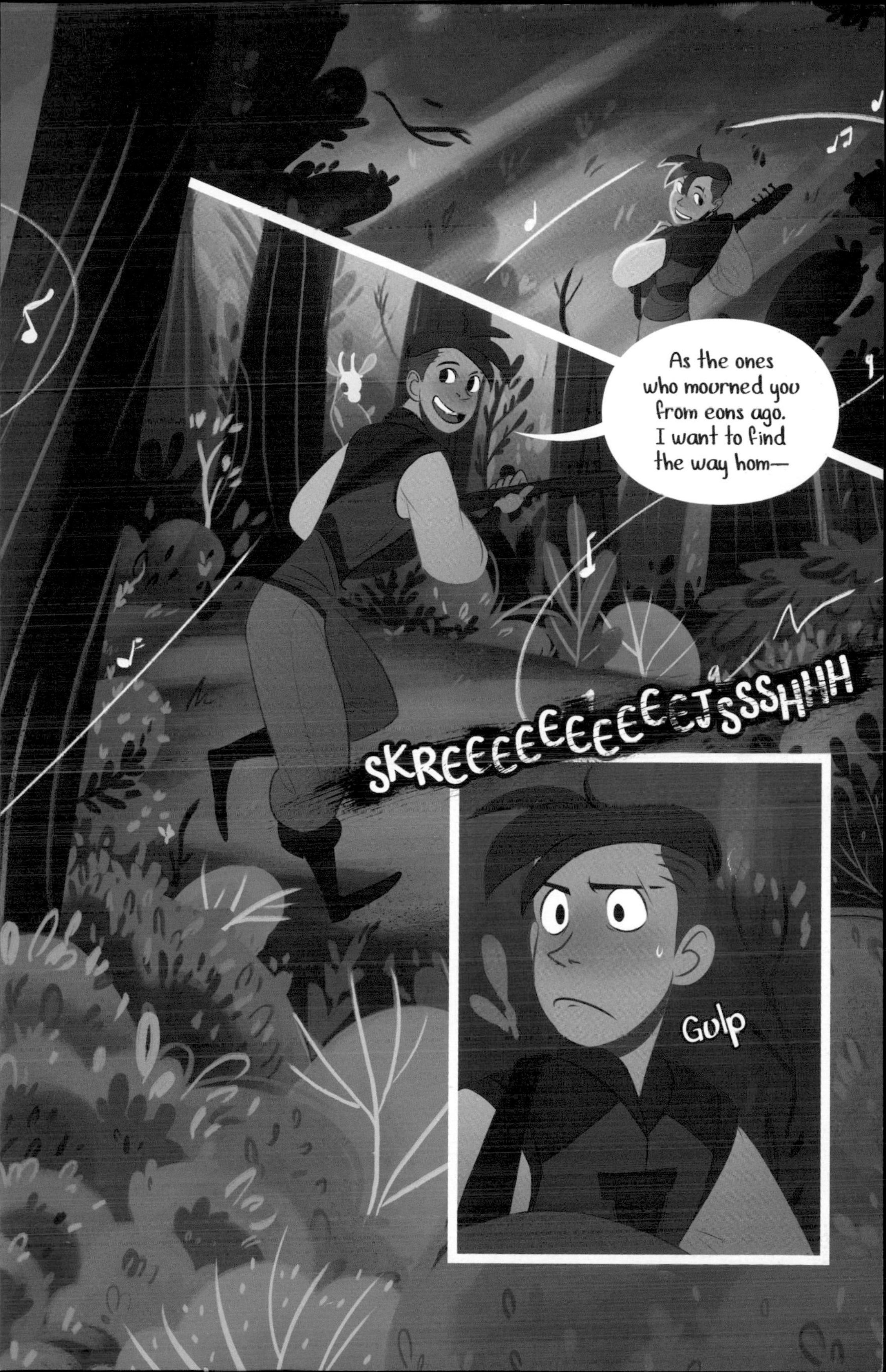
As the ones who mourned you from eons ago. I want to find the way hom—
SKREEEEEEEEEEEJSSSHHH
Gulp

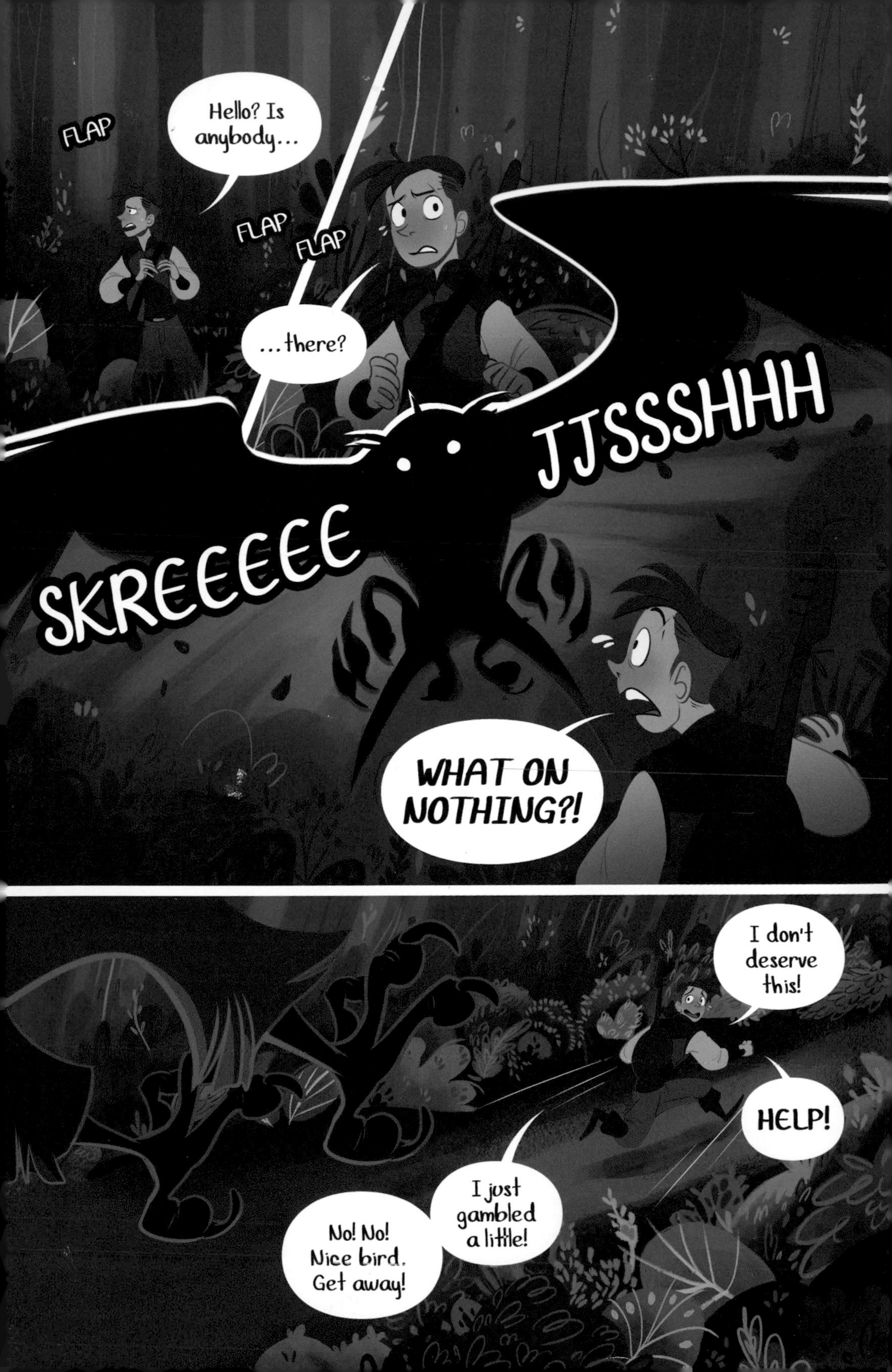
FLAP
Hello? Is anybody...
FLAP
FLAP
...there?
JJSSSHHH
SKREEEEEE
WHAT ON NOTHING?!
I don't deserve this!
HELP!
I just gambled a little!
No! No! Nice bird. Get away!

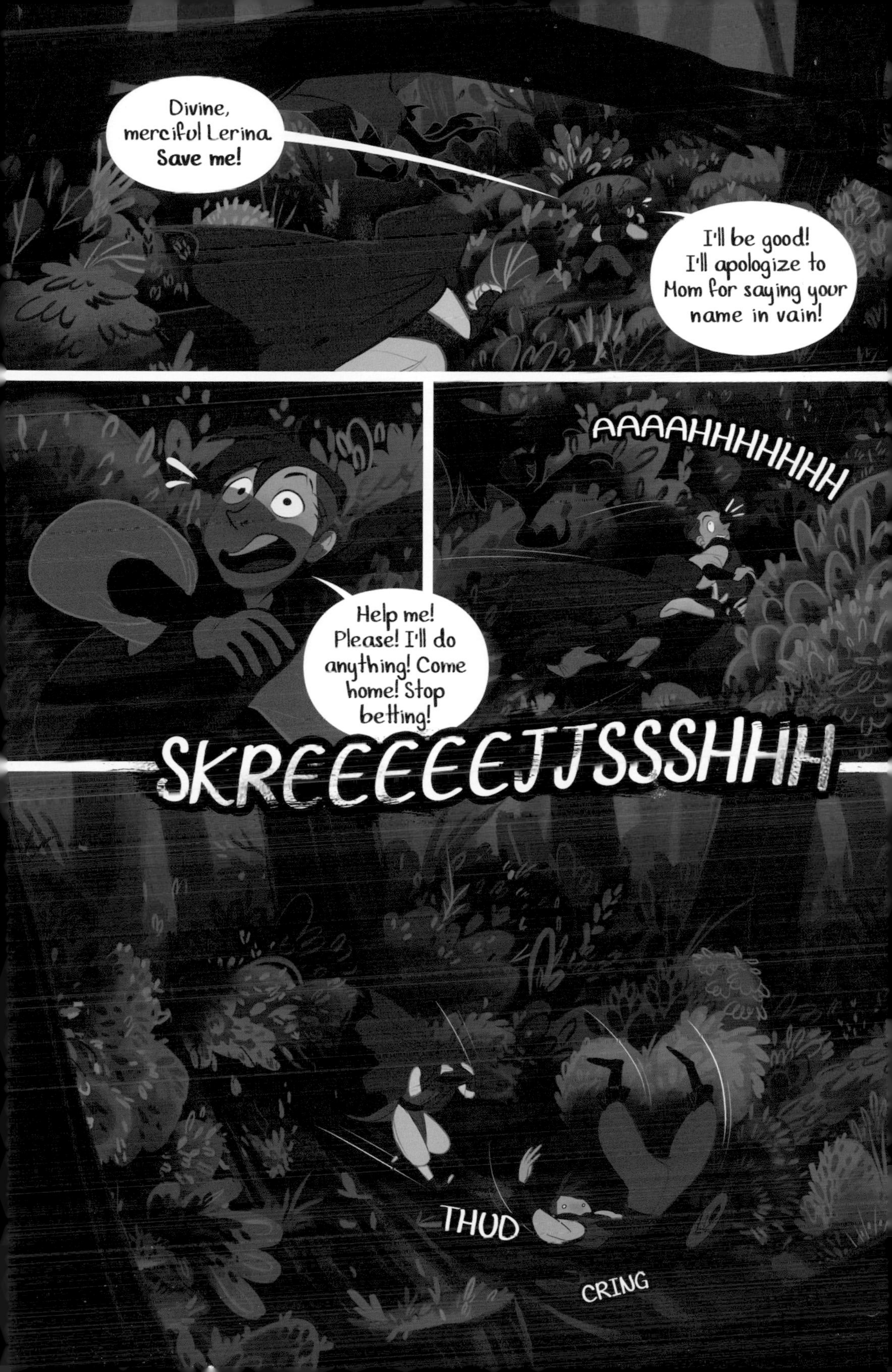
Divine, merciful Lerina. Save me!
I'll be good! I'll apologize to Mom for saying your name in vain!
Help me! Please! I'll do anything! Come home! Stop betting!
AAAAHHHHHHH
SKREEEEEEJJSSSHHH
THUD
CRING

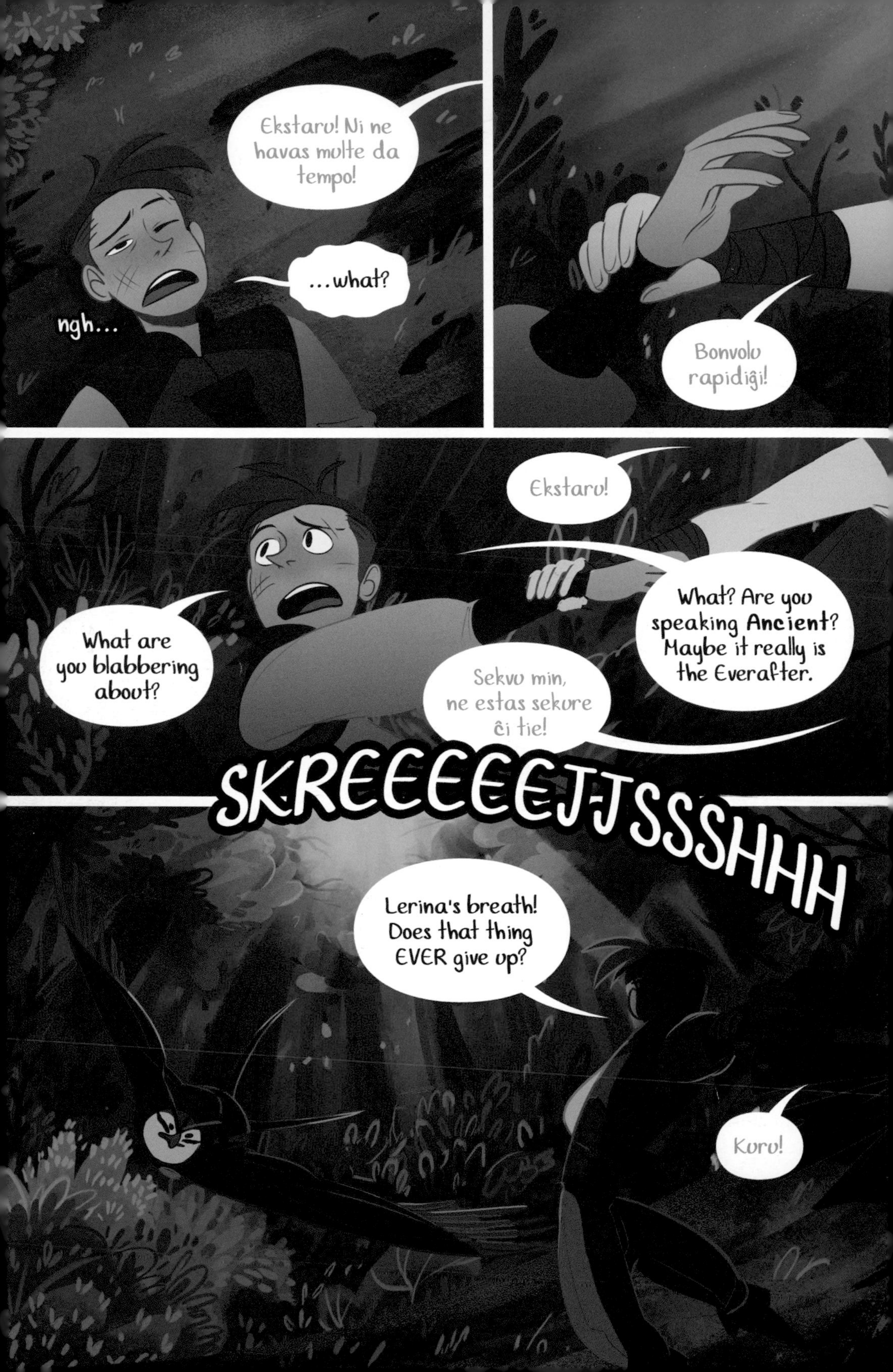

Ekstaru! Ni ne havas multe da tempo!
ngh...
...what?
Bonvolu rapidiĝi!
Ekstaru!
What are you blabbering about?
What? Are you speaking **Ancient**? Maybe it really is the Everafter.
Sekvu min, ne estas sekure ĉi tie!
SKREEEEEEJJSSSHHH
Lerina's breath! Does that thing EVER give up?
Kuru!

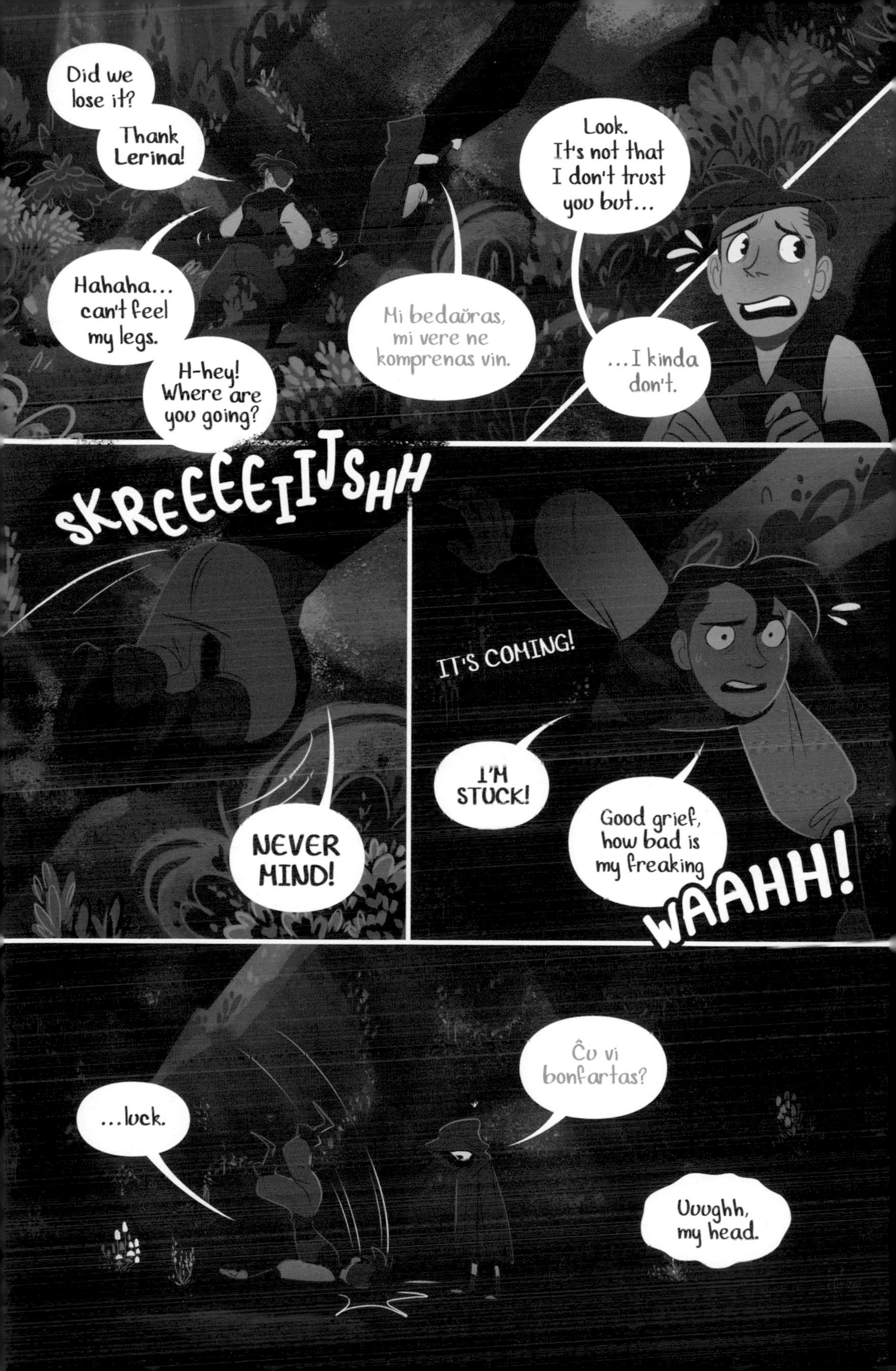
Did we lose it?
Thank Lerina!
Hahaha... can't feel my legs.
H-hey! Where are you going?
Mi bedaŭras, mi vere ne komprenas vin.
Look. It's not that I don't trust you but...
...I kinda don't.
SKREEEEIIJSHH
NEVER MIND!
IT'S COMING!
I'M STUCK!
Good grief, how bad is my freaking
WAAHH!
...luck.
Ĉu vi bonfartas?
Uuughh, my head.

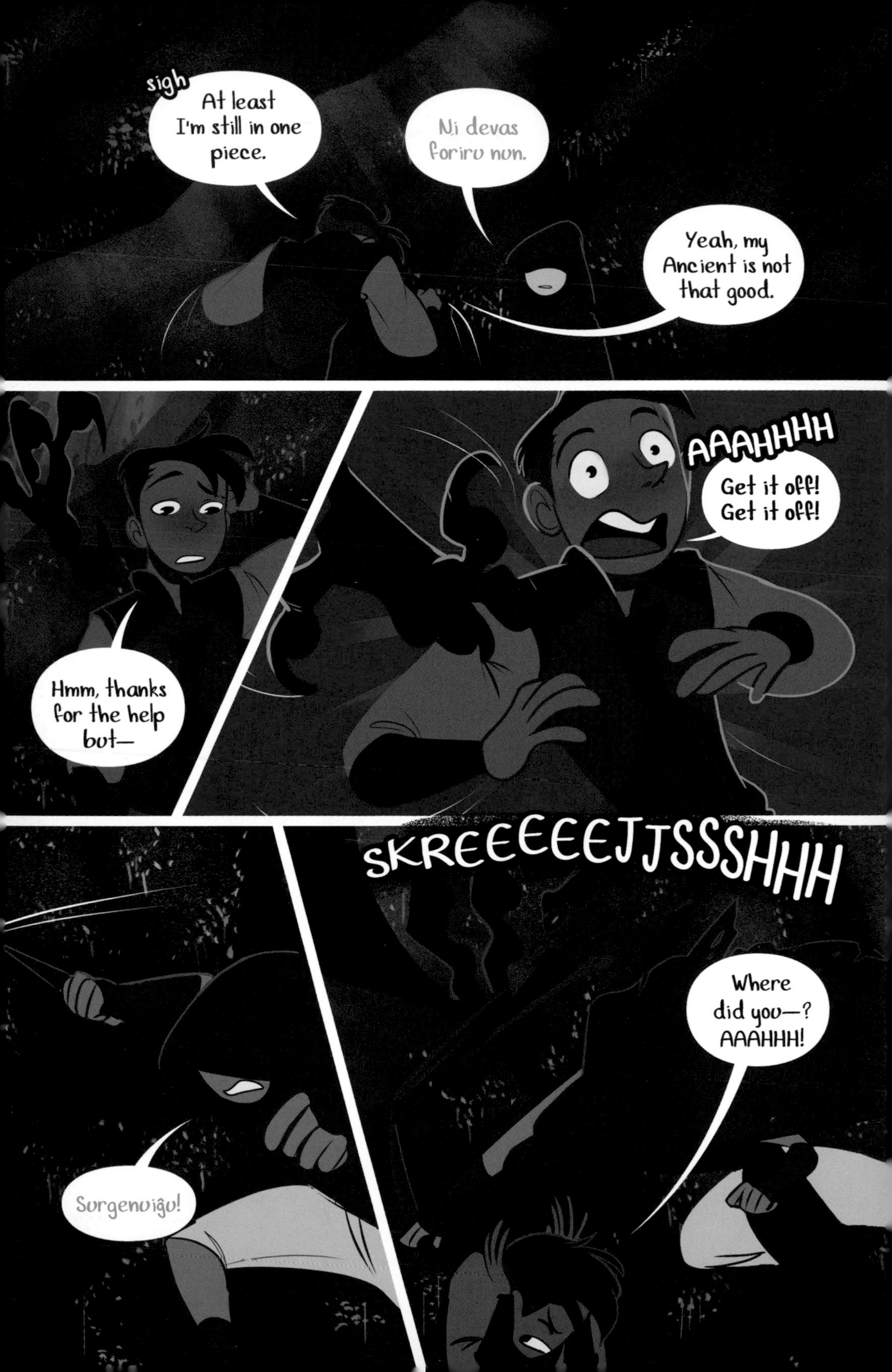
sigh
At least I'm still in one piece.
Ni devas foriru nun.
Yeah, my Ancient is not that good.
Hmm, thanks for the help but—
AAAHHHH
Get it off! Get it off!
SKREEEEEEJJSSSHHH
Surgenuiĝu!
Where did you—? AAAHHH!

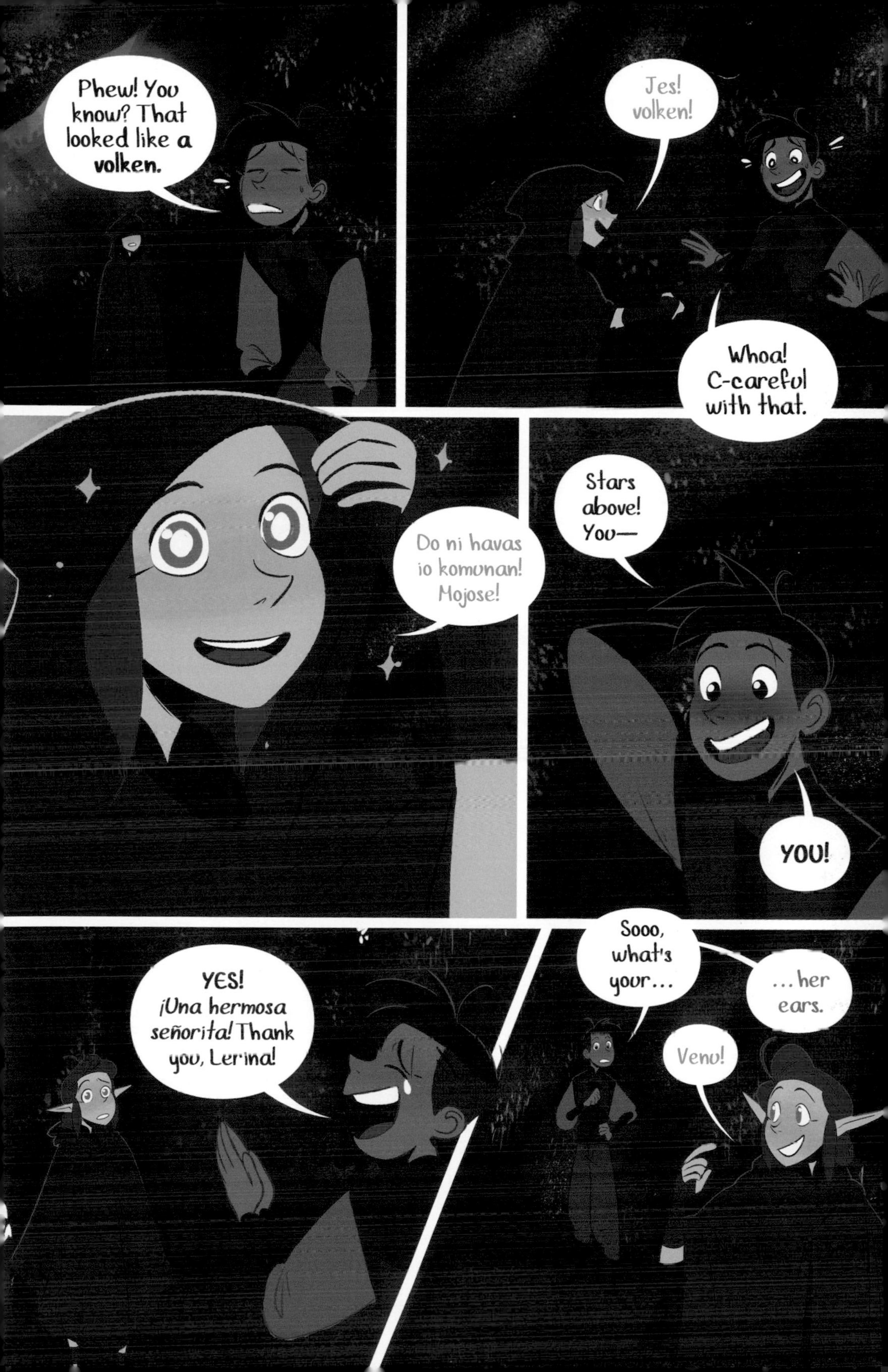
Phew! You know? That looked like a **volken.**
Jes! volken!
Whoa! C-careful with that.
Do ni havas io komunan! Mojose!
Stars above! You—
YOU!
YES! ¡Una hermosa señorita! Thank you, Lerina!
Sooo, what's your...
...her ears.
Venu!

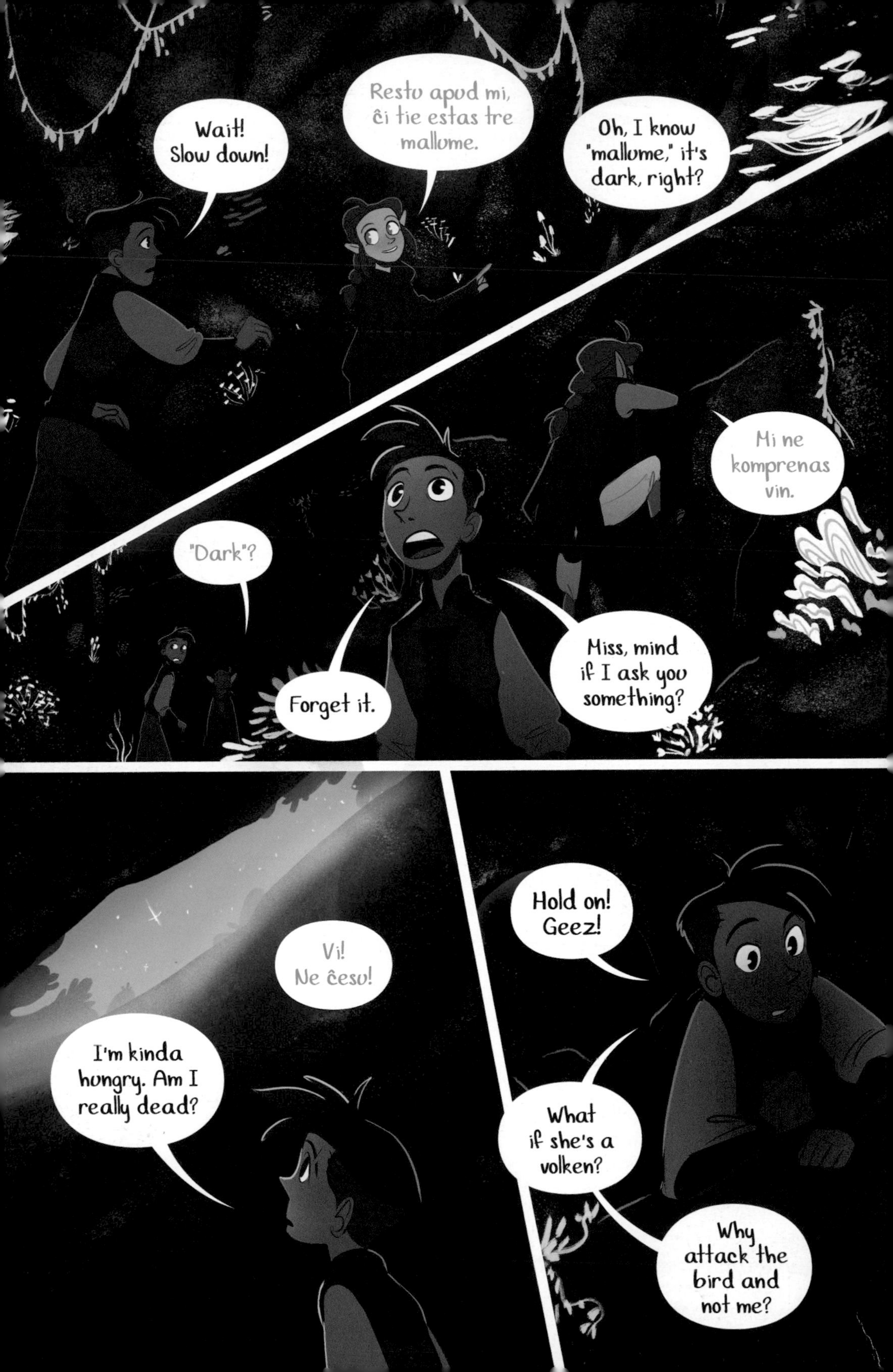
Wait! Slow down!
Restu apud mi, ĉi tie estas tre mallume.
Oh, I know "mallume," it's dark, right?
Mi ne komprenas vin.
Miss, mind if I ask you something?
"Dark"?
Forget it.
Vi! Ne ĉesu!
I'm kinda hungry. Am I really dead?
Hold on! Geez!
What if she's a volken?
Why attack the bird and not me?

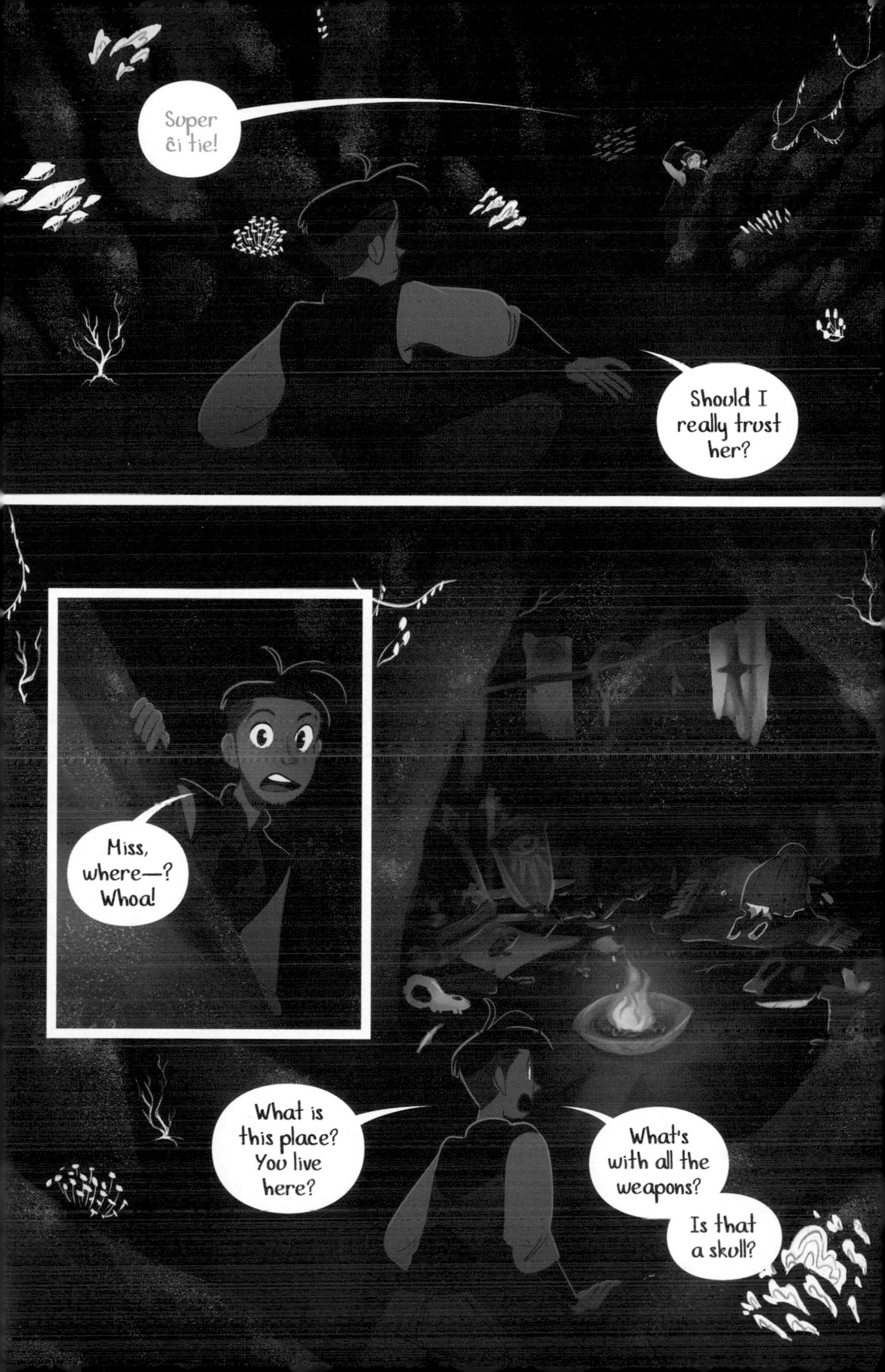

Super ĉi tie!
Should I really trust her?
Miss, where—? Whoa!
What is this place? You live here?
What's with all the weapons?
Is that a skull?

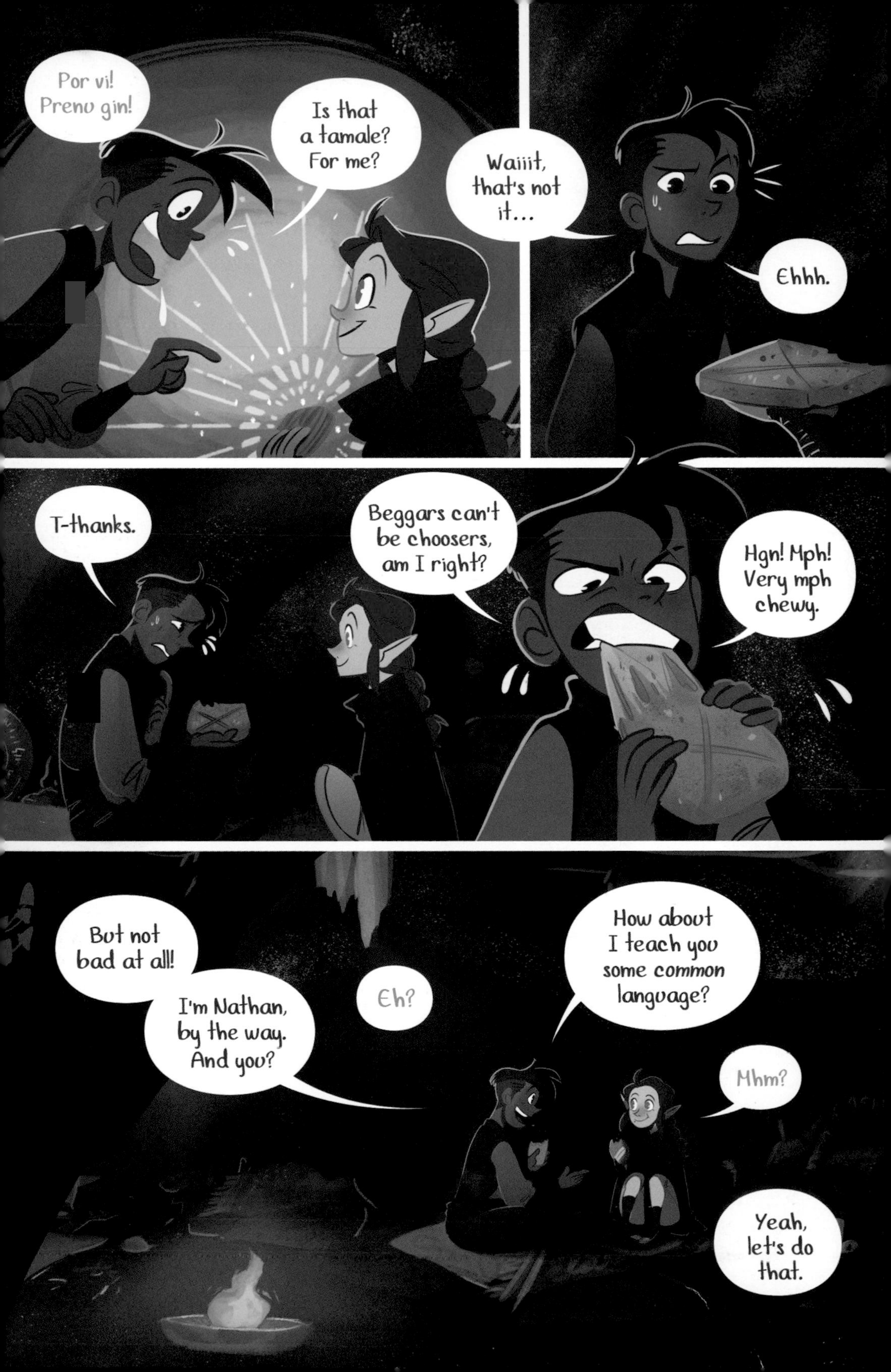
Por vi! Preno gin!
Is that a tamale? For me?
Waiiit, that's not it...
Ehhh.
T-thanks.
Beggars can't be choosers, am I right?
Hgn! Mph! Very mph chewy.
But not bad at all!
I'm Nathan, by the way. And you?
Eh?
How about I teach you some common language?
Mhm?
Yeah, let's do that.

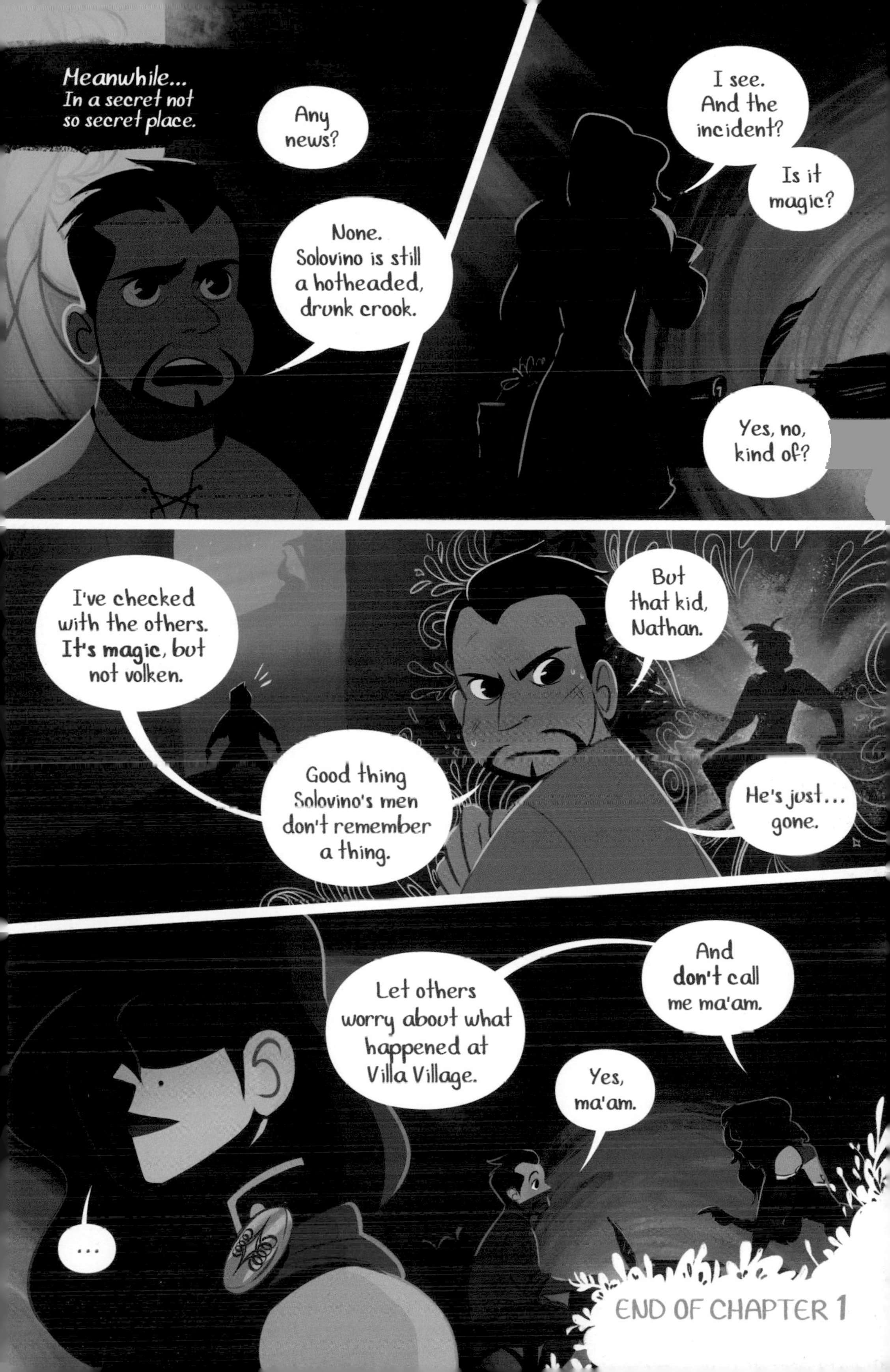

Meanwhile... In a secret not so secret place.
Any news?
None. Solovino is still a hotheaded, drunk crook.
I see. And the incident?
Is it magic?
Yes, no, kind of?
I've checked with the others. It's magic, but not volken.
But that kid, Nathan.
Good thing Solovino's men don't remember a thing.
He's just... gone.
Let others worry about what happened at Villa Village.
And don't call me ma'am.
Yes, ma'am.
...
END OF CHAPTER 1

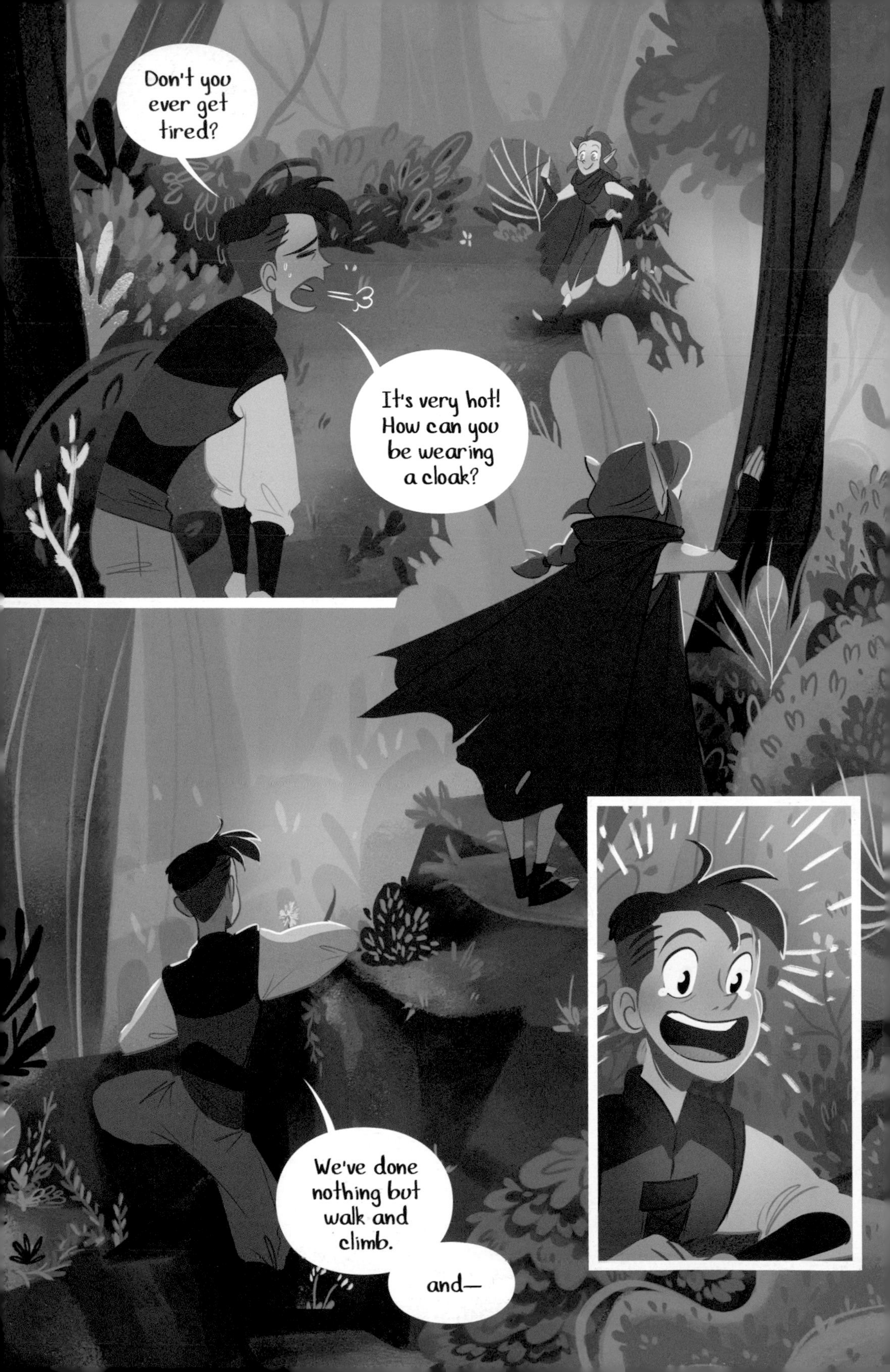

Don't you ever get tired?
It's very hot! How can you be wearing a cloak?
We've done nothing but walk and climb.
and—

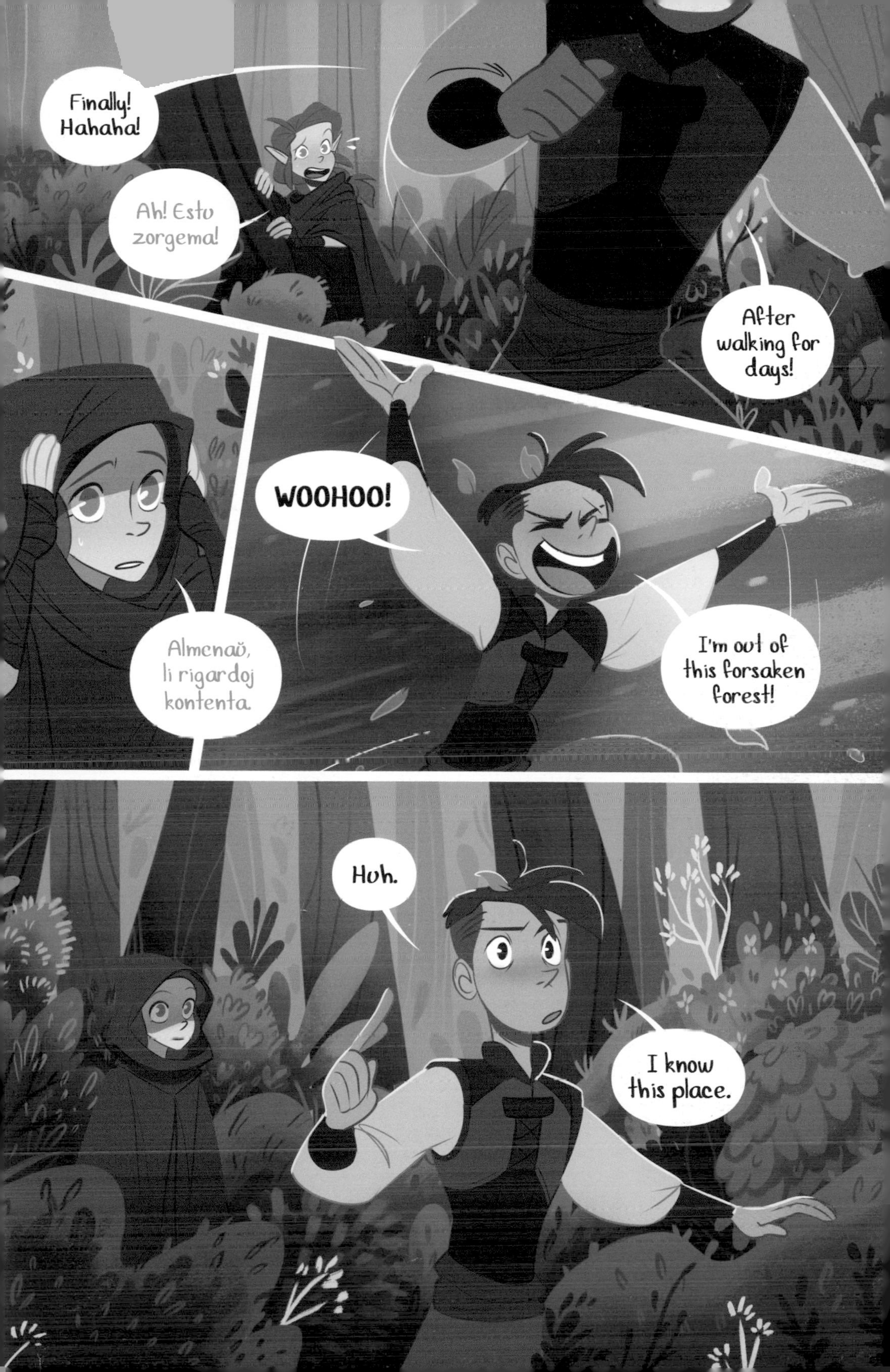
Finally! Hahaha!
Ah! Estu zorgema!
After walking for days!
Almenaŭ, li rigardoj kontenta.
WOOHOO!
I'm out of this forsaken forest!
Huh.
I know this place.

Chapter 2
Still on Nothing

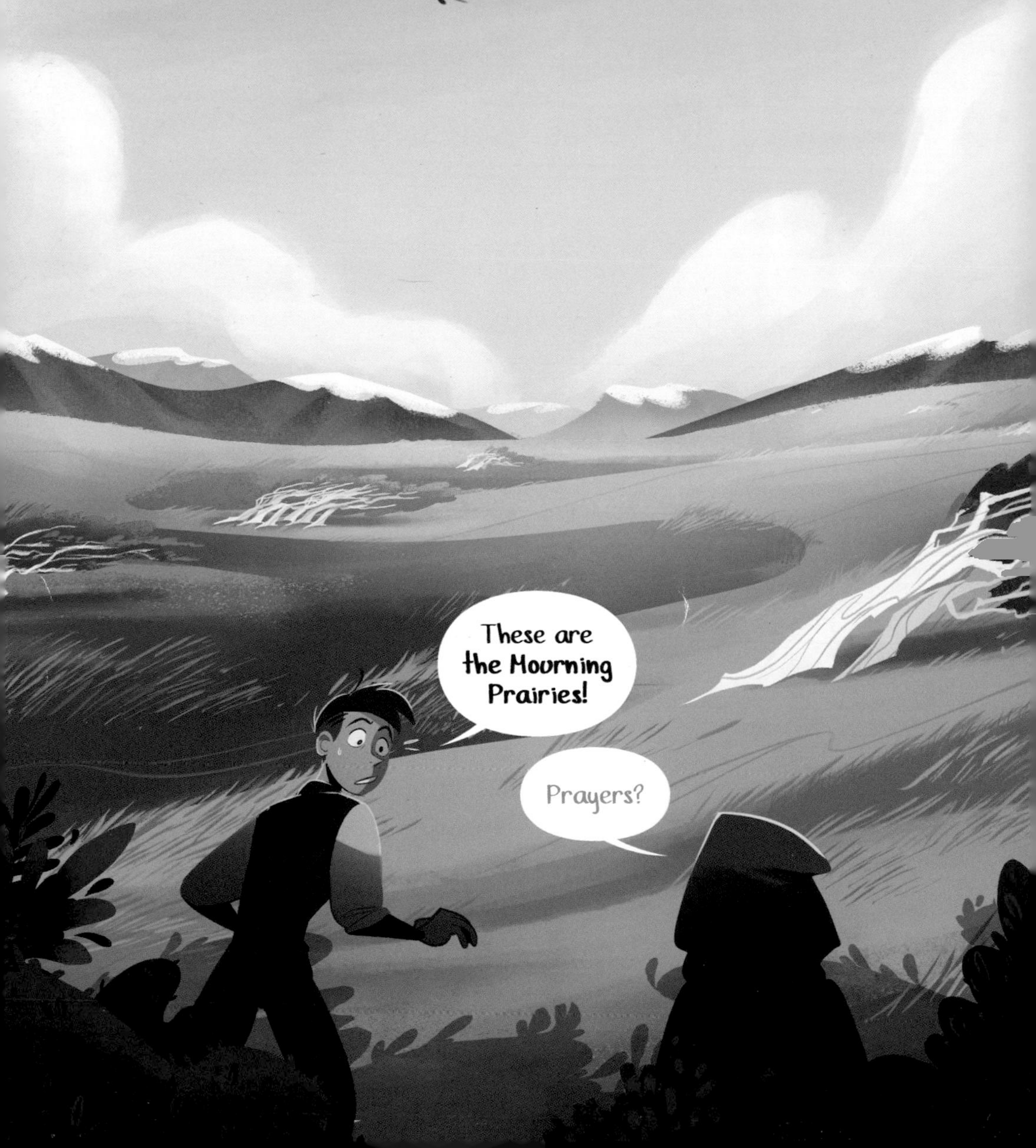
These are the Mourning Prairies!
Prayers?

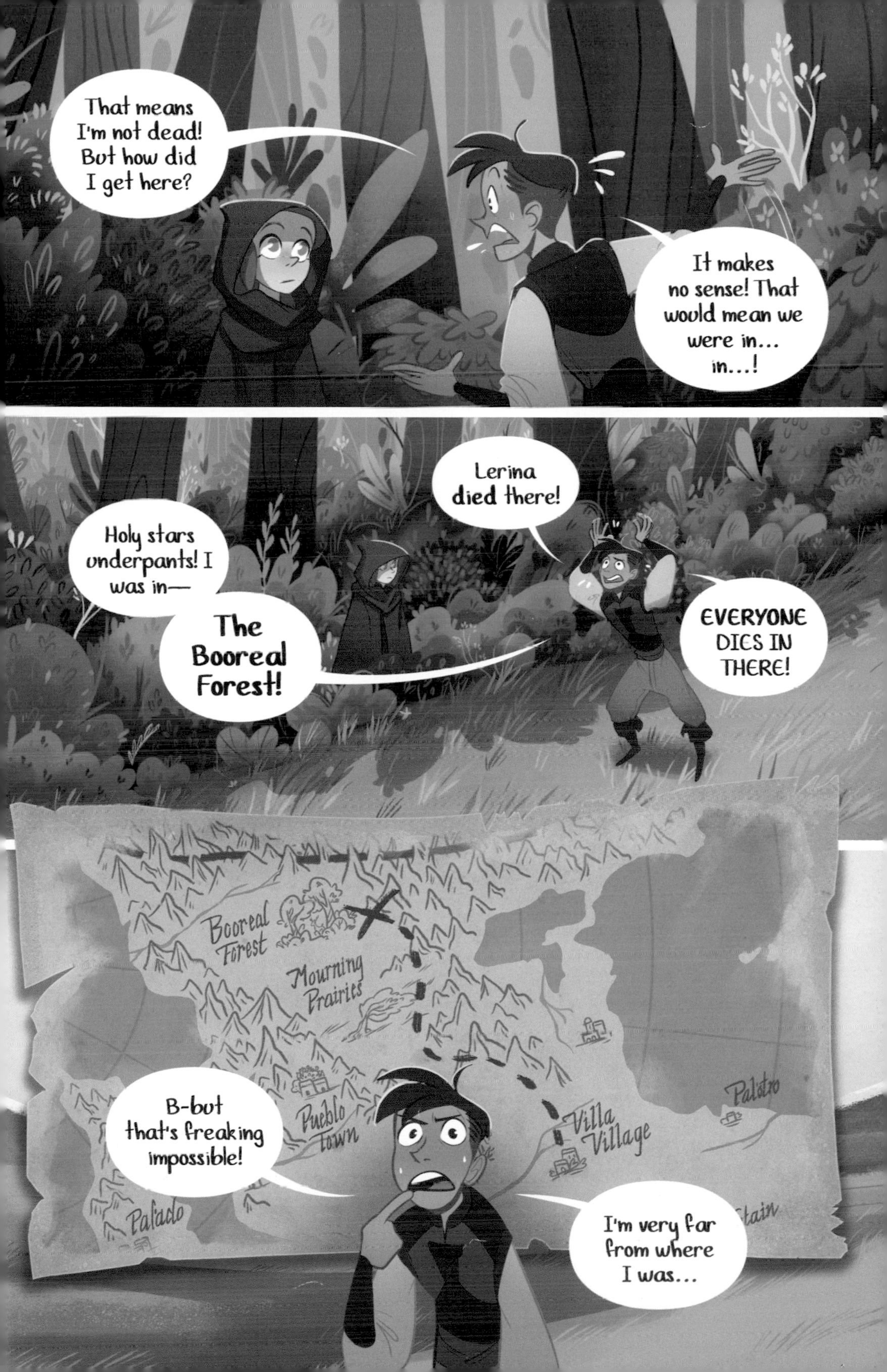
That means I'm not dead! But how did I get here?
It makes no sense! That would mean we were in... in...!
Holy stars underpants! I was in—
The Booreal Forest!
Lerina died there!
EVERYONE DIES IN THERE!
Booreal Forest
Mourning Prairies
Pueblo Town
Villa Village
Palistro
Palado
Stain
B-but that's freaking impossible!
I'm very far from where I was...

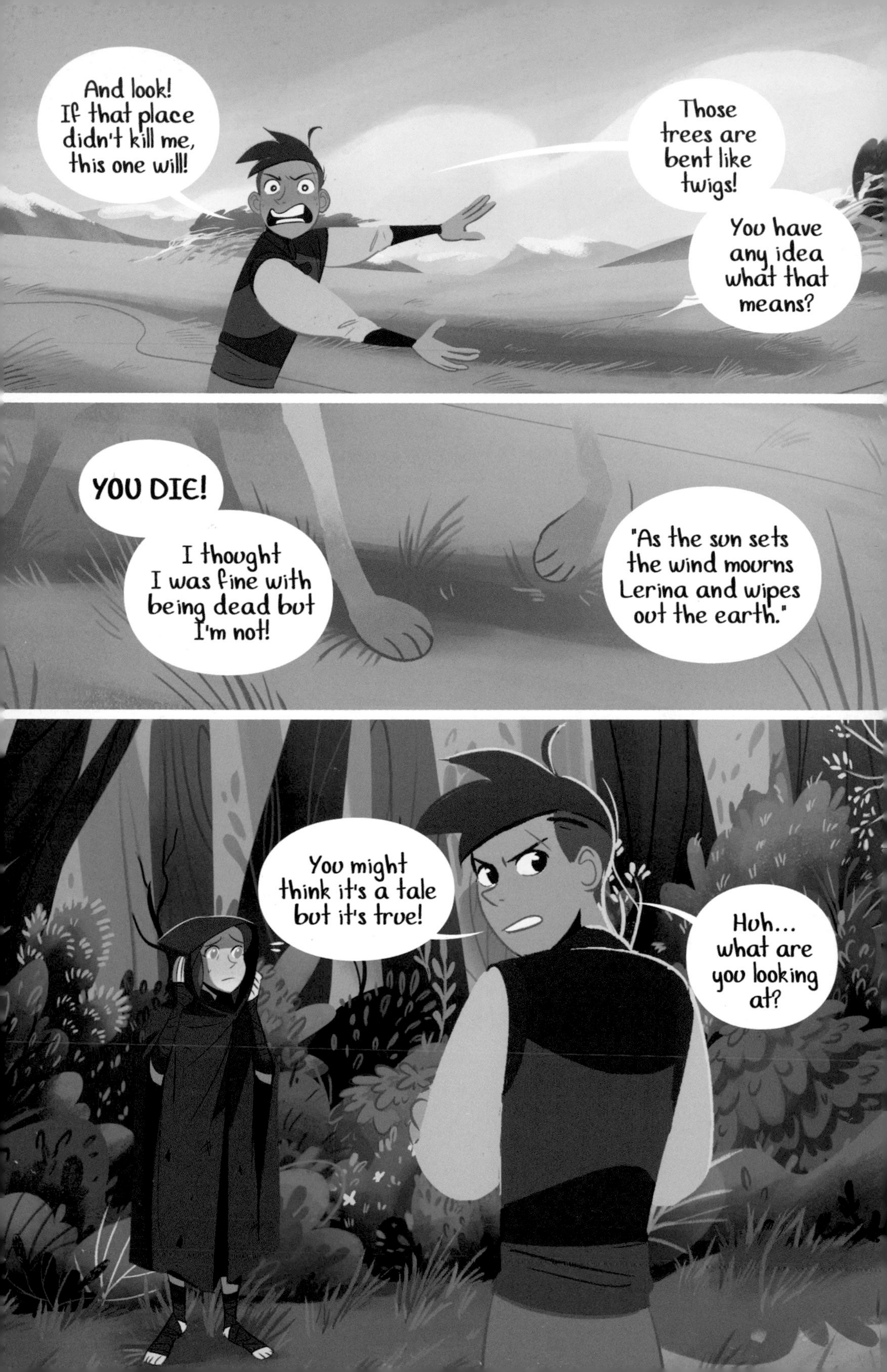
And look! If that place didn't kill me, this one will!
Those trees are bent like twigs!
You have any idea what that means?
YOU DIE!
I thought I was fine with being dead but I'm not!
"As the sun sets the wind mourns Lerina and wipes out the earth."
You might think it's a tale but it's true!
Huh... what are you looking at?

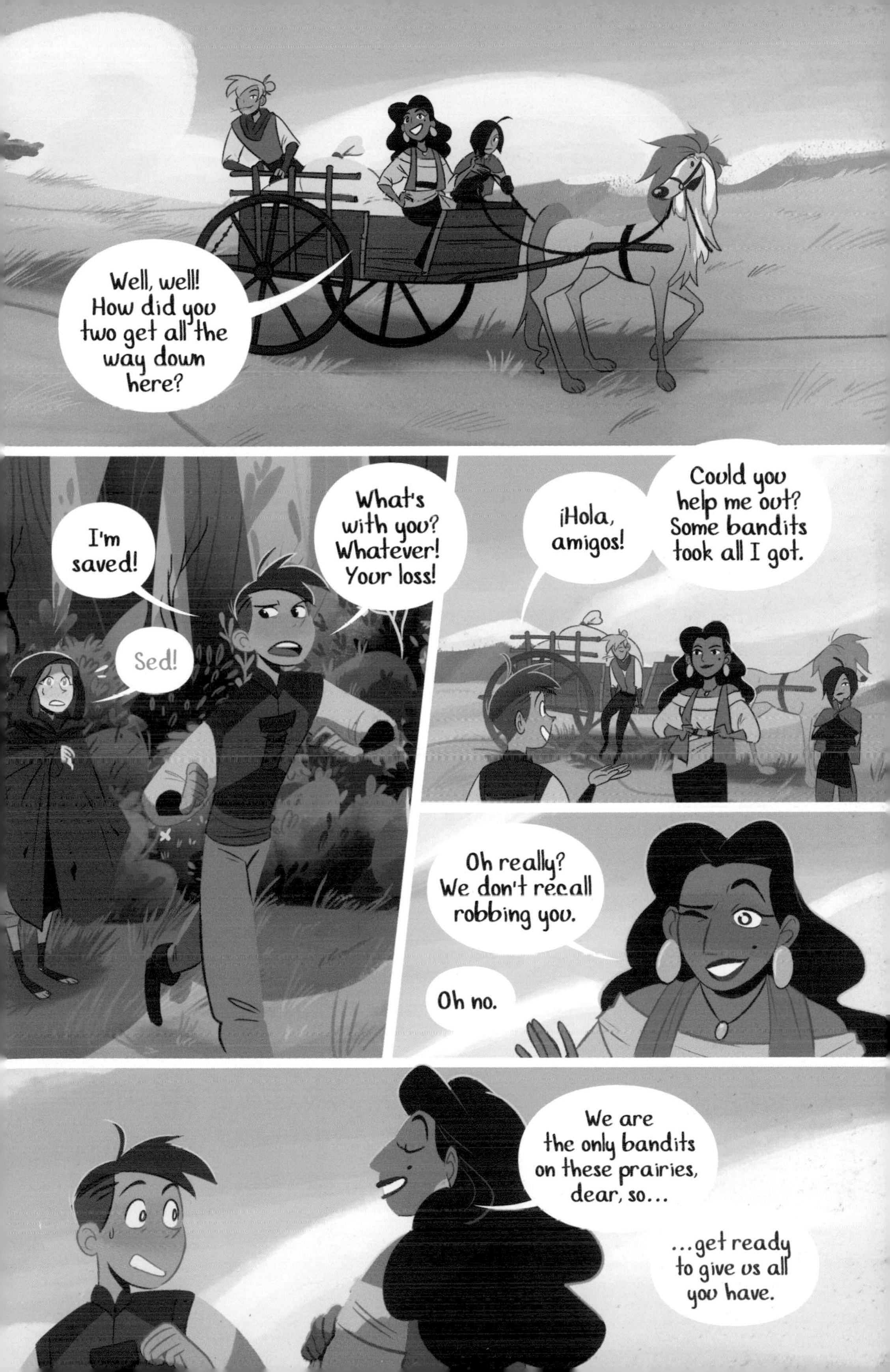
Well, well! How did you two get all the way down here?
I'm saved!
Sed!
What's with you? Whatever! Your loss!
¡Hola, amigos!
Could you help me out? Some bandits took all I got.
Oh really? We don't recall robbing you.
Oh no.
We are the only bandits on these prairies, dear, so...
...get ready to give us all you have.

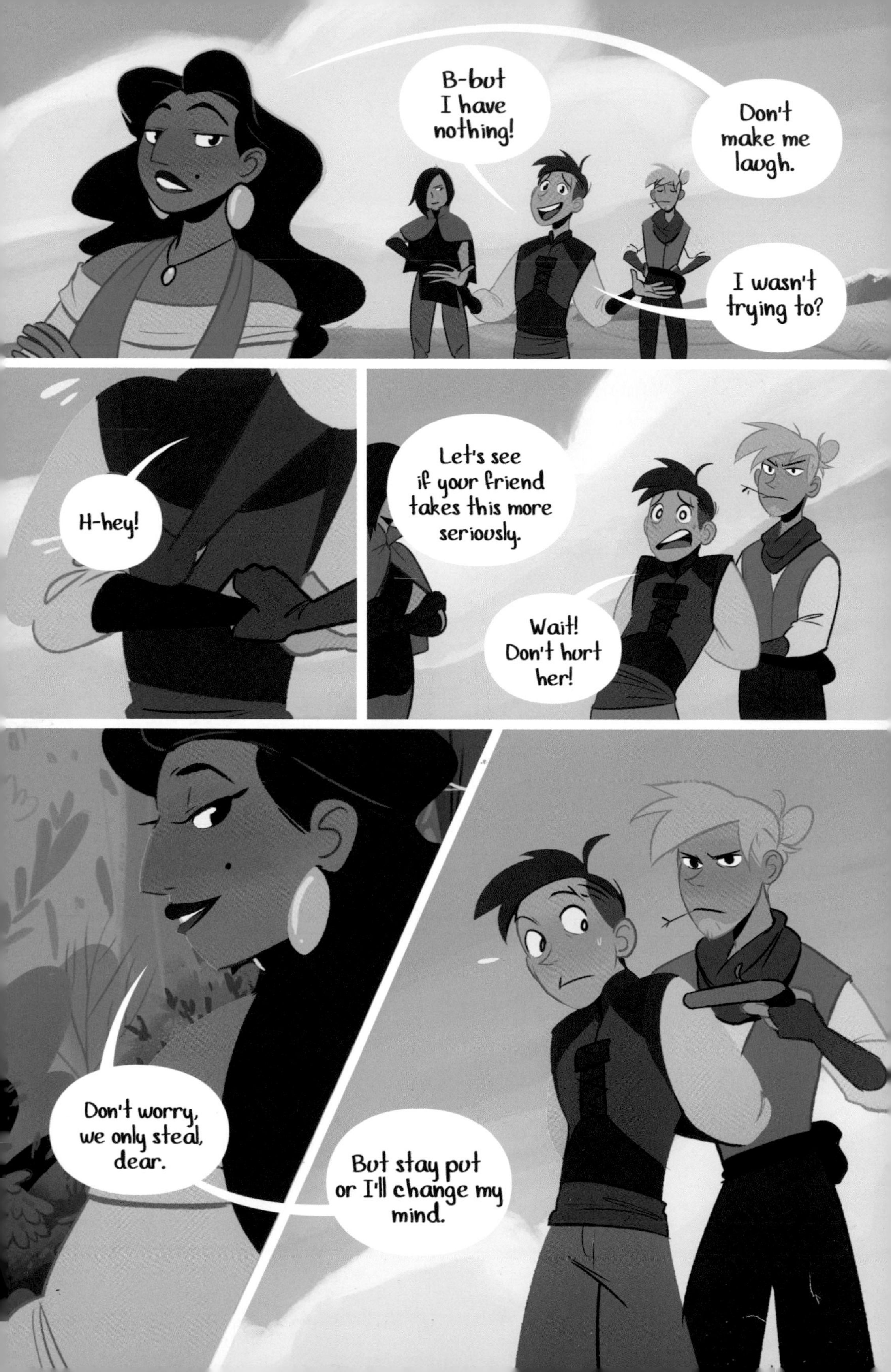
B-but I have nothing!
Don't make me laugh.
I wasn't trying to?
H-hey!
Let's see if your friend takes this more seriously.
Wait! Don't hurt her!
Don't worry, we only steal, dear.
But stay put or I'll change my mind.

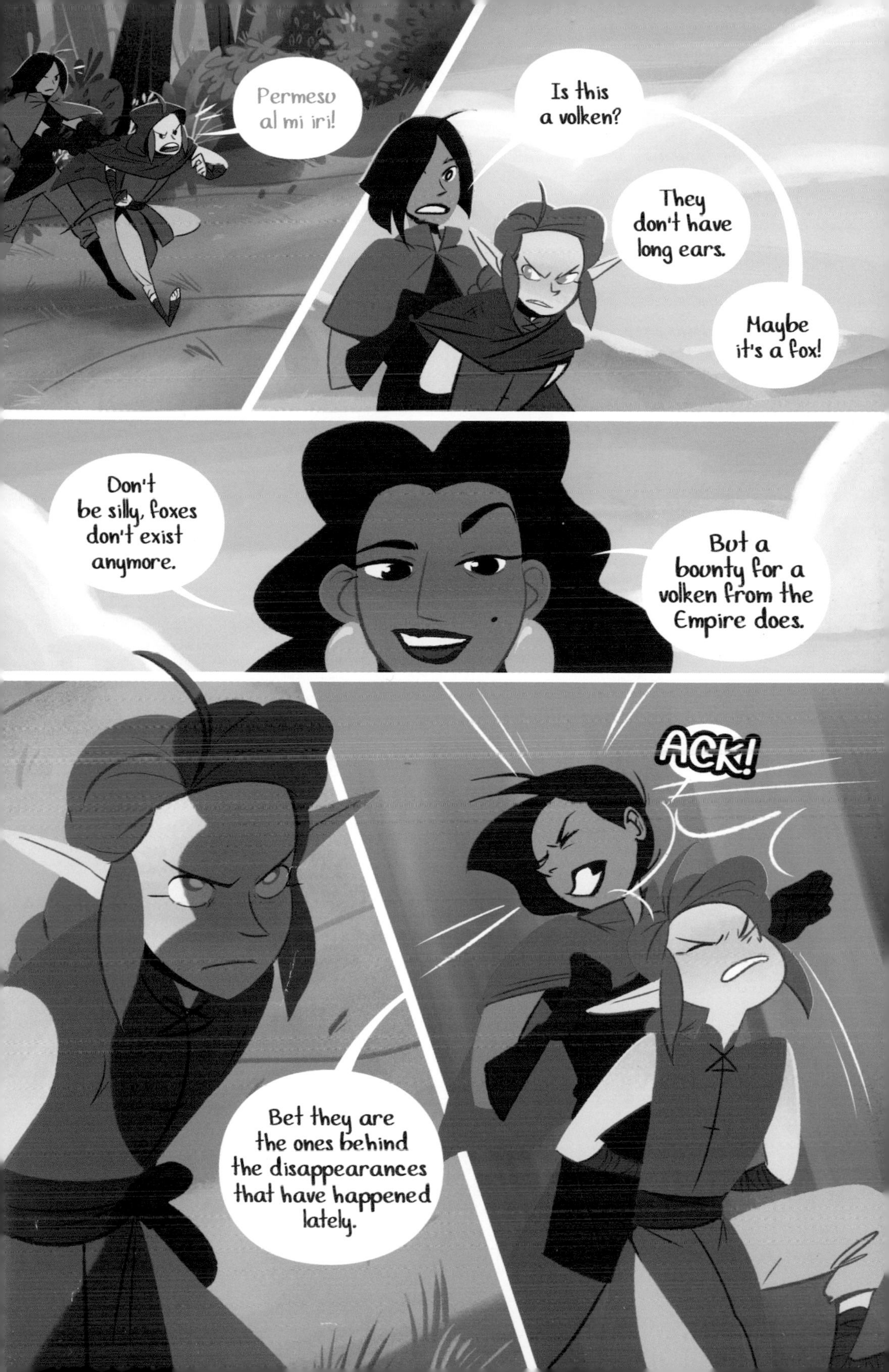
Permeso al mi iri!
Is this a volken?
They don't have long ears.
Maybe it's a fox!
Don't be silly, foxes don't exist anymore.
But a bounty for a volken from the Empire does.
ACK!
Bet they are the ones behind the disappearances that have happened lately.

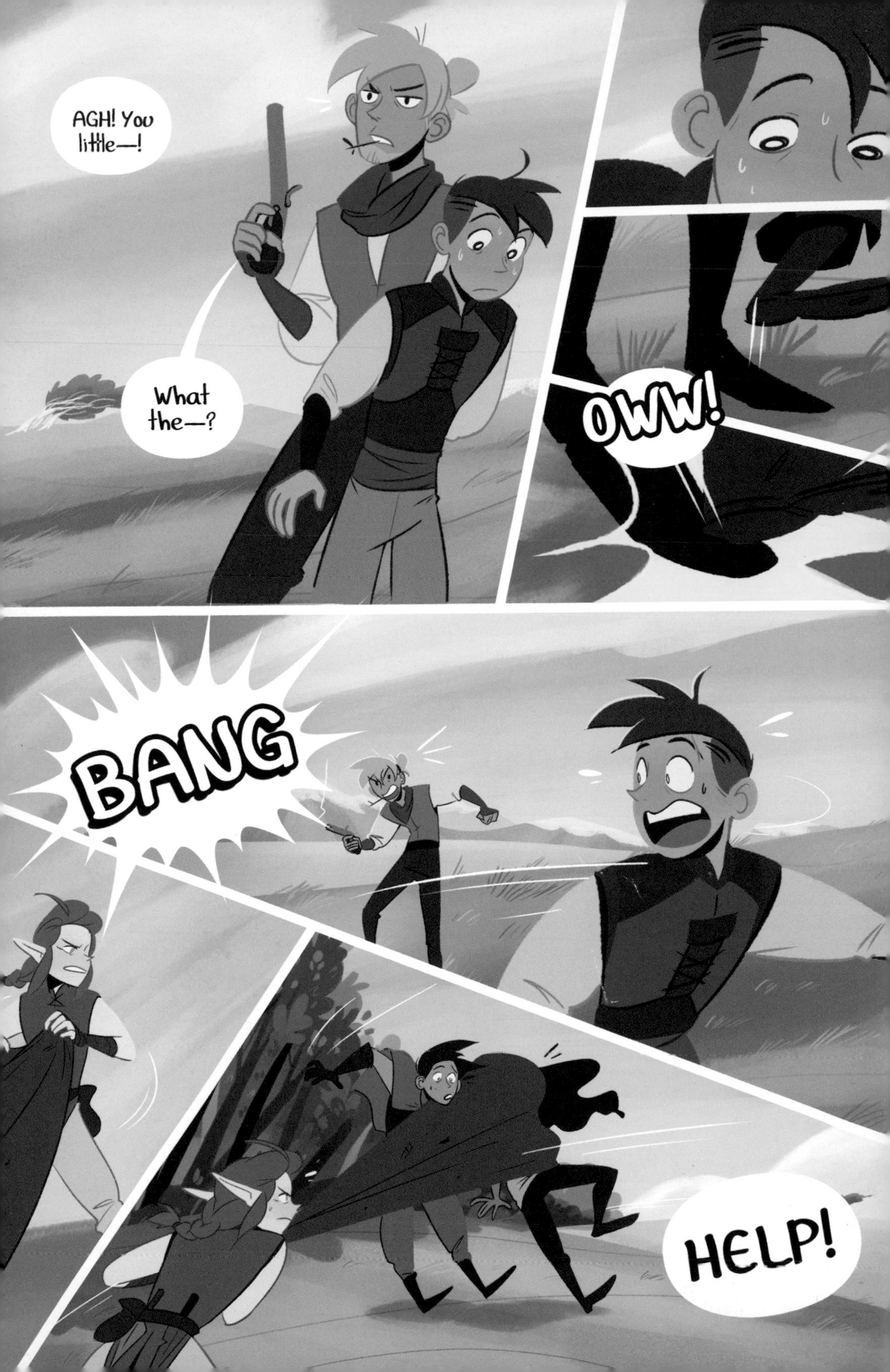

AGH! You little—!
What the—?
OWW!
BANG
HELP!

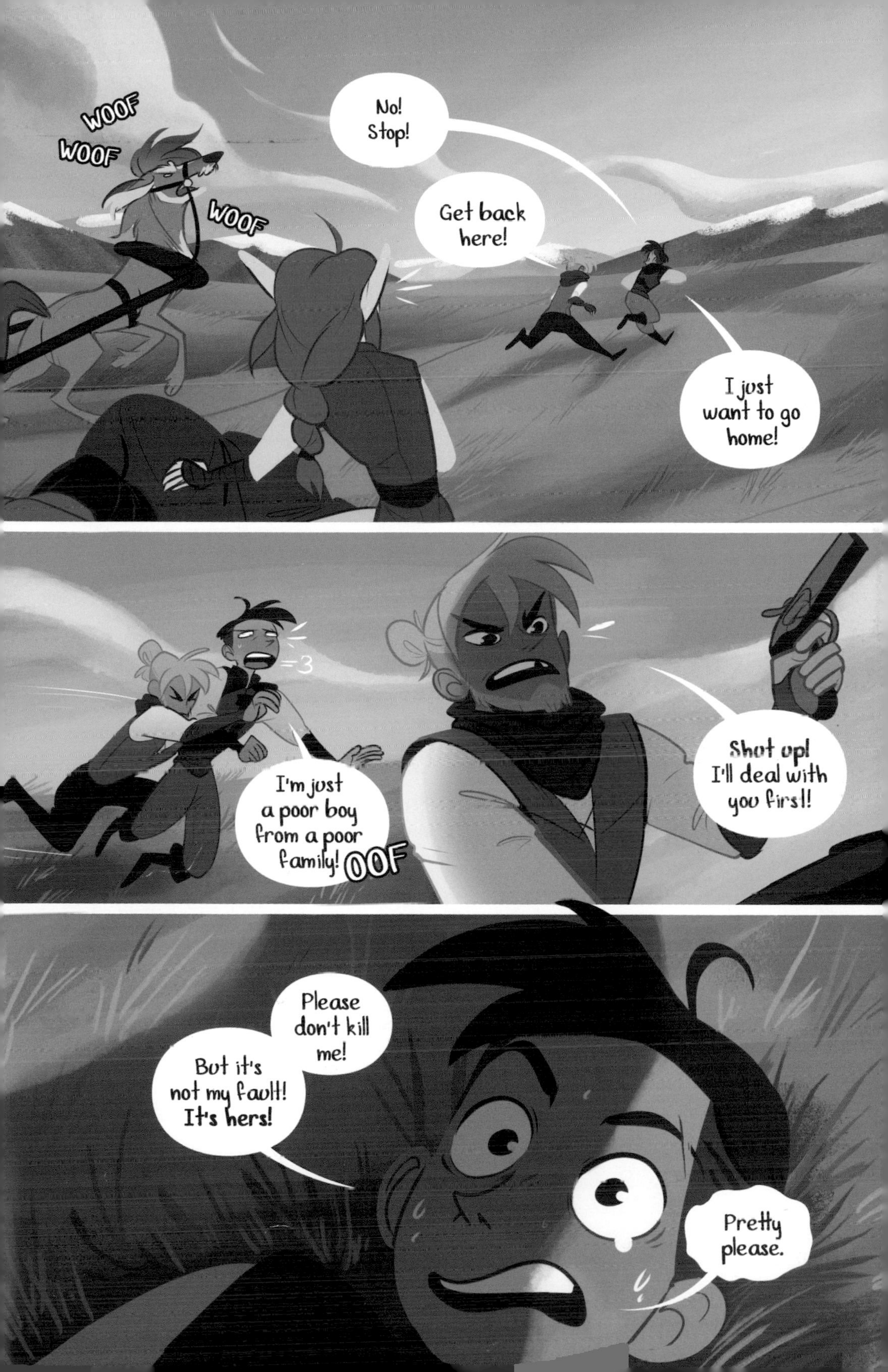
WOOF
WOOF
WOOF
No! Stop!
Get back here!
I just want to go home!
I'm just a poor boy from a poor family!
OOF
Shut up! I'll deal with you first!
Please don't kill me!
But it's not my fault! It's hers!
Pretty please.

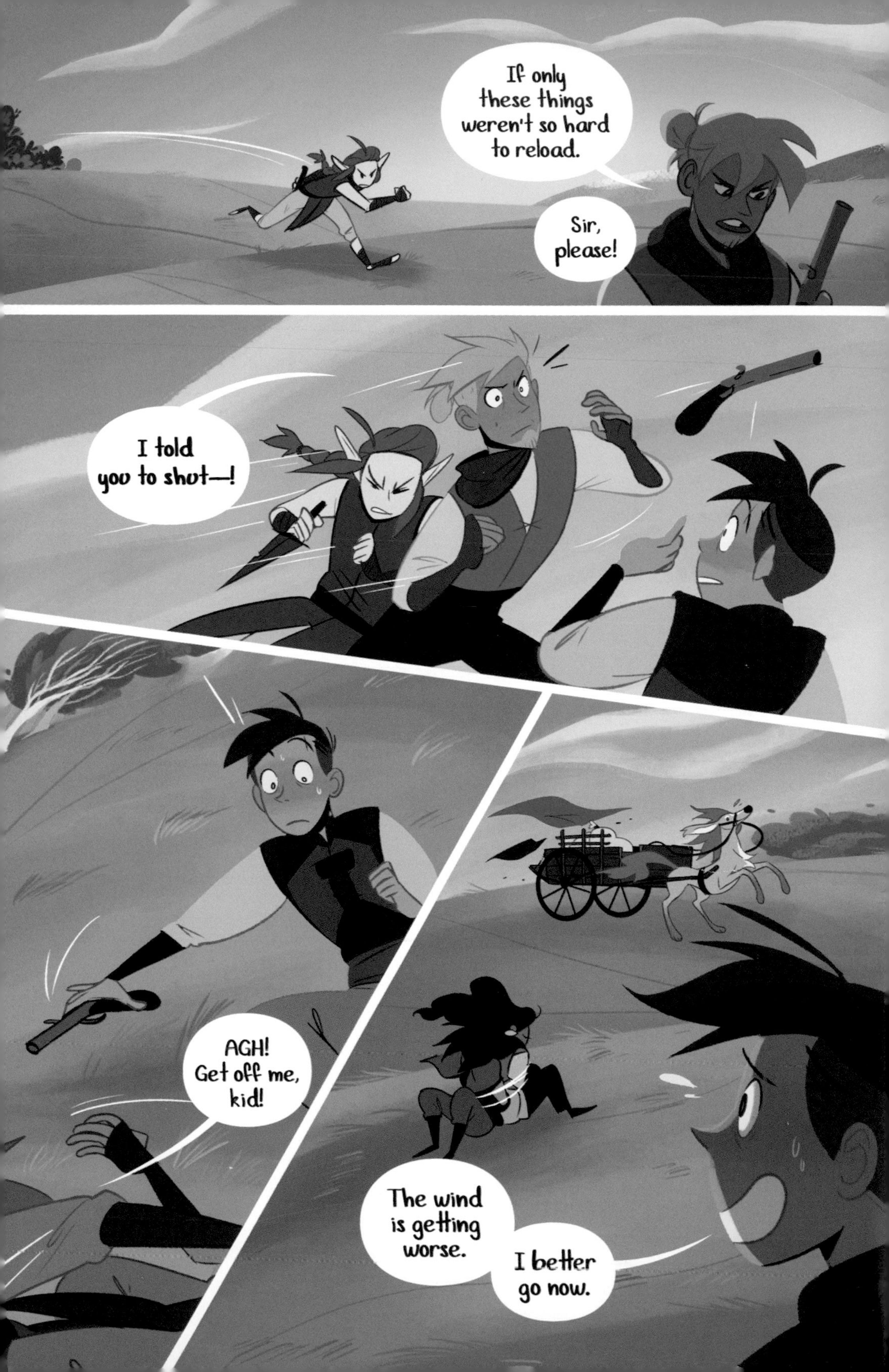
If only these things weren't so hard to reload.
Sir, please!
I told you to shot—!
AGH! Get off me, kid!
The wind is getting worse.
I better go now.

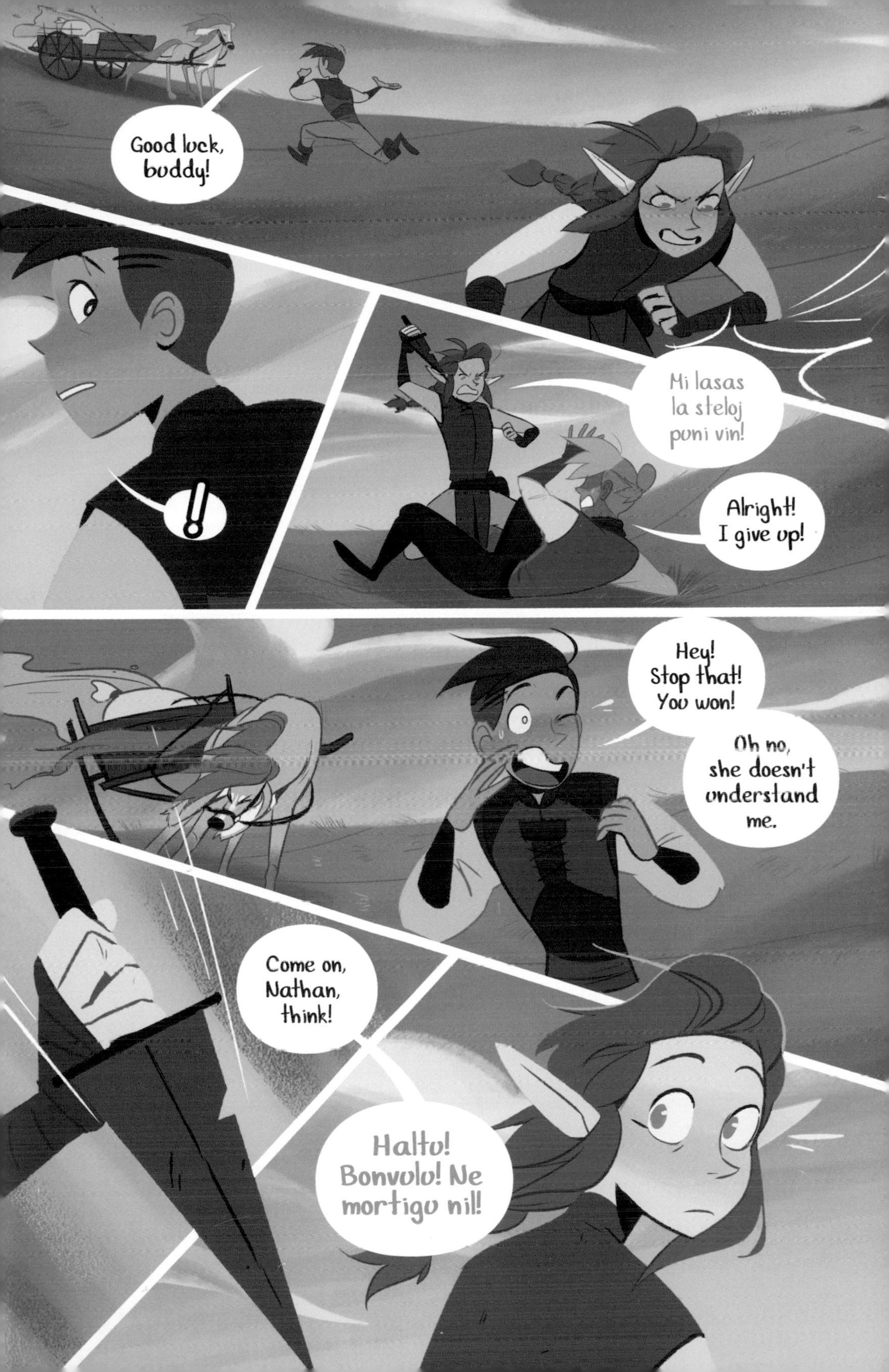
Good luck, buddy!
!
Mi lasas la steloj poni vin!
Alright! I give up!
Hey! Stop that! You won!
Oh no, she doesn't understand me.
Come on, Nathan, think!
Haltu! Bonvolu! Ne mortigu nil!

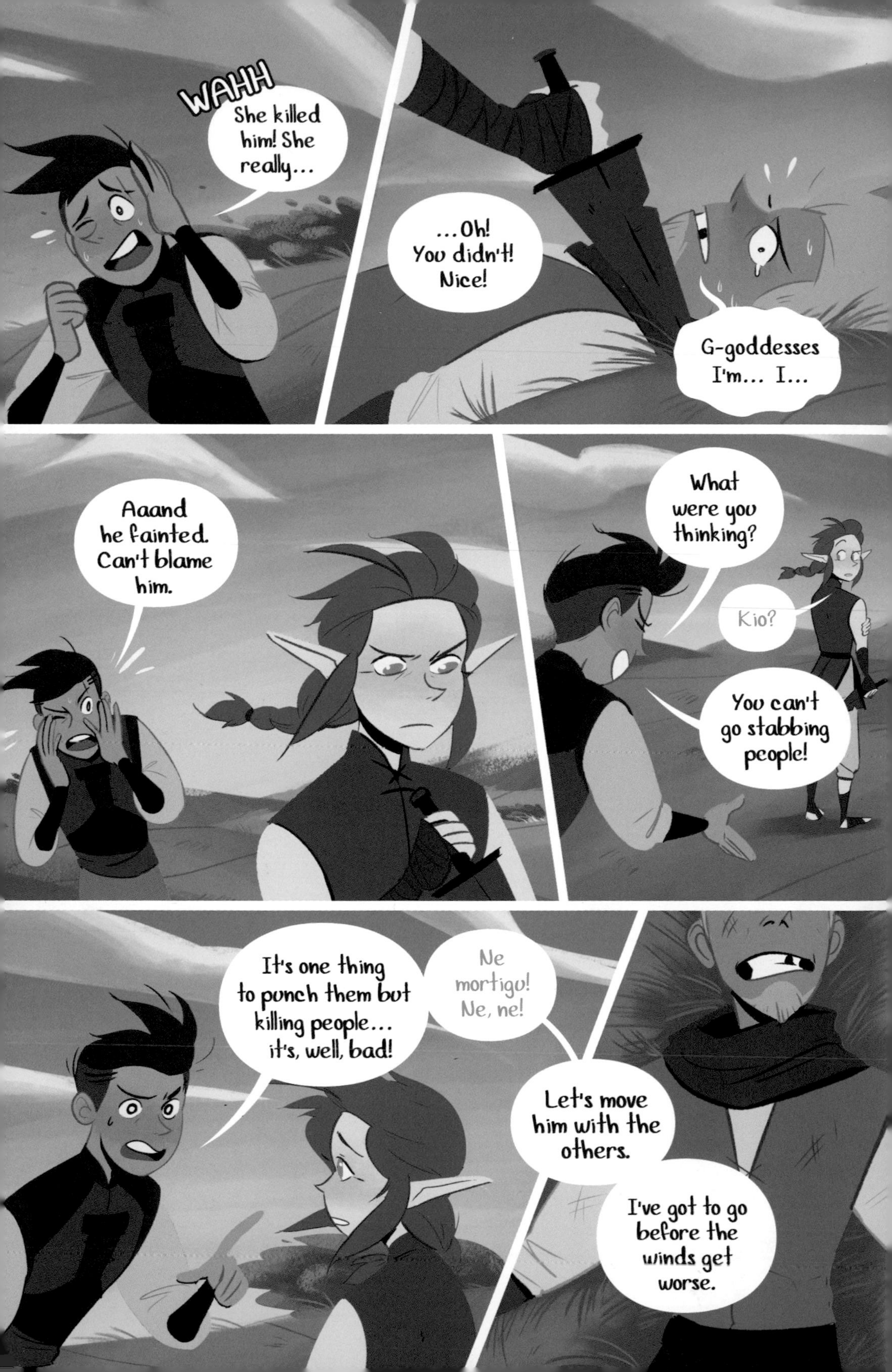
WAHH
She killed him! She really...
...Oh! You didn't! Nice!
G-goddesses I'm... I...
Aaand he fainted. Can't blame him.
What were you thinking?
Kio?
You can't go stabbing people!
It's one thing to punch them but killing people... it's, well, bad!
Ne mortigu! Ne, ne!
Let's move him with the others.
I've got to go before the winds get worse.

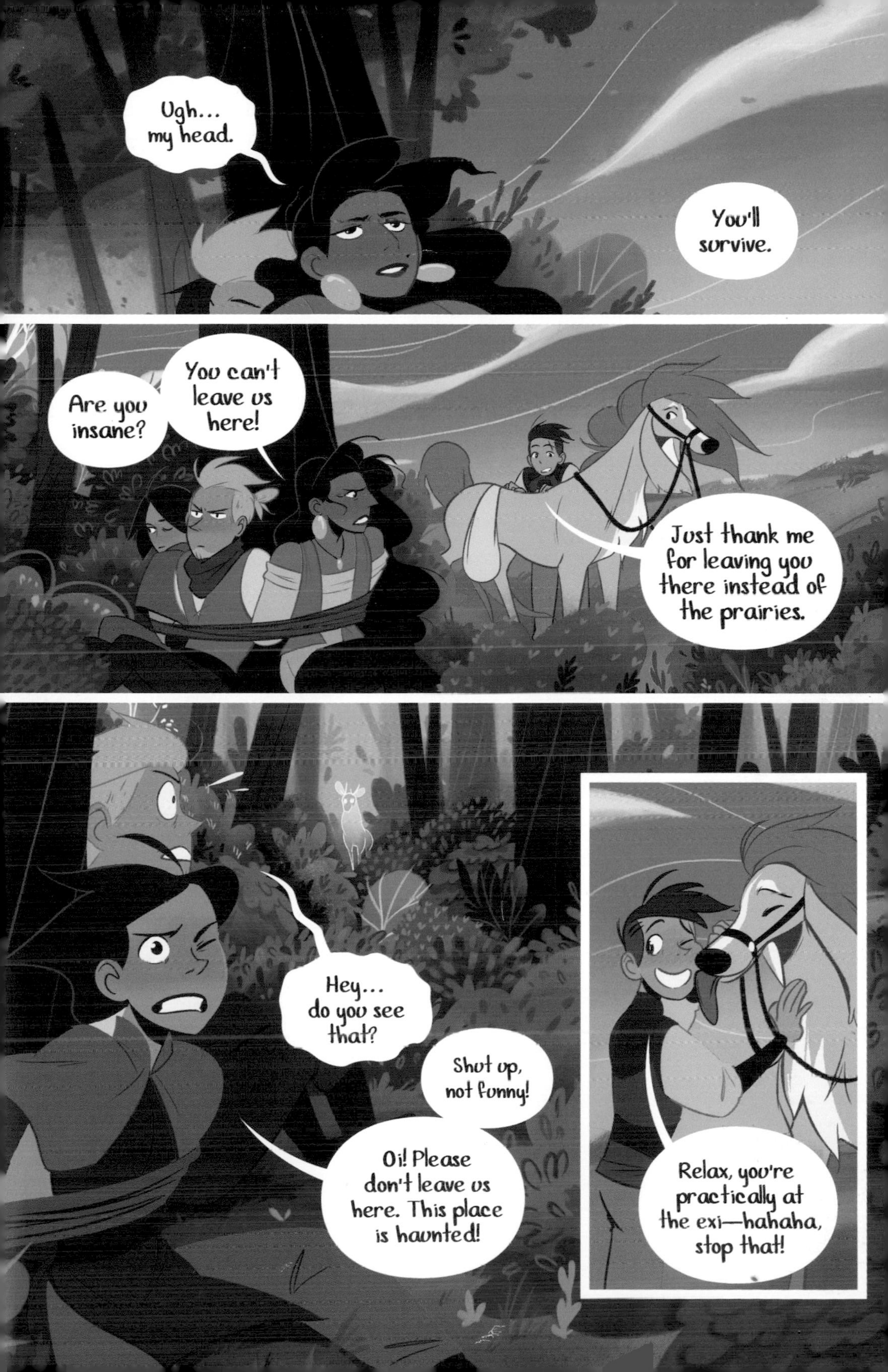
Ugh... my head.
You'll survive.
Are you insane?
You can't leave us here!
Just thank me for leaving you there instead of the prairies.
Hey... do you see that?
Shut up, not funny!
Oi! Please don't leave us here. This place is haunted!
Relax, you're practically at the exi—hahaha, stop that!

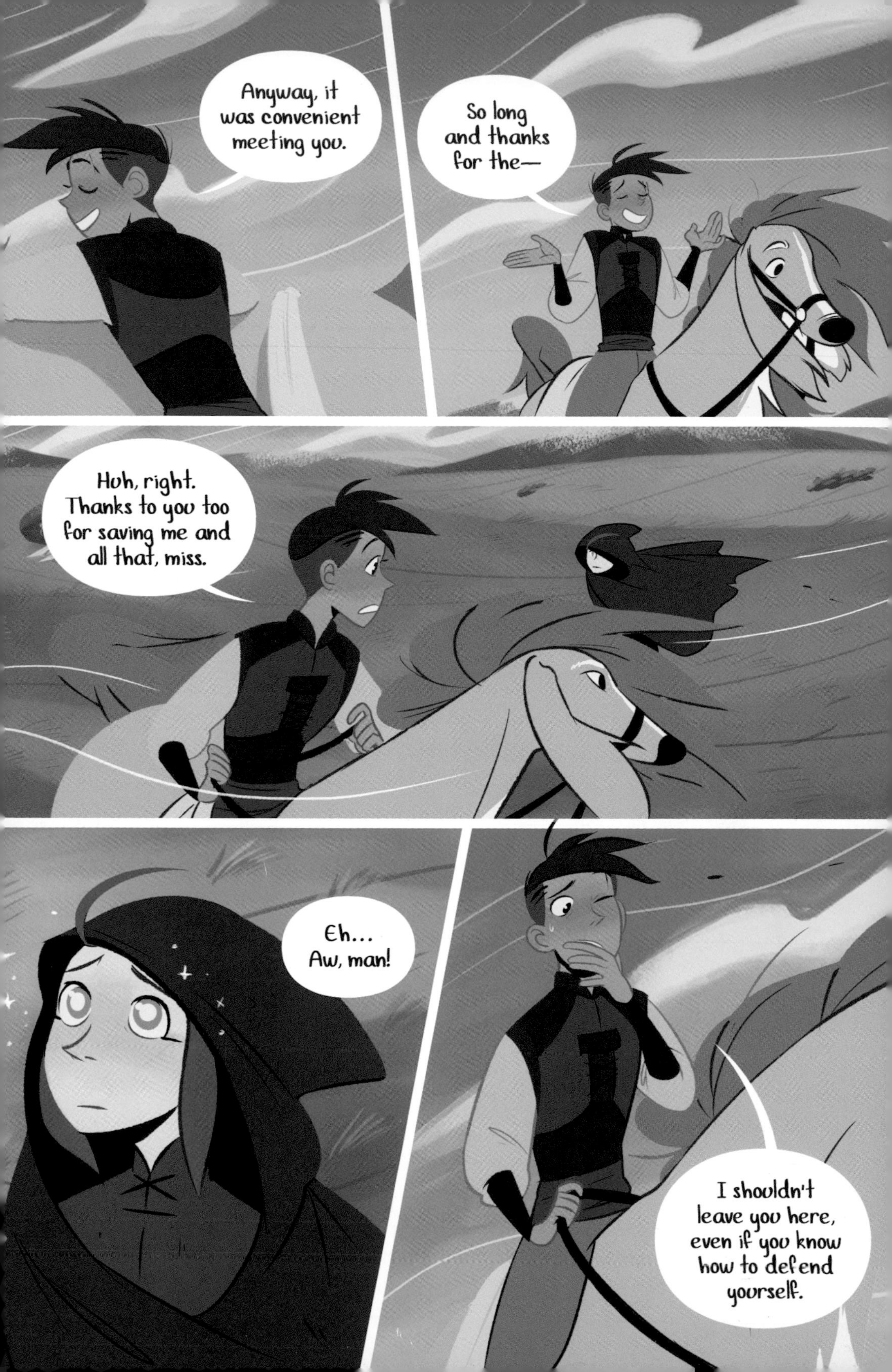
Anyway, it was convenient meeting you.
So long and thanks for the—
Huh, right. Thanks to you too for saving me and all that, miss.
Eh... Aw, man!
I shouldn't leave you here, even if you know how to defend yourself.

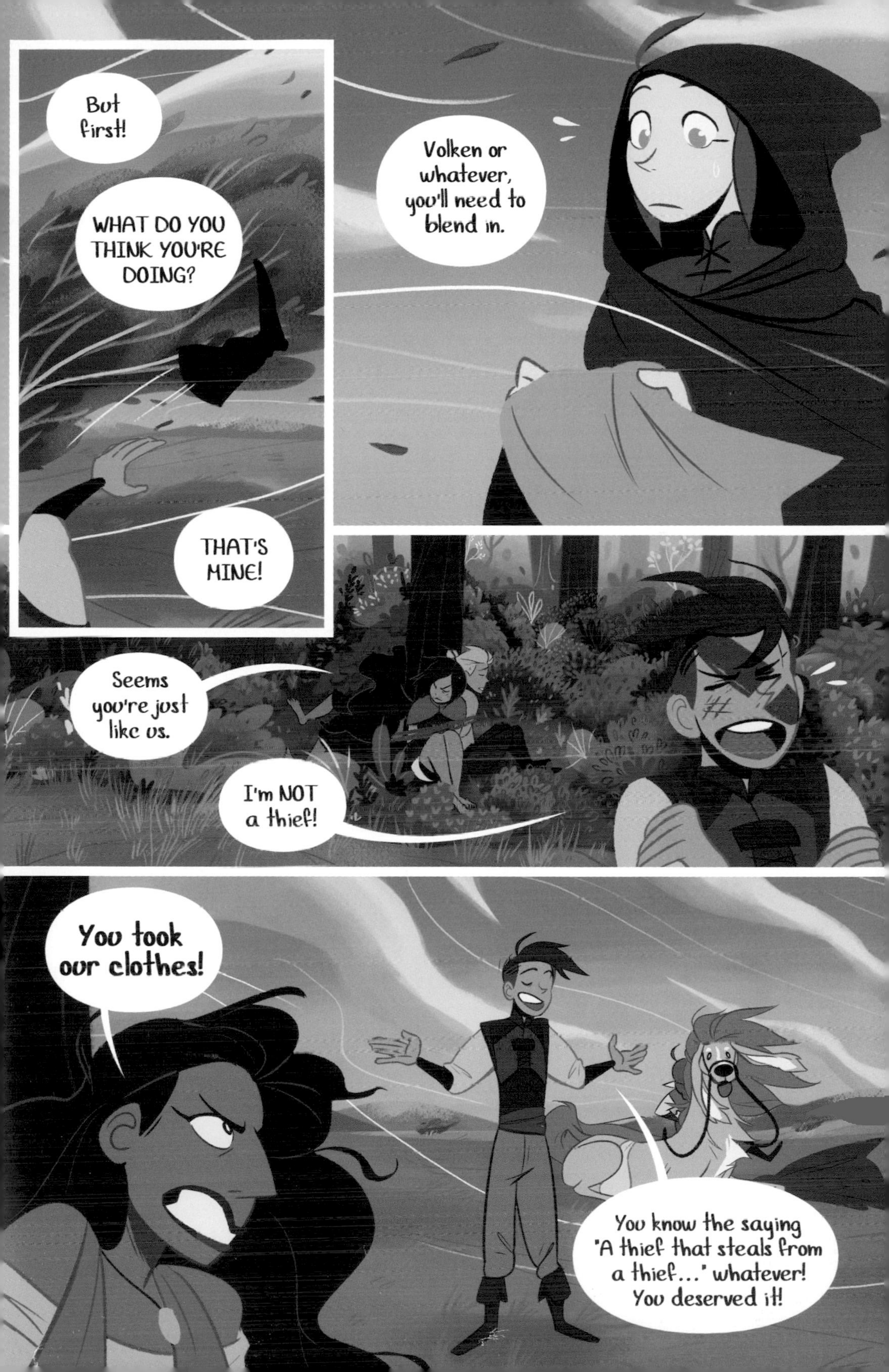
But first!
WHAT DO YOU THINK YOU'RE DOING?
THAT'S MINE!
Volken or whatever, you'll need to blend in.
Seems you're just like us.
I'm NOT a thief!
You took our clothes!
You know the saying "A thief that steals from a thief..." whatever! You deserved it!

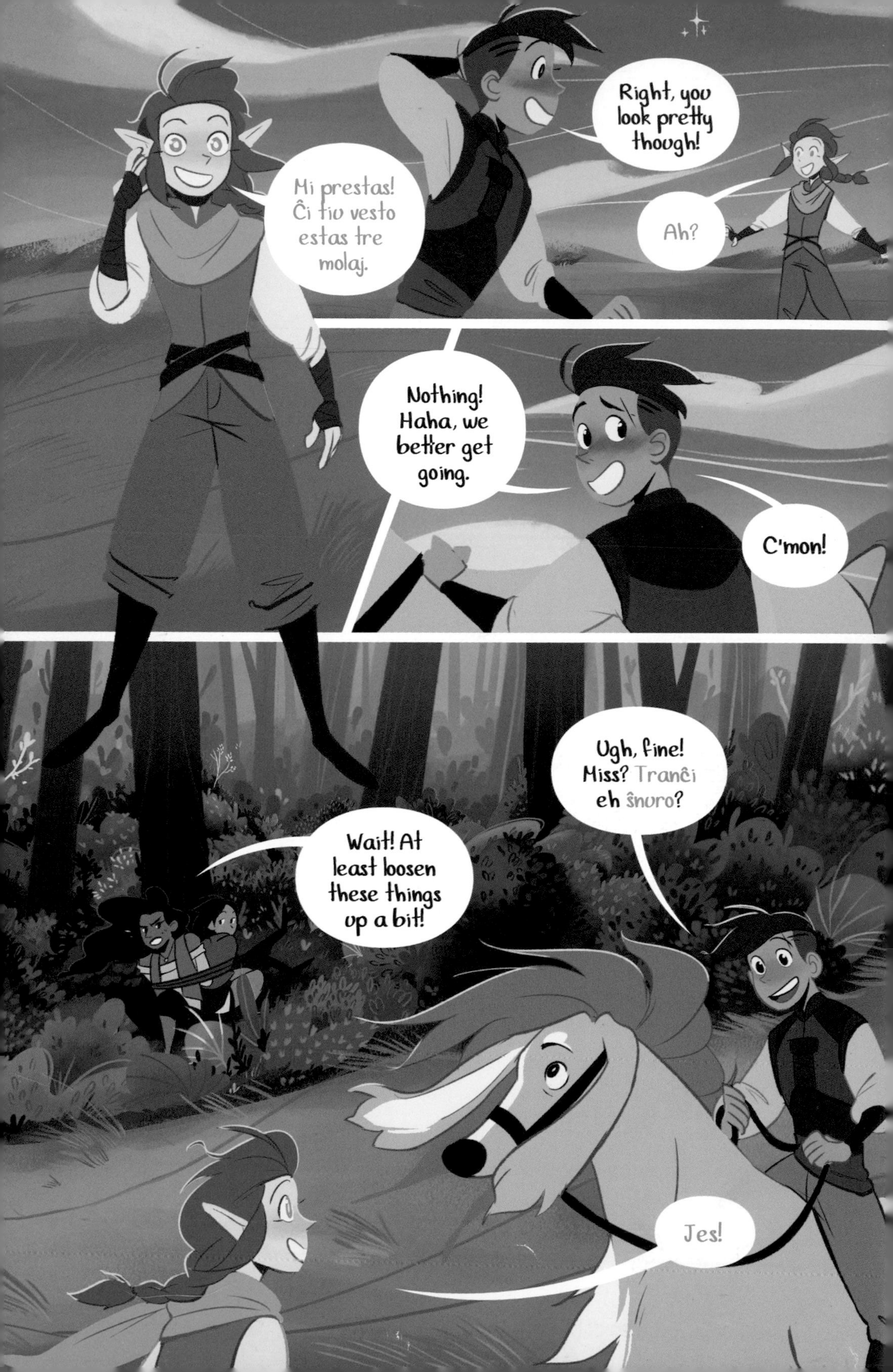
Mi prestas! Ĉi tiu vesto estas tre molaj.
Right, you look pretty though!
Ah?
Nothing! Haha, we better get going.
C'mon!
Ugh, fine! Miss? Tranĉi eh ŝnuro?
Wait! At least loosen these things up a bit!
Jes!

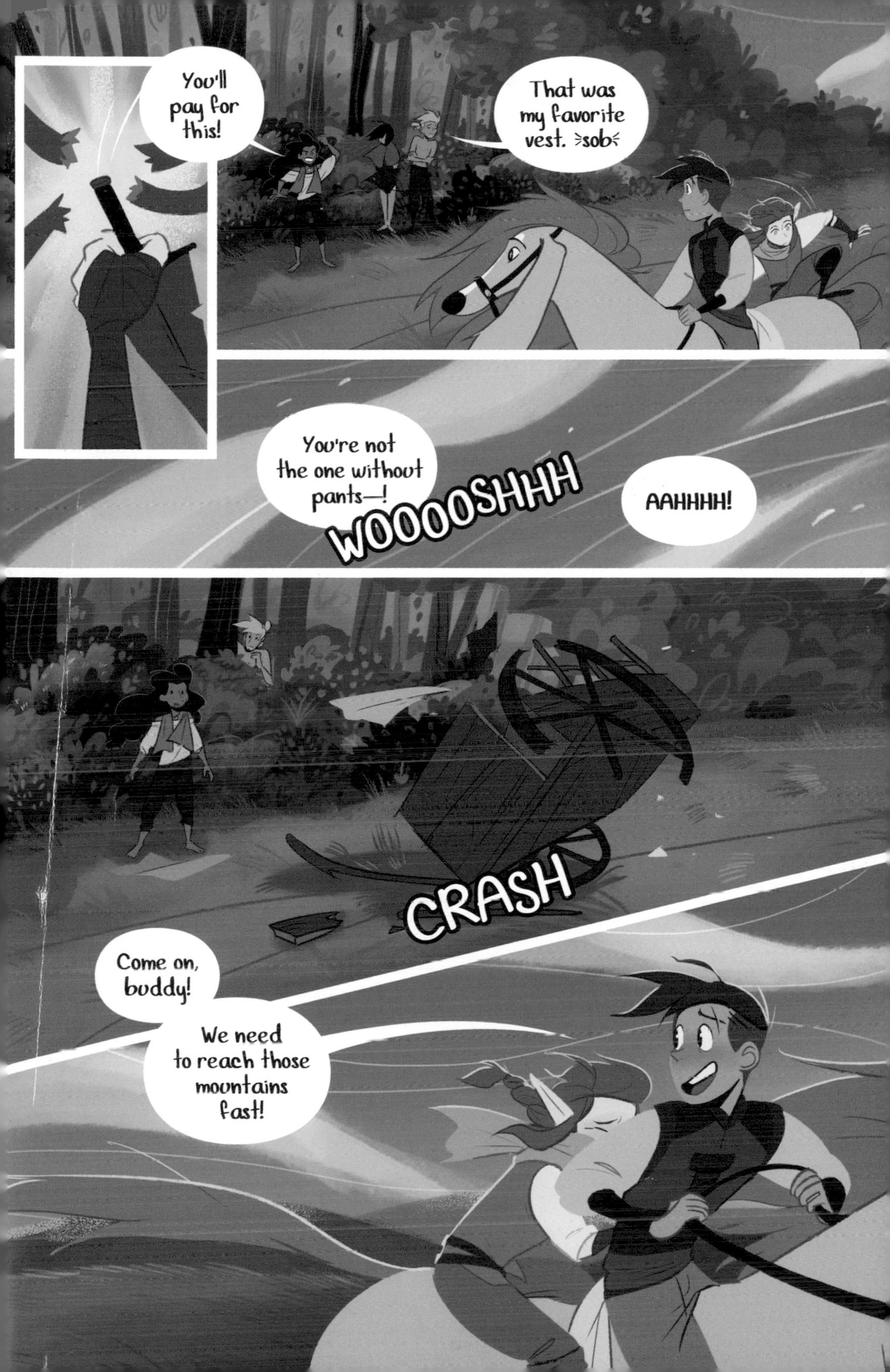

You'll pay for this!
That was my favorite vest. ≽sob≼
You're not the one without pants—!
WOOOOSHHH
AAHHHH!
CRASH
Come on, buddy!
We need to reach those mountains fast!

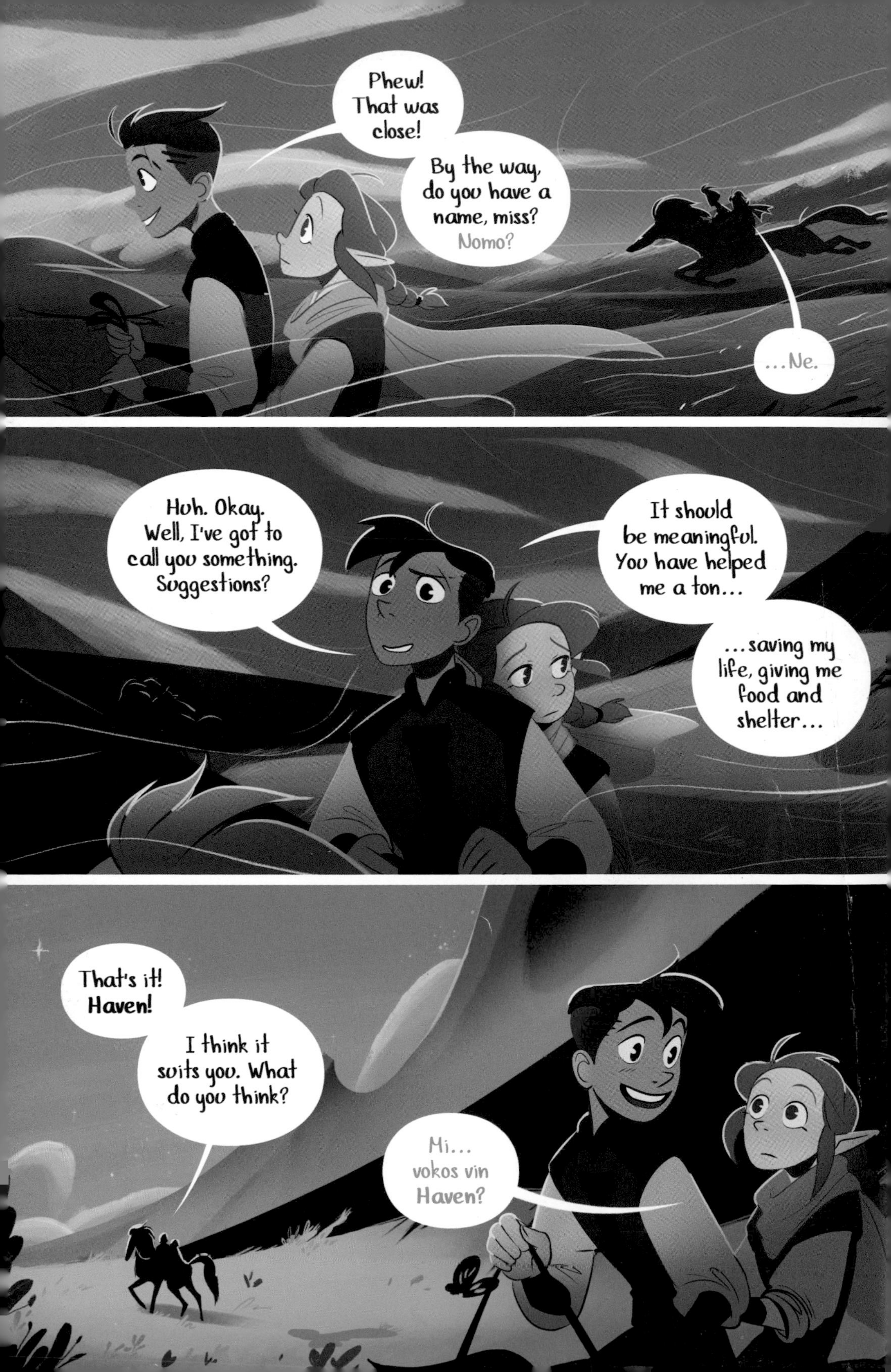
Phew! That was close!
By the way, do you have a name, miss? Nomo?
...Ne.
Huh. Okay. Well, I've got to call you something. Suggestions?
It should be meaningful. You have helped me a ton...
...saving my life, giving me food and shelter...
That's it! Haven!
I think it suits you. What do you think?
Mi... vokos vin Haven?

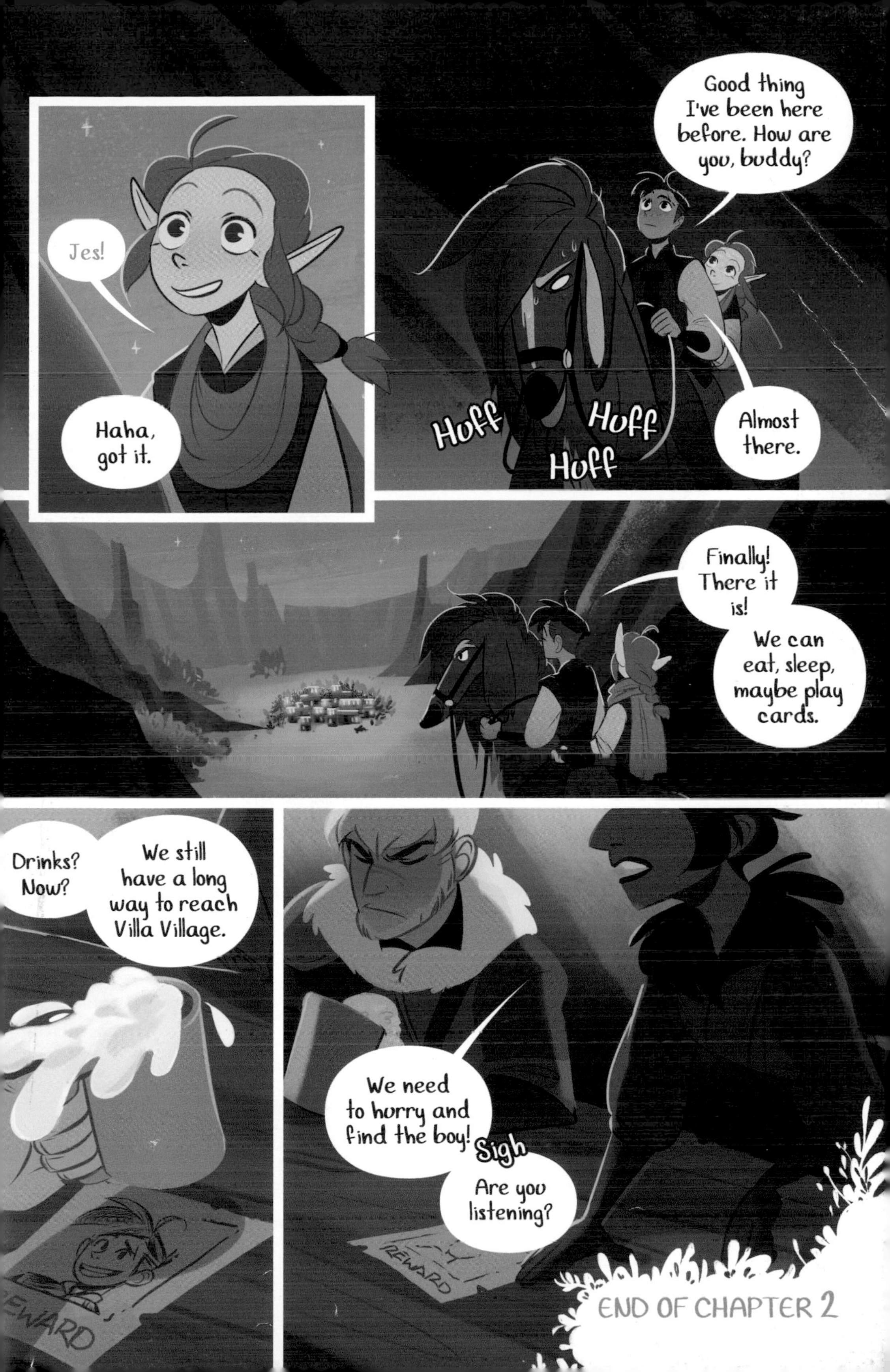
Jes!
Haha, got it.
Good thing I've been here before. How are you, buddy?
Huff
Huff
Huff
Almost there.
Finally! There it is!
We can eat, sleep, maybe play cards.
Drinks? Now?
We still have a long way to reach Villa Village.
REWARD
We need to hurry and find the boy!
Sigh
Are you listening?
REWARD
END OF CHAPTER 2

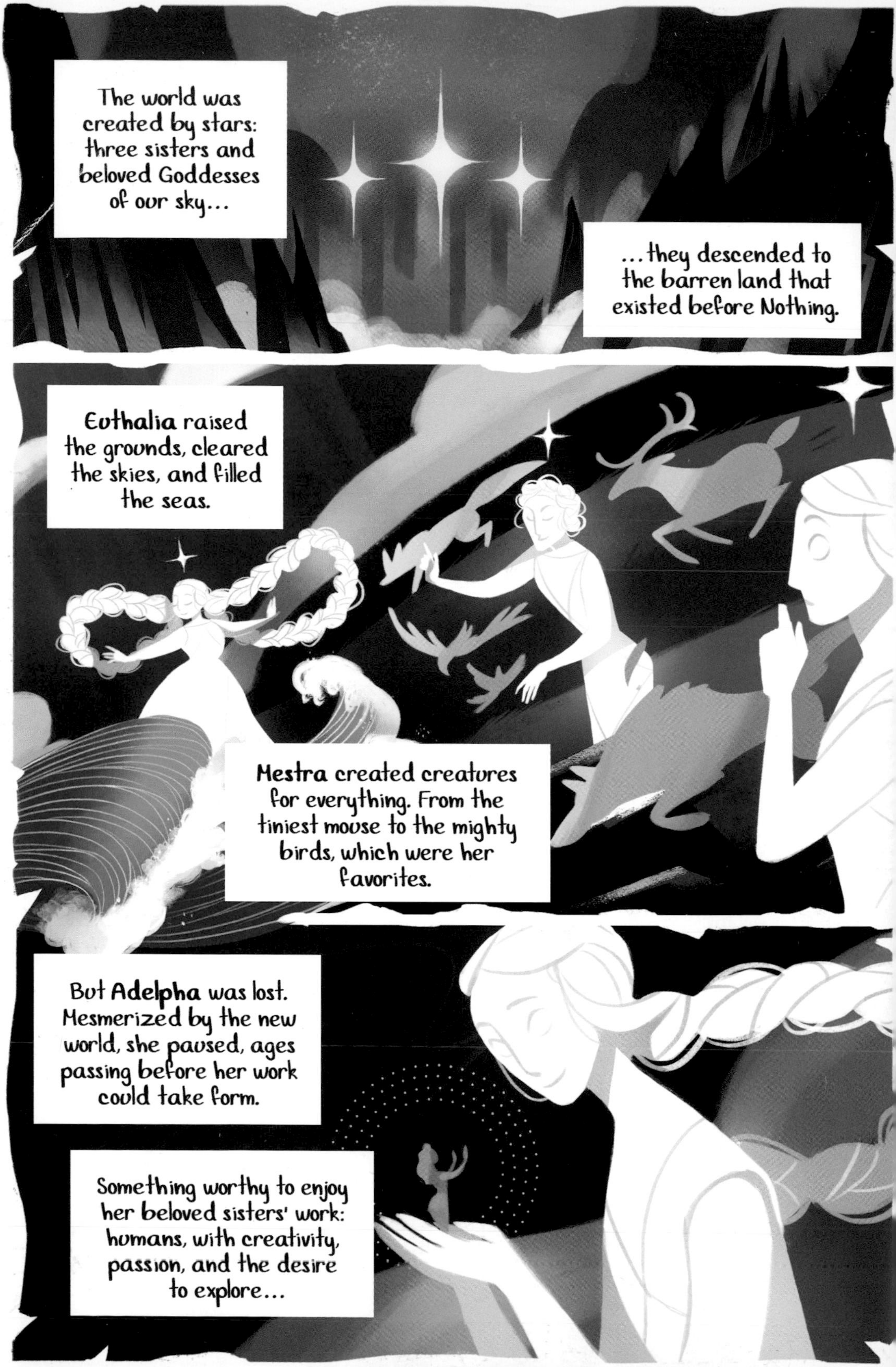
The world was created by stars: three sisters and beloved Goddesses of our sky...
...they descended to the barren land that existed before Nothing.
Euthalia raised the grounds, cleared the skies, and filled the seas.
Mestra created creatures for everything. From the tiniest mouse to the mighty birds, which were her favorites.
But Adelpha was lost. Mesmerized by the new world, she paused, ages passing before her work could take form.
Something worthy to enjoy her beloved sisters' work: humans, with creativity, passion, and the desire to explore...

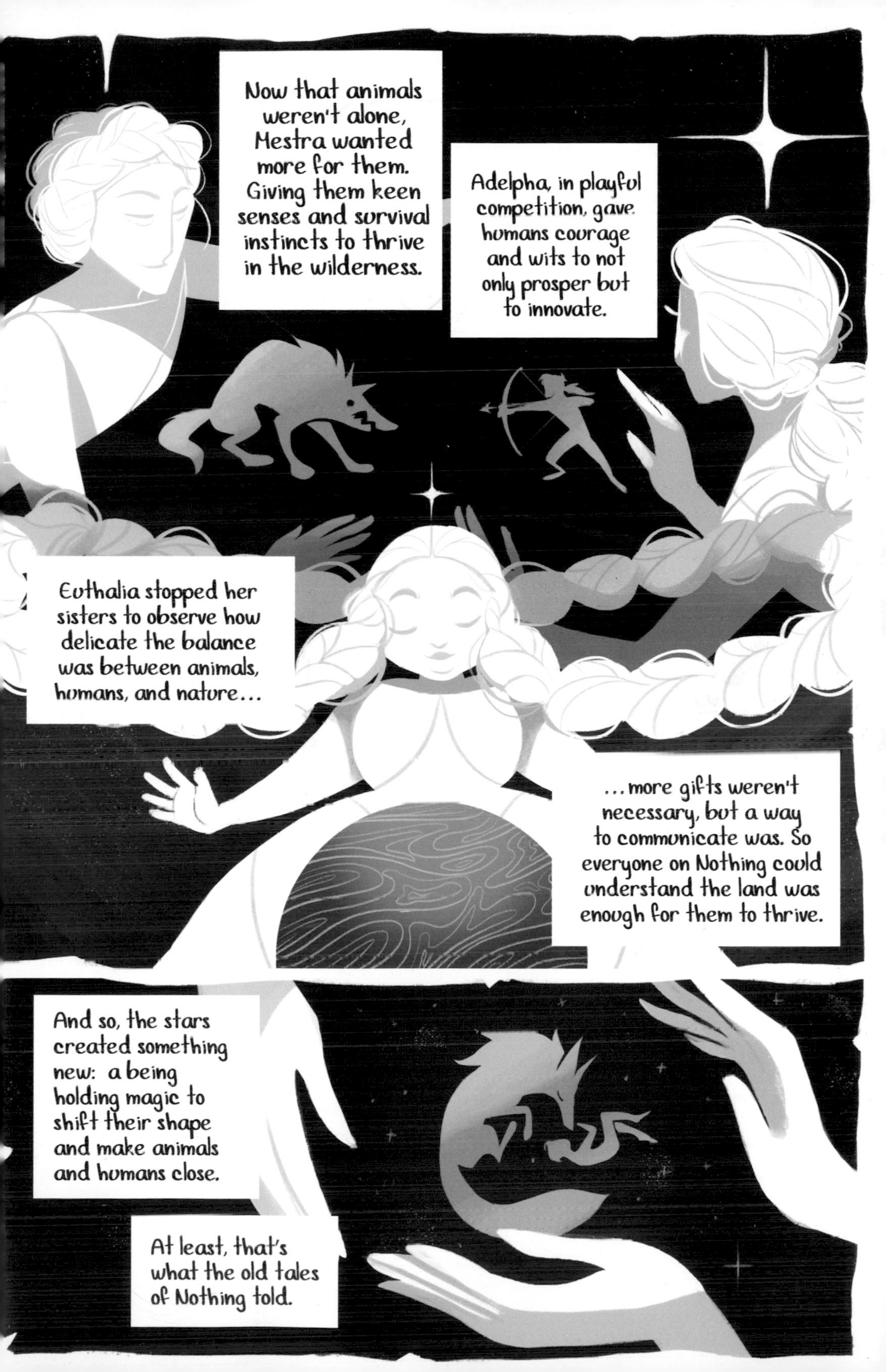
Now that animals weren't alone, Mestra wanted more for them. Giving them keen senses and survival instincts to thrive in the wilderness.
Adelpha, in playful competition, gave humans courage and wits to not only prosper but to innovate.
Euthalia stopped her sisters to observe how delicate the balance was between animals, humans, and nature...
...more gifts weren't necessary, but a way to communicate was. So everyone on Nothing could understand the land was enough for them to thrive.
And so, the stars created something new: a being holding magic to shift their shape and make animals and humans close.
At least, that's what the old tales of Nothing told.

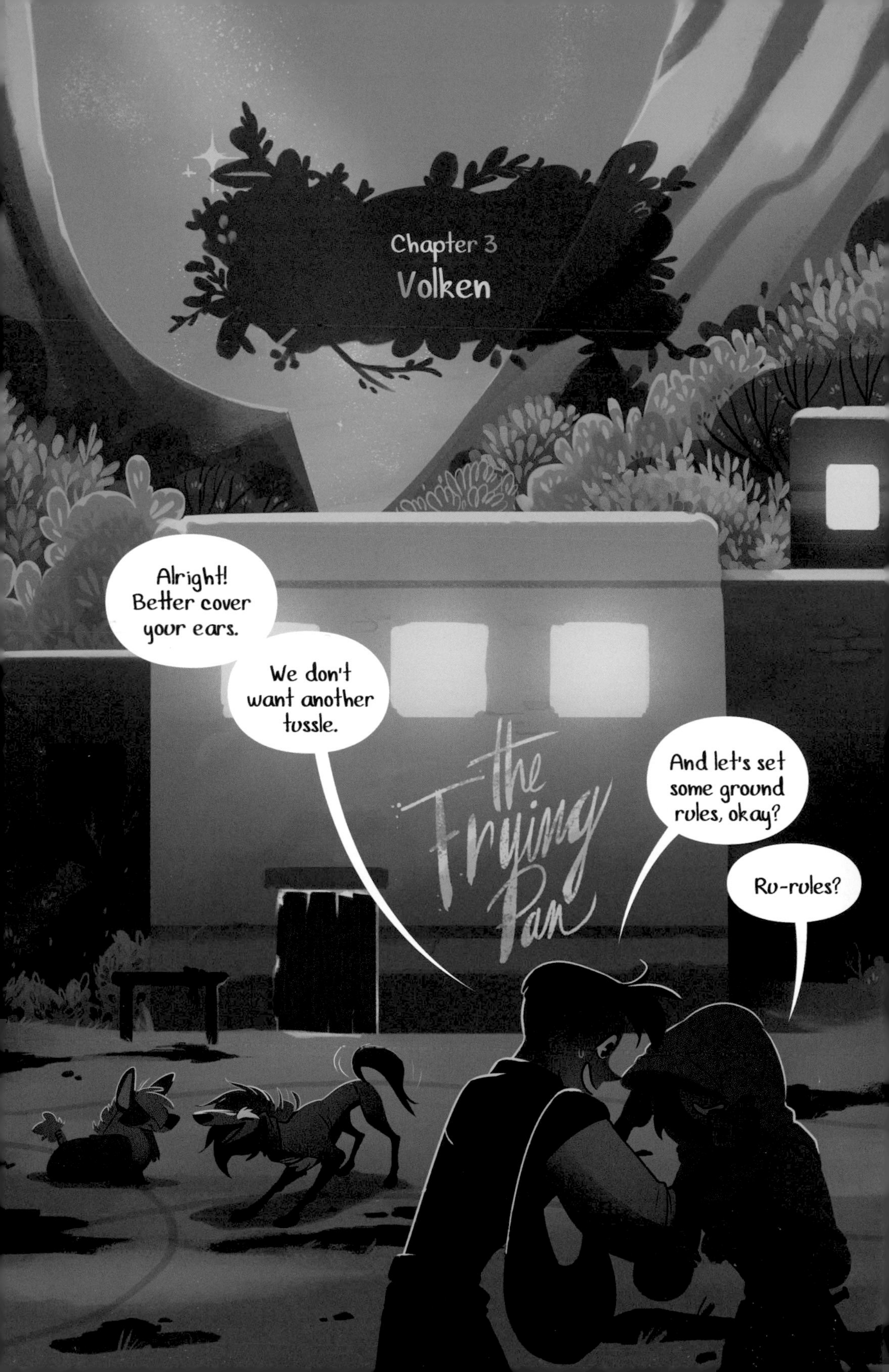
Chapter 3
Volken
Alright! Better cover your ears.
We don't want another tussle.
The Frying Pan
And let's set some ground rules, okay?
Ru-rules?

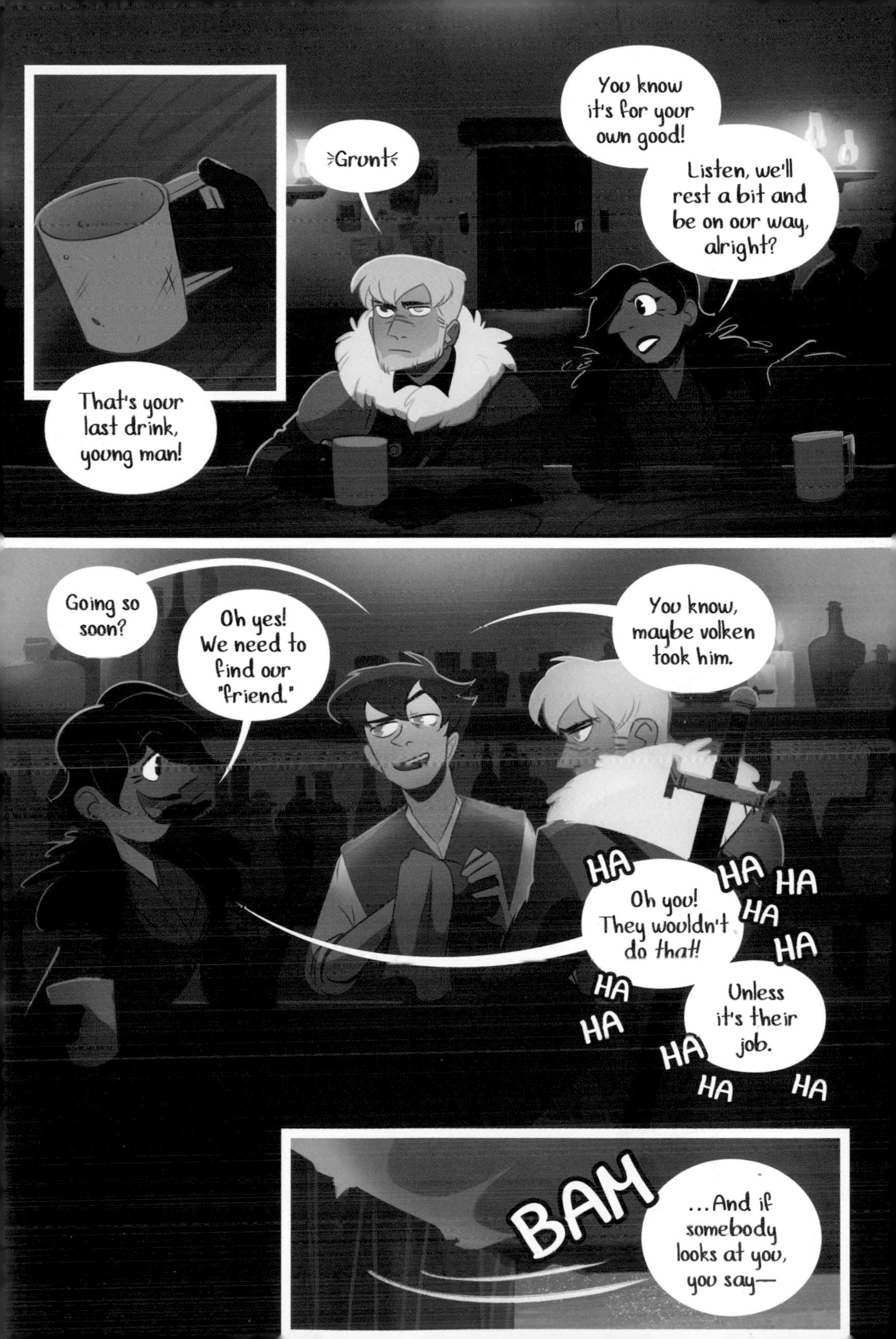
That's your last drink, young man!
⋟Grunt⋞
You know it's for your own good!
Listen, we'll rest a bit and be on our way, alright?
Going so soon?
Oh yes! We need to find our "friend."
You know, maybe volken took him.
HA HA HA HA HA HA HA HA HA HA
Oh you! They wouldn't do that!
Unless it's their job.
BAM
...And if somebody looks at you, you say—

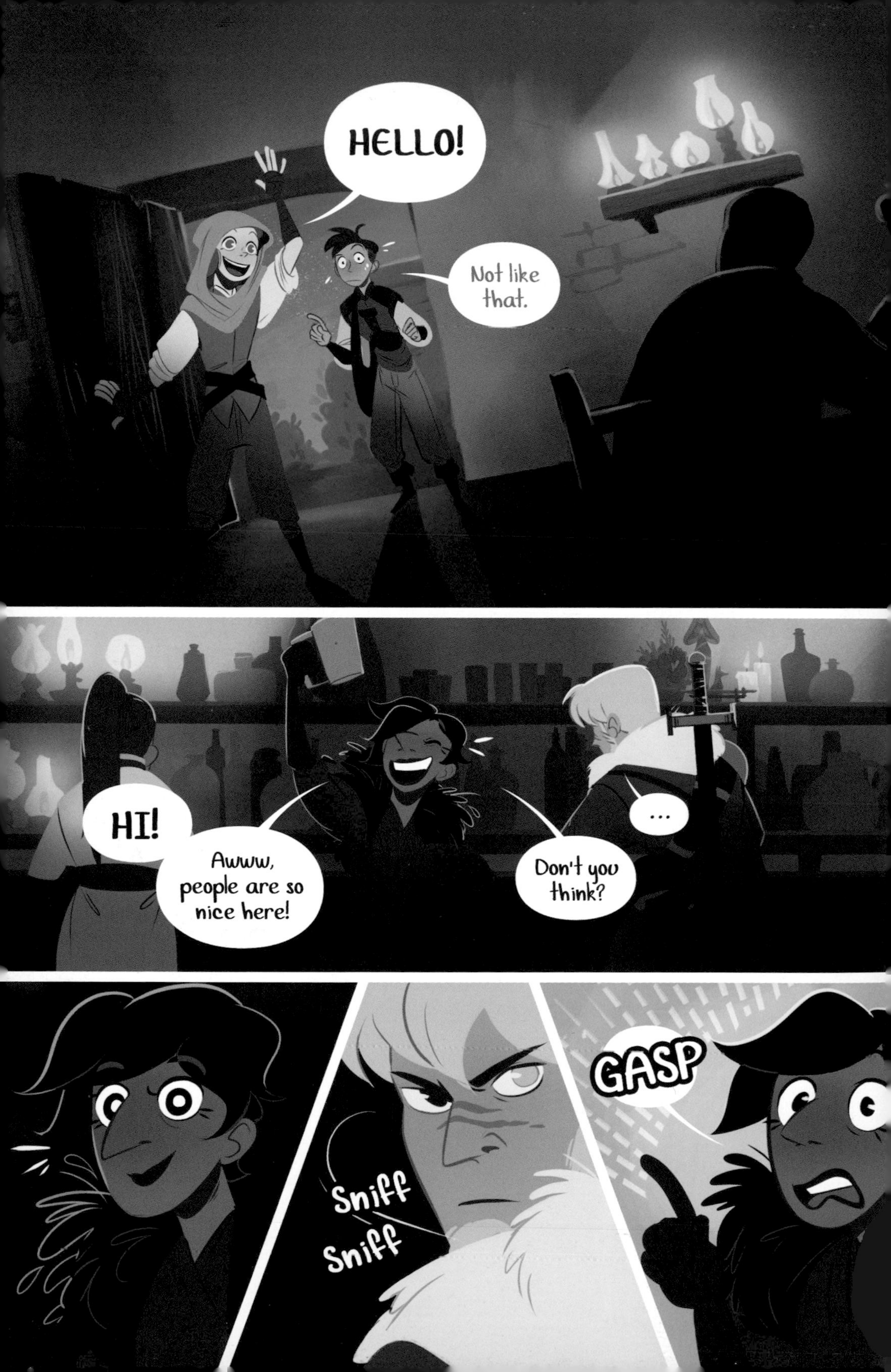
HELLO!
Not like that.
HI!
Awww, people are so nice here!
Don't you think?
...
Sniff
Sniff
GASP

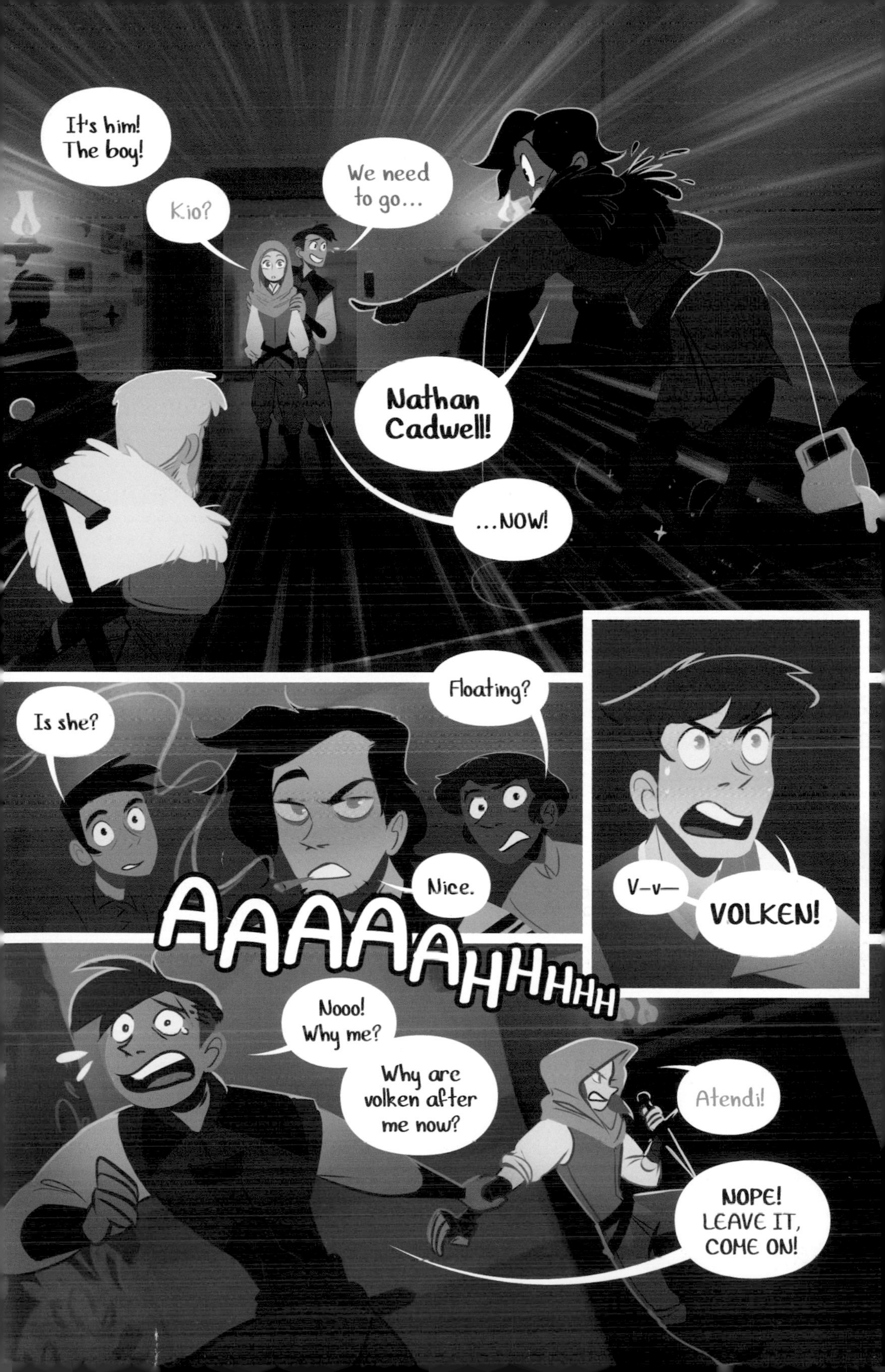

It's him! The boy!
Kio?
We need to go...
Nathan Cadwell!
...NOW!
Is she?
Floating?
Nice.
V–v—
VOLKEN!
AAAAAAHHHHH
Nooo! Why me?
Why are volken after me now?
Atendi!
NOPE! LEAVE IT, COME ON!

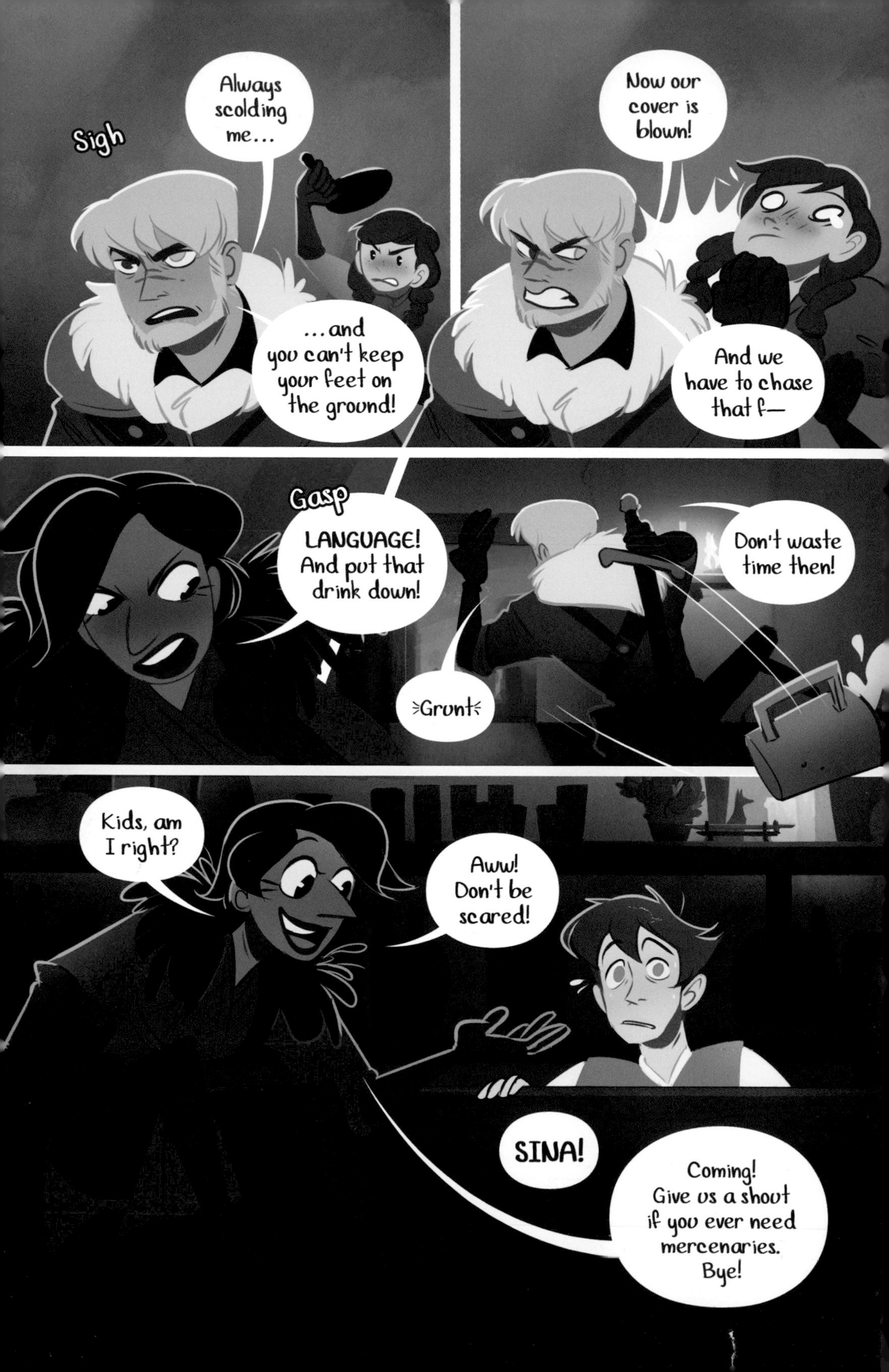
Sigh
Always scolding me...
...and you can't keep your feet on the ground!
Now our cover is blown!
And we have to chase that f—
Gasp
LANGUAGE! And put that drink down!
Don't waste time then!
Grunt
Kids, am I right?
Aww! Don't be scared!
SINA!
Coming! Give us a shout if you ever need mercenaries. Bye!

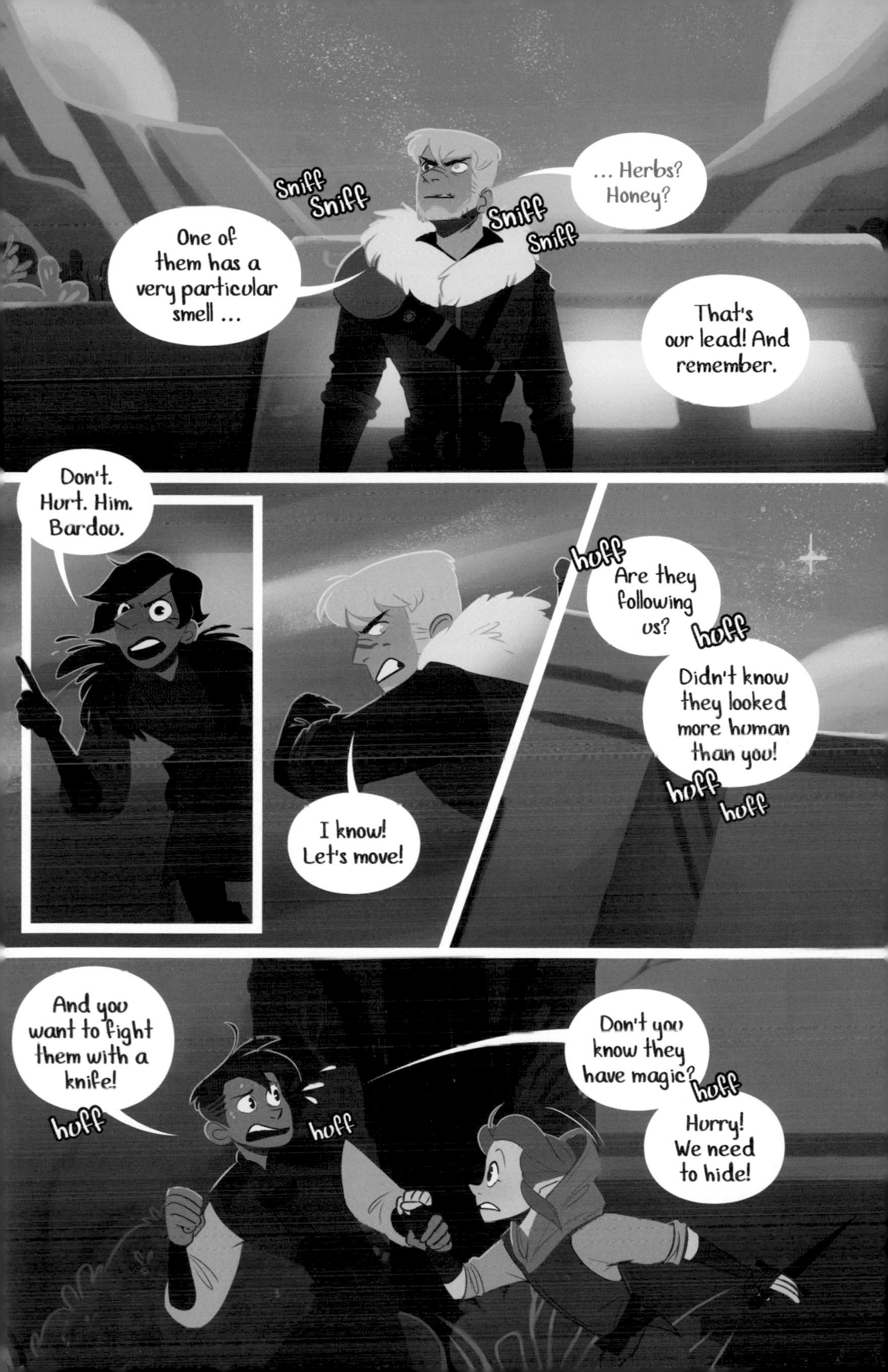
Sniff
Sniff
One of them has a very particular smell ...
Sniff
Sniff
... Herbs? Honey?
That's our lead! And remember.
Don't. Hurt. Him. Bardou.
I know! Let's move!
hoff
Are they following us?
hoff
Didn't know they looked more human than you!
hoff
hoff
And you want to fight them with a knife!
hoff
hoff
Don't you know they have magic?
hoff
Hurry! We need to hide!

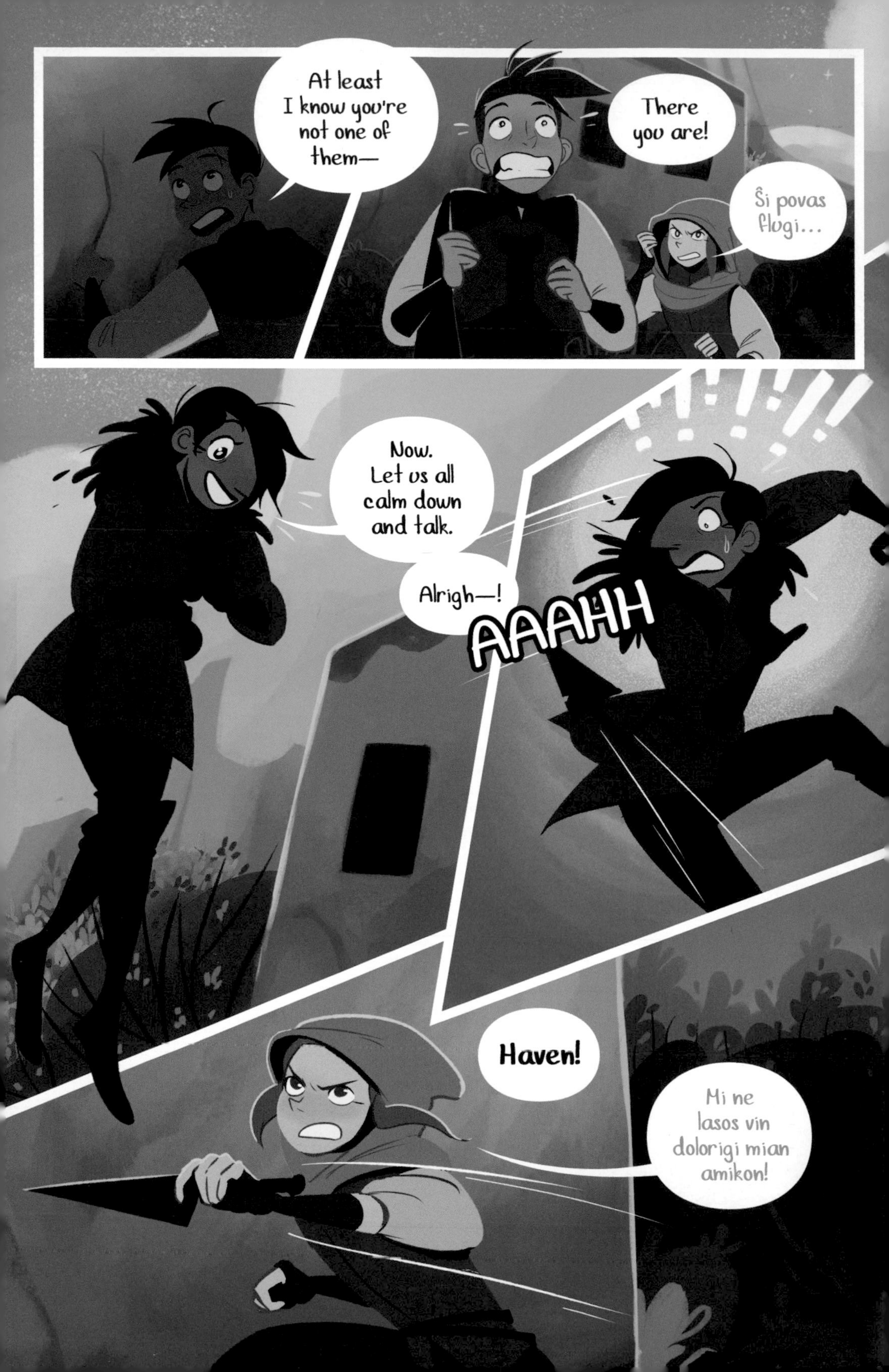
At least I know you're not one of them—
There you are!
Ŝi povas flugi...
Now. Let us all calm down and talk.
Alrigh—!
AAAHH
Haven!
Mi ne lasos vin dolorigi mian amikon!

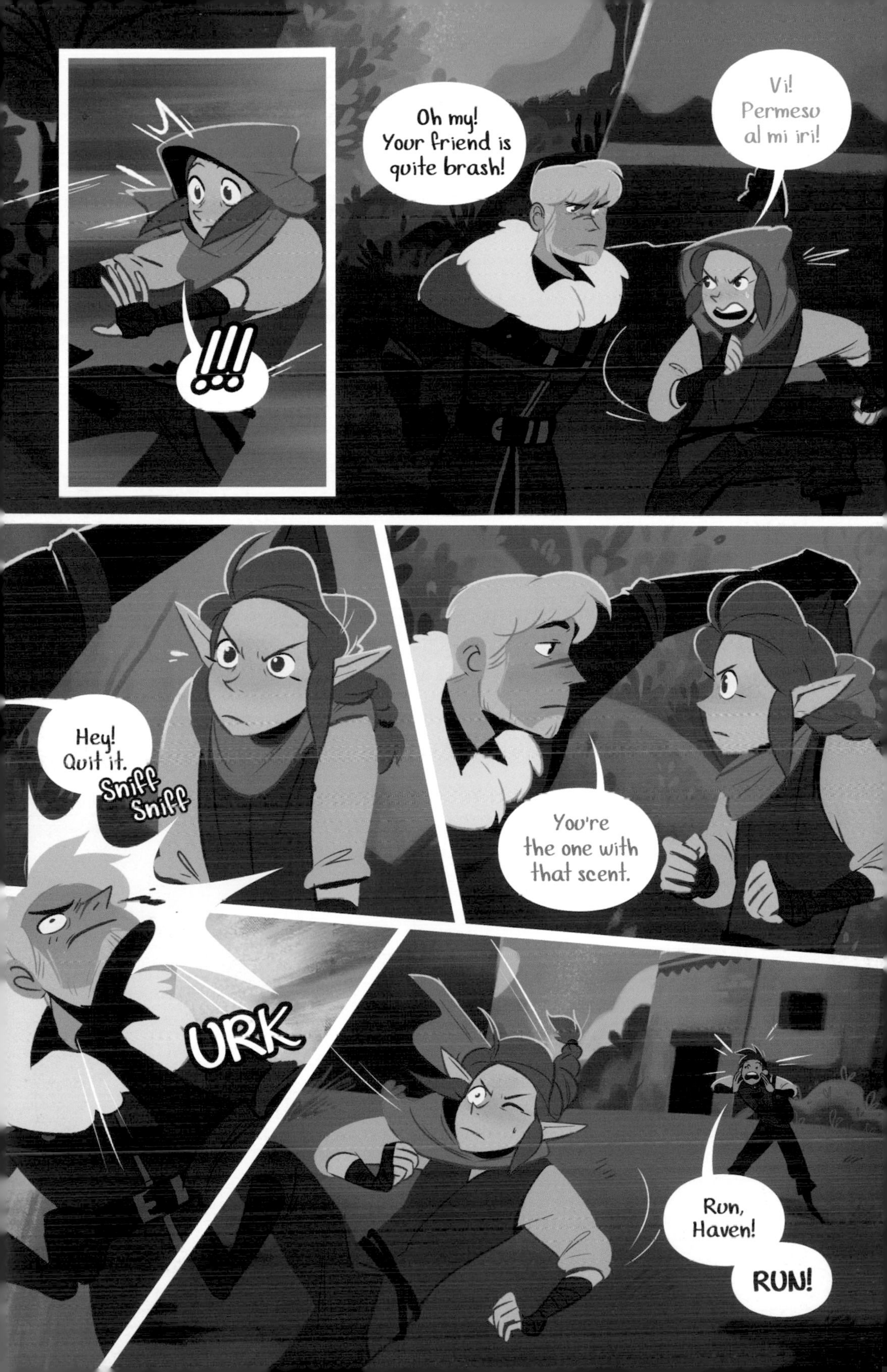
!!!
Oh my! Your friend is quite brash!
Vi! Permeso al mi iri!
Hey! Quit it.
Sniff Sniff
You're the one with that scent.
URK
Run, Haven!
RUN!

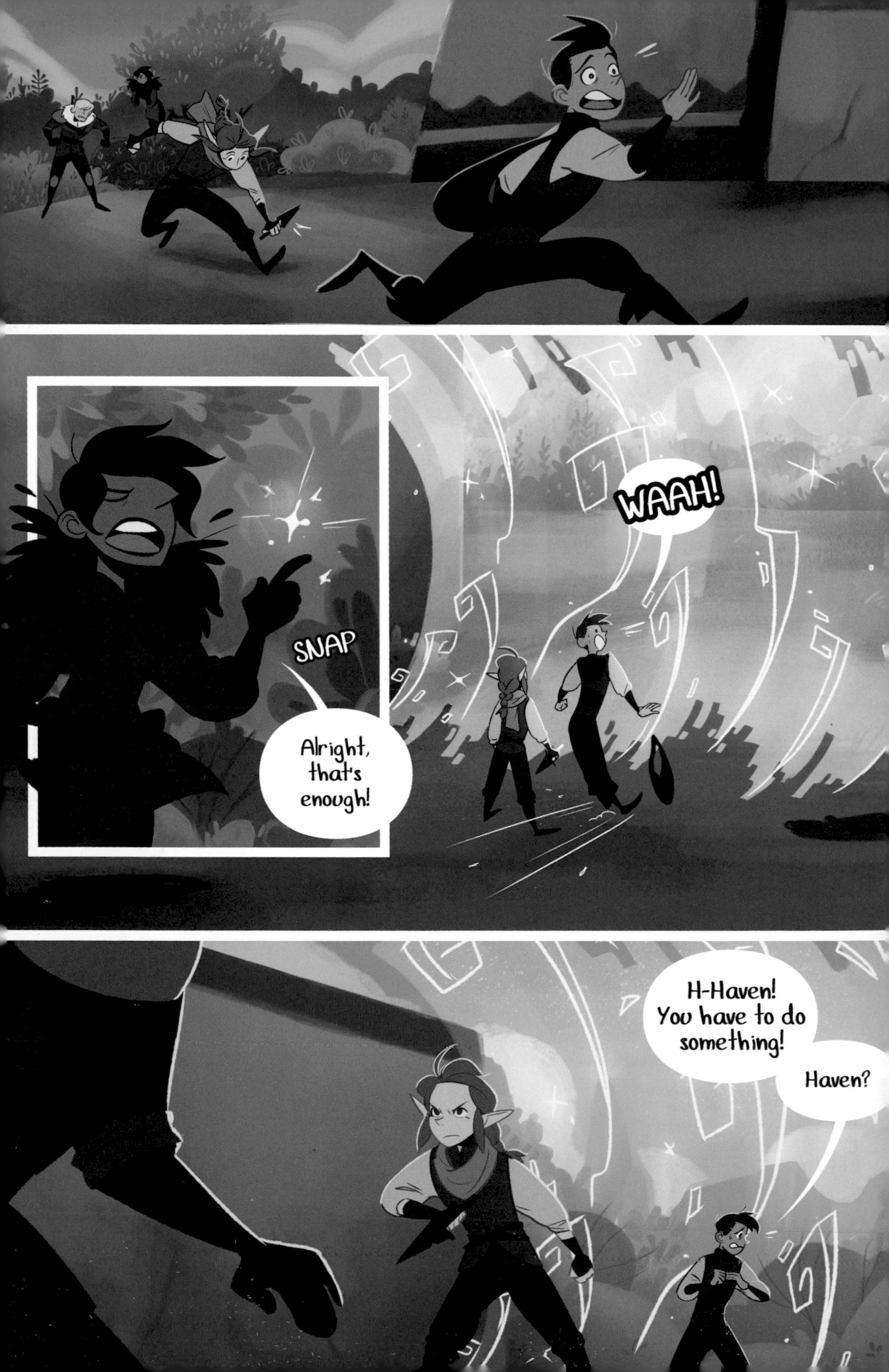
SNAP
Alright, that's enough!
WAAH!
H-Haven! You have to do something!
Haven?

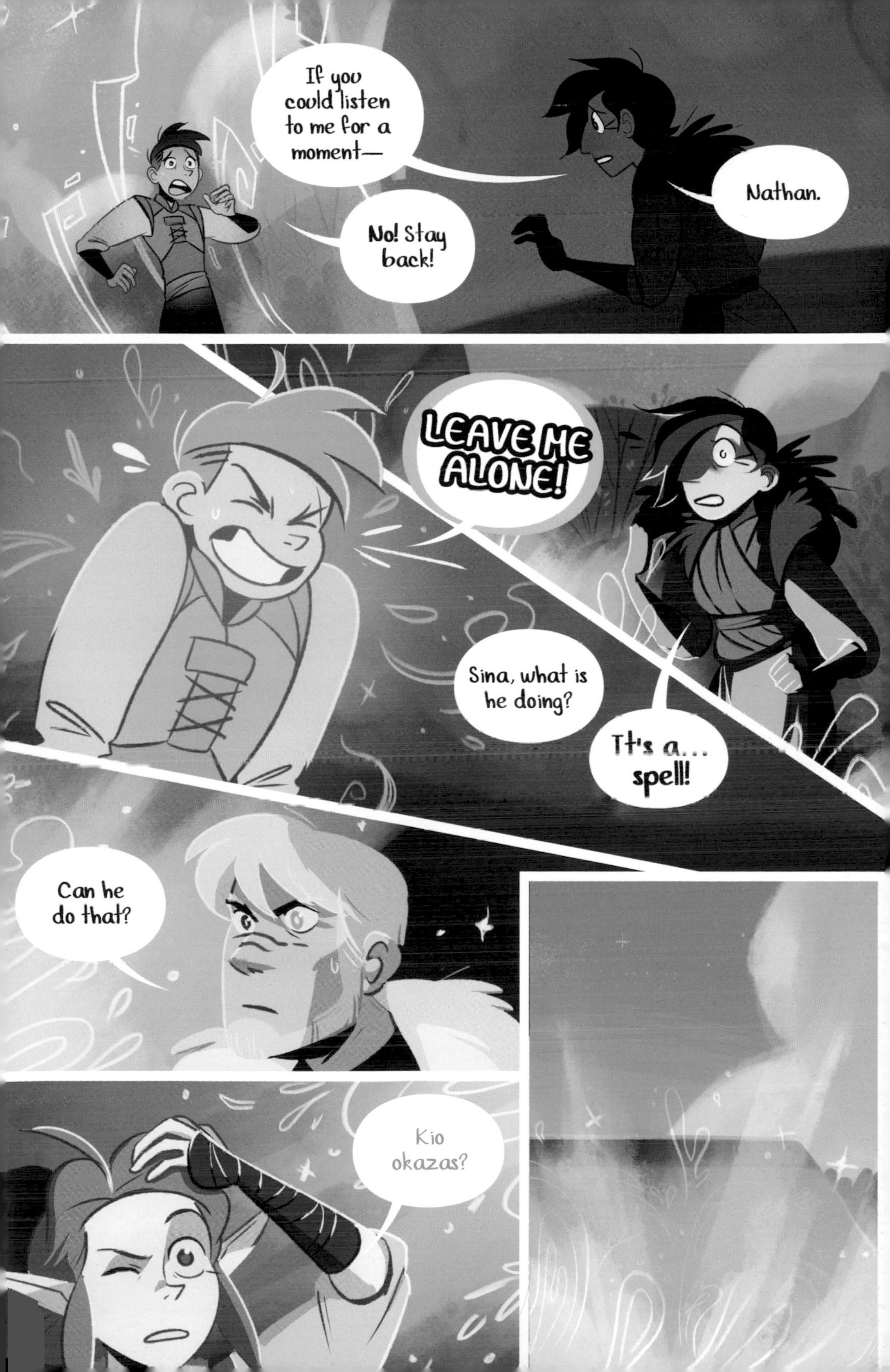

If you could listen to me for a moment—
No! Stay back!
Nathan.
LEAVE ME ALONE!
Sina, what is he doing?
It's a... spell!
Can he do that?
Kio okazas?

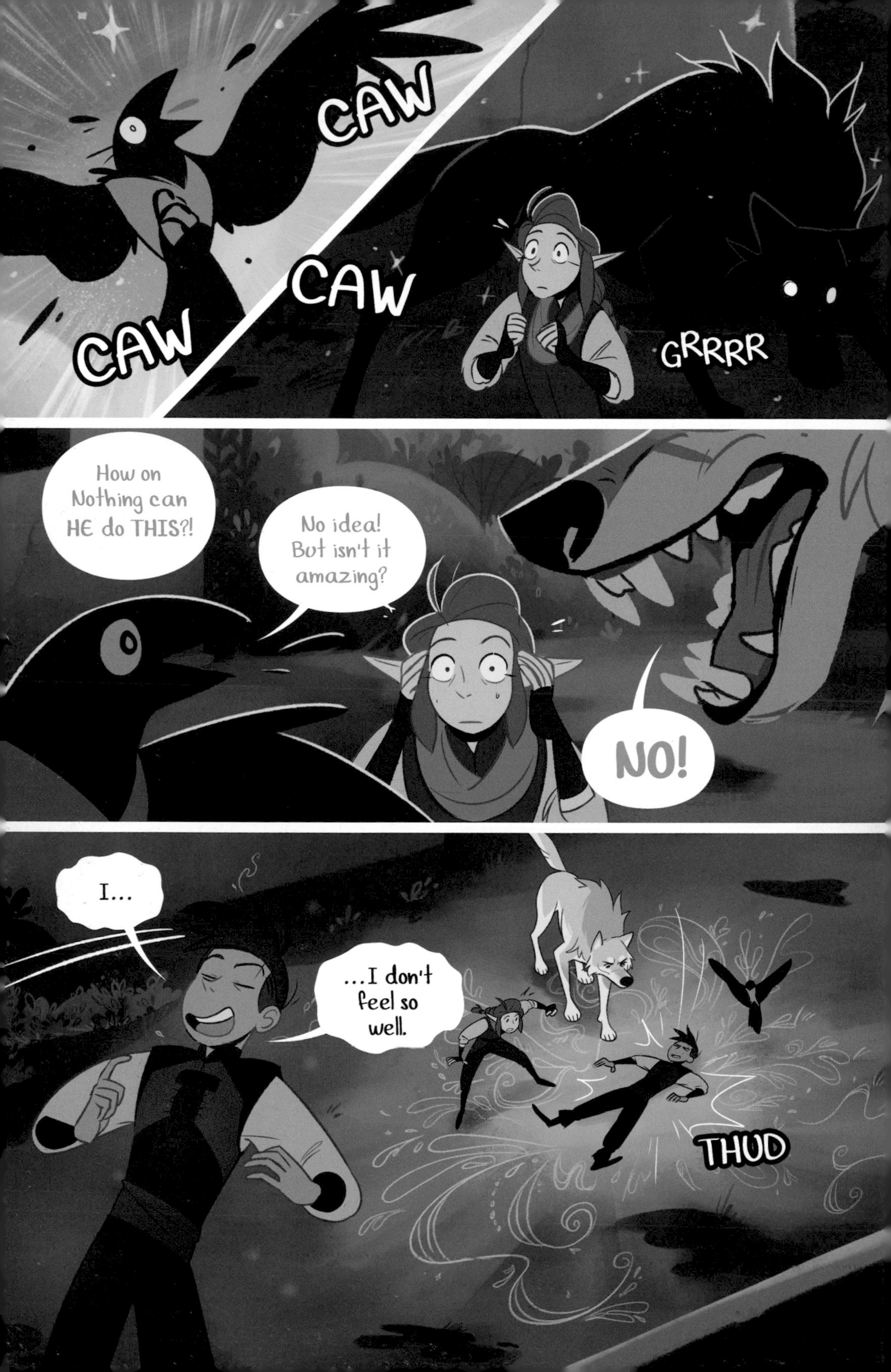
CAW
CAW
CAW
GRRRR
How on Nothing can HE do THIS?!
No idea! But isn't it amazing?
NO!
I...
...I don't feel so well.
THUD

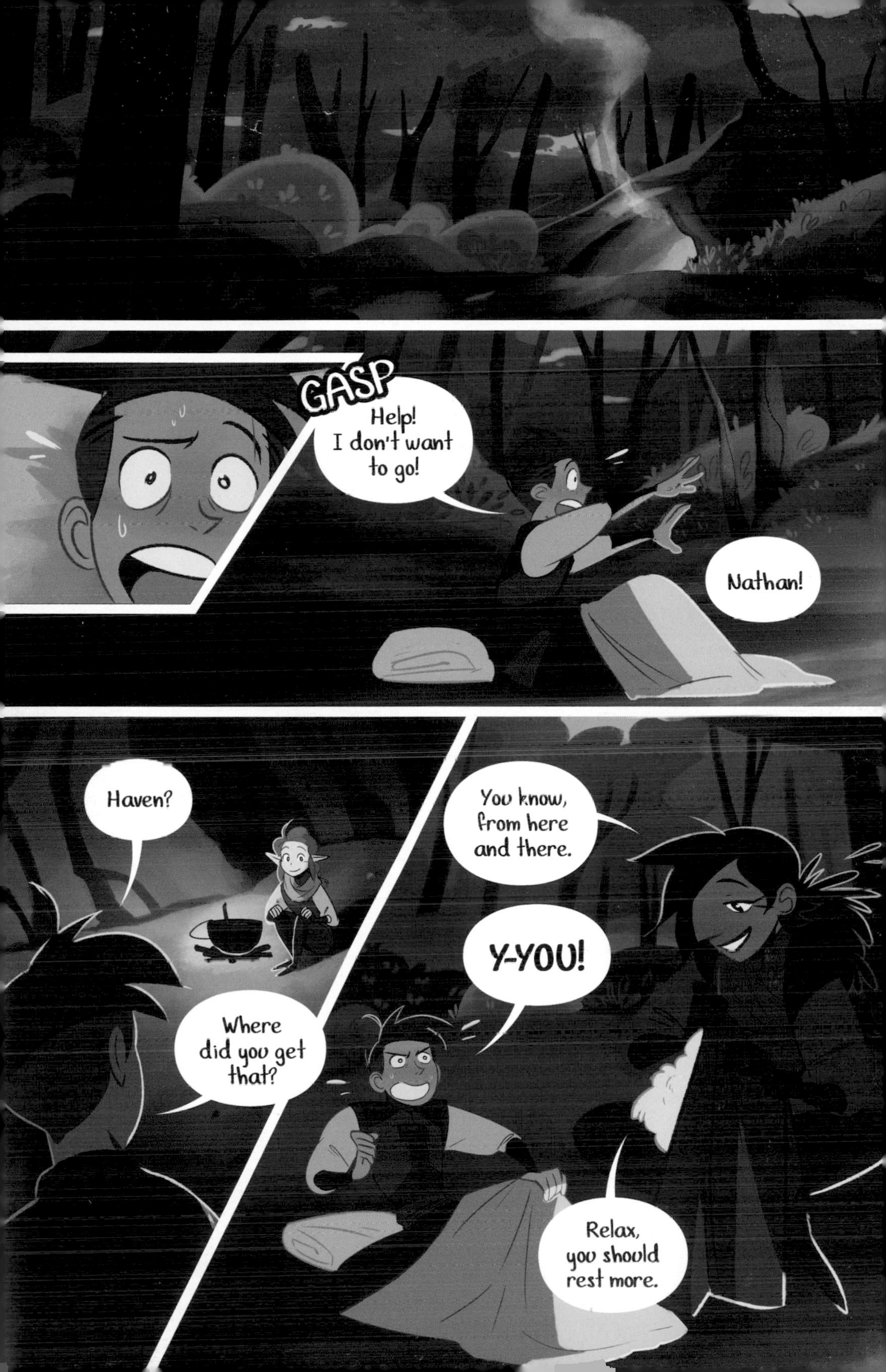
GASP
Help! I don't want to go!
Nathan!
Haven?
Where did you get that?
You know, from here and there.
Y-YOU!
Relax, you should rest more.

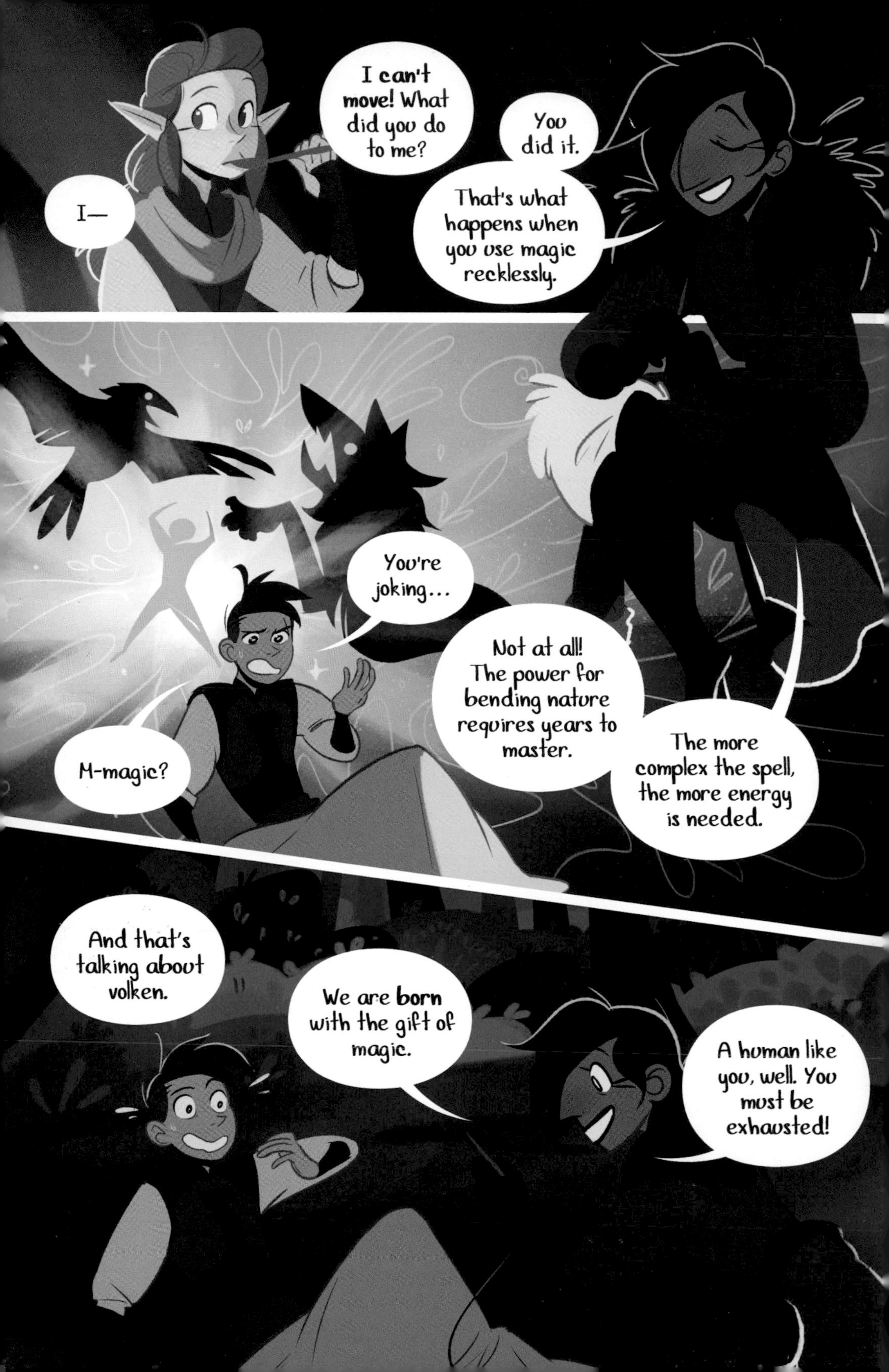

I can't move! What did you do to me?
I—
You did it.
That's what happens when you use magic recklessly.
You're joking...
M-magic?
Not at all! The power for bending nature requires years to master.
The more complex the spell, the more energy is needed.
And that's talking about volken.
We are born with the gift of magic.
A human like you, well. You must be exhausted!

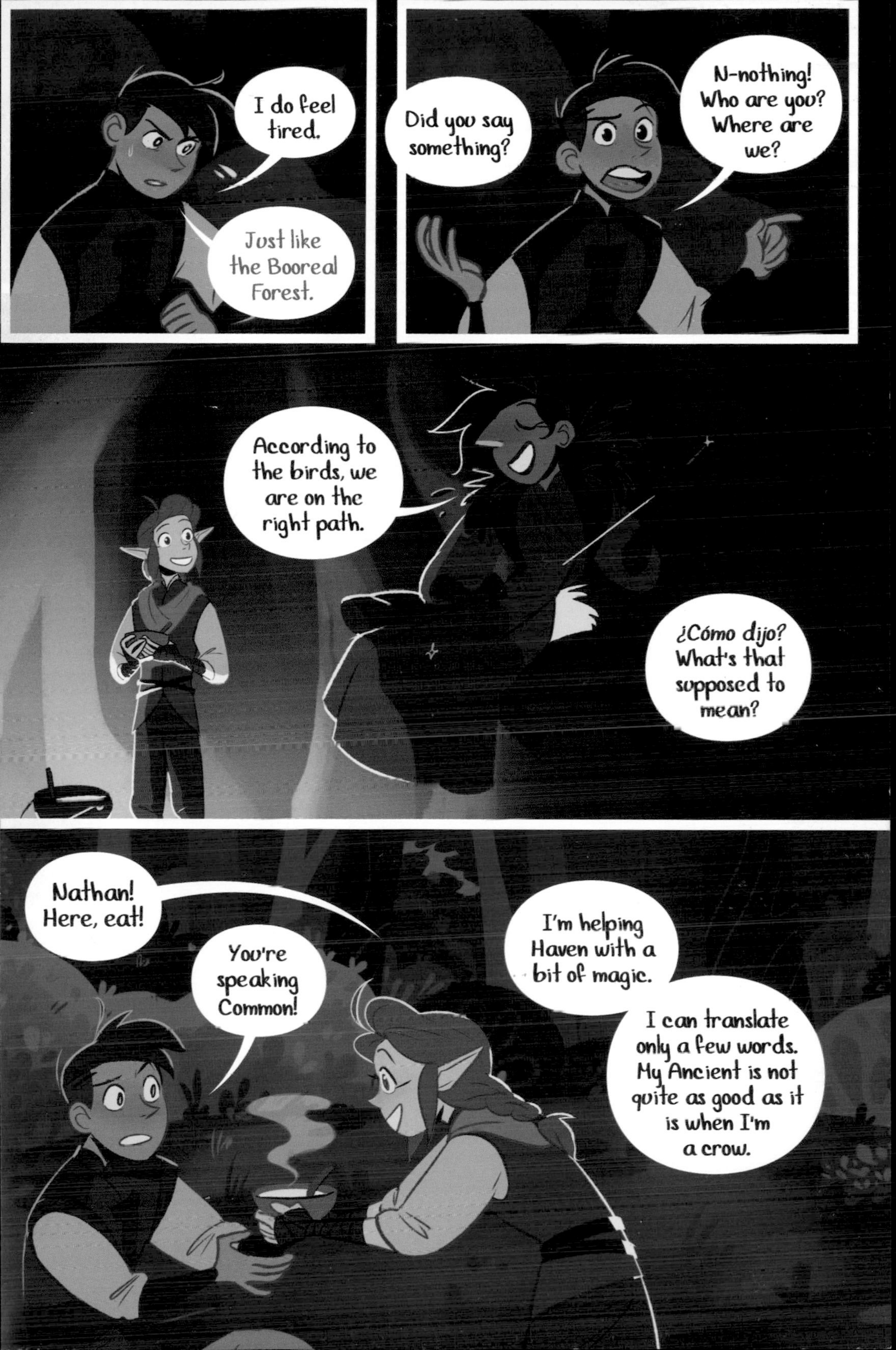
I do feel tired.
Just like the Booreal Forest.
Did you say something?
N-nothing! Who are you? Where are we?
According to the birds, we are on the right path.
¿Cómo dijo? What's that supposed to mean?
Nathan! Here, eat!
You're speaking Common!
I'm helping Haven with a bit of magic.
I can translate only a few words. My Ancient is not quite as good as it is when I'm a crow.

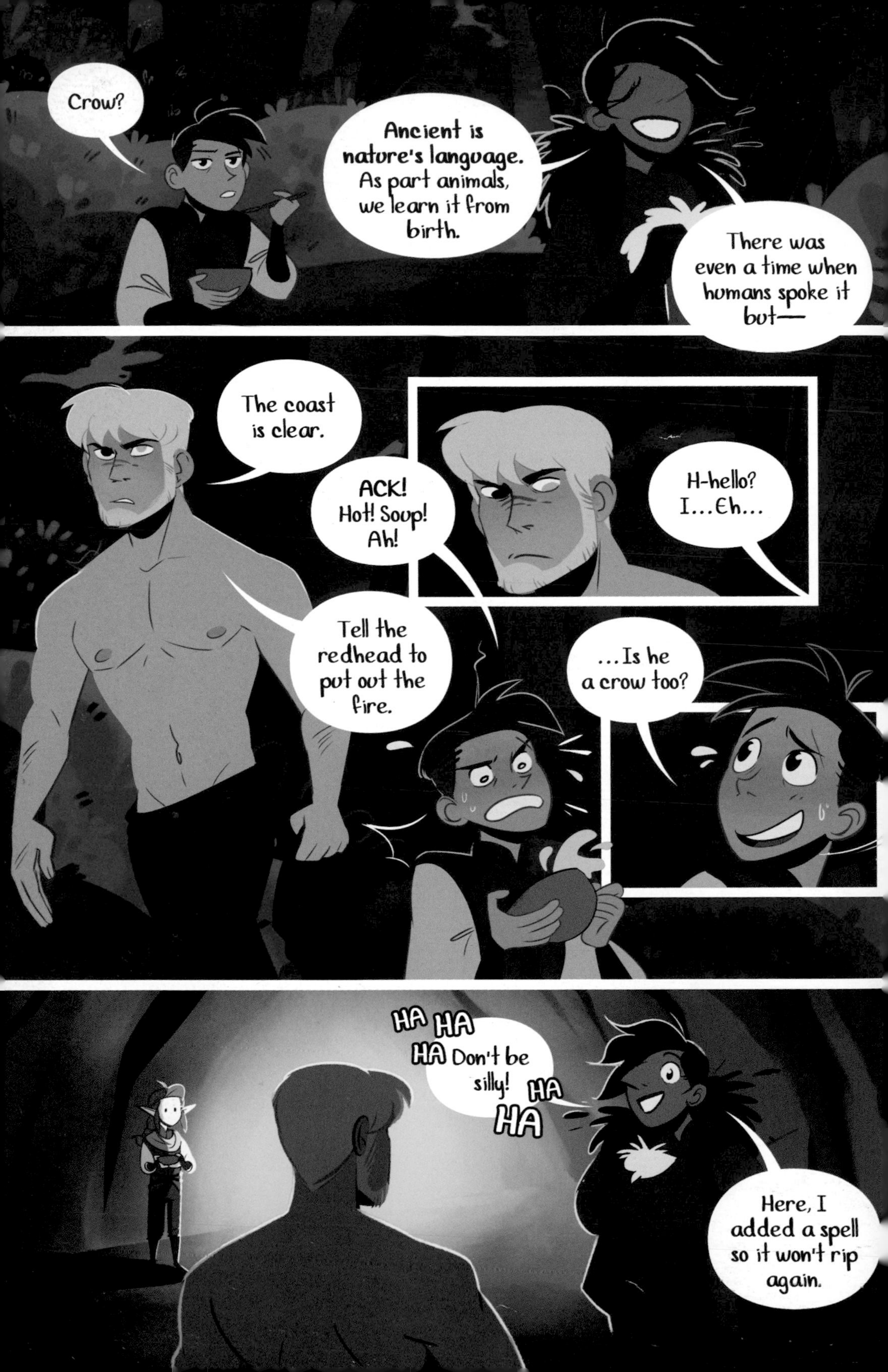

Crow?
Ancient is nature's language. As part animals, we learn it from birth.
There was even a time when humans spoke it but—
The coast is clear.
ACK! Hot! Soup! Ah!
H-hello? I...Eh...
Tell the redhead to put out the fire.
...Is he a crow too?
HA HA HA Don't be silly! HA HA
Here, I added a spell so it won't rip again.

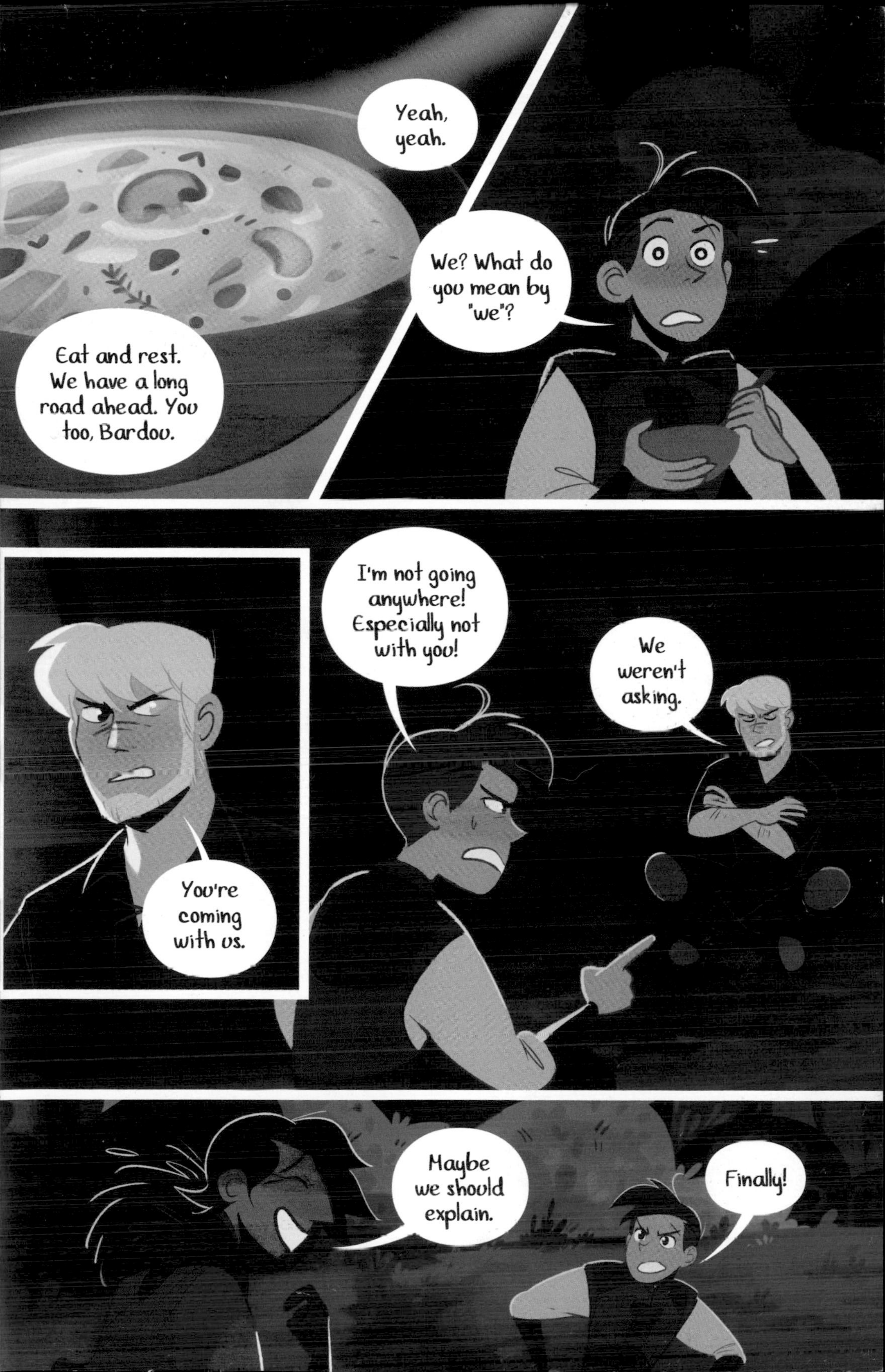
Yeah, yeah.
Eat and rest. We have a long road ahead. You too, Bardou.
We? What do you mean by "we"?
You're coming with us.
I'm not going anywhere! Especially not with you!
We weren't asking.
Maybe we should explain.
Finally!

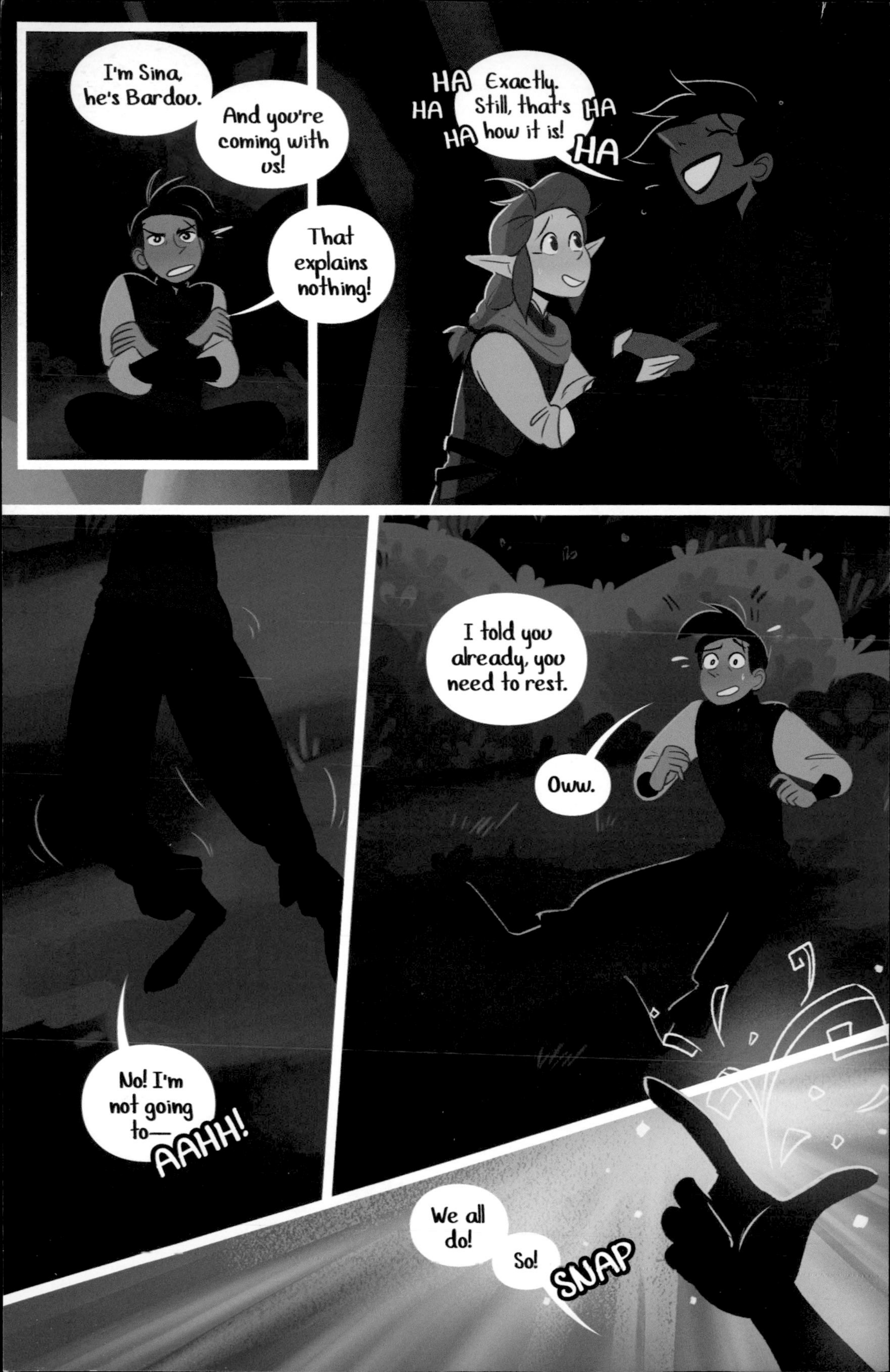
I'm Sina, he's Bardou.
And you're coming with us!
That explains nothing!
HA HA HA
Exactly. Still, that's how it is!
HA HA
No! I'm not going to—
AAHH!
I told you already, you need to rest.
Oww.
We all do!
So!
SNAP

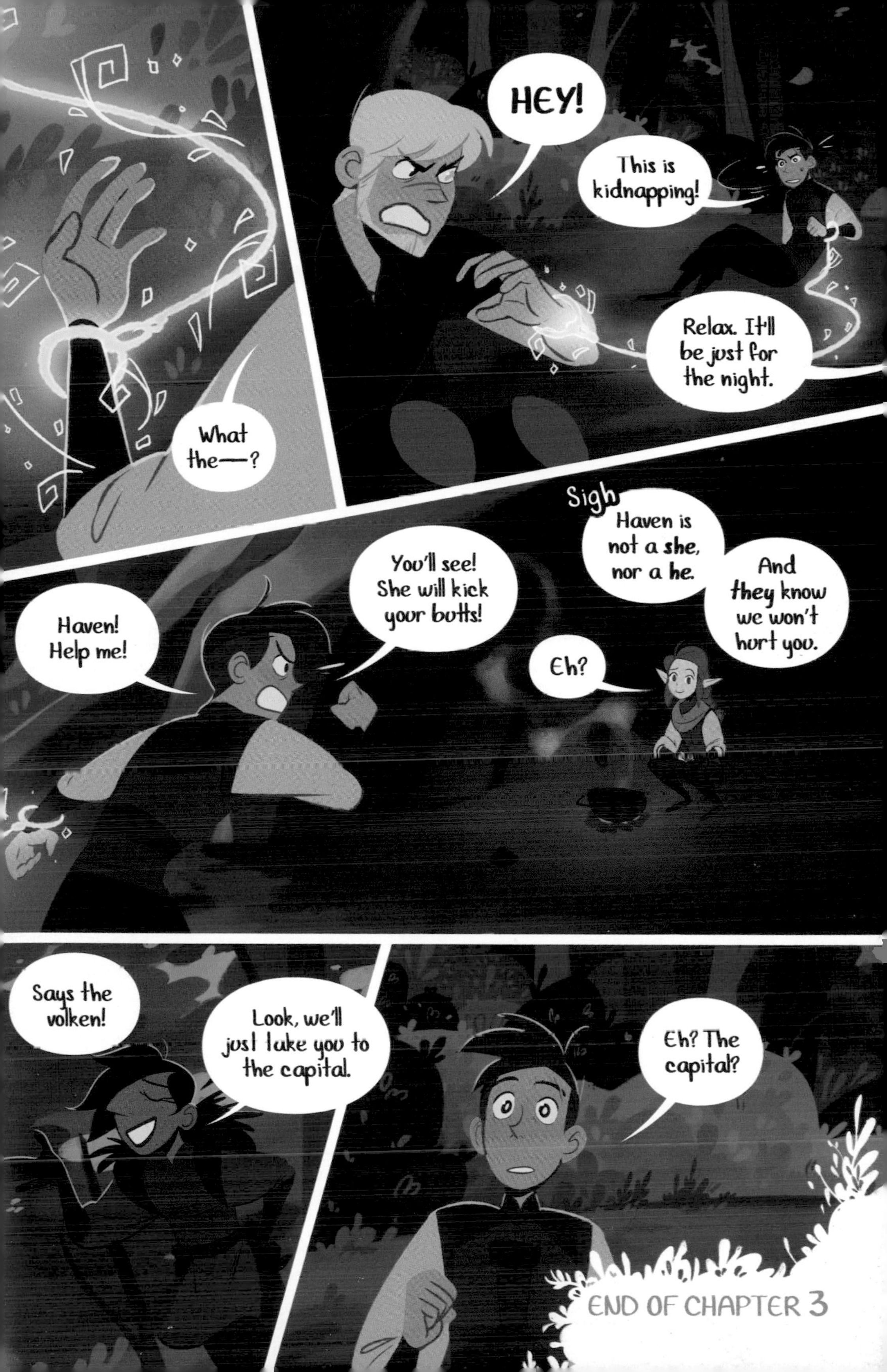
HEY!
This is kidnapping!
Relax. It'll be just for the night.
What the—?
Sigh
Haven is not a she, nor a he.
You'll see! She will kick your butts!
Haven! Help me!
And they know we won't hurt you.
Eh?
Says the volken!
Look, we'll just take you to the capital.
Eh? The capital?
END OF CHAPTER 3

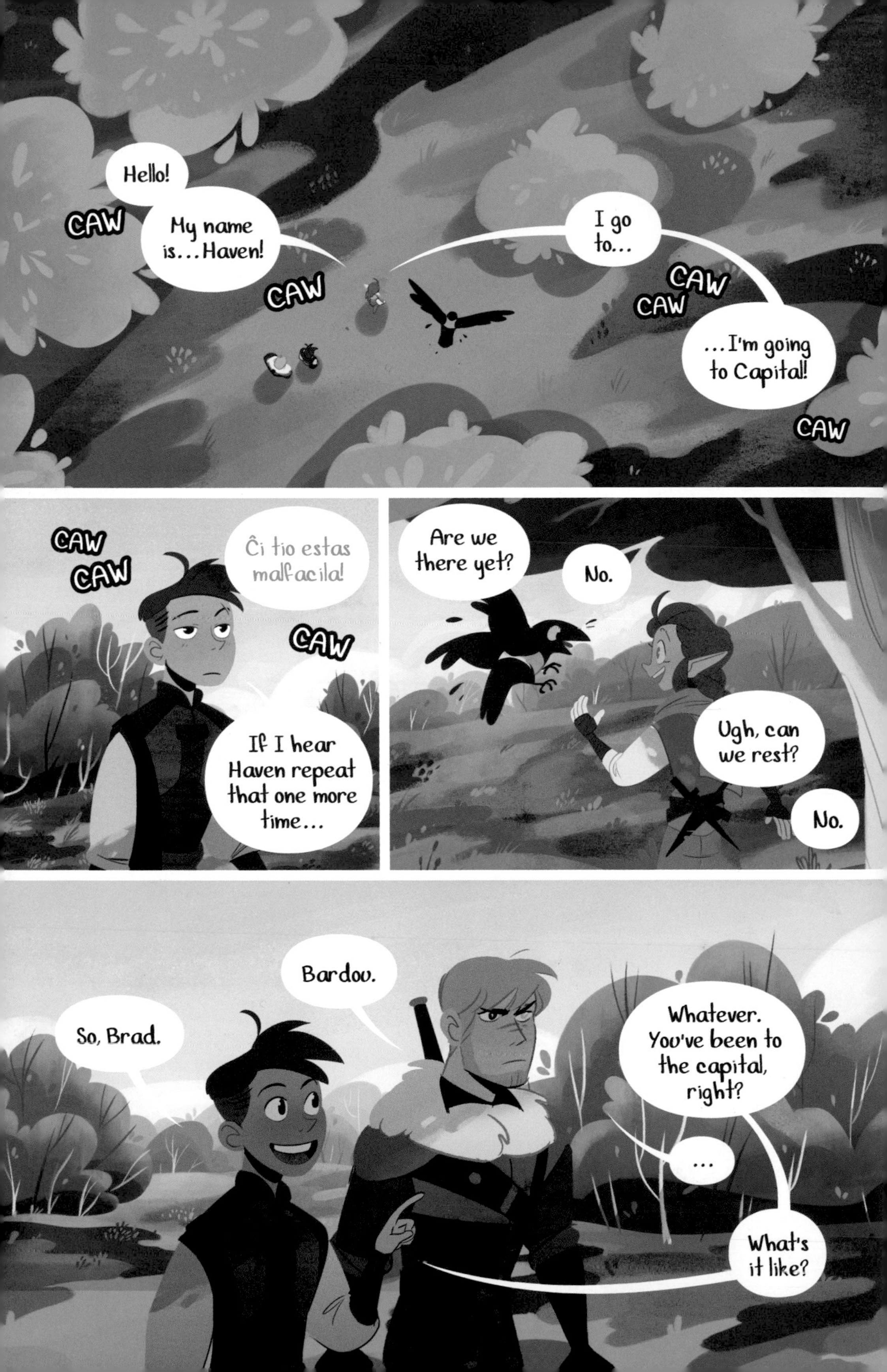

Hello!
CAW
My name is... Haven!
CAW
I go to...
CAW
CAW
...I'm going to Capital!
CAW
CAW
CAW
Ĉi tio estas malfacila!
CAW
If I hear Haven repeat that one more time...
Are we there yet?
No.
Ugh, can we rest?
No.
So, Brad.
Bardov.
Whatever. You've been to the capital, right?
...
What's it like?

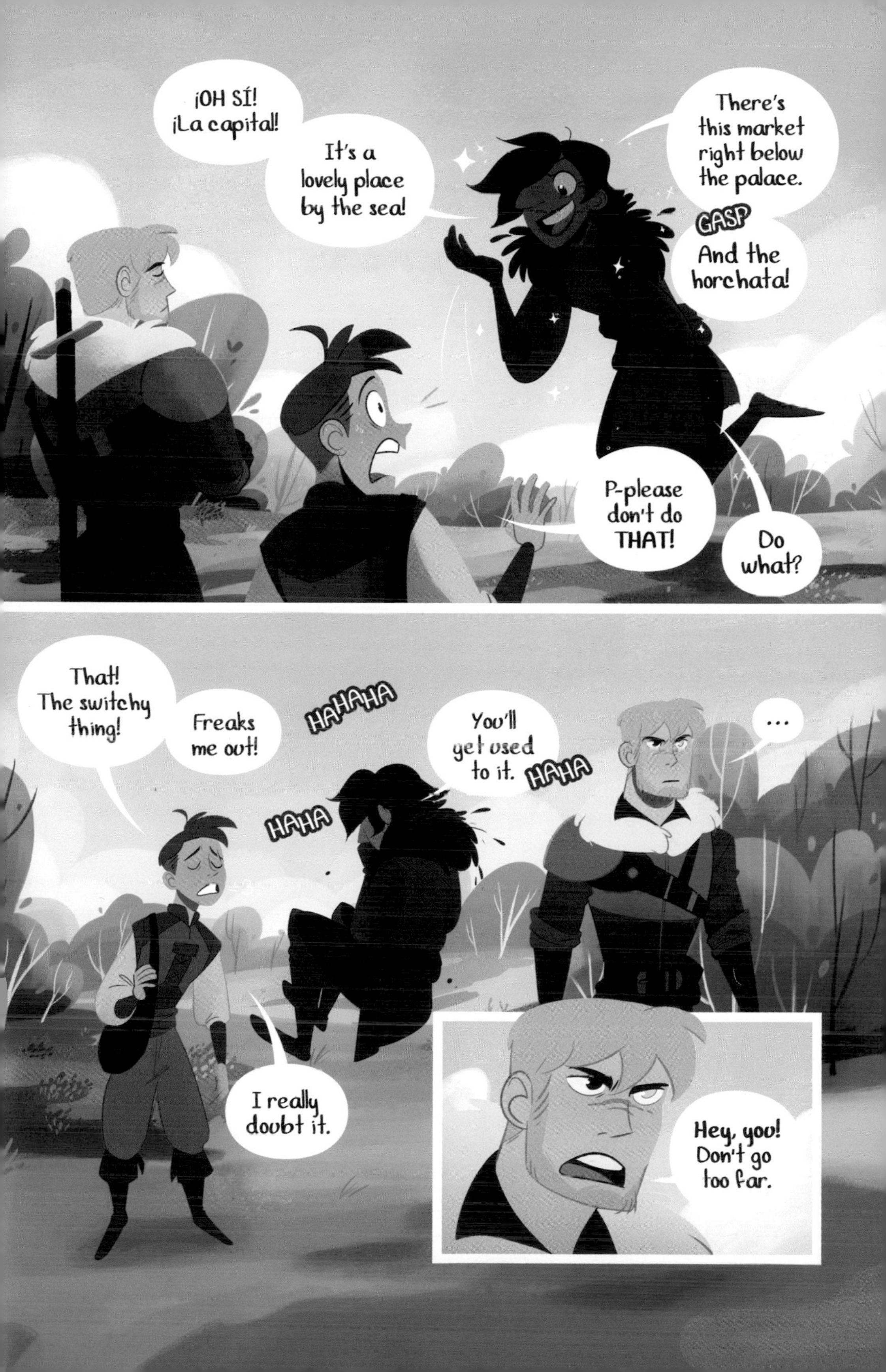
¡OH SÍ! ¡La capital!
It's a lovely place by the sea!
There's this market right below the palace.
GASP
And the horchata!
P-please don't do THAT!
Do what?
That! The switchy thing!
Freaks me out!
HAHAHA
HAHA
You'll get used to it.
HAHA
...
I really doubt it.
Hey, you! Don't go too far.

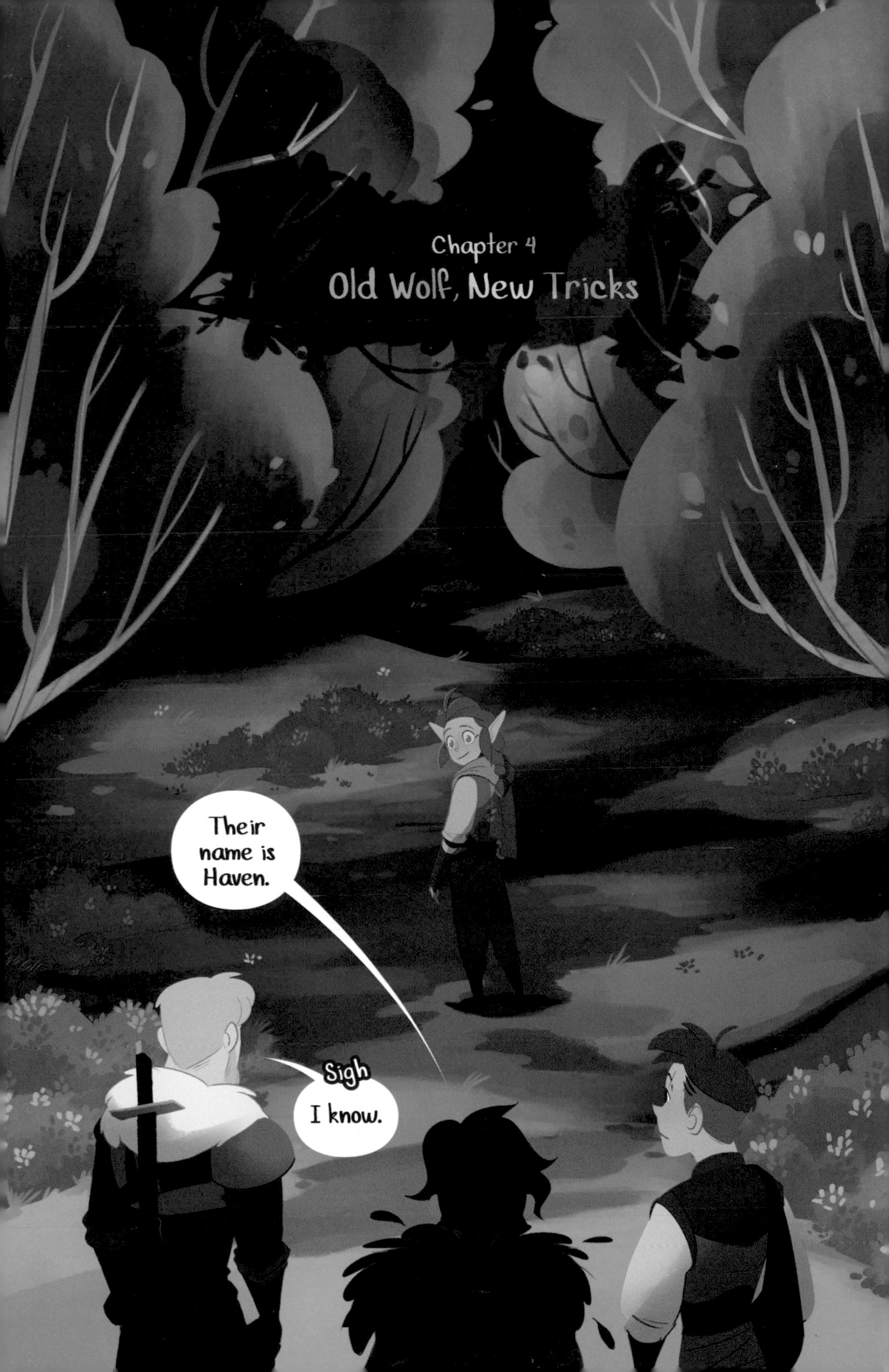
Chapter 4
Old Wolf, New Tricks
Their name is Haven.
Sigh
I know.

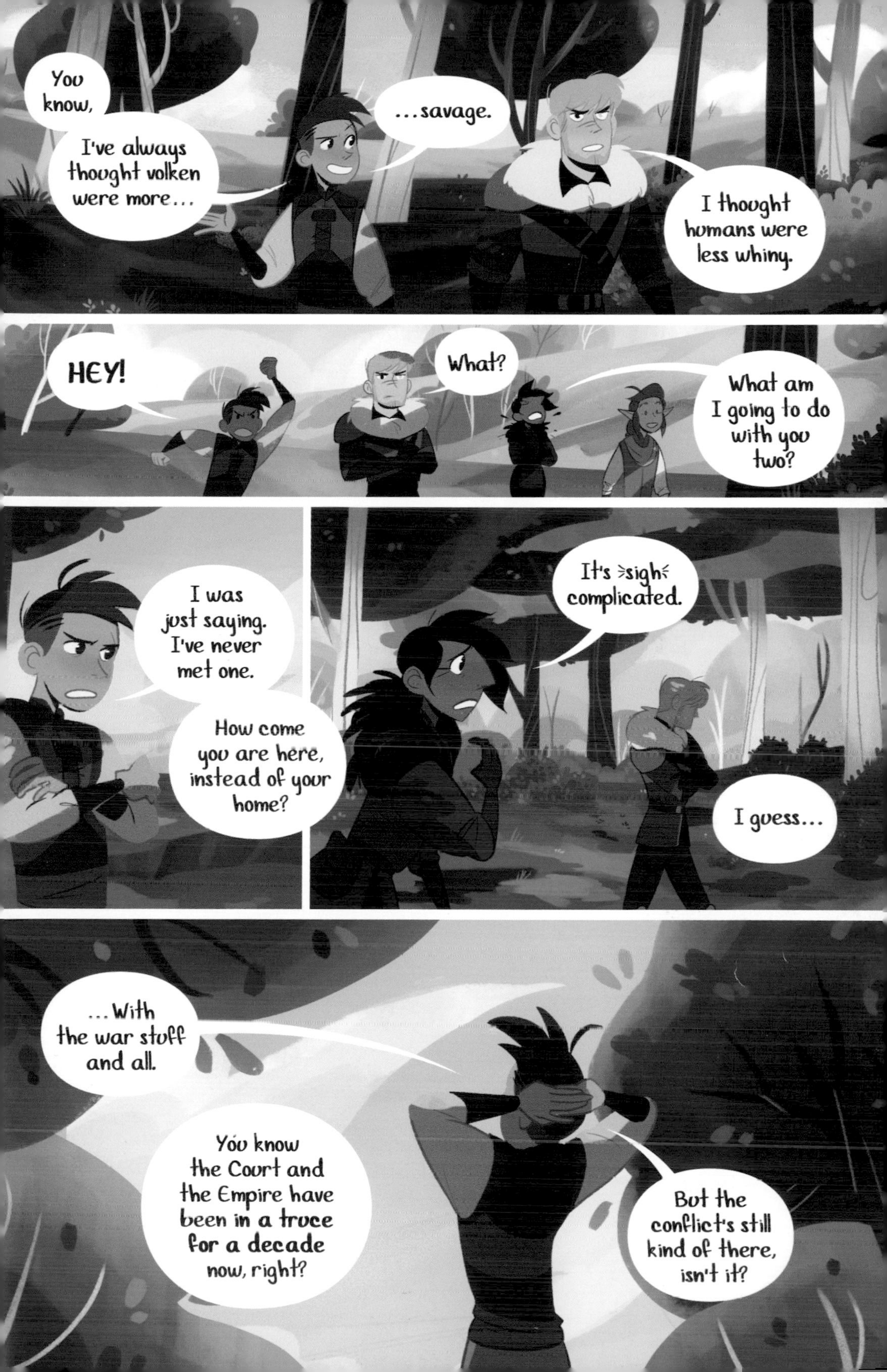
You know,
I've always thought volken were more...
...savage.
I thought humans were less whiny.
HEY!
What?
What am I going to do with you two?
I was just saying. I've never met one.
How come you are here, instead of your home?
It's ⪢sigh⪡ complicated.
I guess...
...With the war stuff and all.
You know the Court and the Empire have been in a truce for a decade now, right?
But the conflict's still kind of there, isn't it?

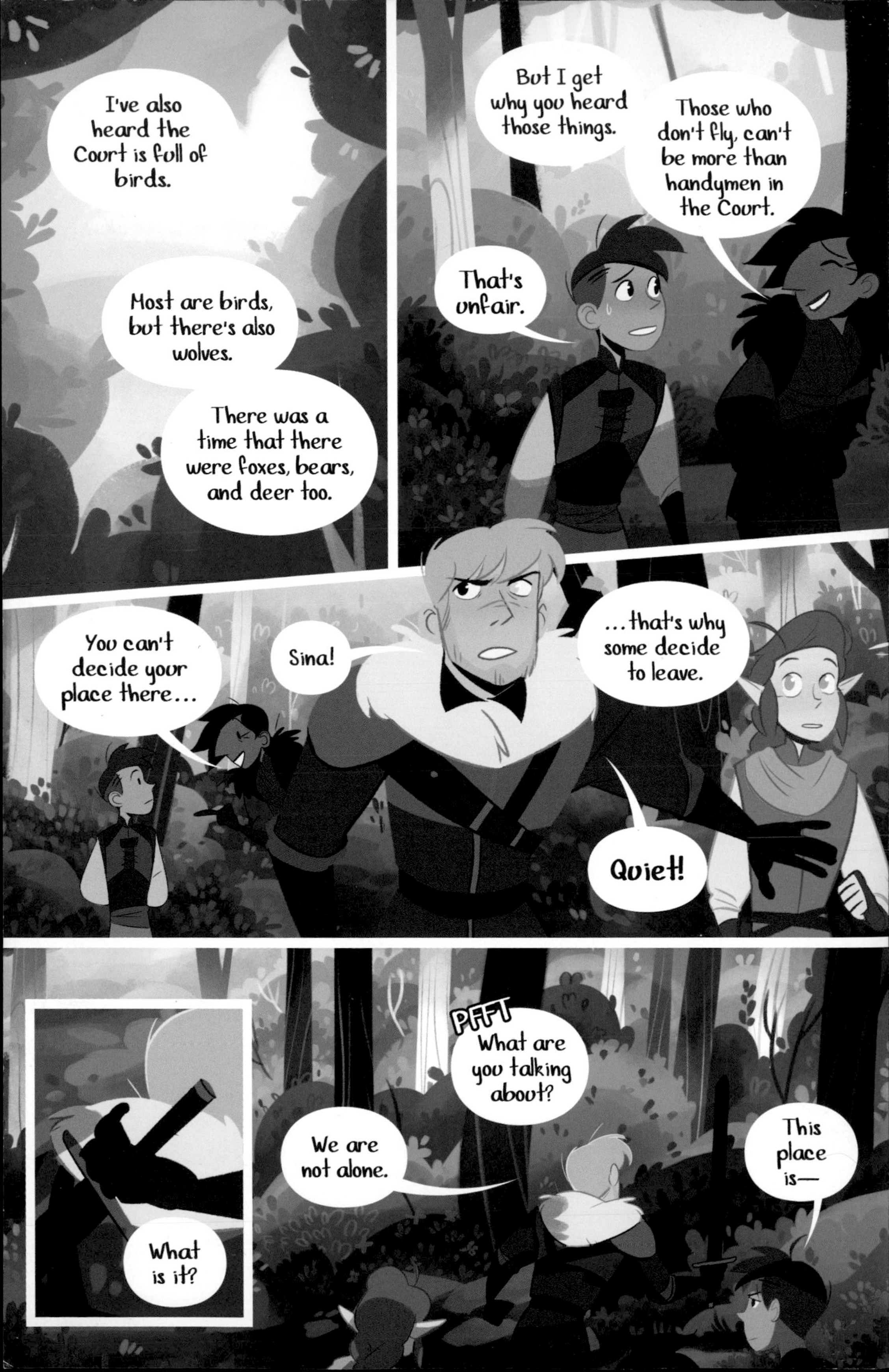
I've also heard the Court is full of birds.
Most are birds, but there's also wolves.
There was a time that there were foxes, bears, and deer too.
But I get why you heard those things.
Those who don't fly, can't be more than handymen in the Court.
That's unfair.
You can't decide your place there...
Sina!
...that's why some decide to leave.
Quiet!
PFFT
What are you talking about?
We are not alone.
This place is—
What is it?

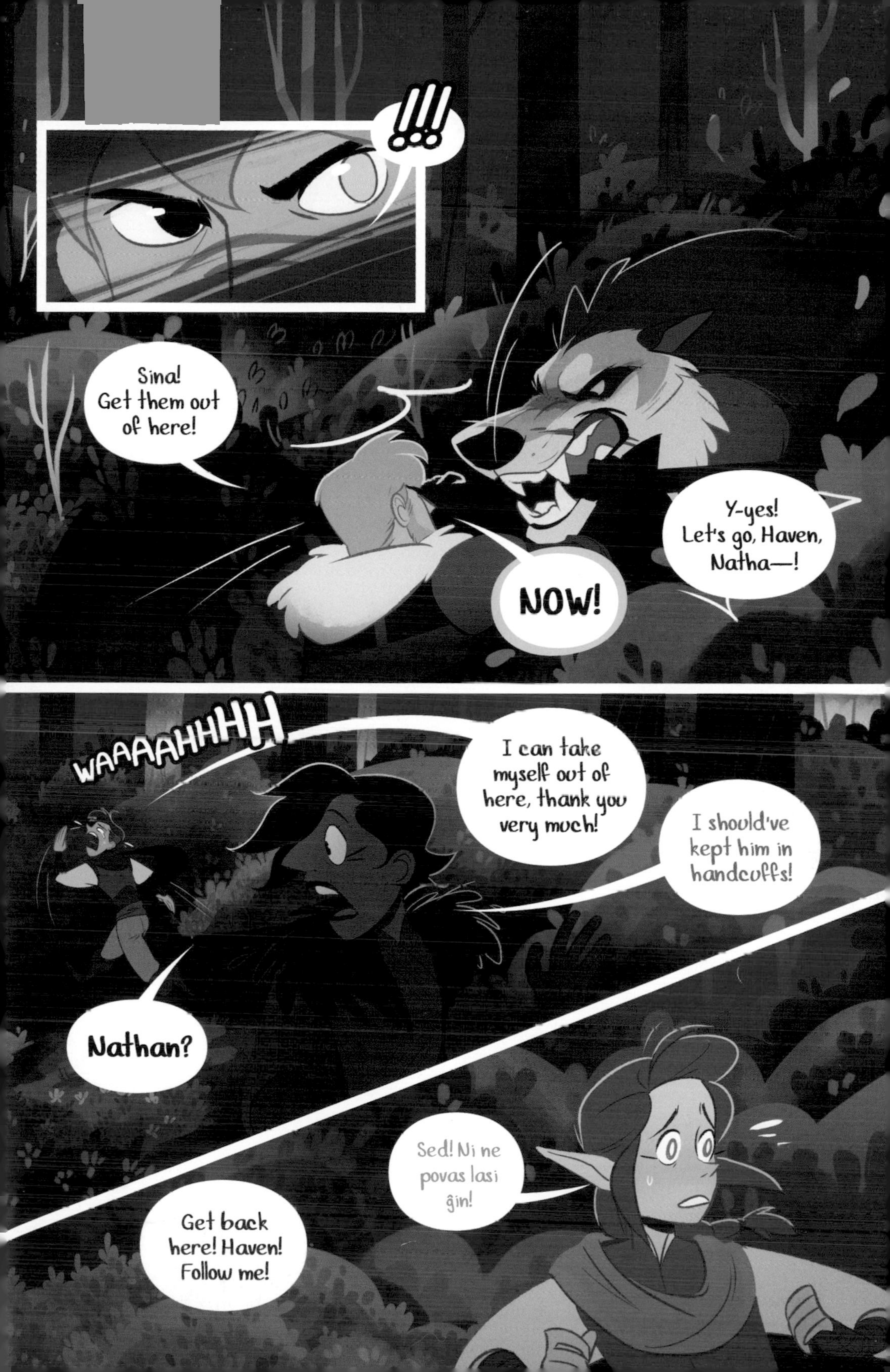
!!!
Sina! Get them out of here!
NOW!
Y-yes! Let's go, Haven, Natha—!
WAAAAHHHH
I can take myself out of here, thank you very much!
I should've kept him in handcuffs!
Nathan?
Sed! Ni ne povas lasi ĝin!
Get back here! Haven! Follow me!

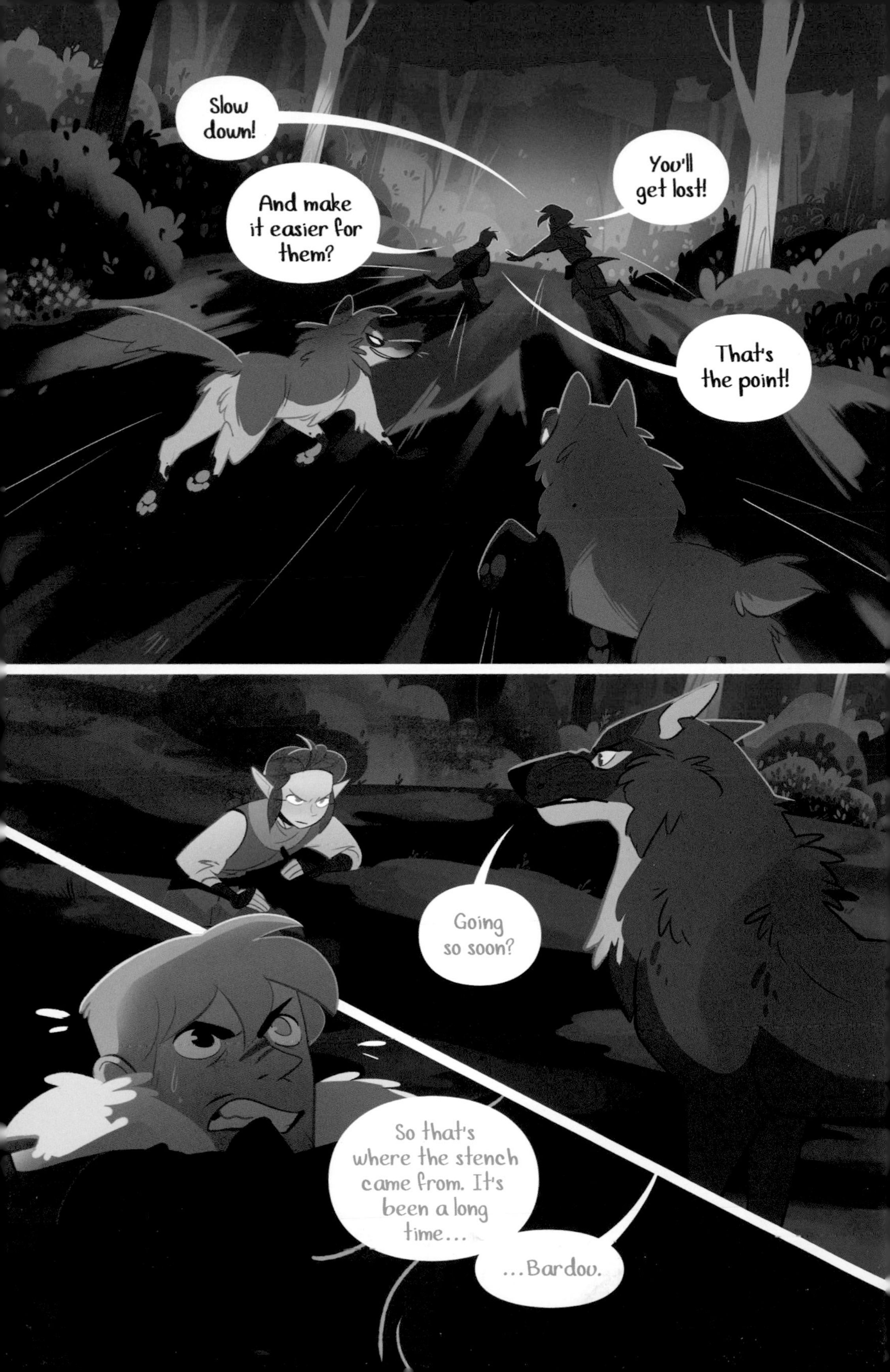
Slow down!
You'll get lost!
And make it easier for them?
That's the point!
Going so soon?
So that's where the stench came from. It's been a long time...
...Bardou.

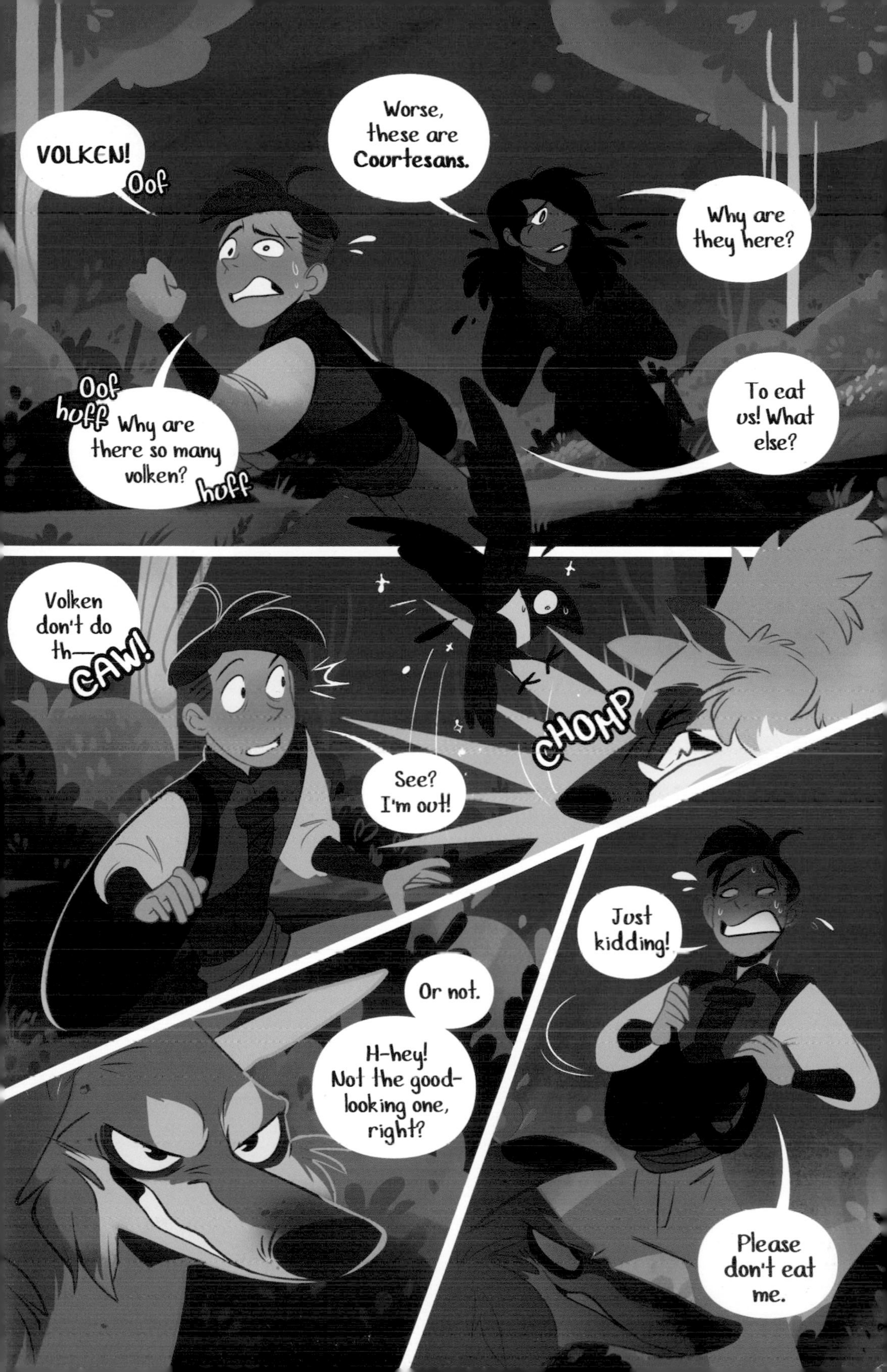
VOLKEN! Oof
Worse, these are Courtesans.
Why are they here?
Oof huff
Why are there so many volken? huff
To eat us! What else?
Volken don't do th—
CAW!
CHOMP
See? I'm out!
Or not.
H-hey! Not the good-looking one, right?
Just kidding!
Please don't eat me.

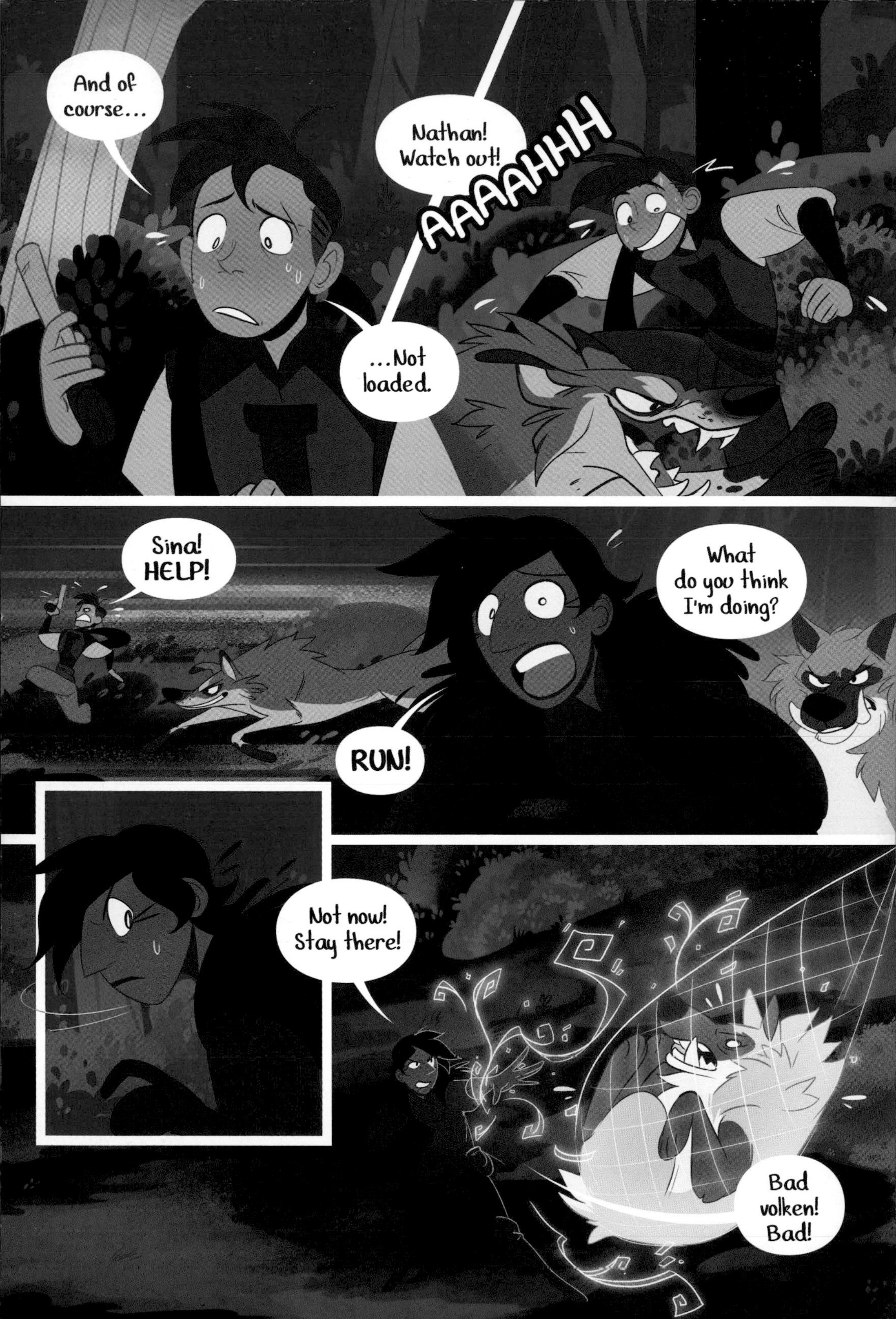
And of course...
...Not loaded.
Nathan! Watch out!
AAAAHHH
Sina! HELP!
RUN!
What do you think I'm doing?
Not now! Stay there!
Bad volken! Bad!

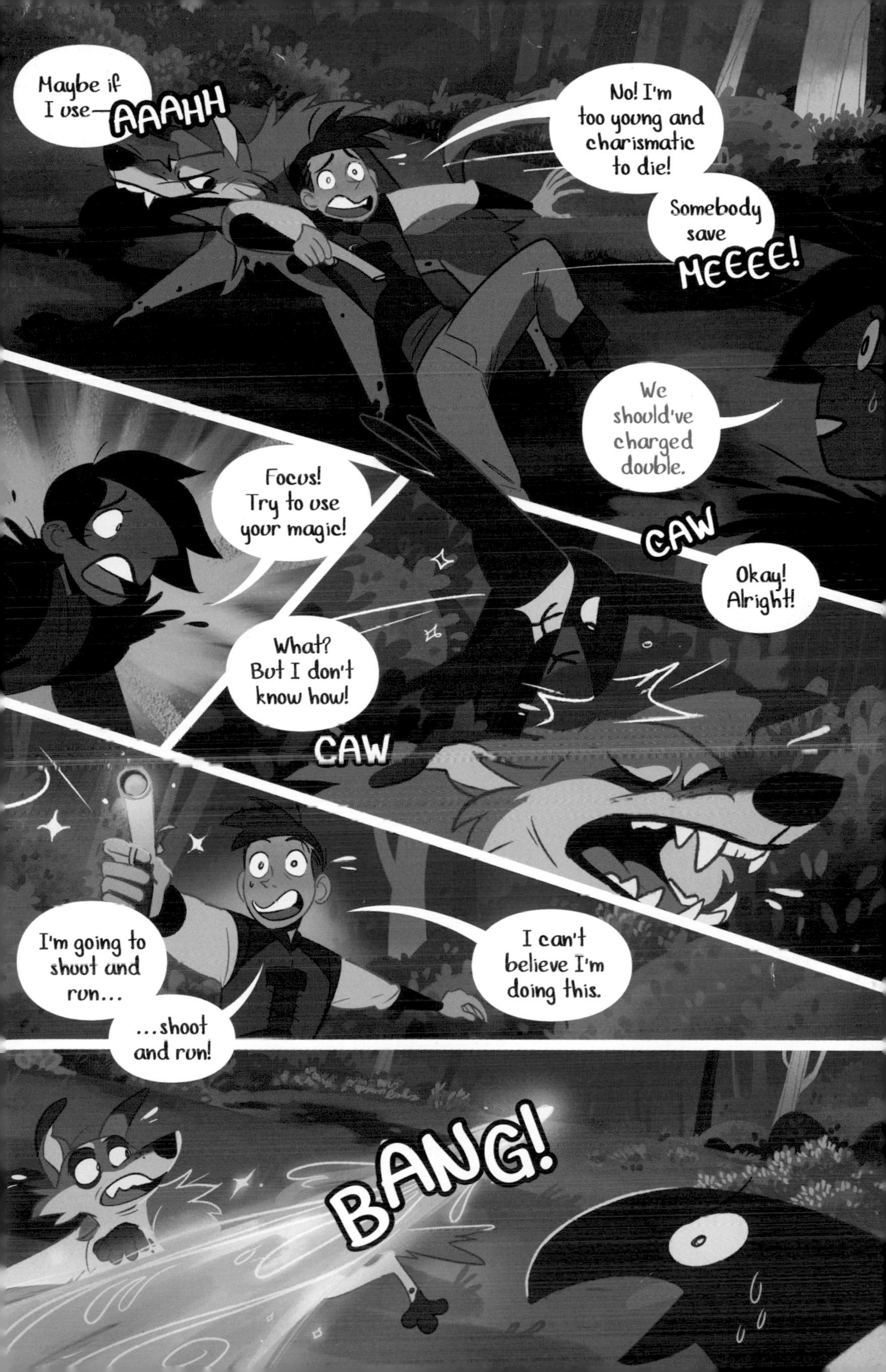

Maybe if I use—
AAAHH
No! I'm too young and charismatic to die!
Somebody save
MEEEE!
We should've charged double.
Focus! Try to use your magic!
CAW
Okay! Alright!
What? But I don't know how!
CAW
I'm going to shoot and run...
...shoot and run!
I can't believe I'm doing this.
BANG!

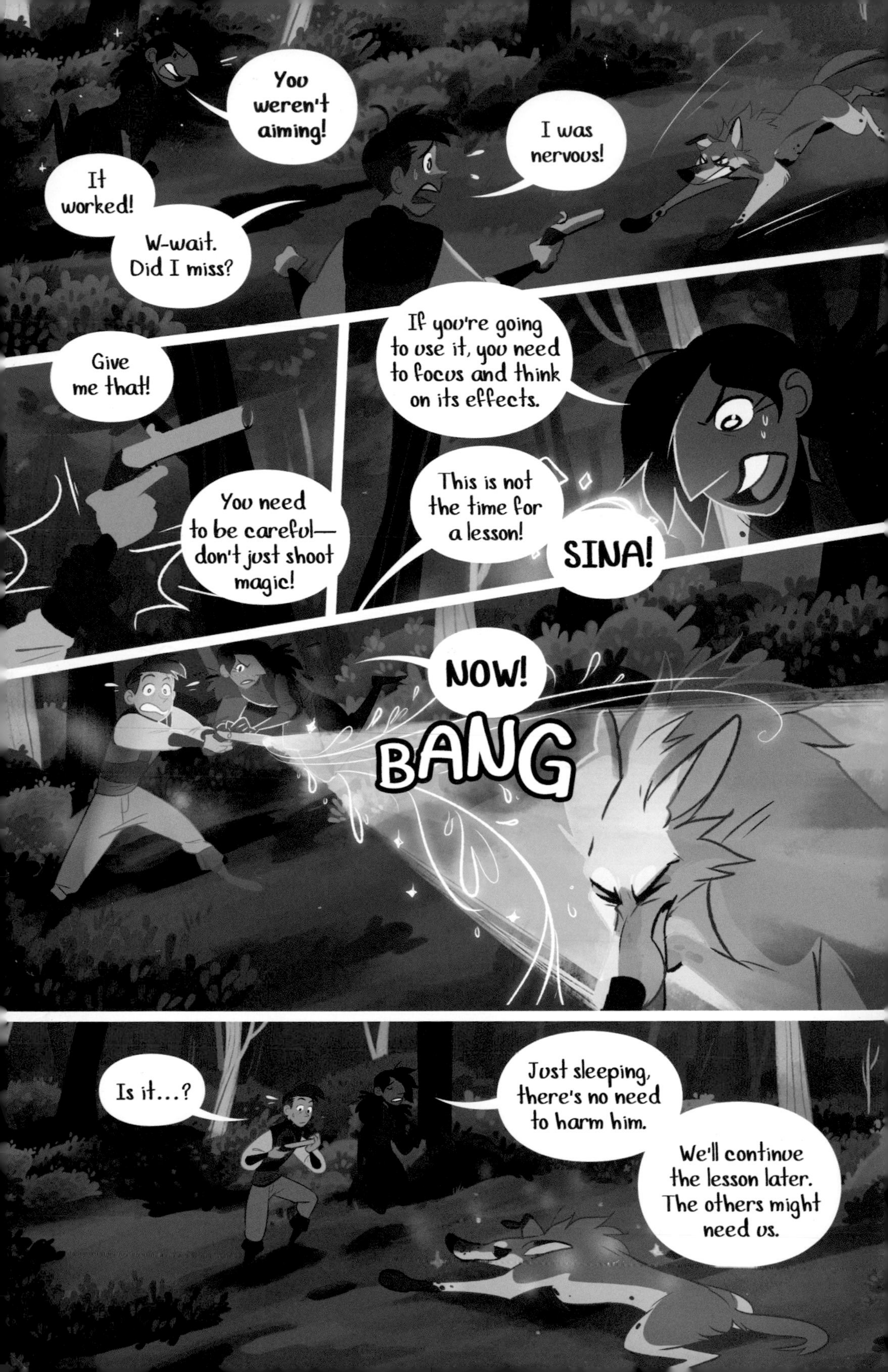
You weren't aiming!
I was nervous!
It worked!
W-wait. Did I miss?
Give me that!
If you're going to use it, you need to focus and think on its effects.
You need to be careful— don't just shoot magic!
This is not the time for a lesson!
SINA!
NOW!
BANG
Is it...?
Just sleeping, there's no need to harm him.
We'll continue the lesson later. The others might need us.

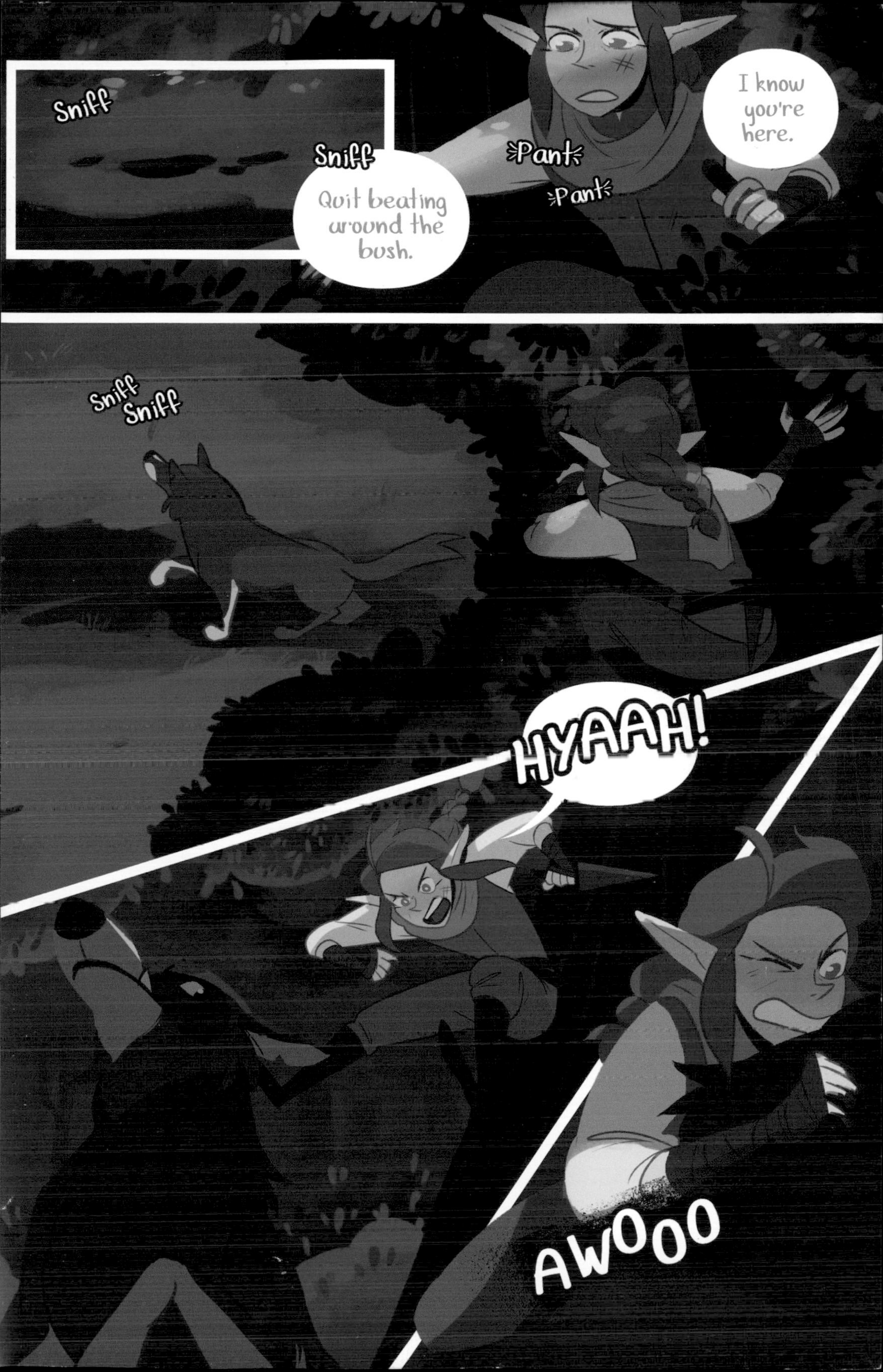

Sniff
Sniff
Quit beating around the bush.
Pant
Pant
I know you're here.
Sniff Sniff
HYAAH!
AWOOO

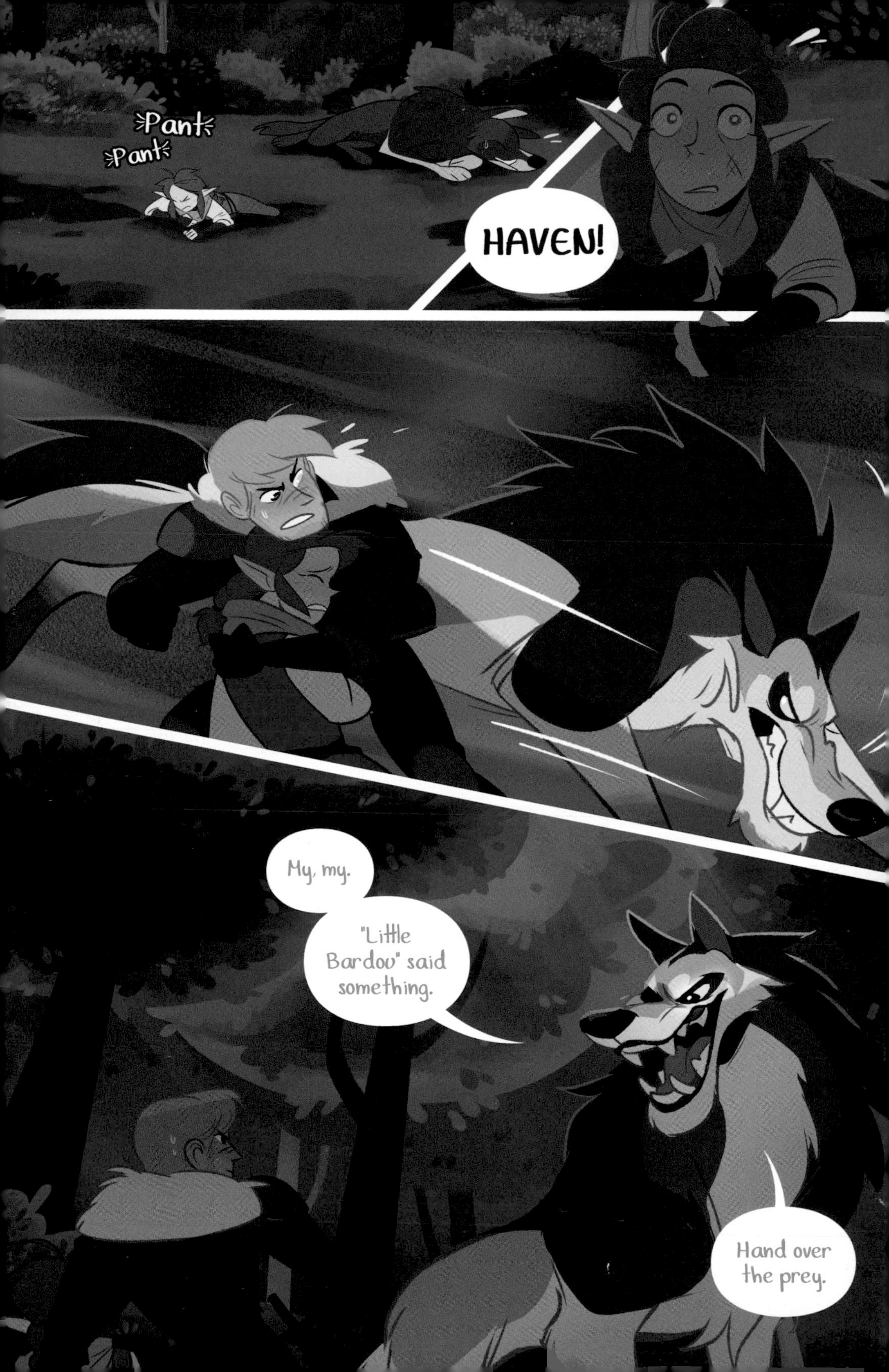
Pant
Pant
HAVEN!
My, my.
"Little Bardov" said something.
Hand over the prey.

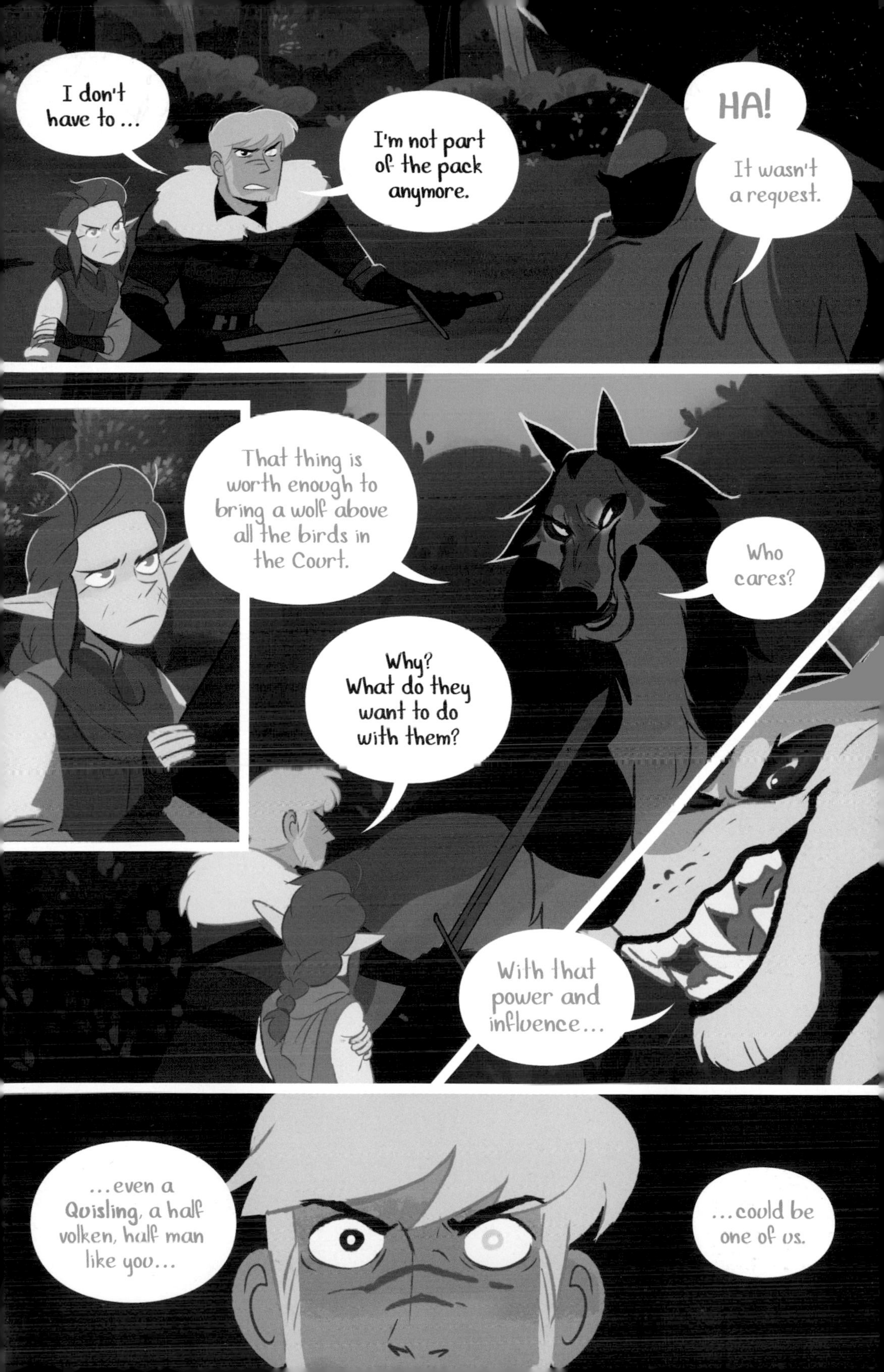
I don't have to ...
I'm not part of the pack anymore.
HA!
It wasn't a request.
That thing is worth enough to bring a wolf above all the birds in the Court.
Who cares?
Why? What do they want to do with them?
With that power and influence...
...even a Quisling, a half volken, half man like you...
...could be one of us.

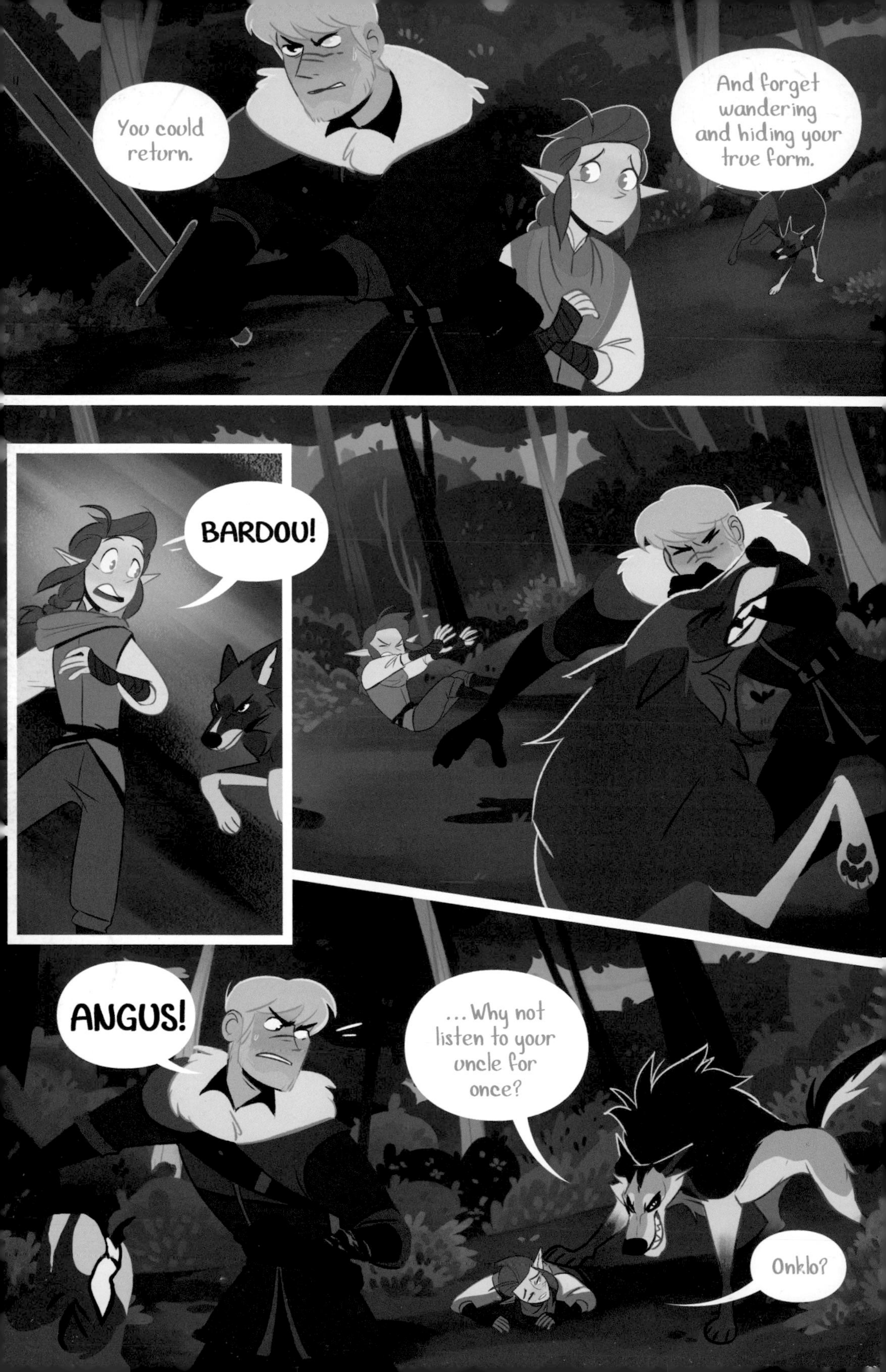
You could return.
And forget wandering and hiding your true form.
BARDOU!
ANGUS!
...Why not listen to your uncle for once?
Onklo?

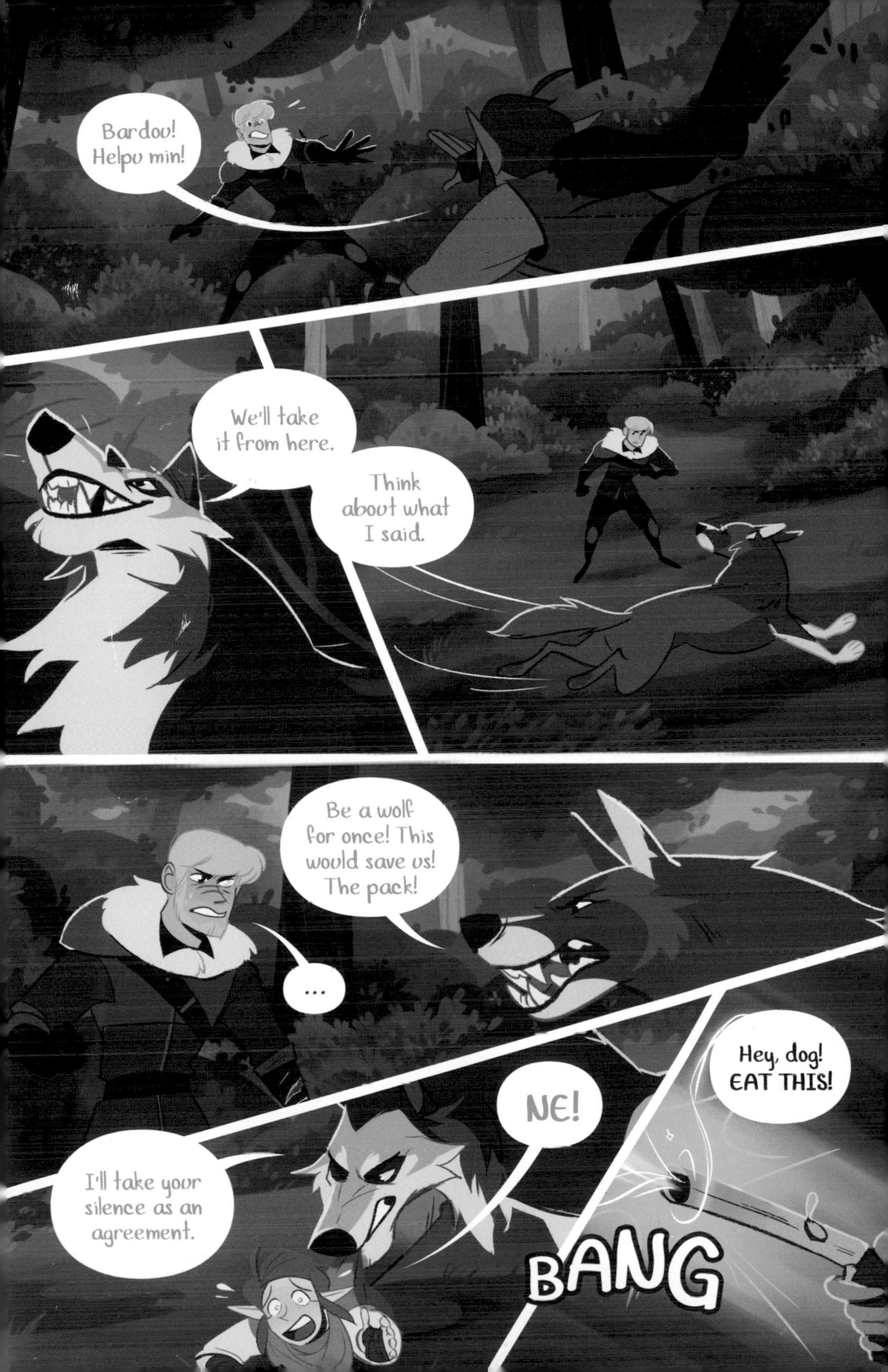
Bardou!
Helpu min!
We'll take
it from here.
Think
about what
I said.
Be a wolf
for once! This
would save us!
The pack!
...
I'll take your
silence as an
agreement.
NE!
Hey, dog!
EAT THIS!
BANG

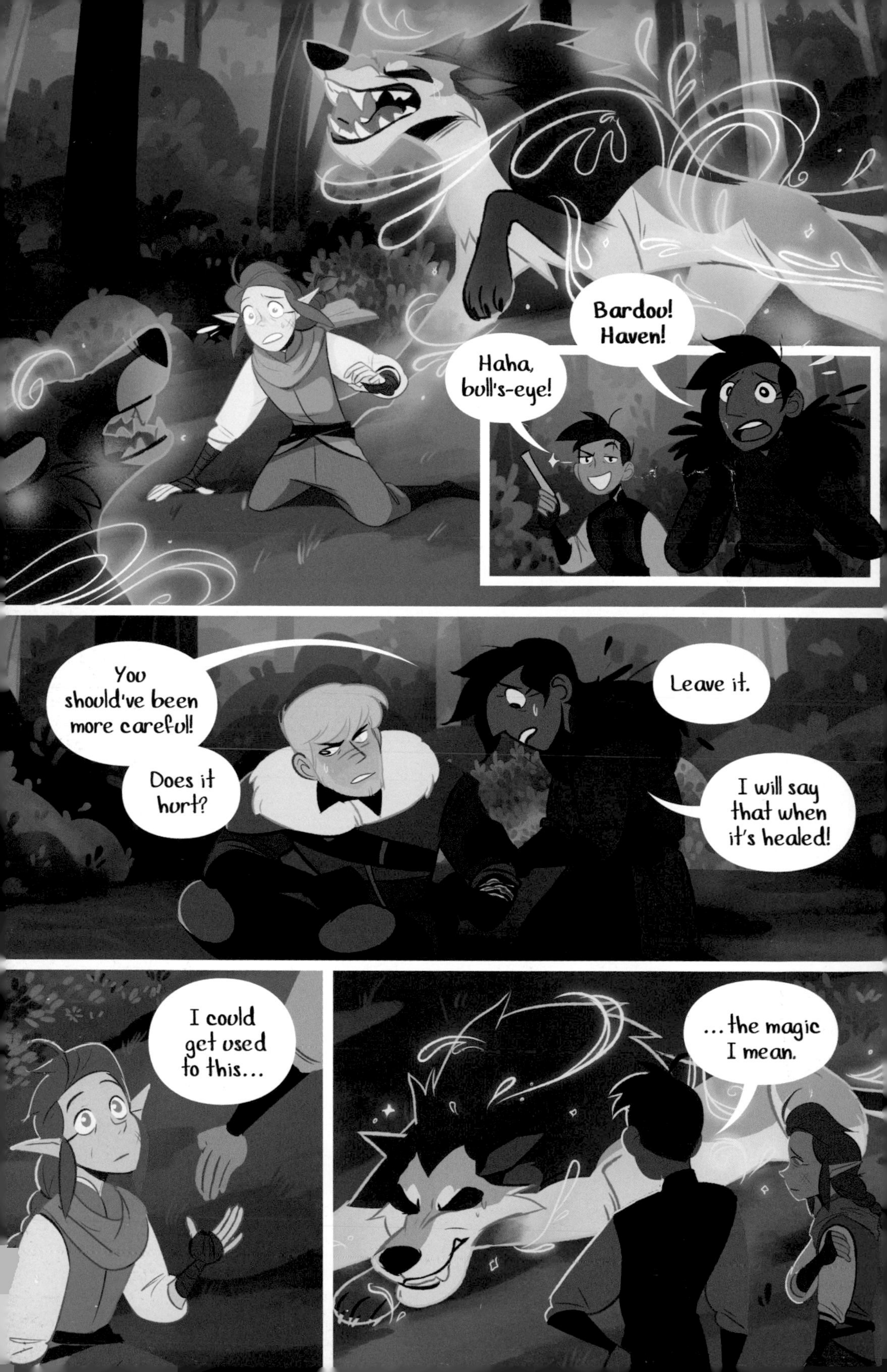
Haha, bull's-eye!
Bardou! Haven!
You should've been more careful!
Does it hurt?
Leave it.
I will say that when it's healed!
I could get used to this...
...the magic I mean.

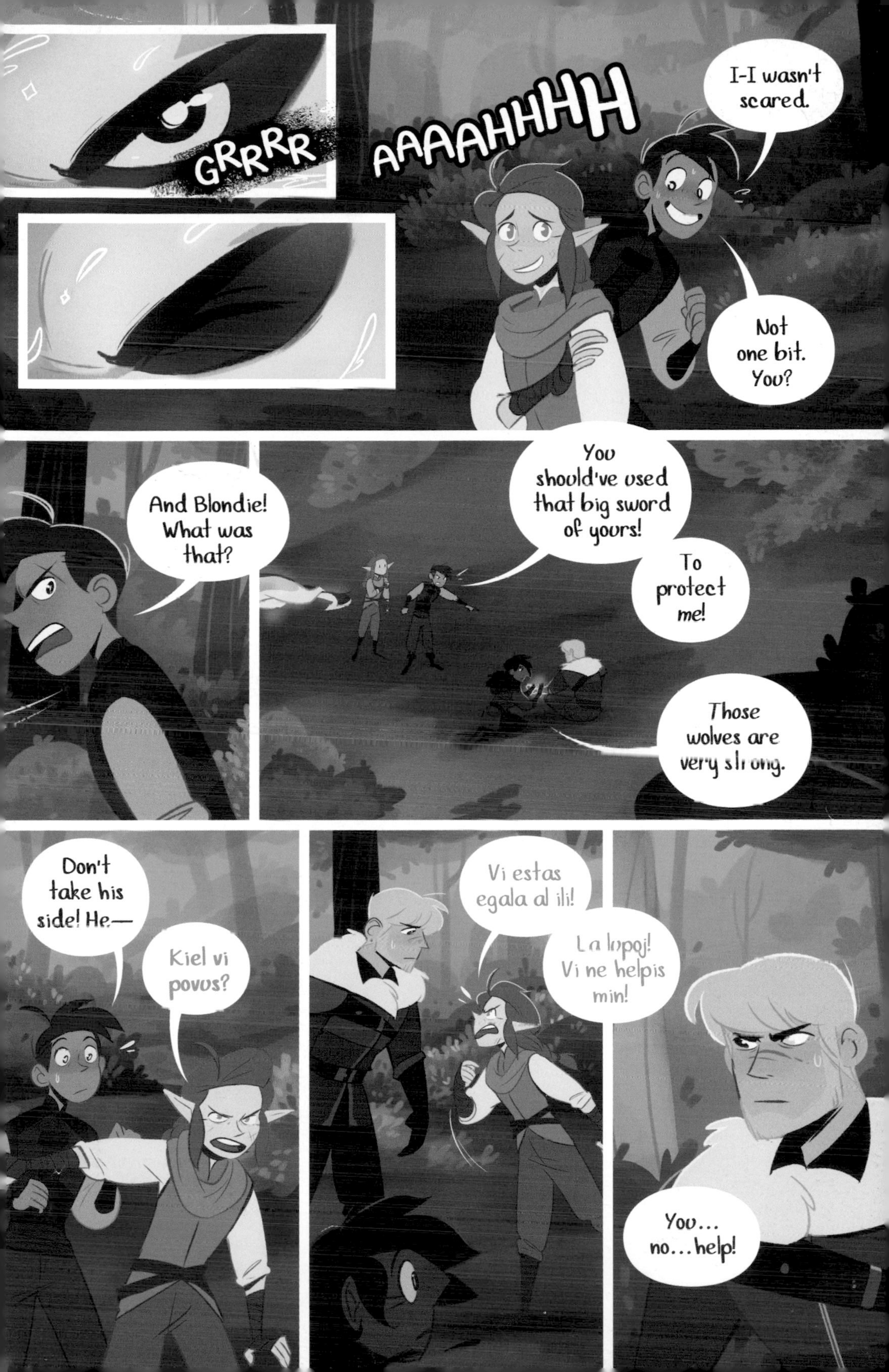
GRRRR
AAAAHHHH
I-I wasn't scared.
Not one bit. You?
And Blondie! What was that?
You should've used that big sword of yours!
To protect me!
Those wolves are very strong.
Don't take his side! He—
Kiel vi povus?
Vi estas egala al ili!
La lupoj! Vi ne helpis min!
You... no... help!

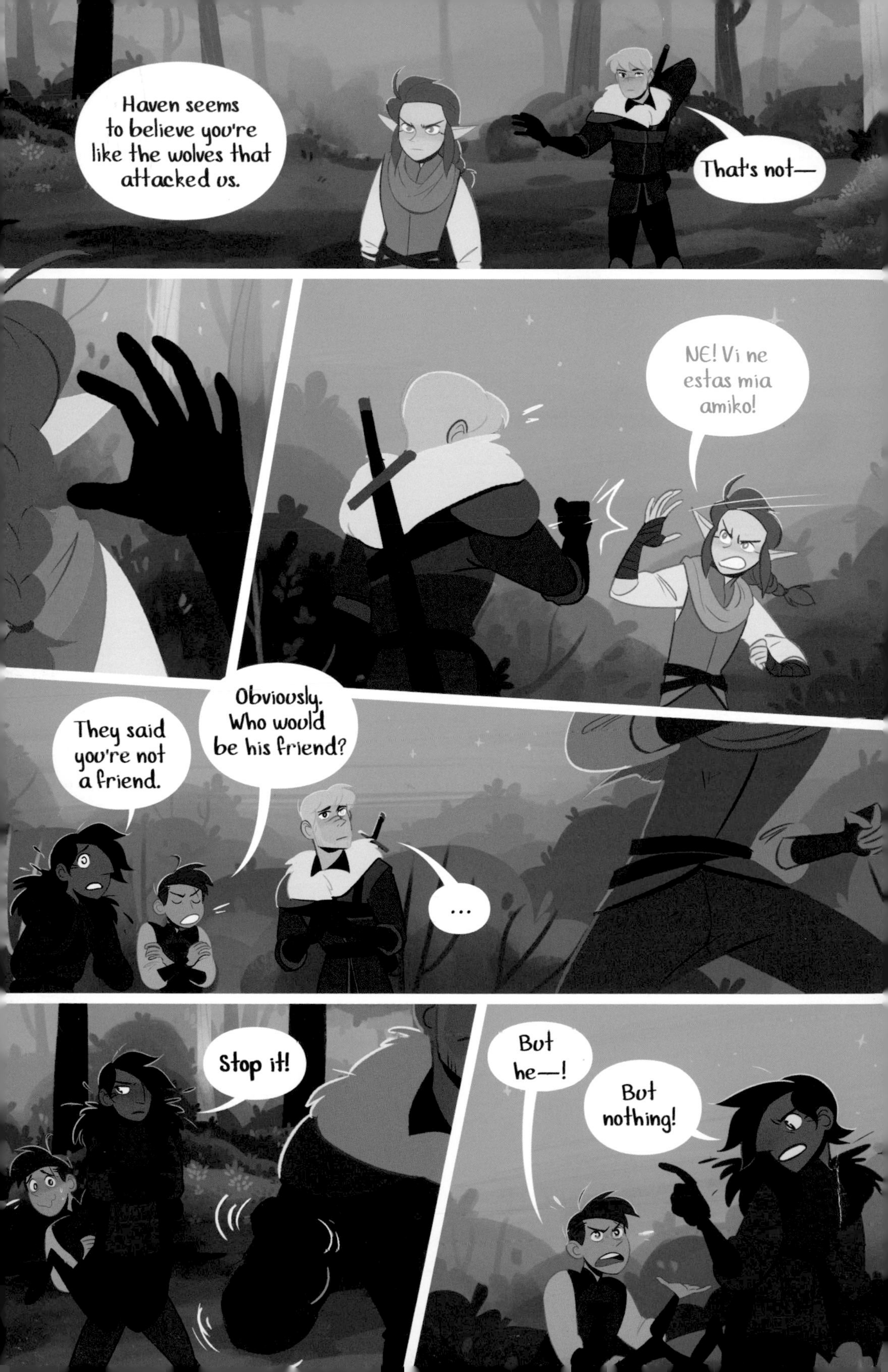

Haven seems to believe you're like the wolves that attacked us.
That's not—
NE! Vi ne estas mia amiko!
They said you're not a friend.
Obviously. Who would be his friend?
...
Stop it!
But he—!
But nothing!

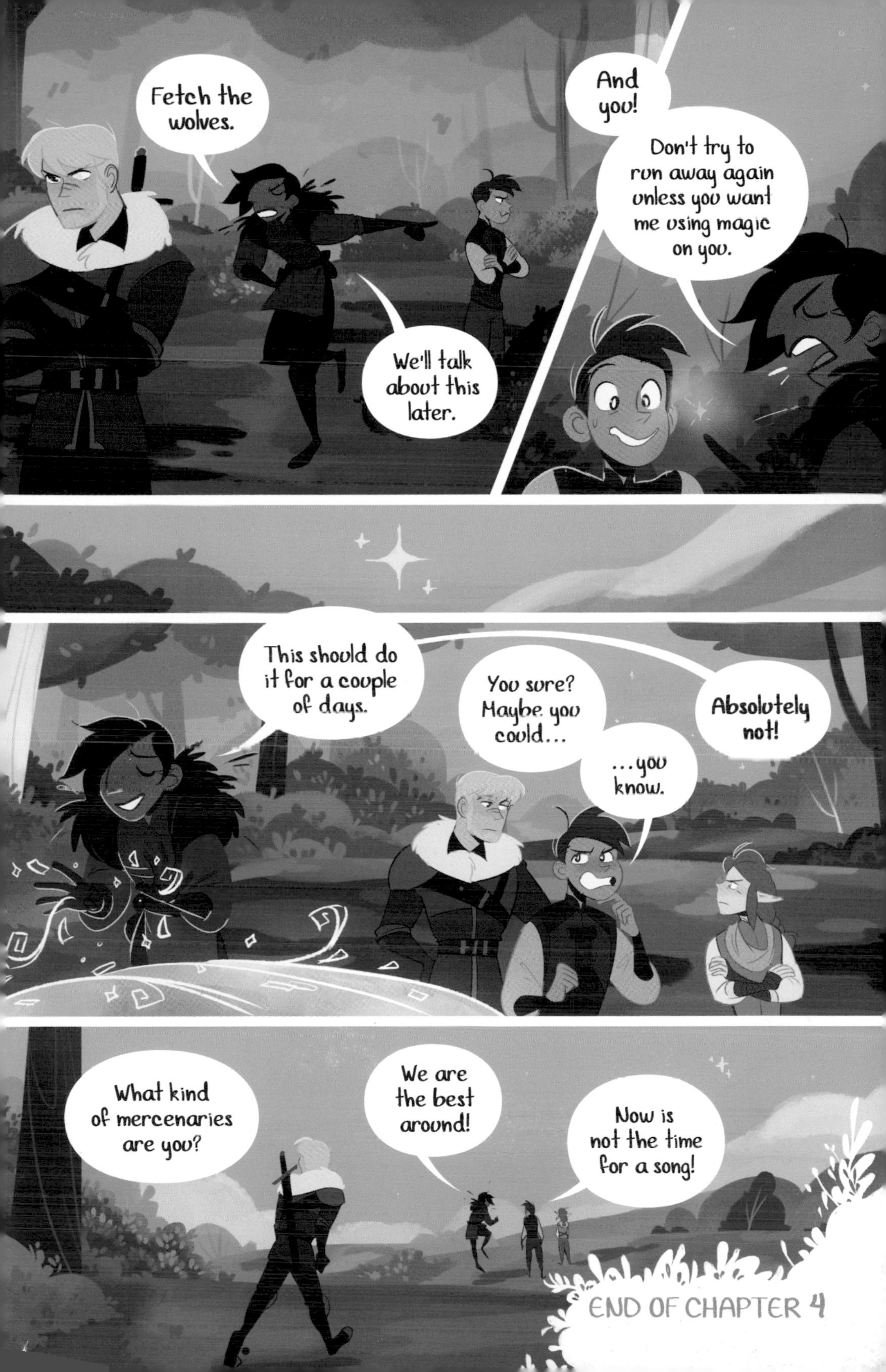

Fetch the wolves.
We'll talk about this later.
And you!
Don't try to run away again unless you want me using magic on you.
This should do it for a couple of days.
You sure? Maybe you could...
...you know.
Absolutely not!
What kind of mercenaries are you?
We are the best around!
Now is not the time for a song!
END OF CHAPTER 4

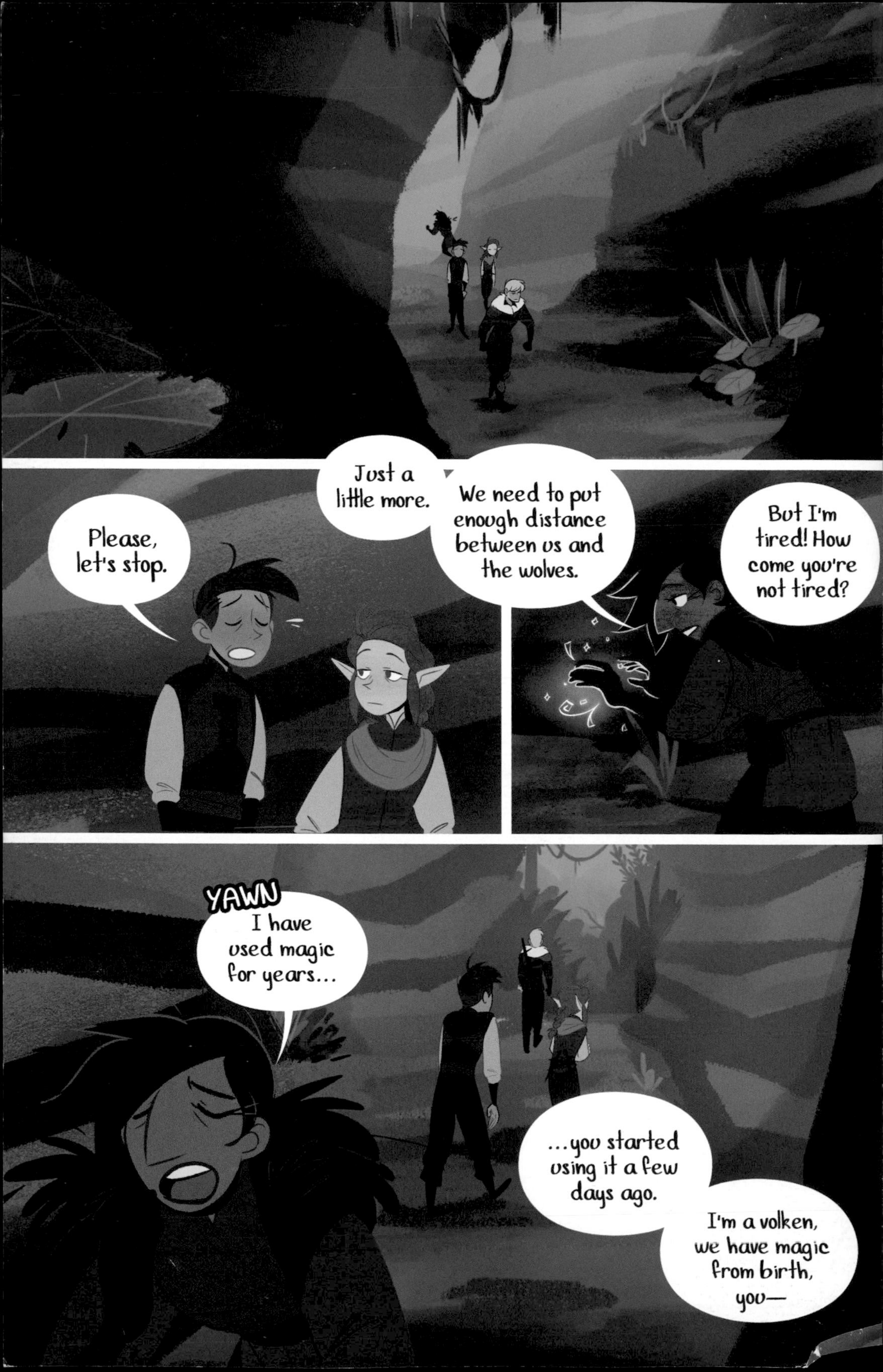
Please, let's stop.
Just a little more.
We need to put enough distance between us and the wolves.
But I'm tired! How come you're not tired?
YAWN
I have used magic for years...
...you started using it a few days ago.
I'm a volken, we have magic from birth, you—

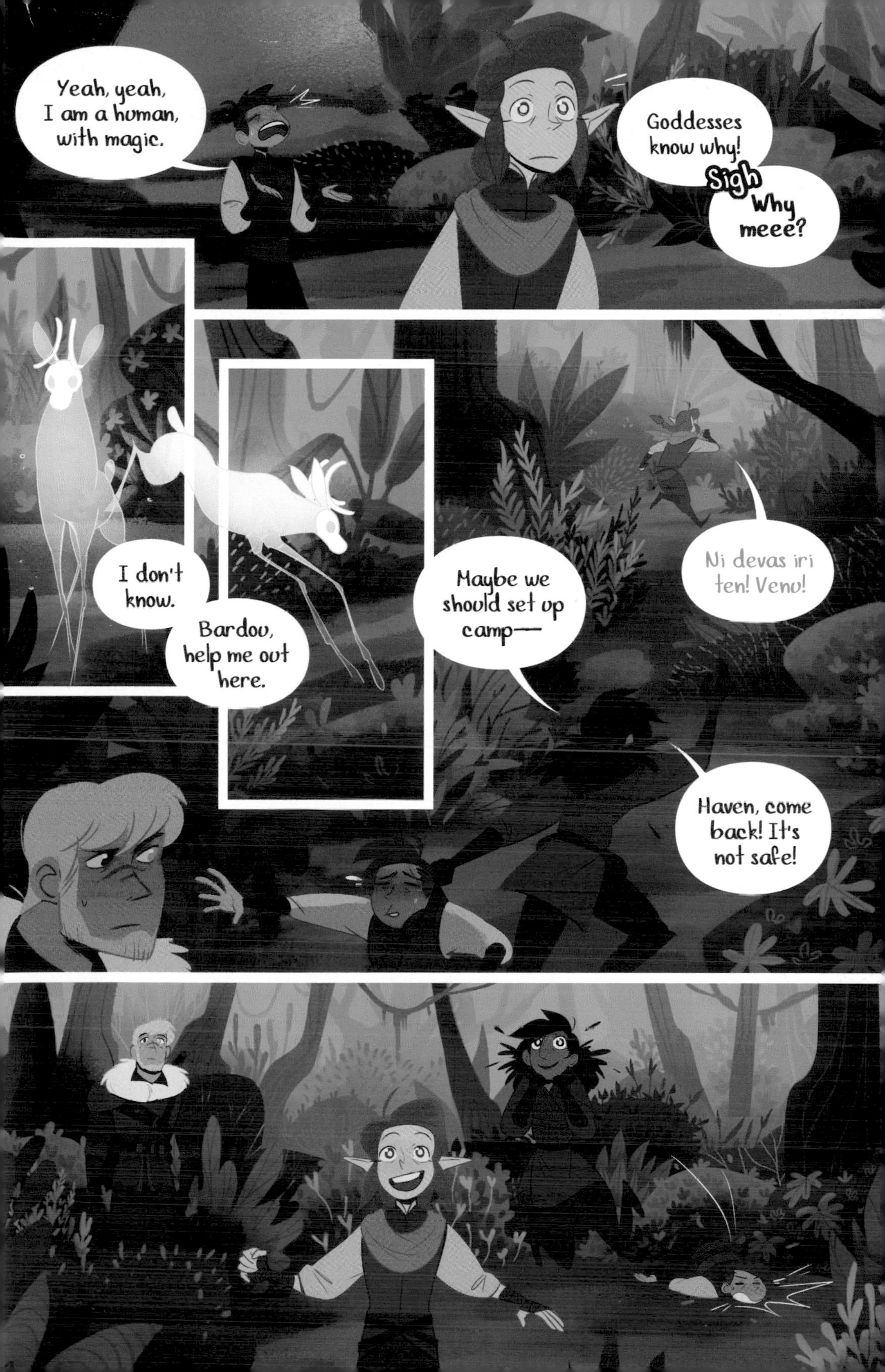
Yeah, yeah, I am a human, with magic.
Goddesses know why!
Sigh
Why meee?
I don't know.
Bardou, help me out here.
Maybe we should set up camp—
Ni devas iri ten! Venu!
Haven, come back! It's not safe!

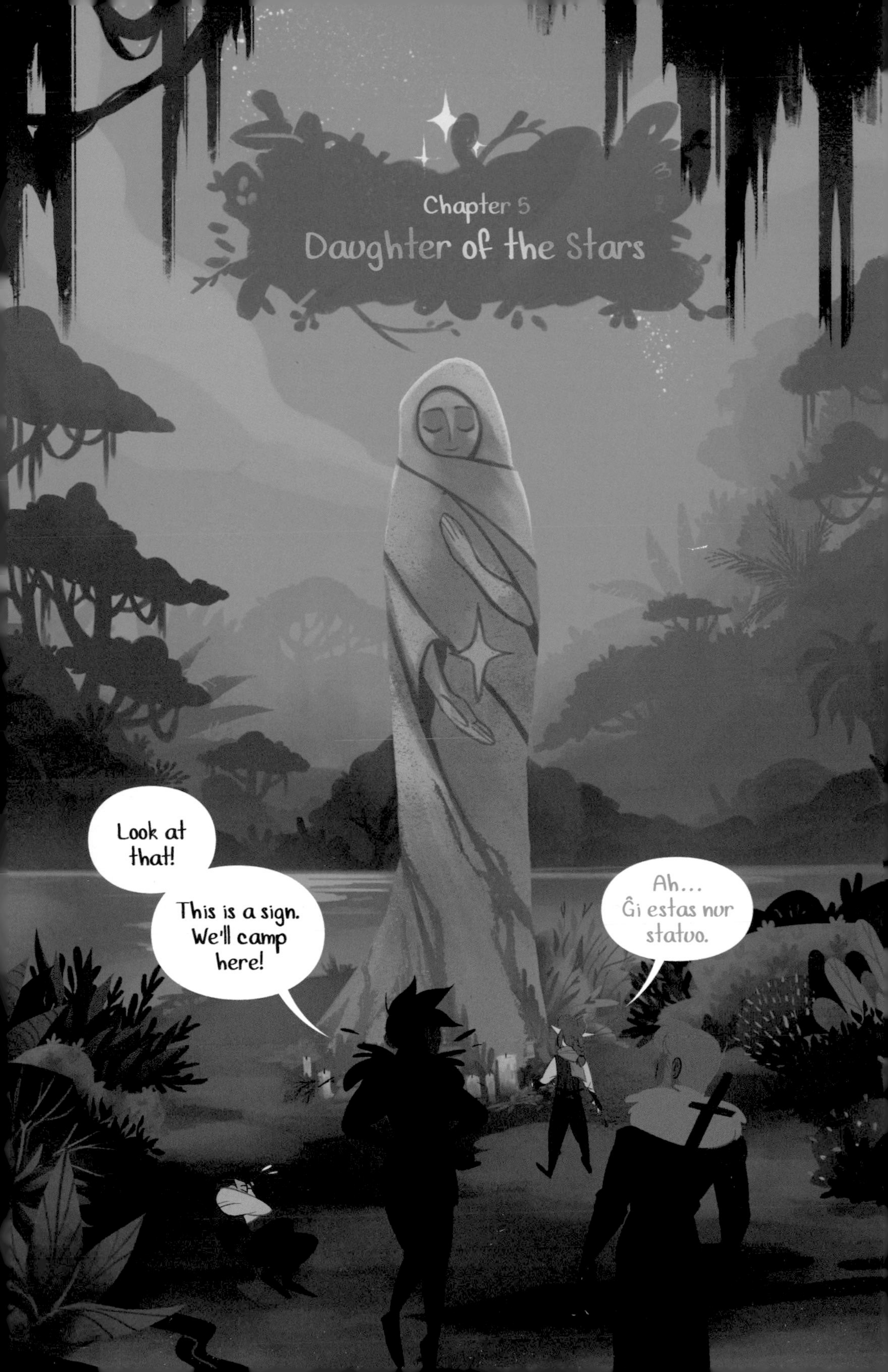
Chapter 5
Daughter of the Stars
Look at that!
This is a sign. We'll camp here!
Ah... Ĝi estas nur statuo.

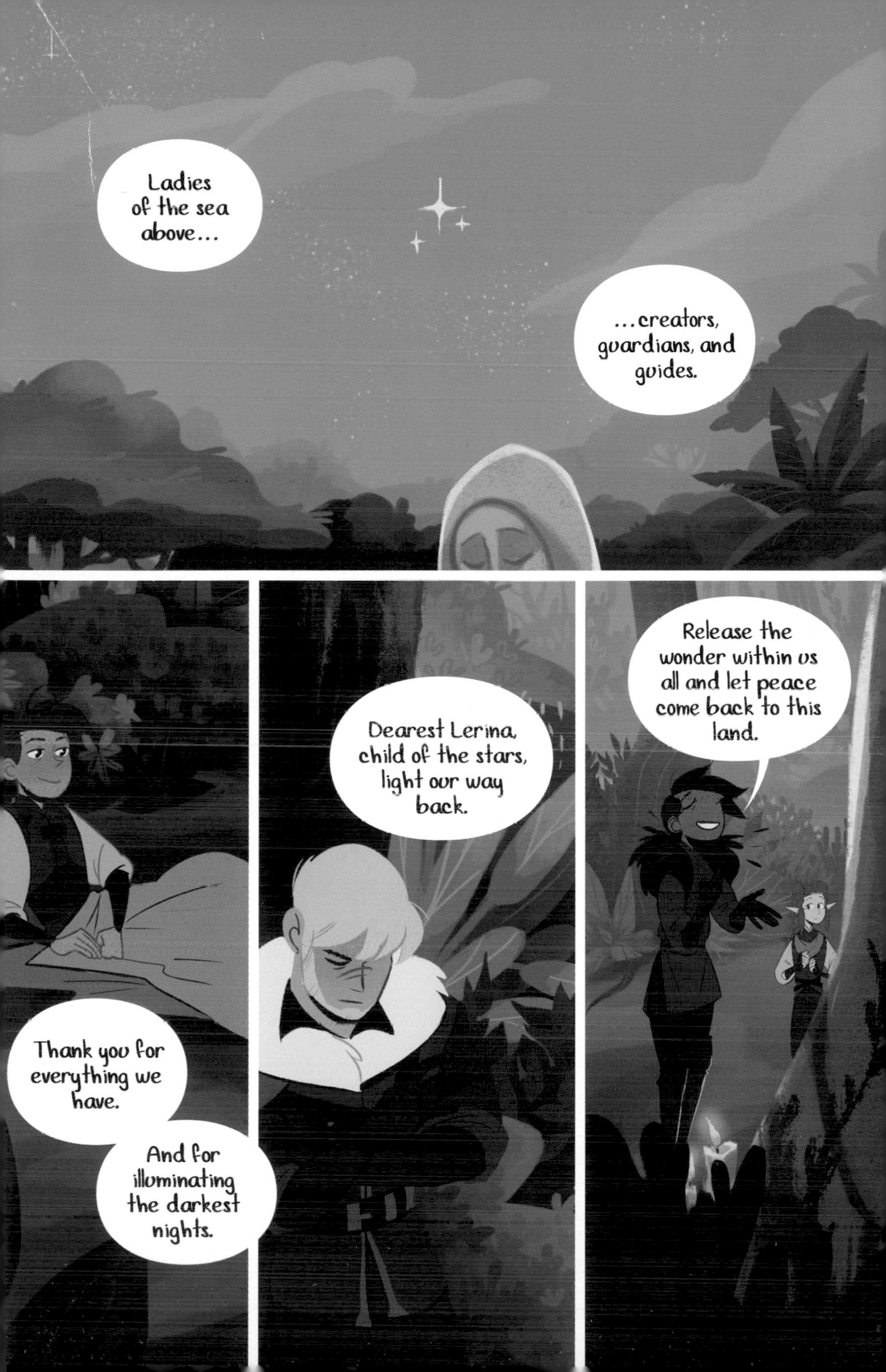
Ladies of the sea above...
...creators, guardians, and guides.
Thank you for everything we have.
And for illuminating the darkest nights.
Dearest Lerina, child of the stars, light our way back.
Release the wonder within us all and let peace come back to this land.

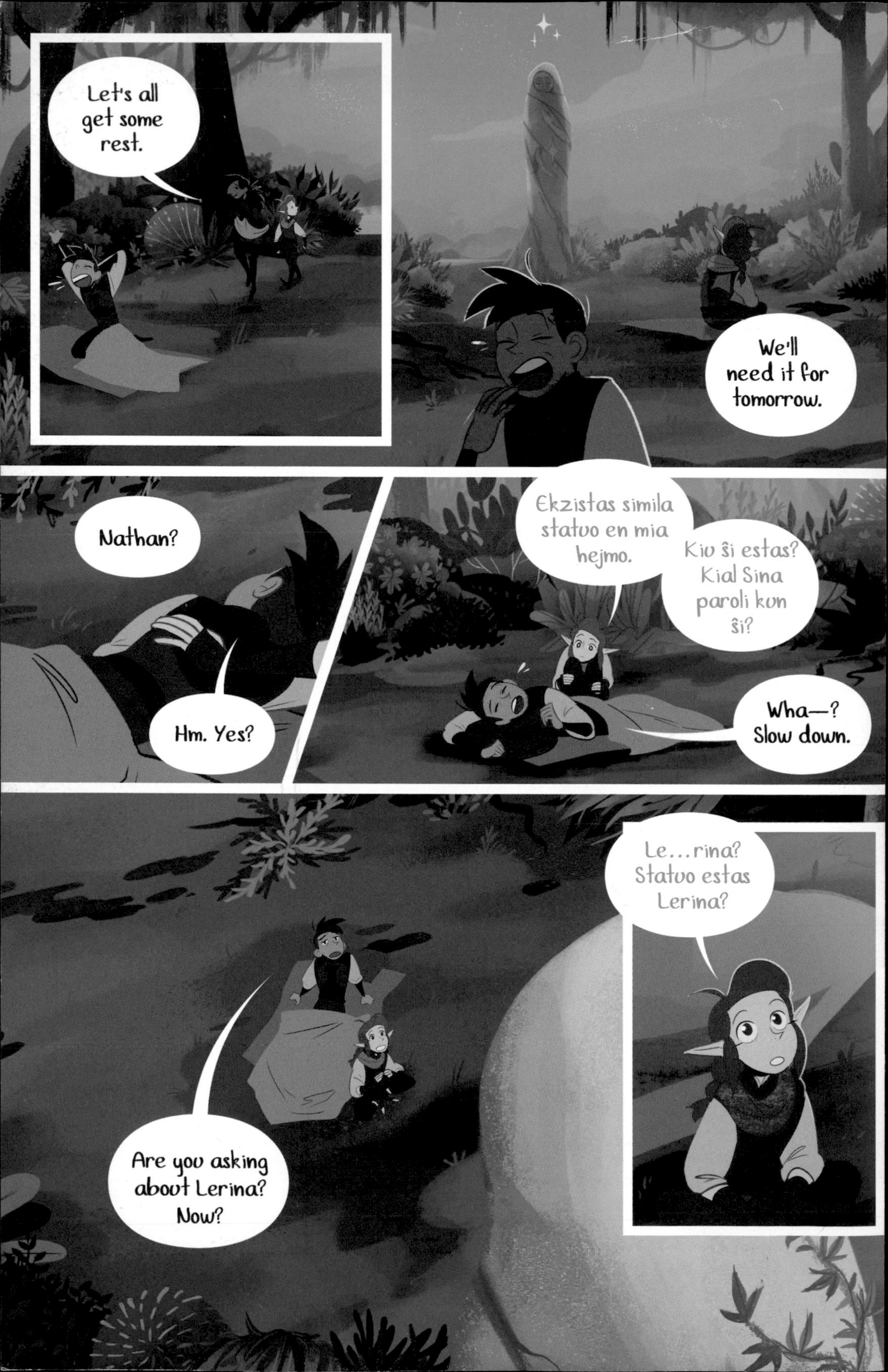

Let's all get some rest.
We'll need it for tomorrow.
Nathan?
Hm. Yes?
Ekzistas simila statuo en mia hejmo.
Kiu ŝi estas? Kial Sina paroli kun ŝi?
Wha—? Slow down.
Are you asking about Lerina? Now?
Le...rina? Statuo estas Lerina?

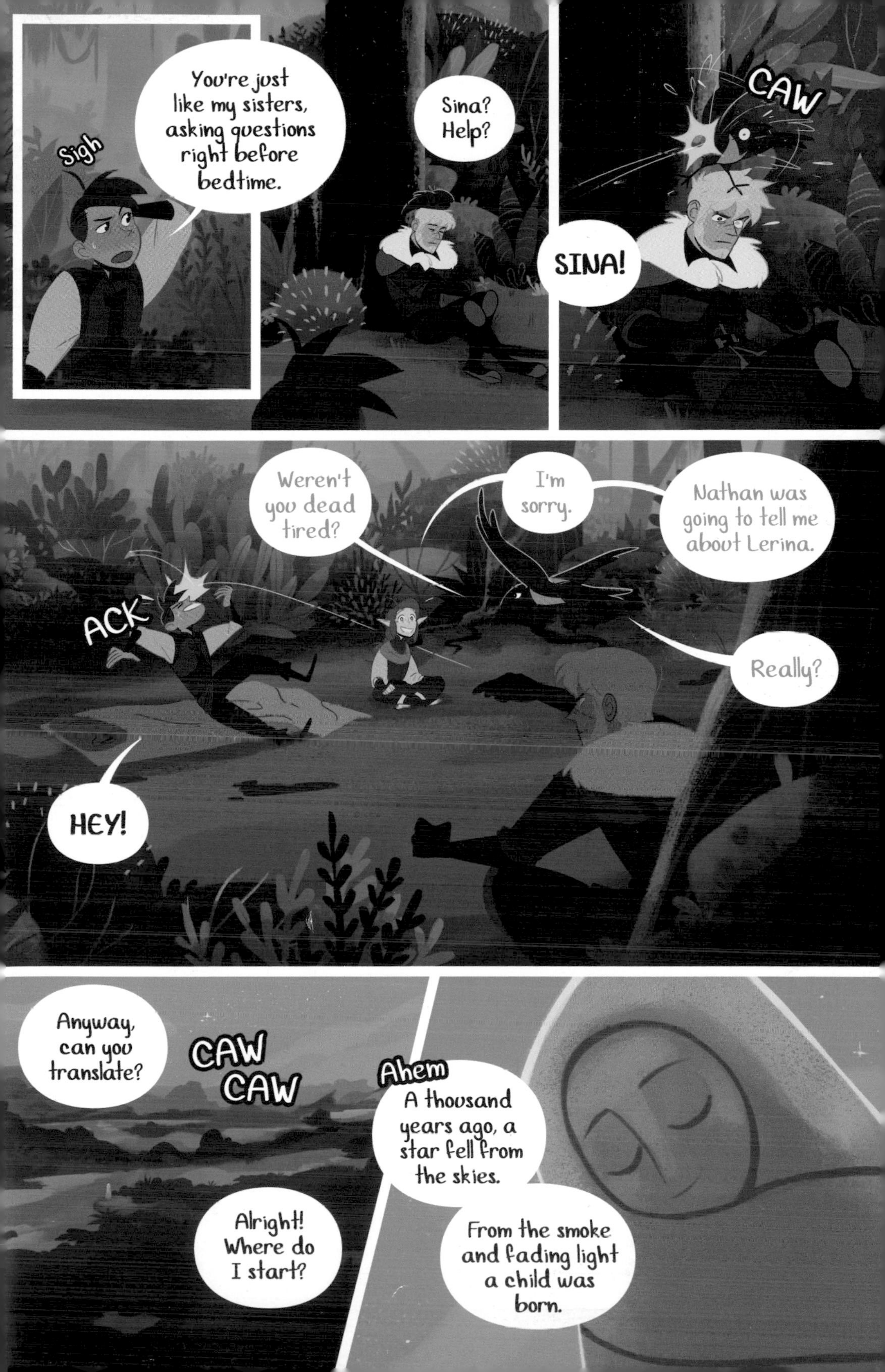
Sigh
You're just like my sisters, asking questions right before bedtime.
Sina? Help?
CAW
SINA!
ACK
Weren't you dead tired?
I'm sorry.
Nathan was going to tell me about Lerina.
Really?
HEY!
Anyway, can you translate?
CAW
CAW
Alright! Where do I start?
Ahem
A thousand years ago, a star fell from the skies.
From the smoke and fading light a child was born.

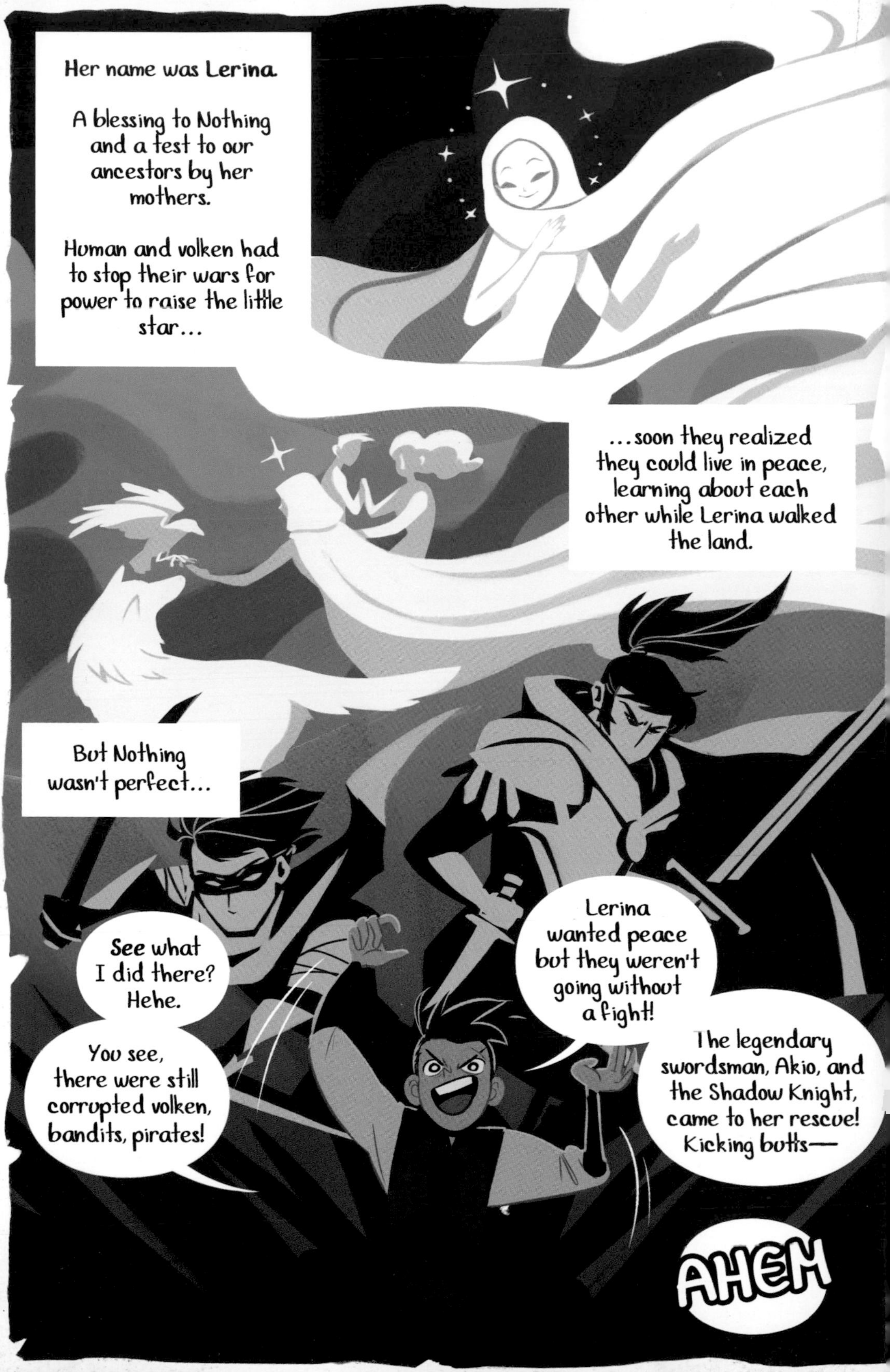
Her name was Lerina.
A blessing to Nothing and a test to our ancestors by her mothers.
Human and volken had to stop their wars for power to raise the little star...
...soon they realized they could live in peace, learning about each other while Lerina walked the land.
But Nothing wasn't perfect...
See what I did there? Hehe.
You see, there were still corrupted volken, bandits, pirates!
Lerina wanted peace but they weren't going without a fight!
The legendary swordsman, Akio, and the Shadow Knight, came to her rescue! Kicking butts—
AHEM

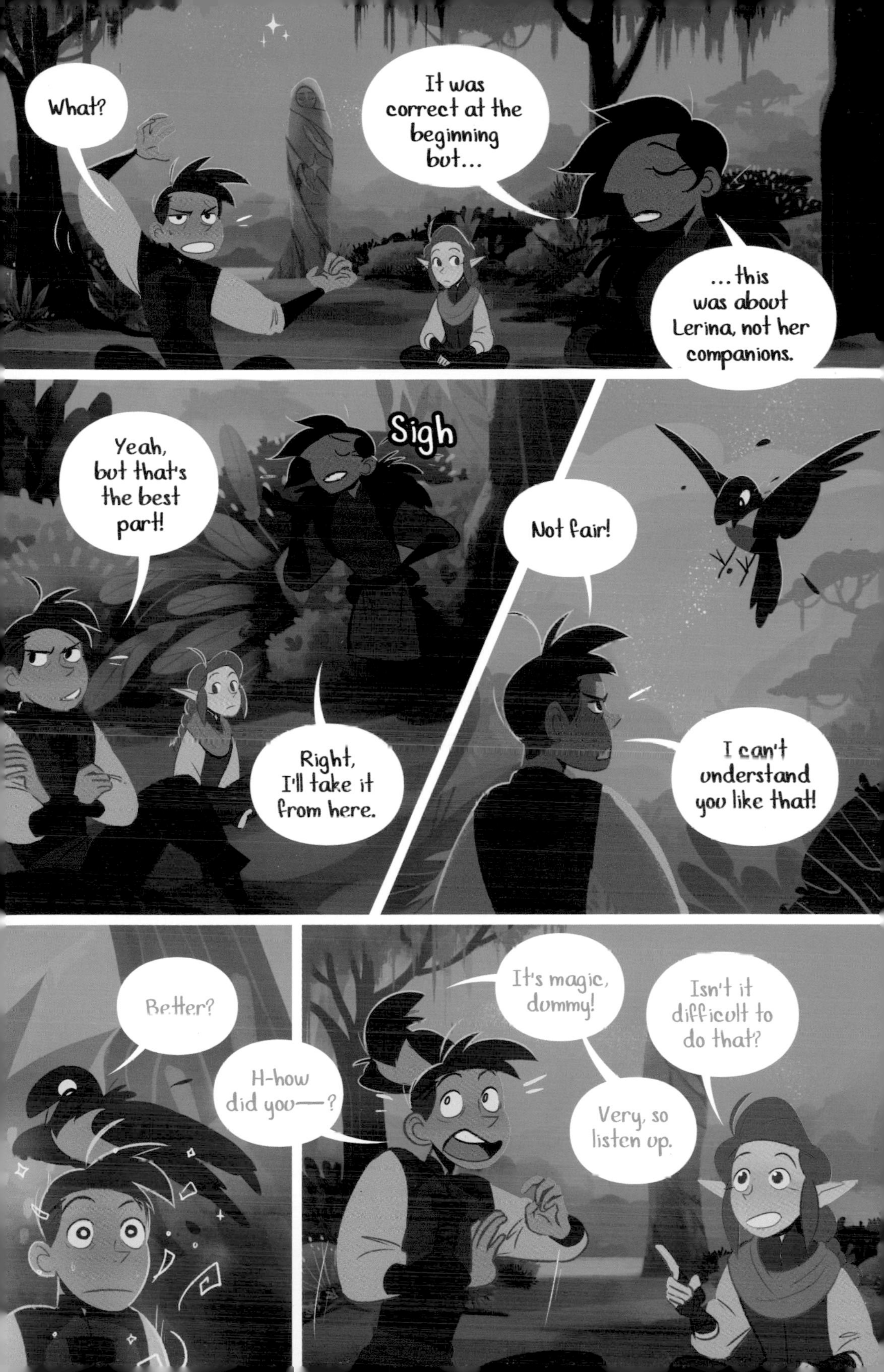
What?
It was correct at the beginning but...
...this was about Lerina, not her companions.
Yeah, but that's the best part!
Sigh
Right, I'll take it from here.
Not fair!
I can't understand you like that!
Better?
H-how did you—?
It's magic, dummy!
Isn't it difficult to do that?
Very, so listen up.

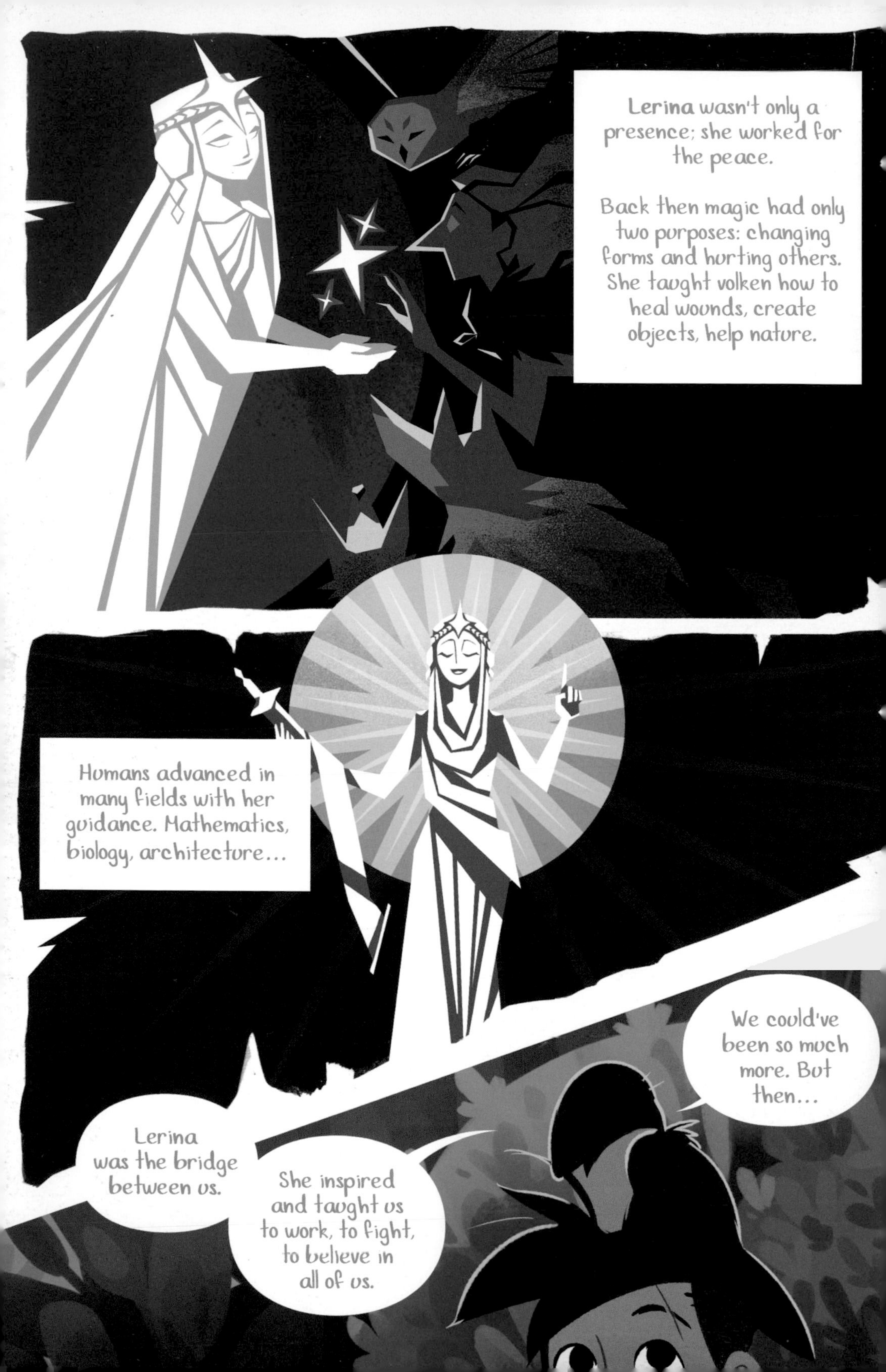
Lerina wasn't only a presence; she worked for the peace.
Back then magic had only two purposes: changing forms and hurting others. She taught volken how to heal wounds, create objects, help nature.
Humans advanced in many fields with her guidance. Mathematics, biology, architecture...
We could've been so much more. But then...
Lerina was the bridge between us.
She inspired and taught us to work, to fight, to believe in all of us.

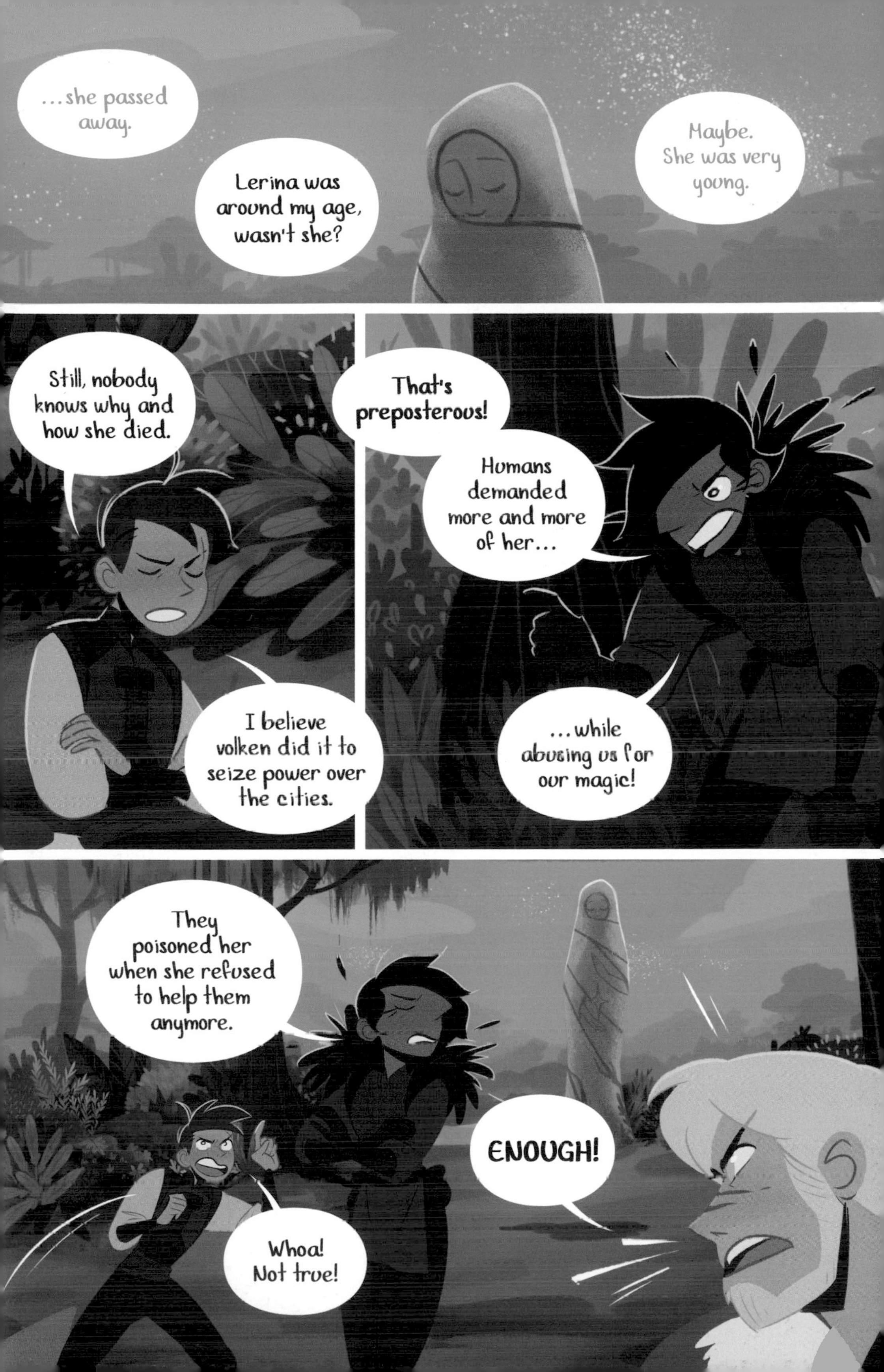
...she passed away.
Lerina was around my age, wasn't she?
Maybe. She was very young.
Still, nobody knows why and how she died.
I believe volken did it to seize power over the cities.
That's preposterous!
Humans demanded more and more of her...
...while abusing us for our magic!
They poisoned her when she refused to help them anymore.
Whoa! Not true!
ENOUGH!

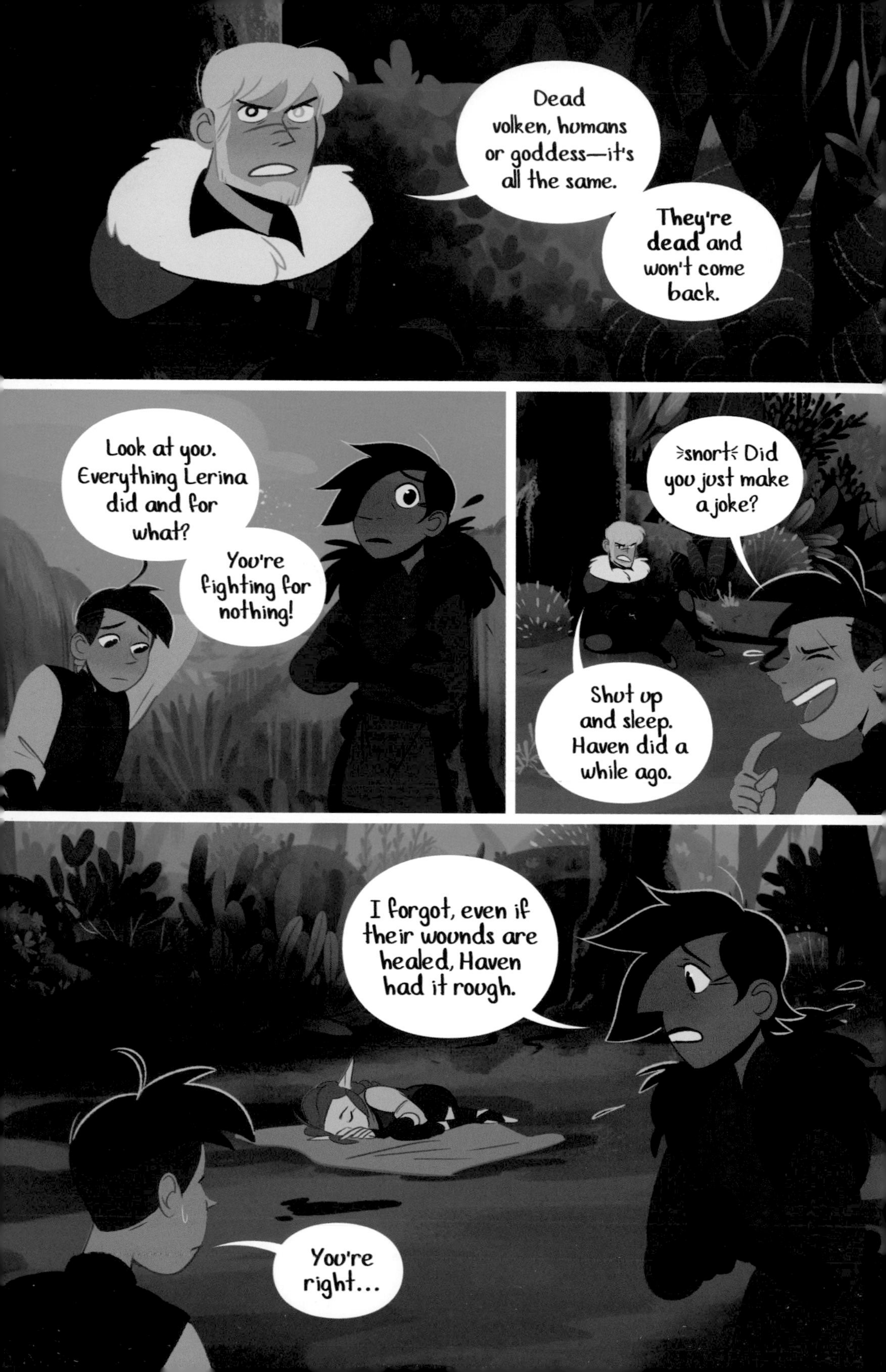
Dead volken, humans or goddess—it's all the same.
They're dead and won't come back.
Look at you. Everything Lerina did and for what?
You're fighting for nothing!
⪢snort⪡ Did you just make a joke?
Shut up and sleep. Haven did a while ago.
I forgot, even if their wounds are healed, Haven had it rough.
You're right...

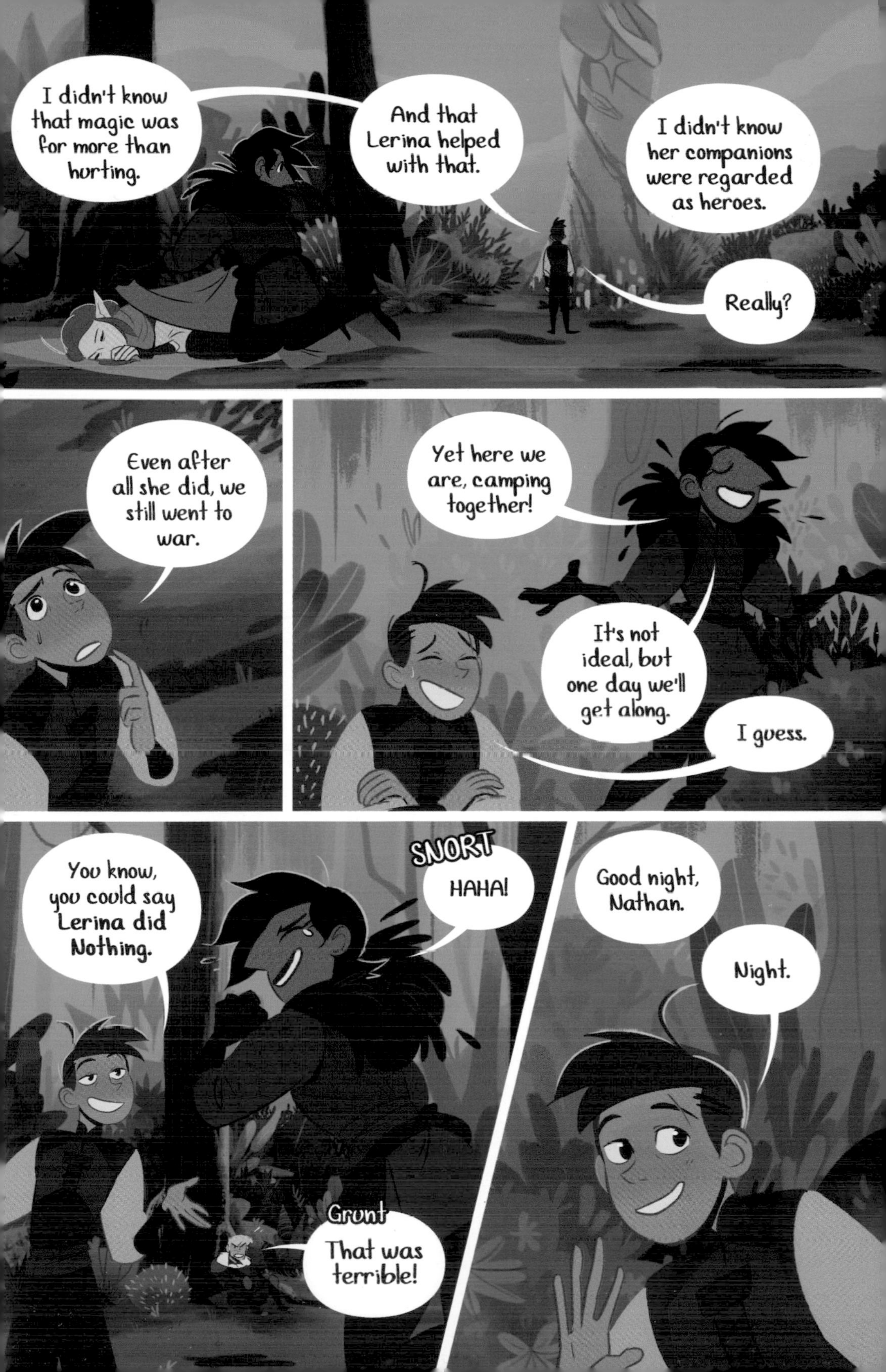

I didn't know that magic was for more than hurting.
And that Lerina helped with that.
I didn't know her companions were regarded as heroes.
Really?
Even after all she did, we still went to war.
Yet here we are, camping together!
It's not ideal, but one day we'll get along.
I guess.
You know, you could say Lerina did Nothing.
SNORT
HAHA!
Grunt
That was terrible!
Good night, Nathan.
Night.

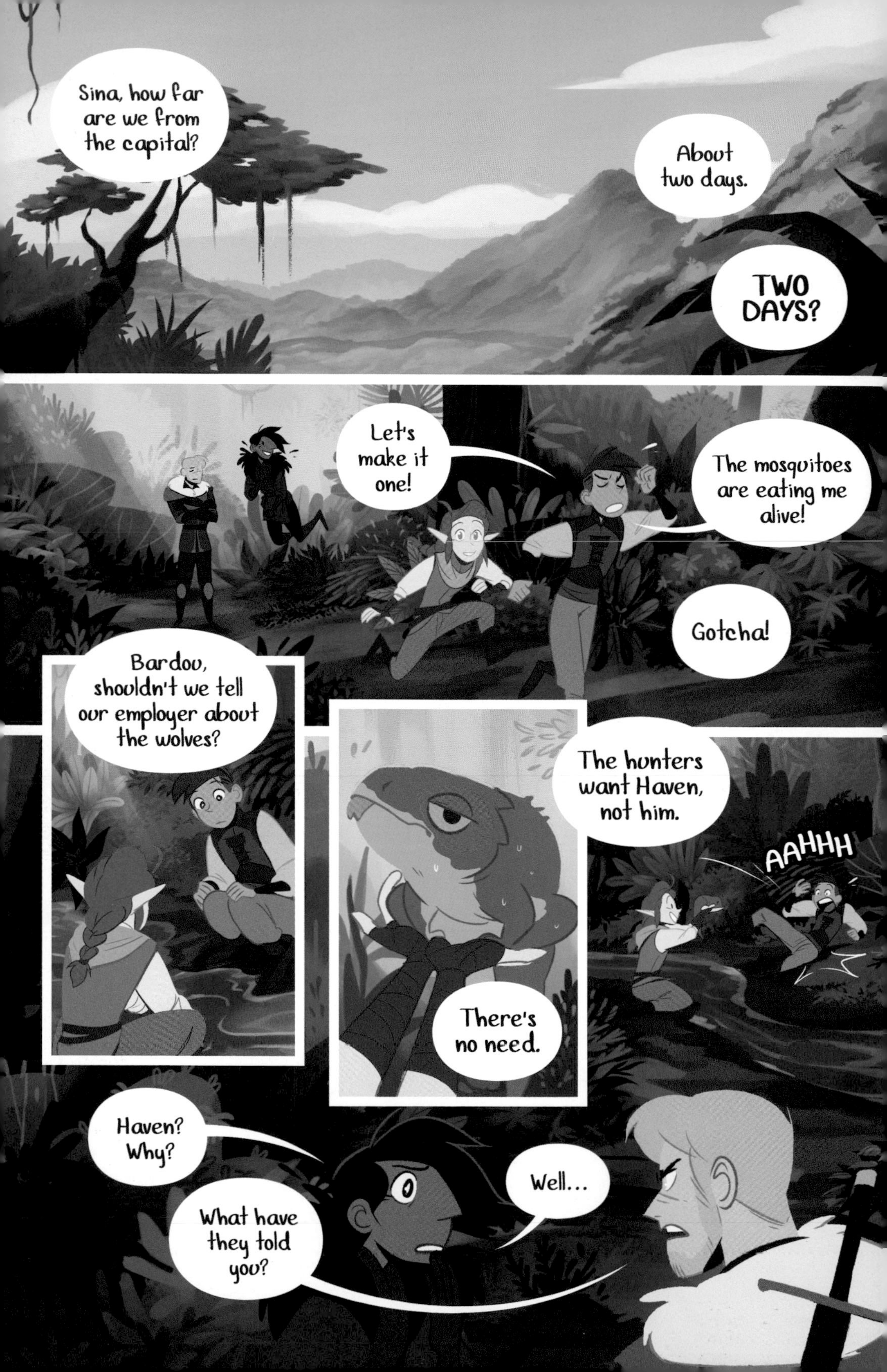
Sina, how far are we from the capital?
About two days.
TWO DAYS?
Let's make it one!
The mosquitoes are eating me alive!
Gotcha!
Bardou, shouldn't we tell our employer about the wolves?
The hunters want Haven, not him.
AAHHH
There's no need.
Haven? Why?
What have they told you?
Well...

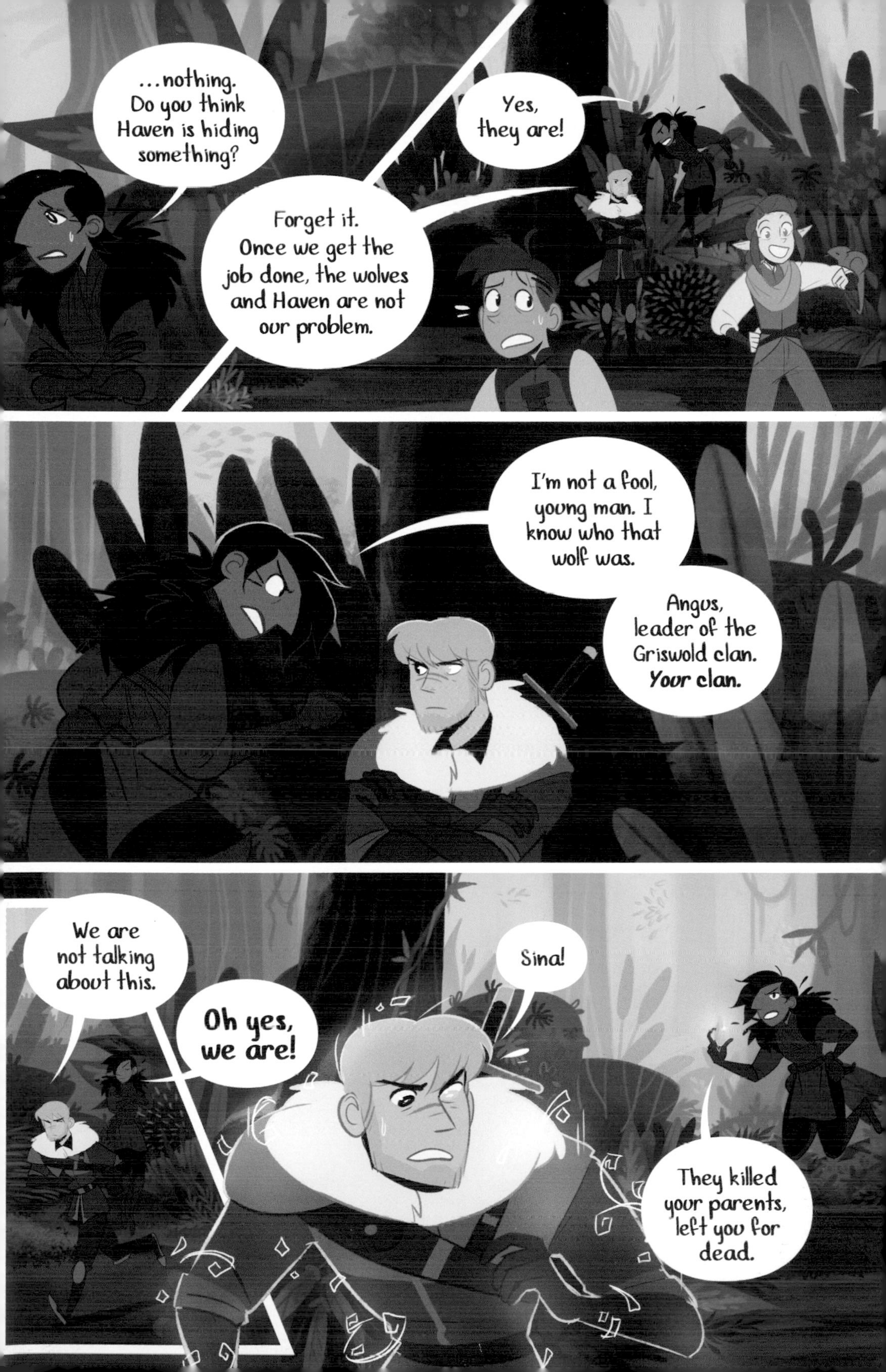
...nothing. Do you think Haven is hiding something?
Yes, they are!
Forget it. Once we get the job done, the wolves and Haven are not our problem.
I'm not a fool, young man. I know who that wolf was.
Angus, leader of the Griswold clan. **Your clan.**
We are not talking about this.
Oh yes, we are!
Sina!
They killed your parents, left you for dead.

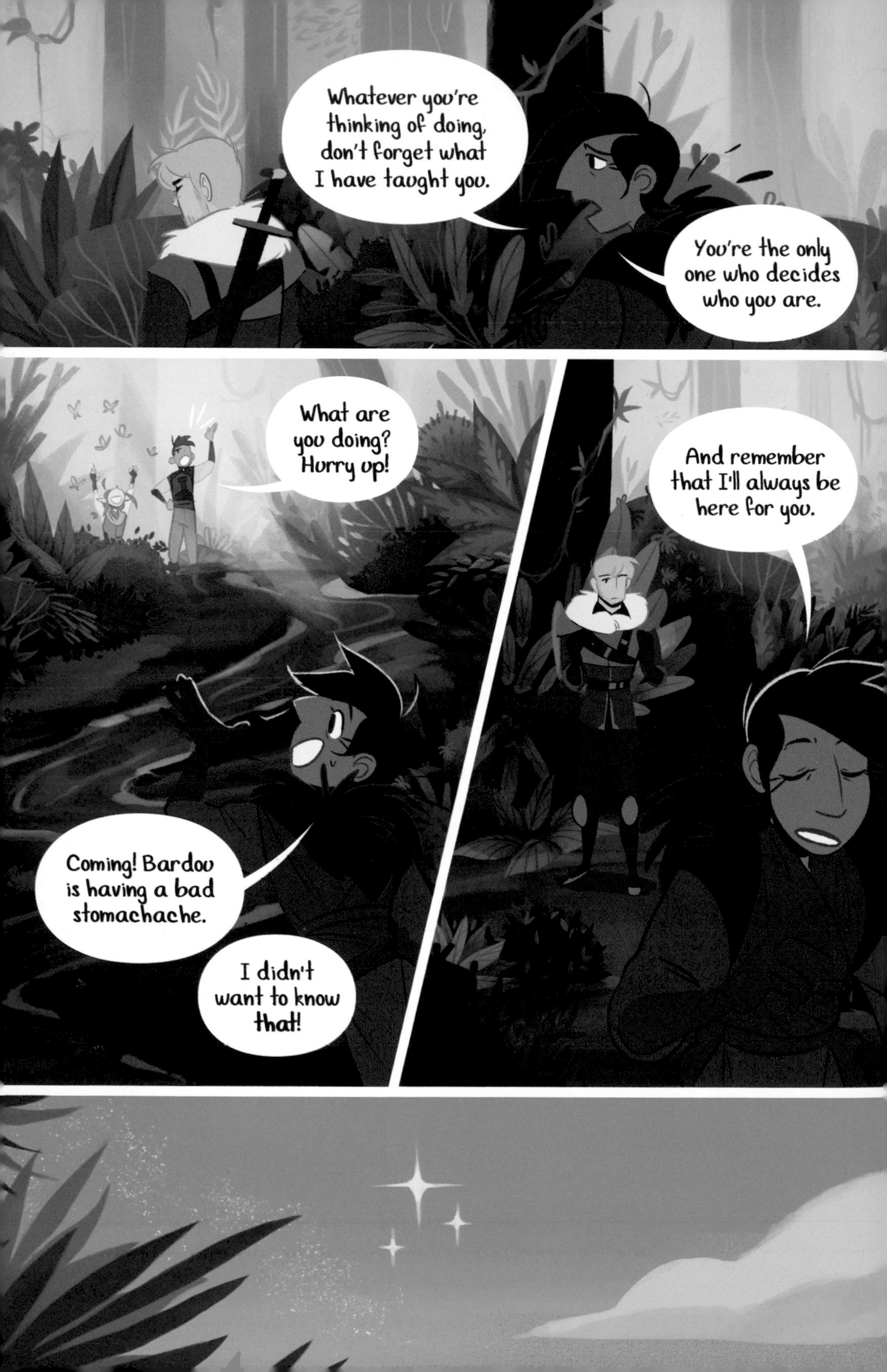
Whatever you're thinking of doing, don't forget what I have taught you.
You're the only one who decides who you are.
What are you doing? Hurry up!
Coming! Bardou is having a bad stomachache.
I didn't want to know that!
And remember that I'll always be here for you.

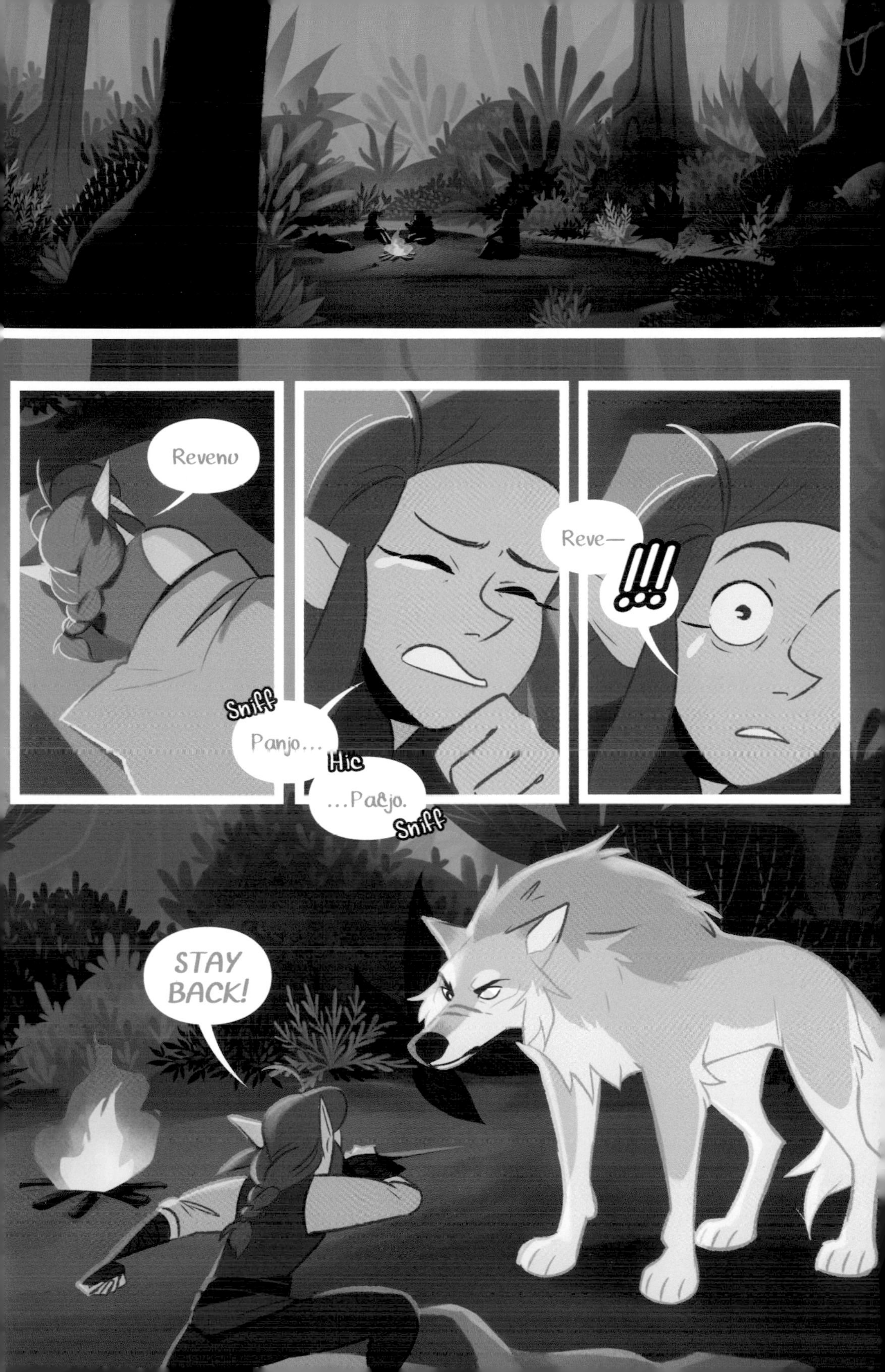

Reveno
Sniff
Panjo...
Hic
...Pacjo.
Sniff
Reve—
!!!
STAY BACK!

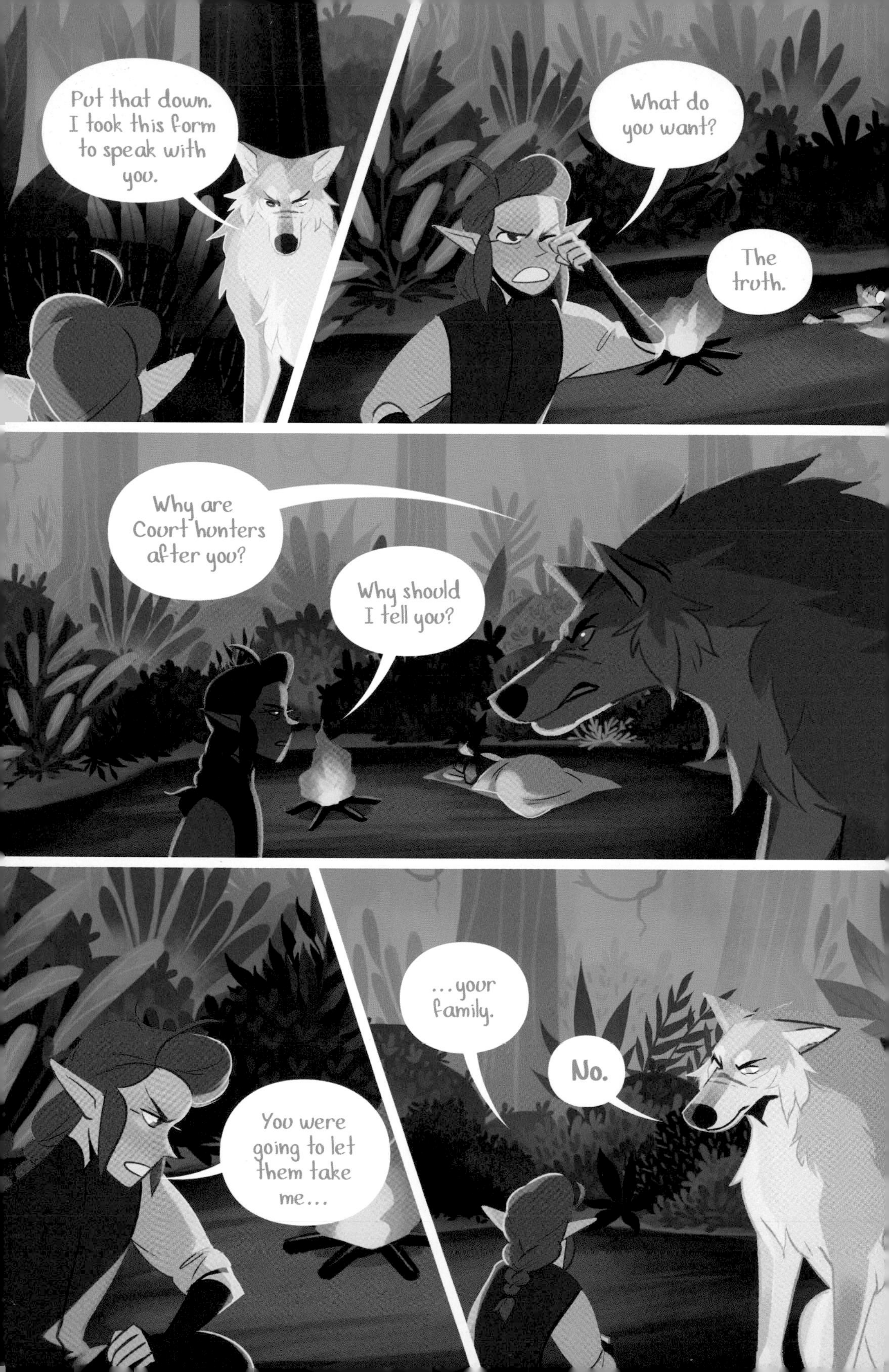

Put that down. I took this form to speak with you.
What do you want?
The truth.
Why are Court hunters after you?
Why should I tell you?
You were going to let them take me...
...your family.
No.

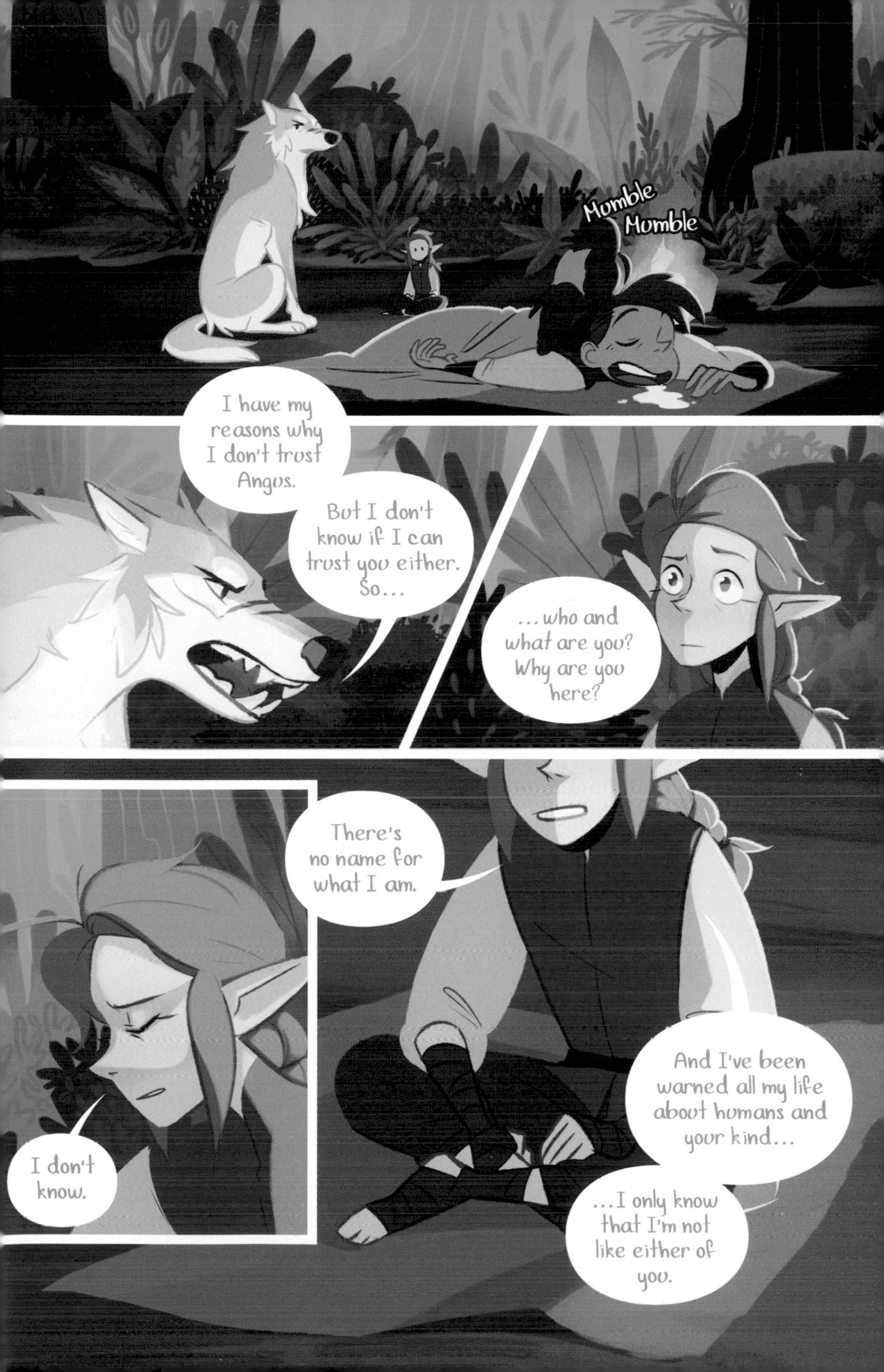
Mumble
Mumble
I have my reasons why I don't trust Angus.
But I don't know if I can trust you either. So...
...who and what are you? Why are you here?
There's no name for what I am.
I don't know.
And I've been warned all my life about humans and your kind...
...I only know that I'm not like either of you.

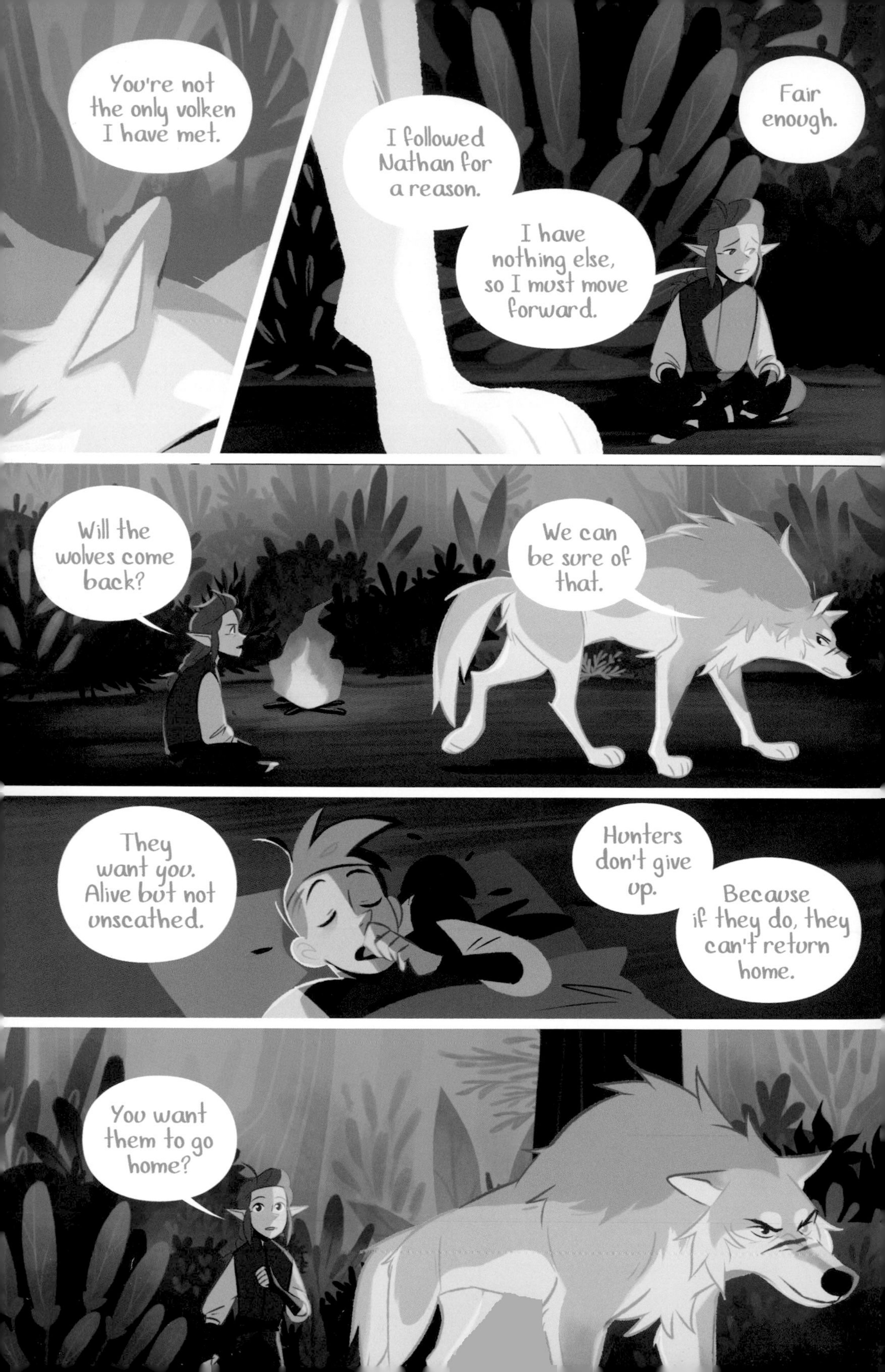
You're not the only volken I have met.
I followed Nathan for a reason.
I have nothing else, so I must move forward.
Fair enough.
Will the wolves come back?
We can be sure of that.
They want you. Alive but not unscathed.
Hunters don't give up.
Because if they do, they can't return home.
You want them to go home?

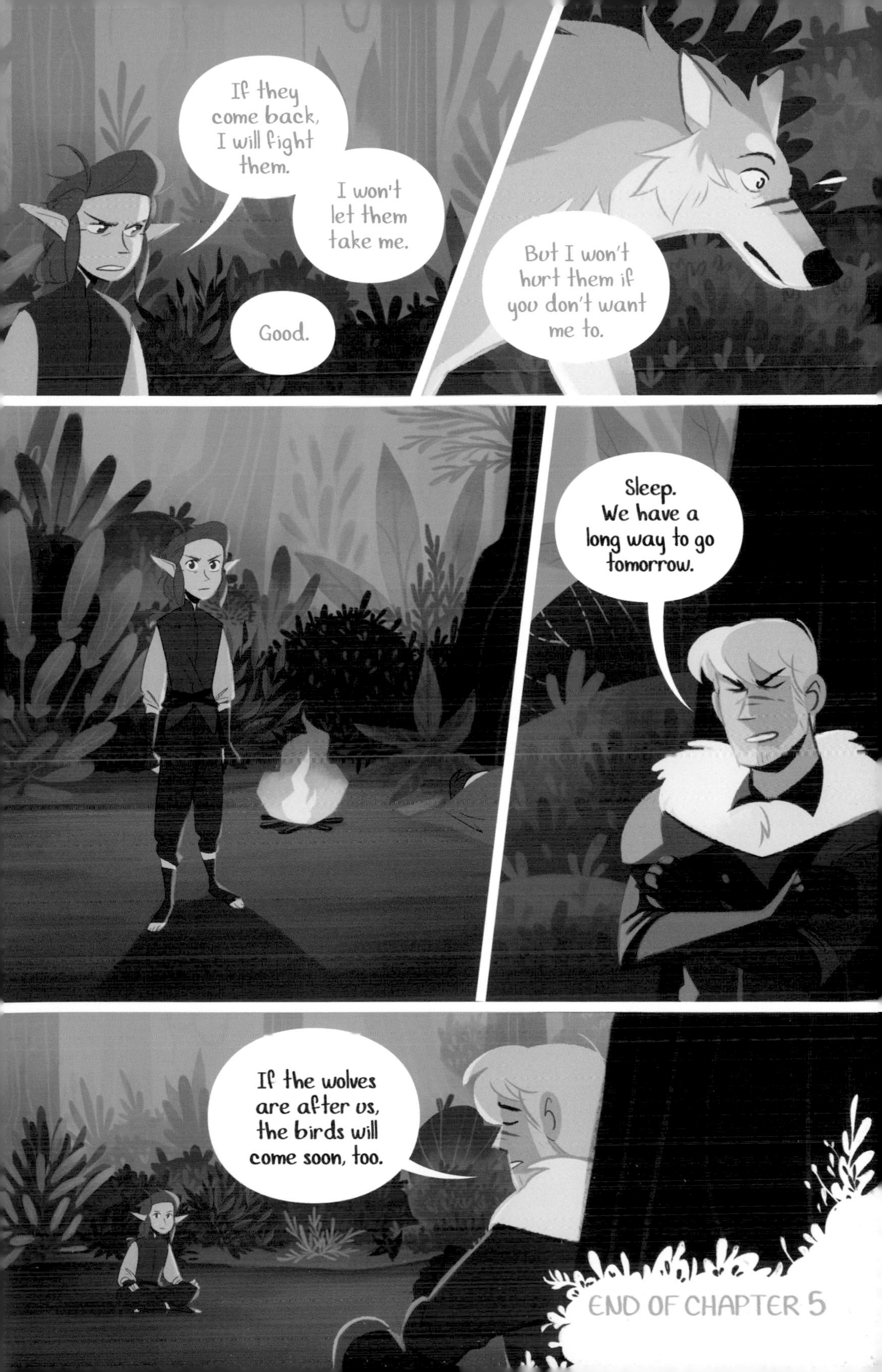
If they come back, I will fight them.
I won't let them take me.
Good.
But I won't hurt them if you don't want me to.
Sleep. We have a long way to go tomorrow.
If the wolves are after us, the birds will come soon, too.
END OF CHAPTER 5

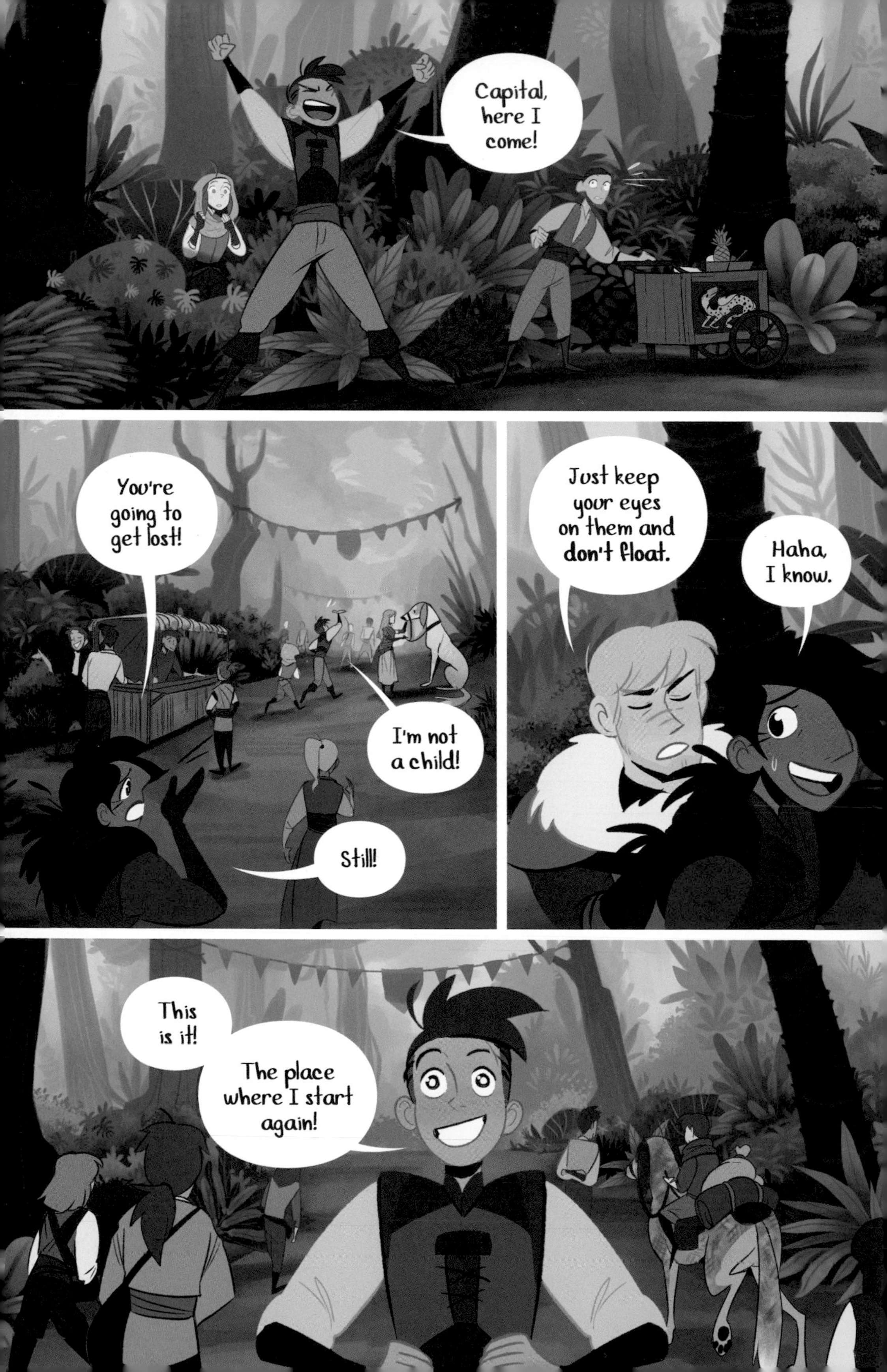

Capital, here I come!
You're going to get lost!
I'm not a child!
Still!
Just keep your eyes on them and **don't float.**
Haha, I know.
This is it!
The place where I start again!

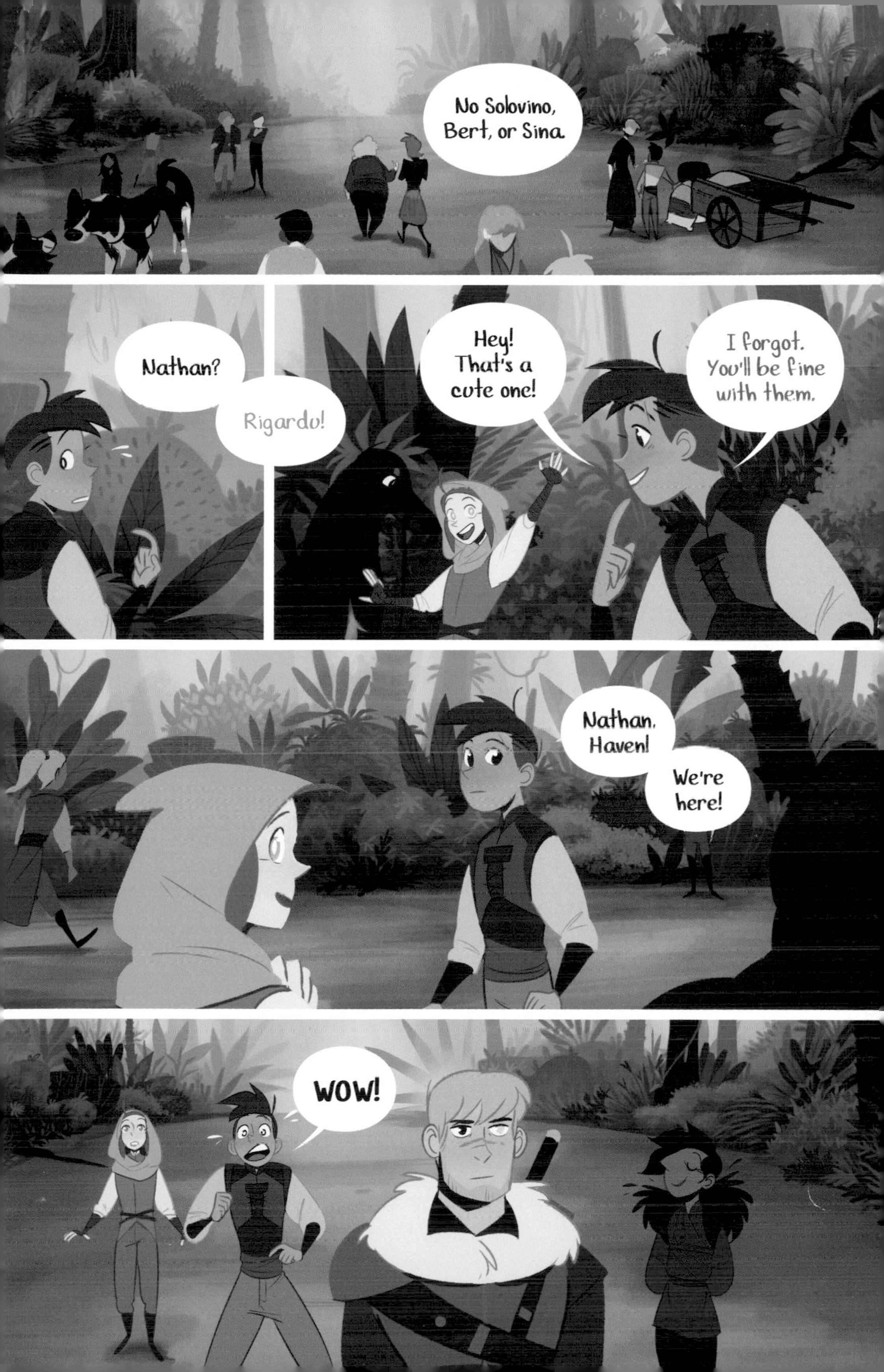
No Solovino, Bert, or Sina.
Nathan?
Rigardo!
Hey! That's a cute one!
I forgot. You'll be fine with them.
Nathan. Haven!
We're here!
WOW!

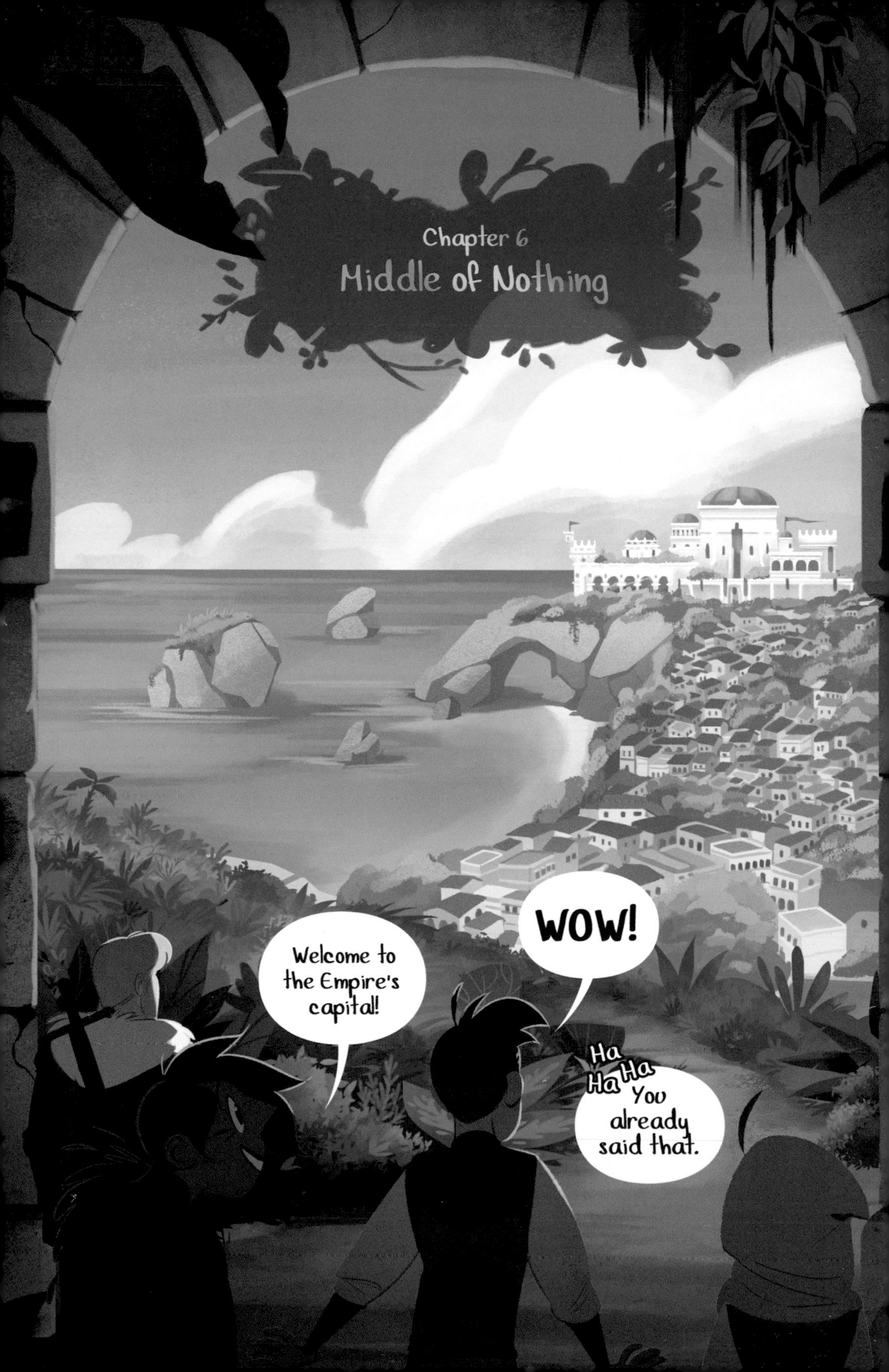
Chapter 6
Middle of Nothing
Welcome to the Empire's capital!
WOW!
Ha Ha Ha
You already said that.

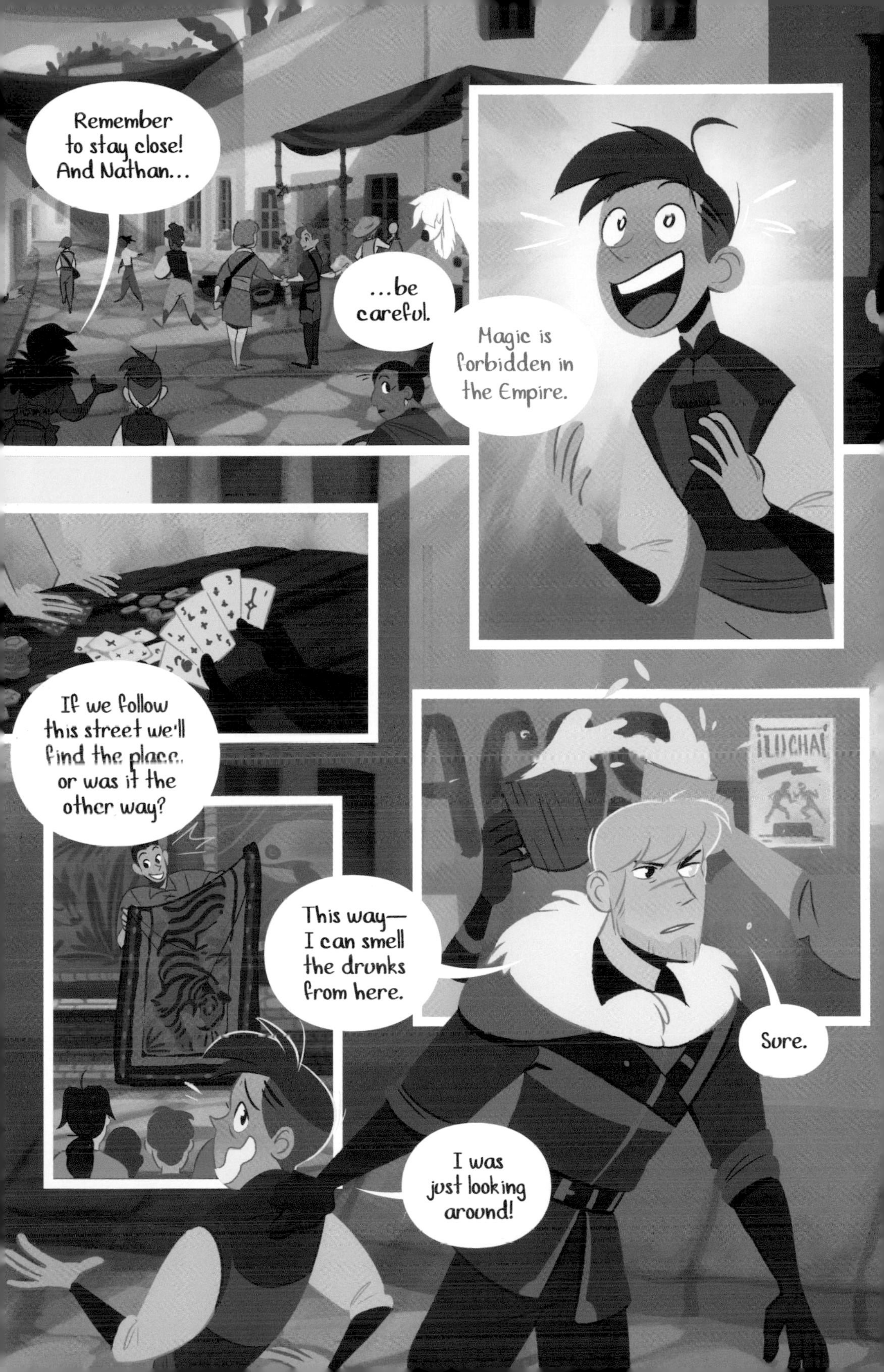
Remember to stay close! And Nathan...
...be careful.
Magic is forbidden in the Empire.
If we follow this street we'll find the place.. or was it the other way?
¡LUCHA!
This way— I can smell the drunks from here.
Sure.
I was just looking around!

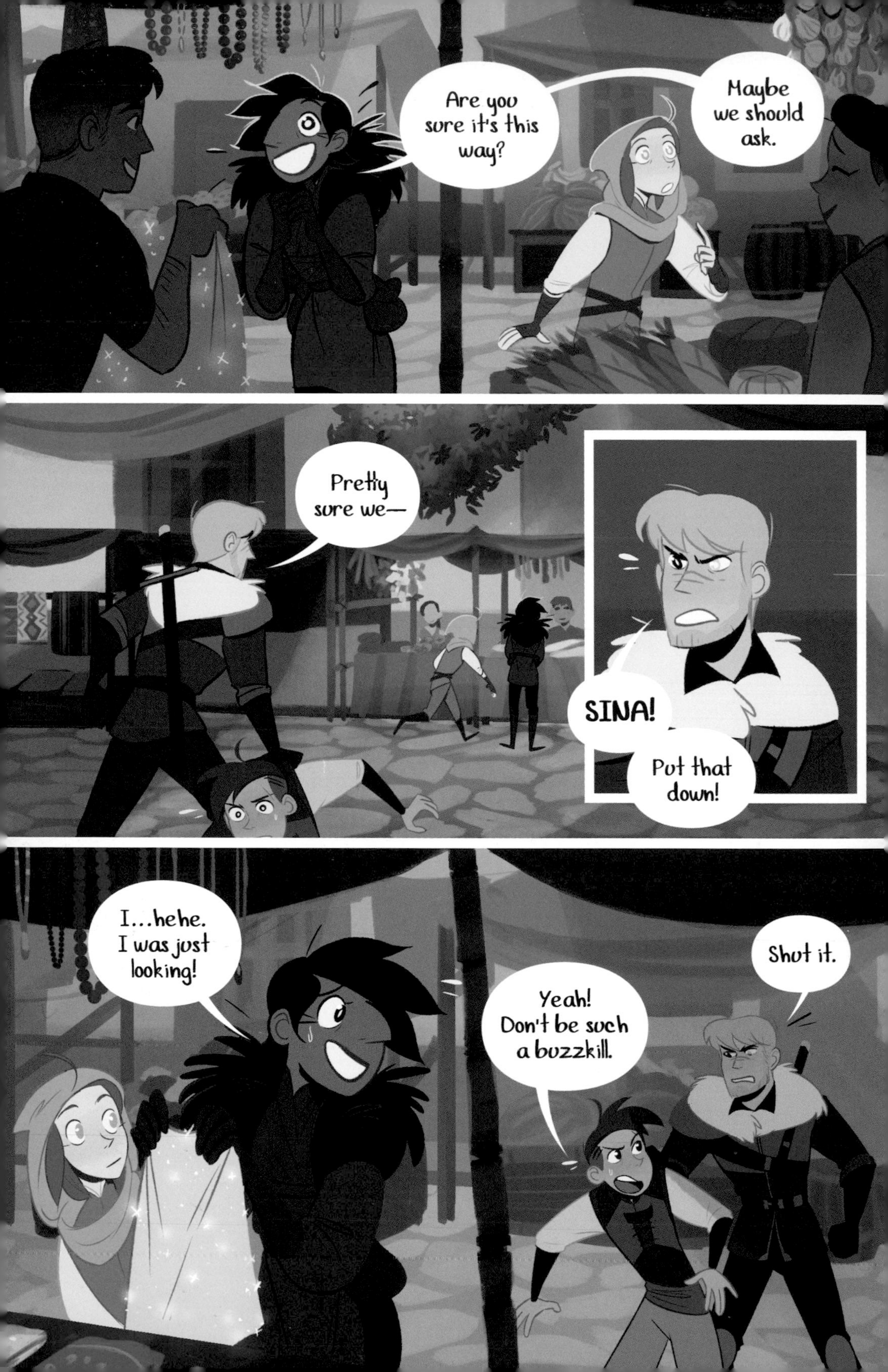
Are you sure it's this way?
Maybe we should ask.
Pretty sure we—
SINA!
Put that down!
I...hehe. I was just looking!
Yeah! Don't be such a buzzkill.
Shut it.

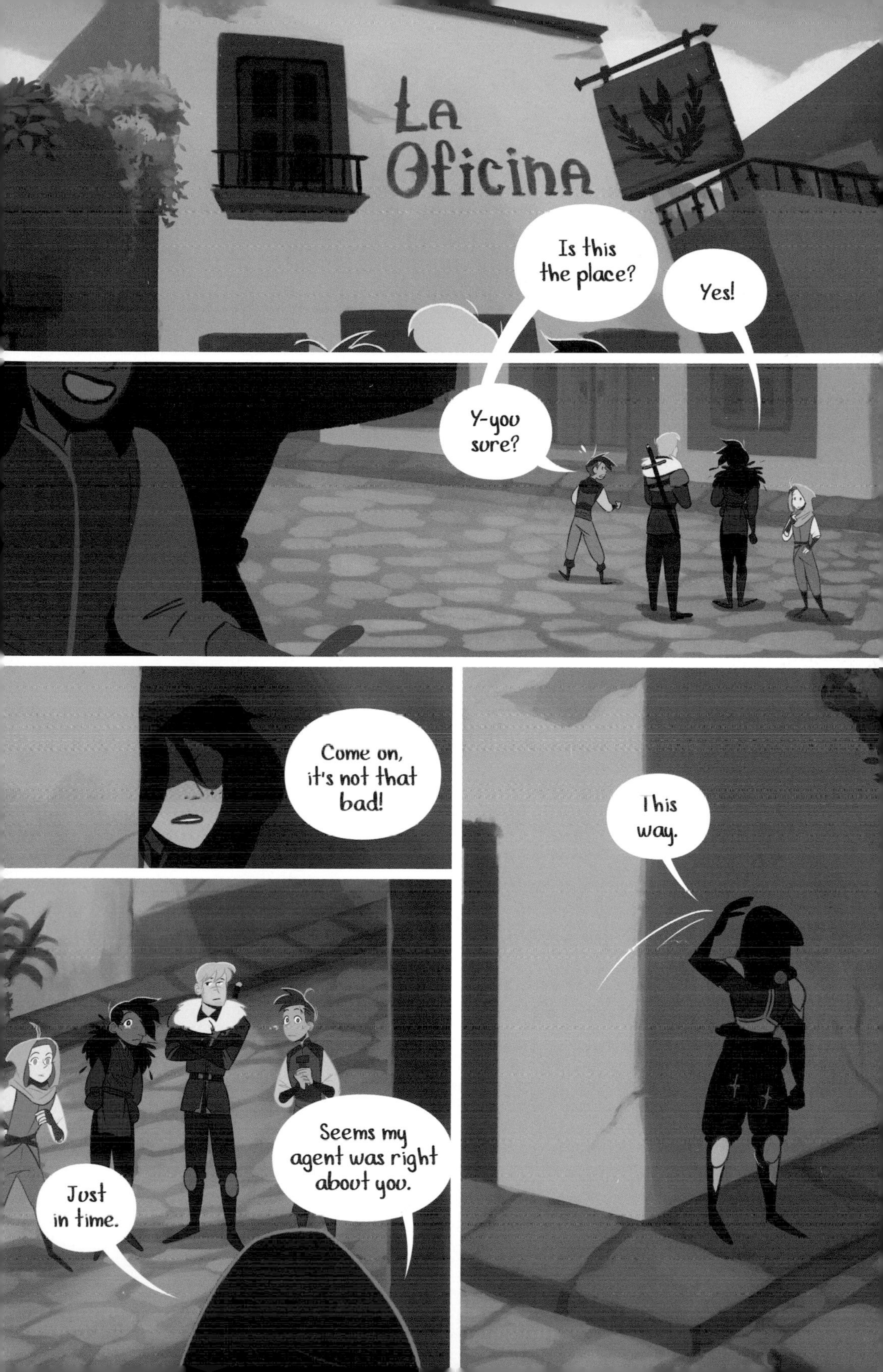
La Oficina
Is this the place?
Yes!
Y-you sure?
Come on, it's not that bad!
This way.
Just in time.
Seems my agent was right about you.

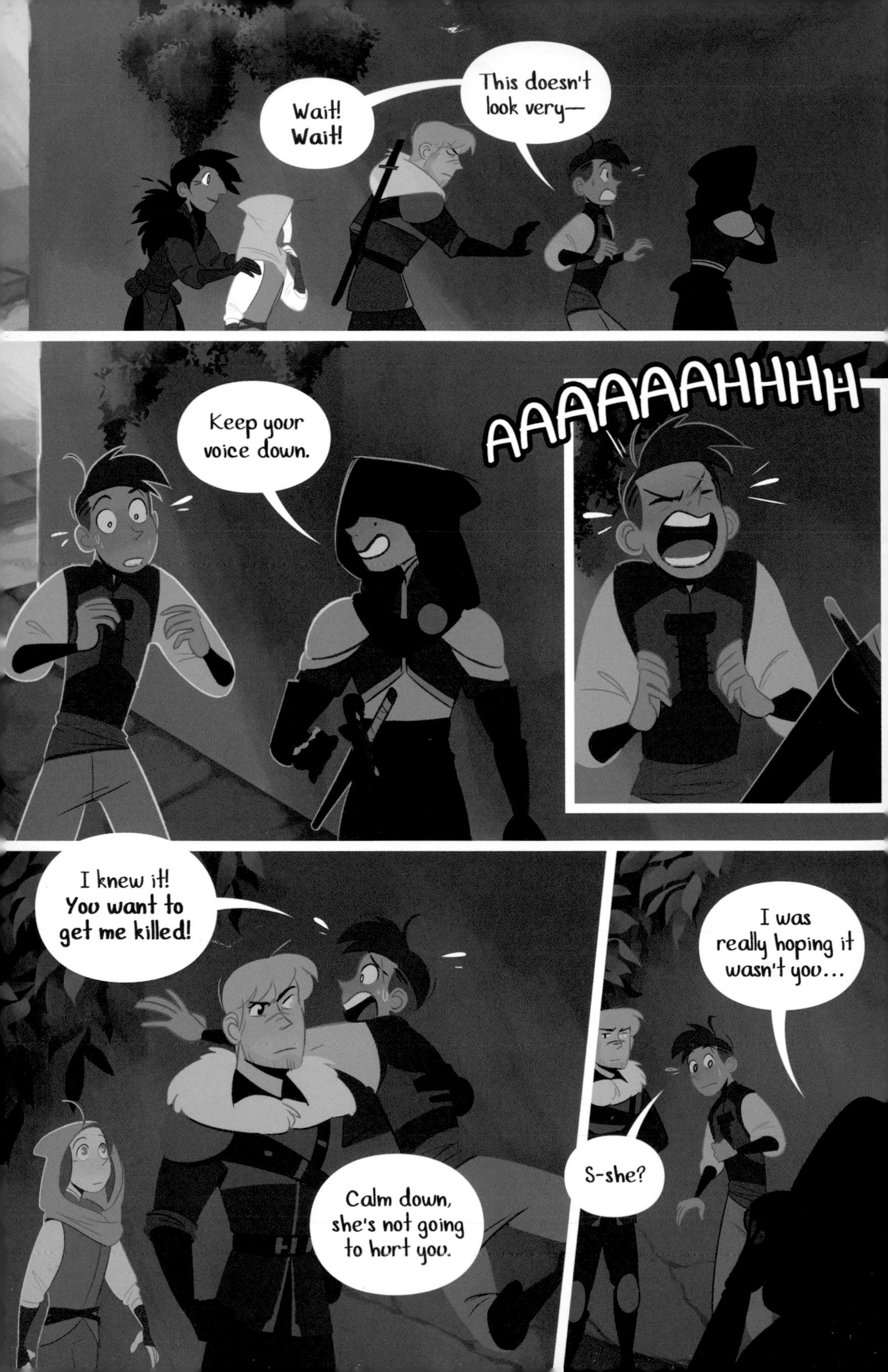
Wait!
Wait!
This doesn't look very—
Keep your voice down.
AAAAAAHHHH
I knew it! You want to get me killed!
Calm down, she's not going to hurt you.
I was really hoping it wasn't you...
S-she?

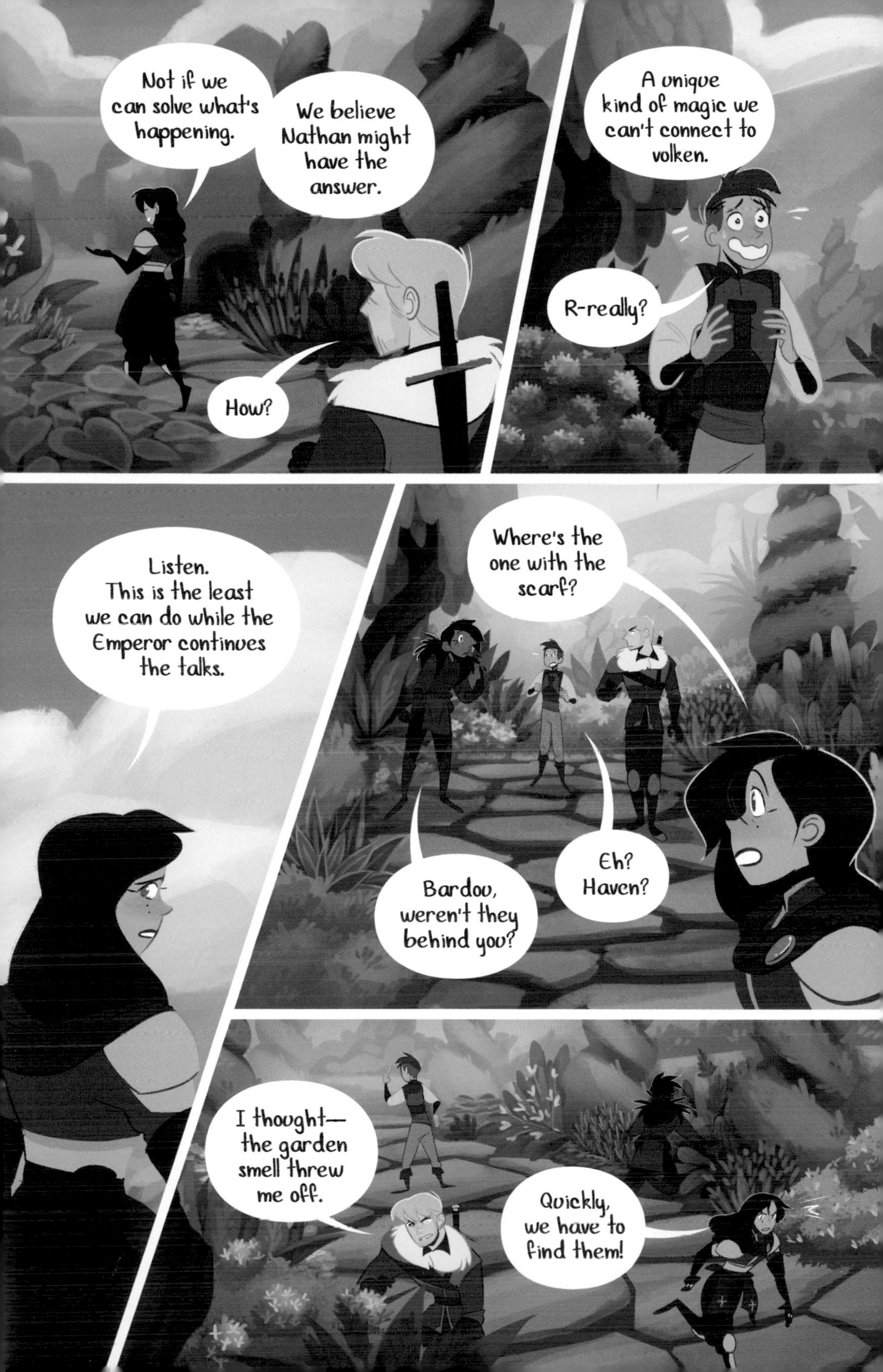
Not if we can solve what's happening.
We believe Nathan might have the answer.
How?
A unique kind of magic we can't connect to volken.
R-really?
Listen. This is the least we can do while the Emperor continues the talks.
Where's the one with the scarf?
Eh? Haven?
Bardou, weren't they behind you?
I thought— the garden smell threw me off.
Quickly, we have to find them!

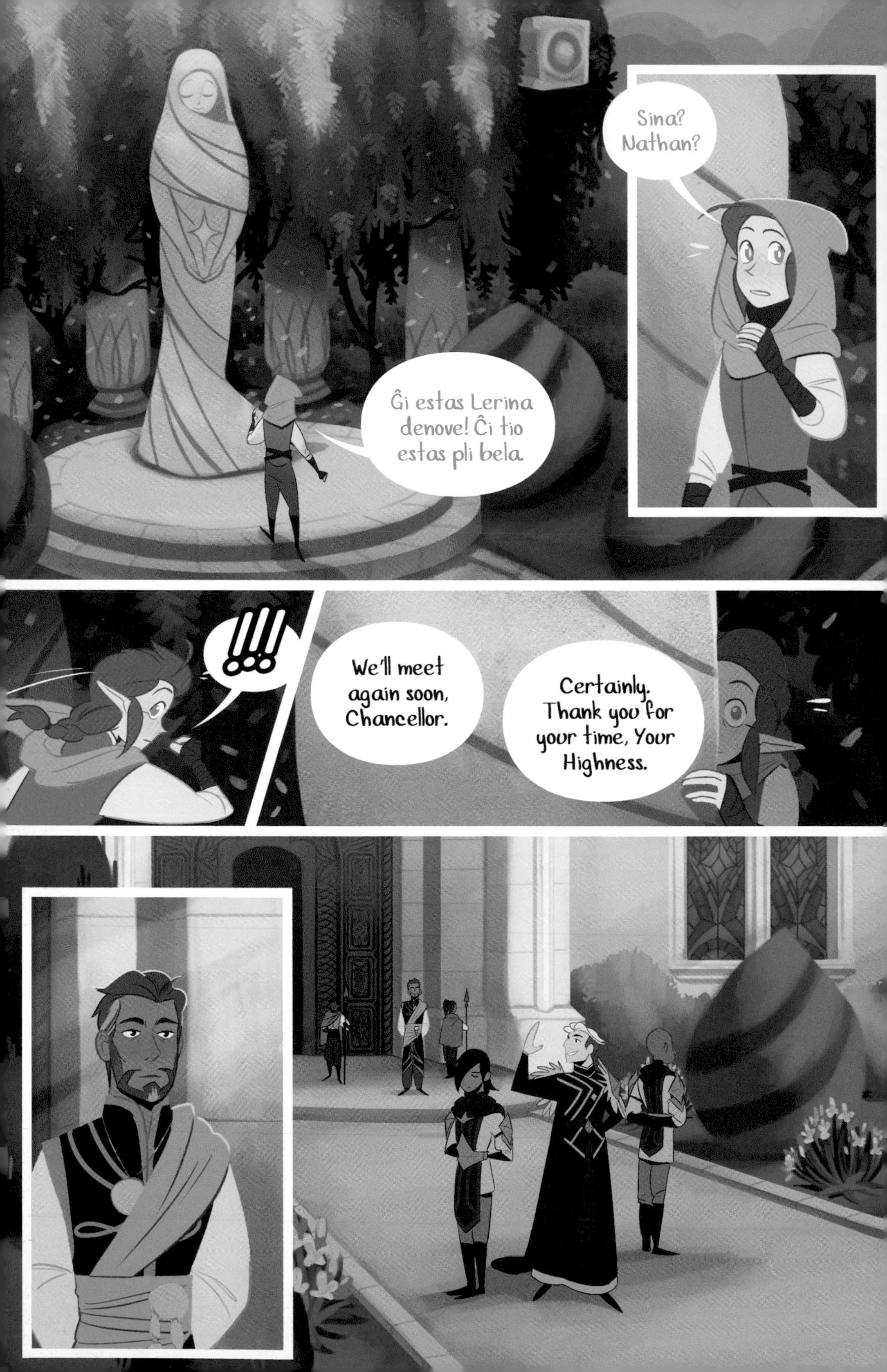
Sina?
Nathan?
Ĝi estas Lerina denove! Ĉi tio estas pli bela
!!!
We'll meet again soon, Chancellor.
Certainly. Thank you for your time, Your Highness.

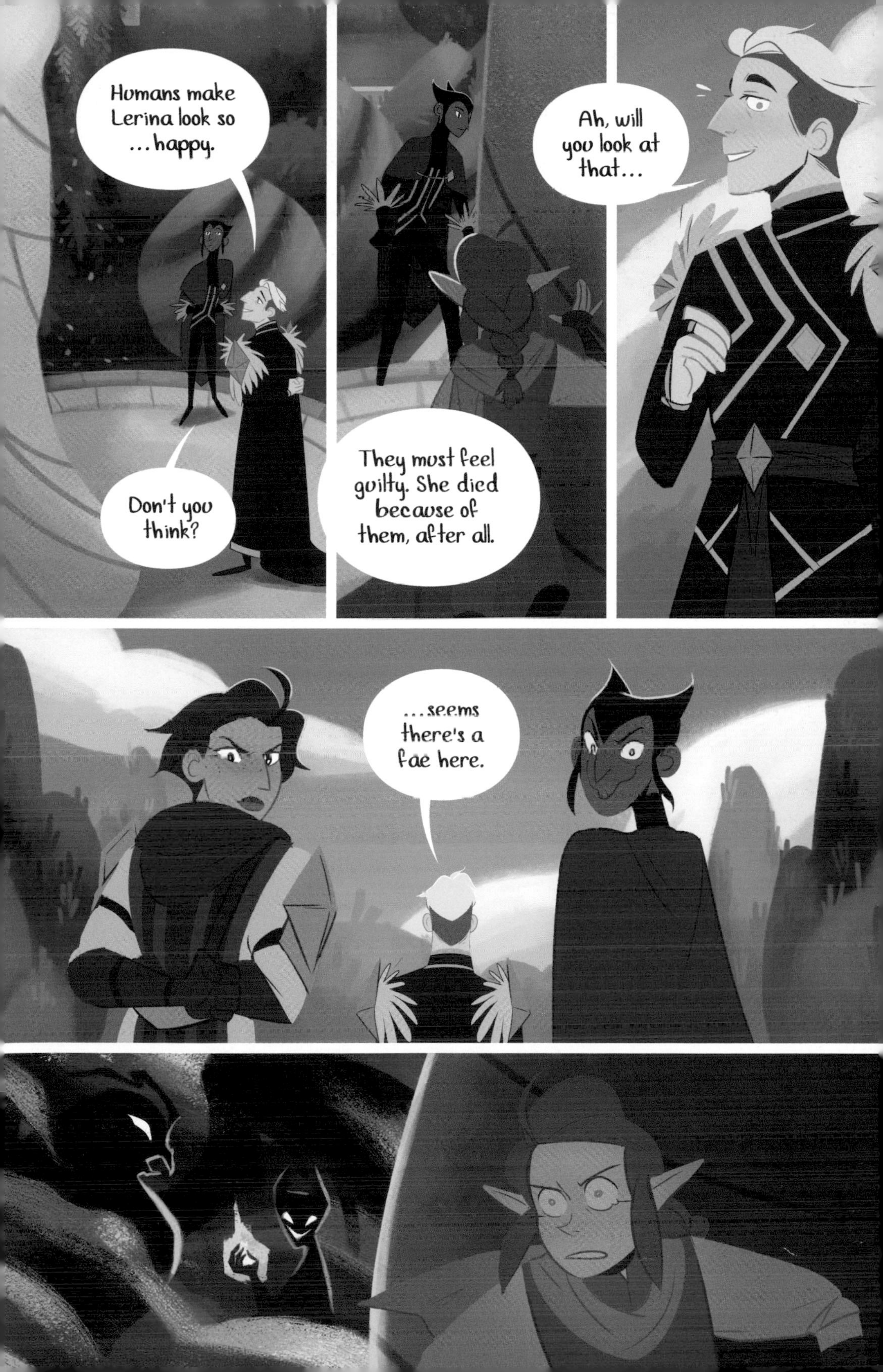
Humans make Lerina look so ...happy.
Don't you think?
They must feel guilty. She died because of them, after all.
Ah, will you look at that...
...seems there's a fae here.

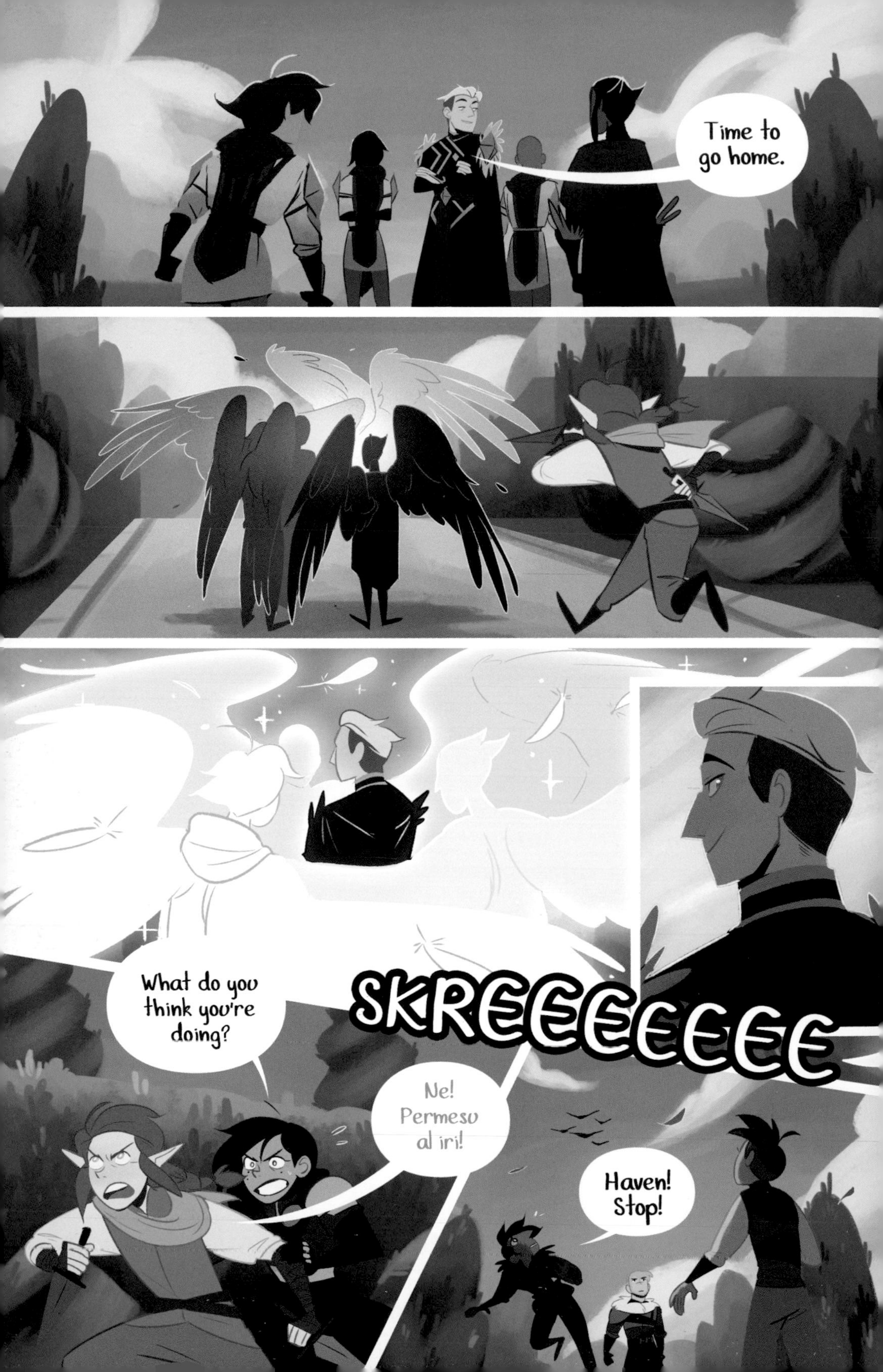
Time to go home.
What do you think you're doing?
SKREEEEEEEE
Ne! Permeso al iri!
Haven! Stop!

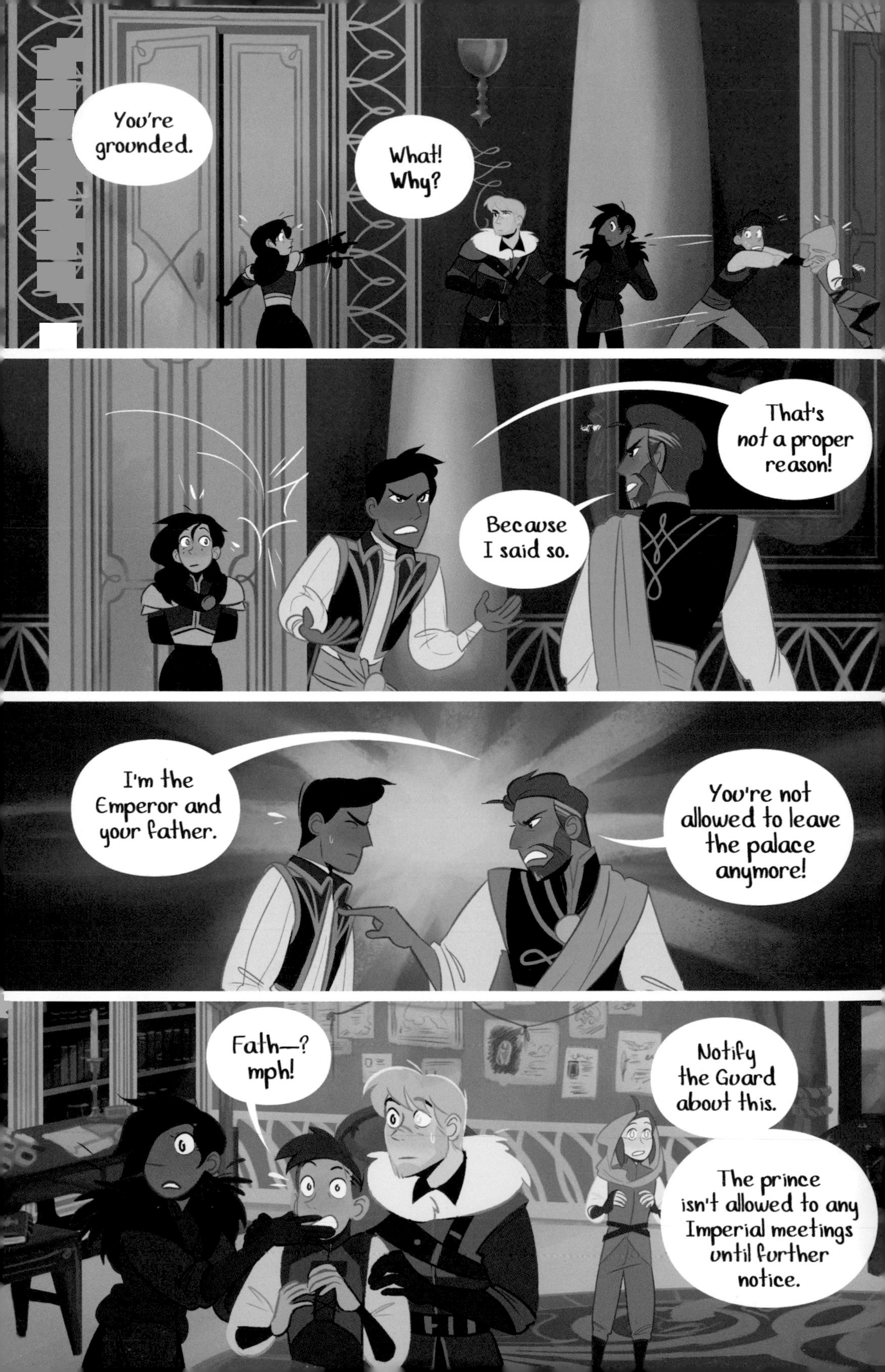
You're grounded.
What! Why?
Because I said so.
That's not a proper reason!
I'm the Emperor and your father.
You're not allowed to leave the palace anymore!
Fath—? mph!
Notify the Guard about this.
The prince isn't allowed to any Imperial meetings until further notice.

END OF CHAPTER 6

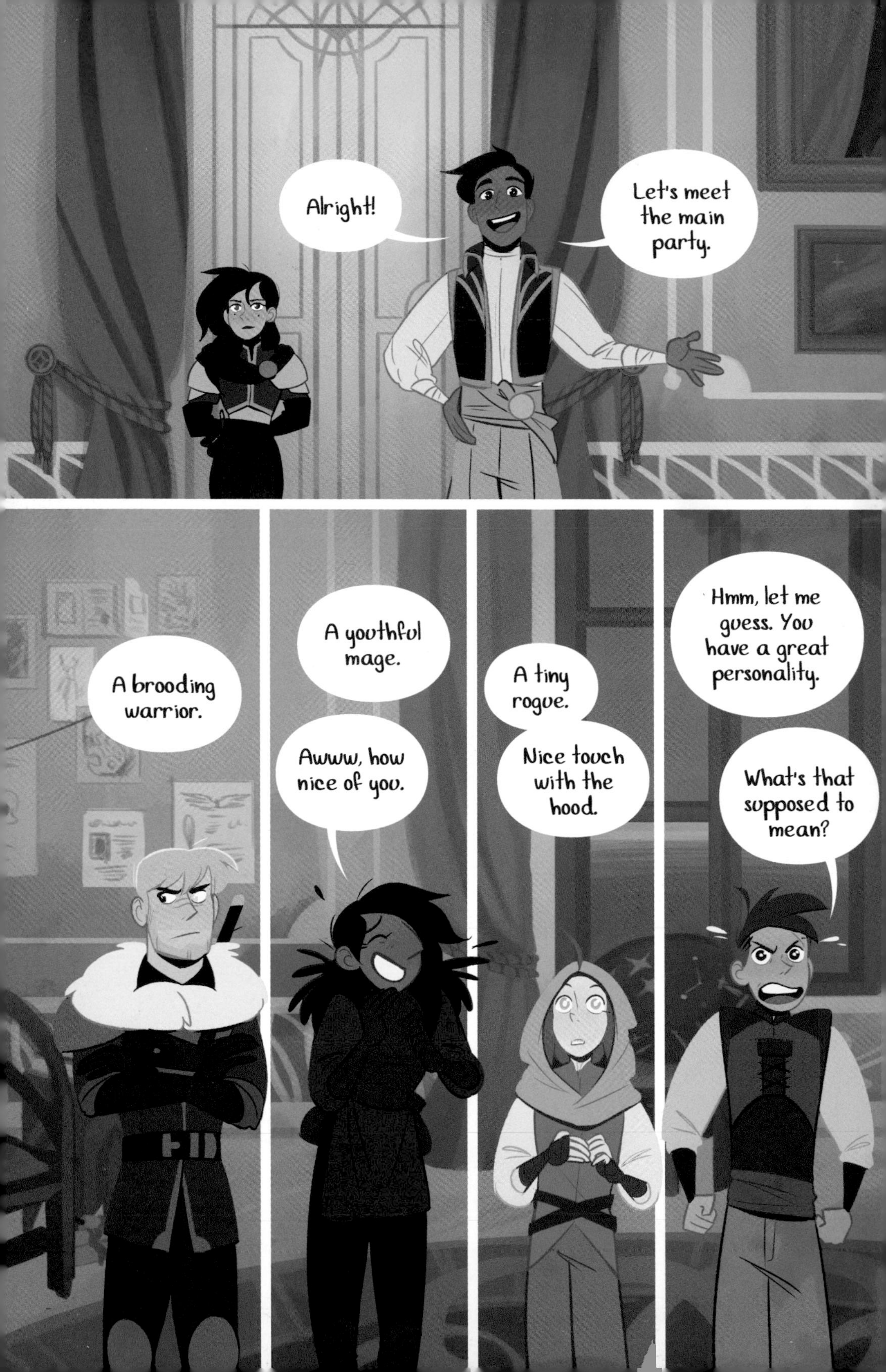
Alright!
Let's meet the main party.
A brooding warrior.
A youthful mage.
Awww, how nice of you.
A tiny rogue.
Nice touch with the hood.
Hmm, let me guess. You have a great personality.
What's that supposed to mean?

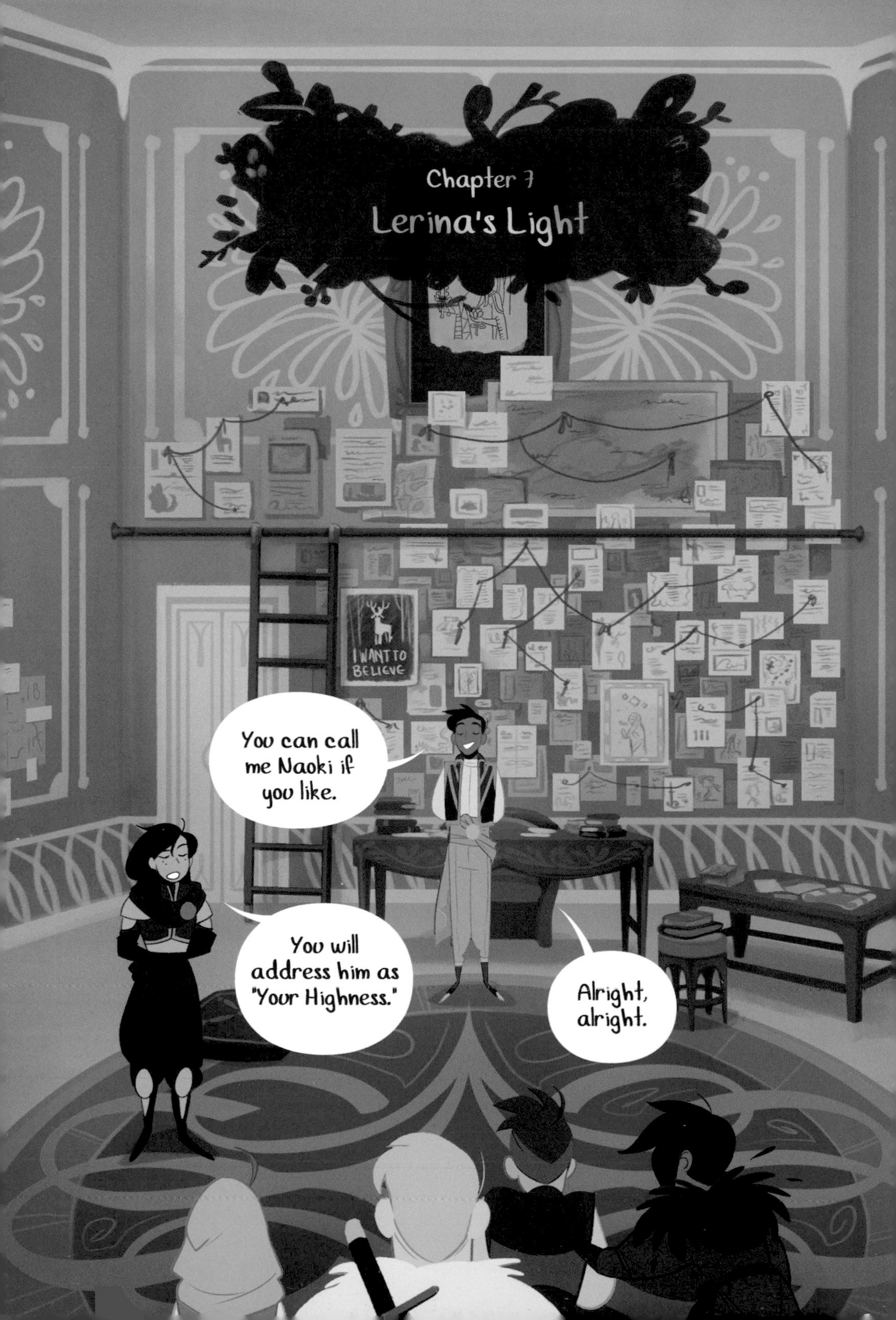
Chapter 7
Lerina's Light
I WANT TO BELIEVE
You can call me Naoki if you like.
You will address him as "Your Highness."
Alright, alright.

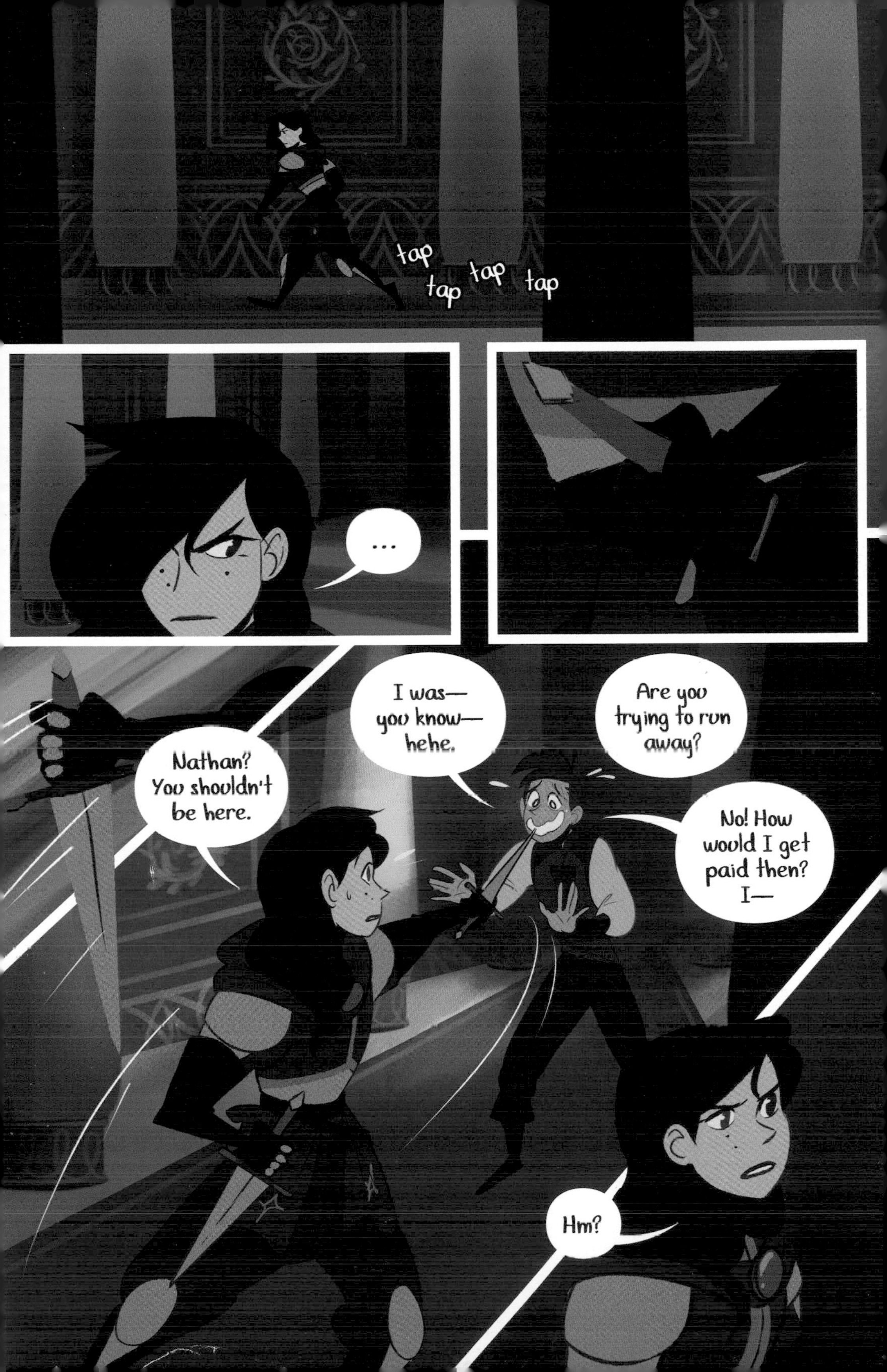
tap
tap tap tap
...
Nathan? You shouldn't be here.
I was— you know— hehe.
Are you trying to run away?
No! How would I get paid then? I—
Hm?

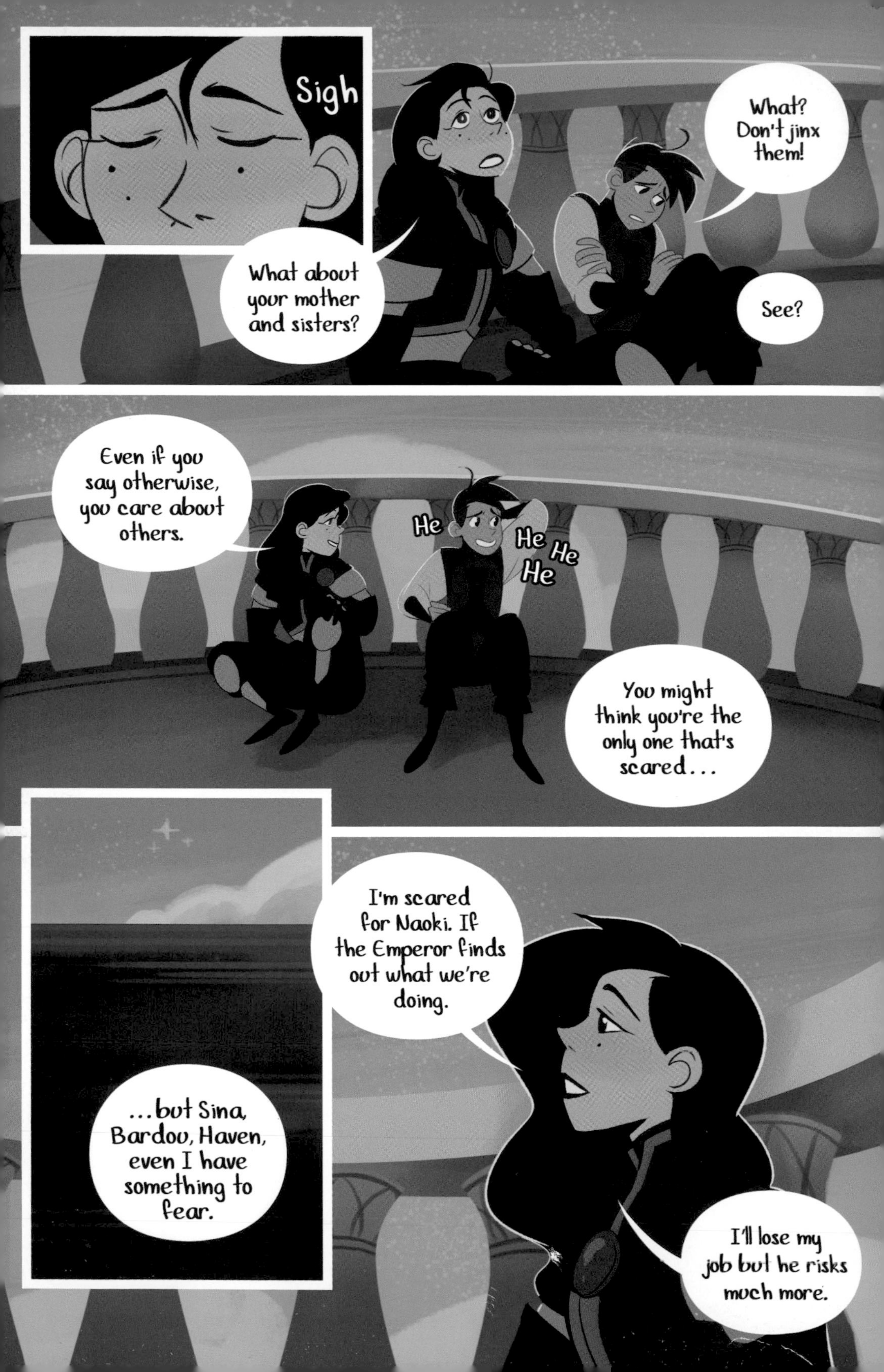
Sigh
What about your mother and sisters?
What? Don't jinx them!
See?
Even if you say otherwise, you care about others.
He
He He He
You might think you're the only one that's scared...
I'm scared for Naoki. If the Emperor finds out what we're doing.
...but Sina, Bardou, Haven, even I have something to fear.
I'll lose my job but he risks much more.

Ahem

So, you call the prince by his name?

Shut up. I'm also worried you'll do something stupid.

Hey, Ren.

What?

Is my family alright?

They are. I check on the village occasionally.

Sigh

That's good to know.

By the way, you and the prince...you know?

You want another scar?

You said this one was an accident!

This one won't be.

Maaaybe. Good night, Nathan.

Y-you're joking, right? Right?

Hehe. Night, Ren.

END OF CHAPTER 7

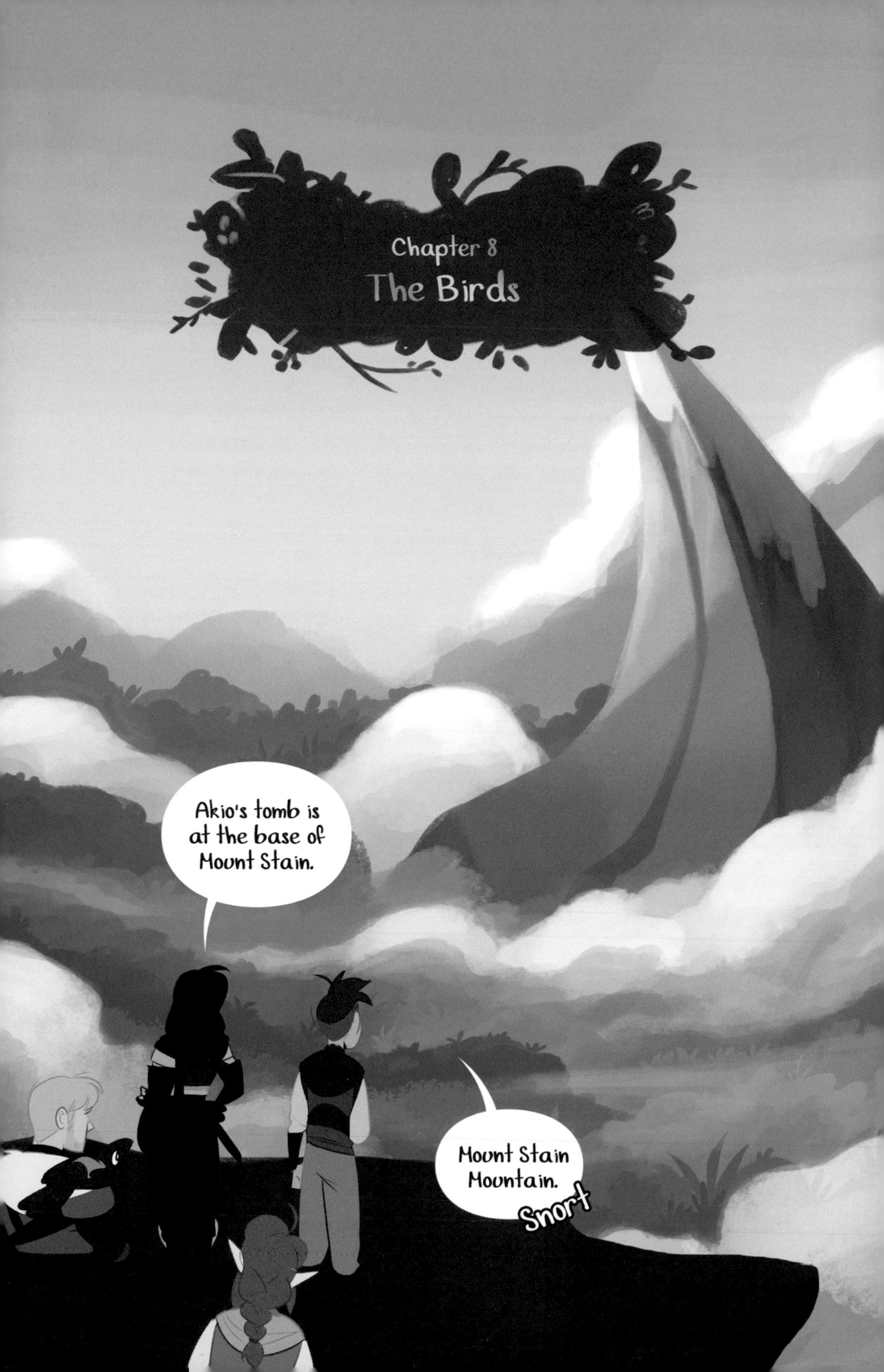
Chapter 8
The Birds
Akio's tomb is at the base of Mount Stain.
Mount Stain Mountain.
Snort

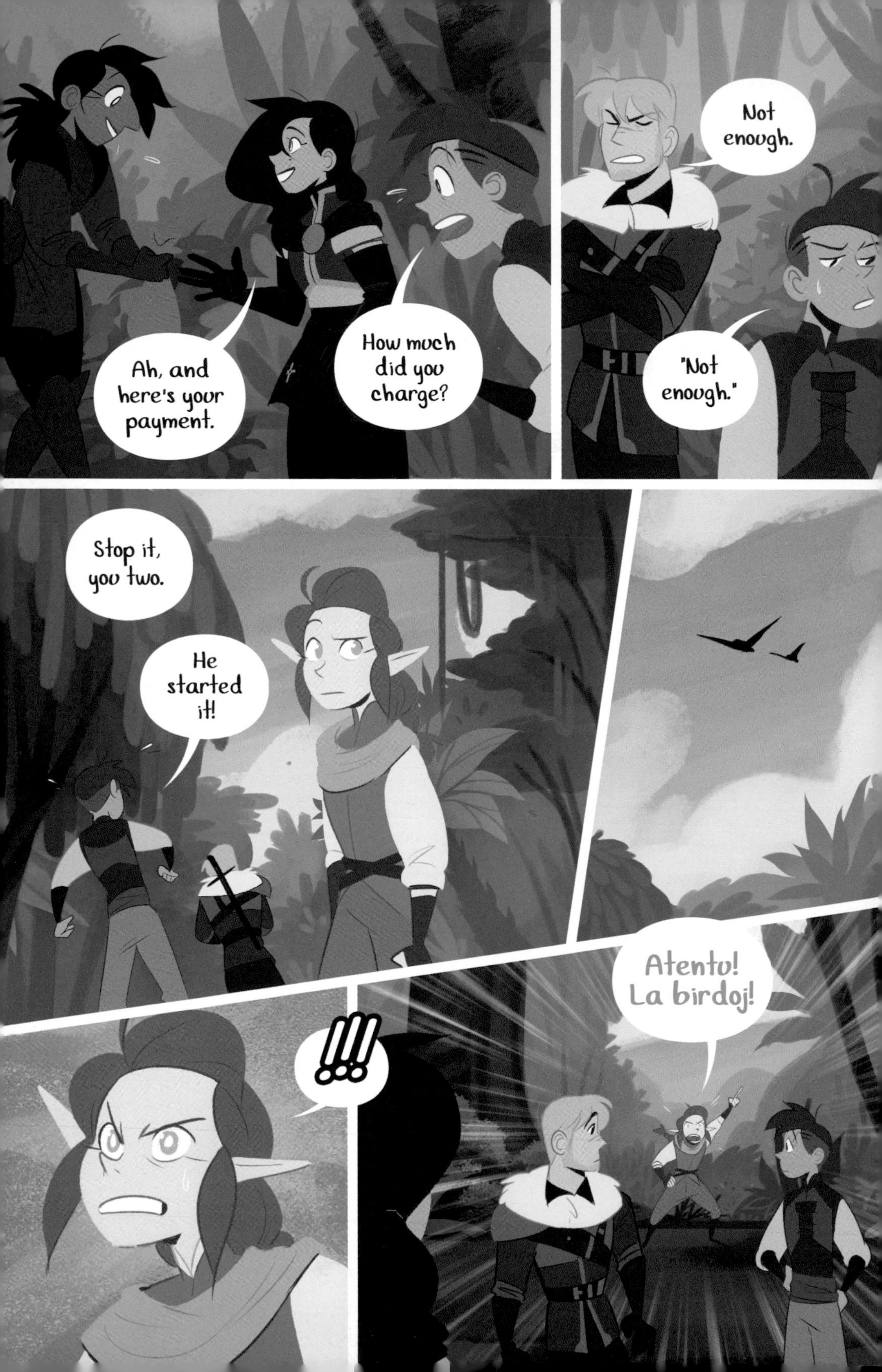
Ah, and here's your payment.
How much did you charge?
Not enough.
"Not enough."
Stop it, you two.
He started it!
!!!
Atentu! La birdoj!

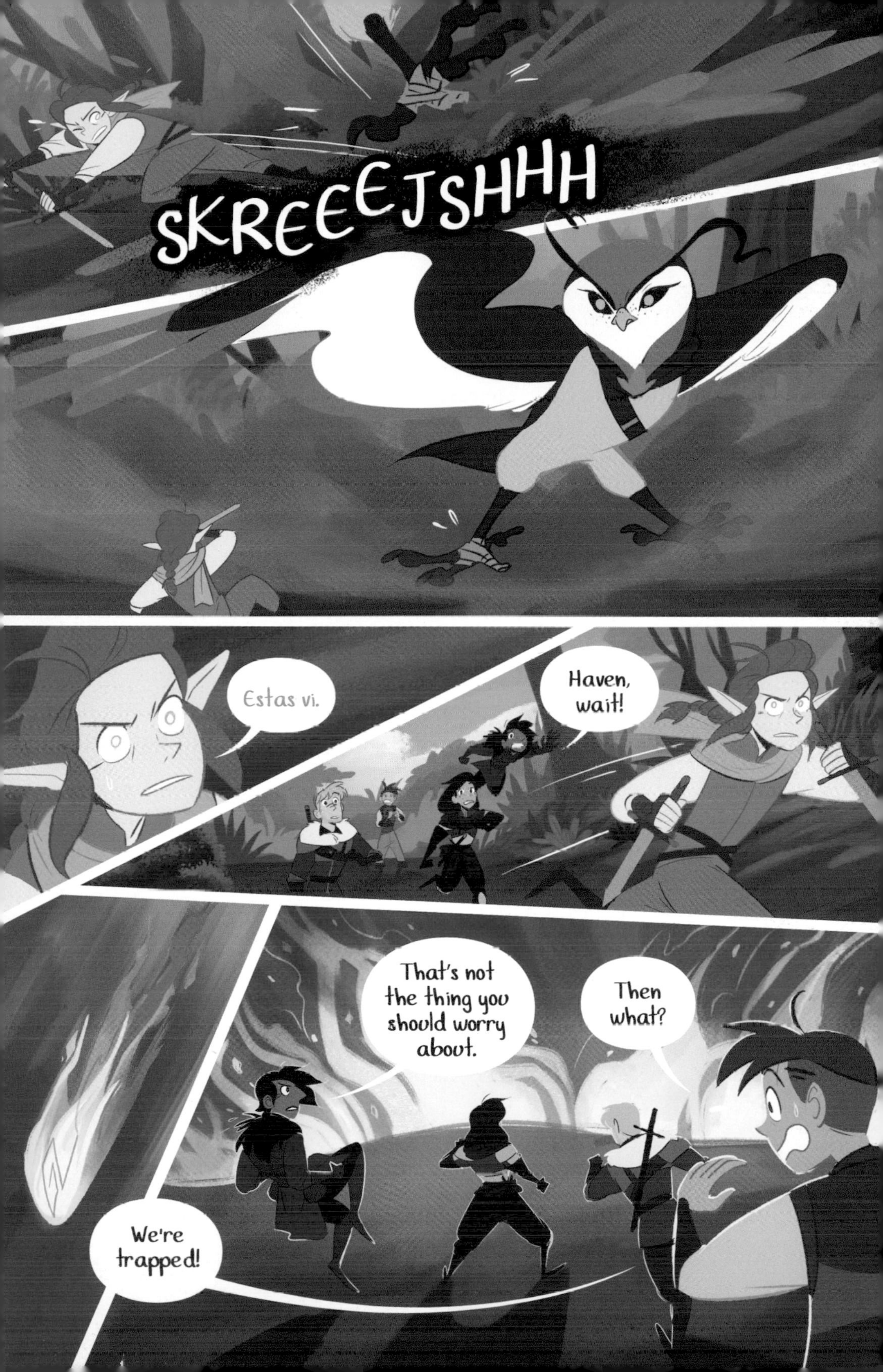
SKREEEJSHHH
Estas vi.
Haven, wait!
That's not the thing you should worry about.
Then what?
We're trapped!

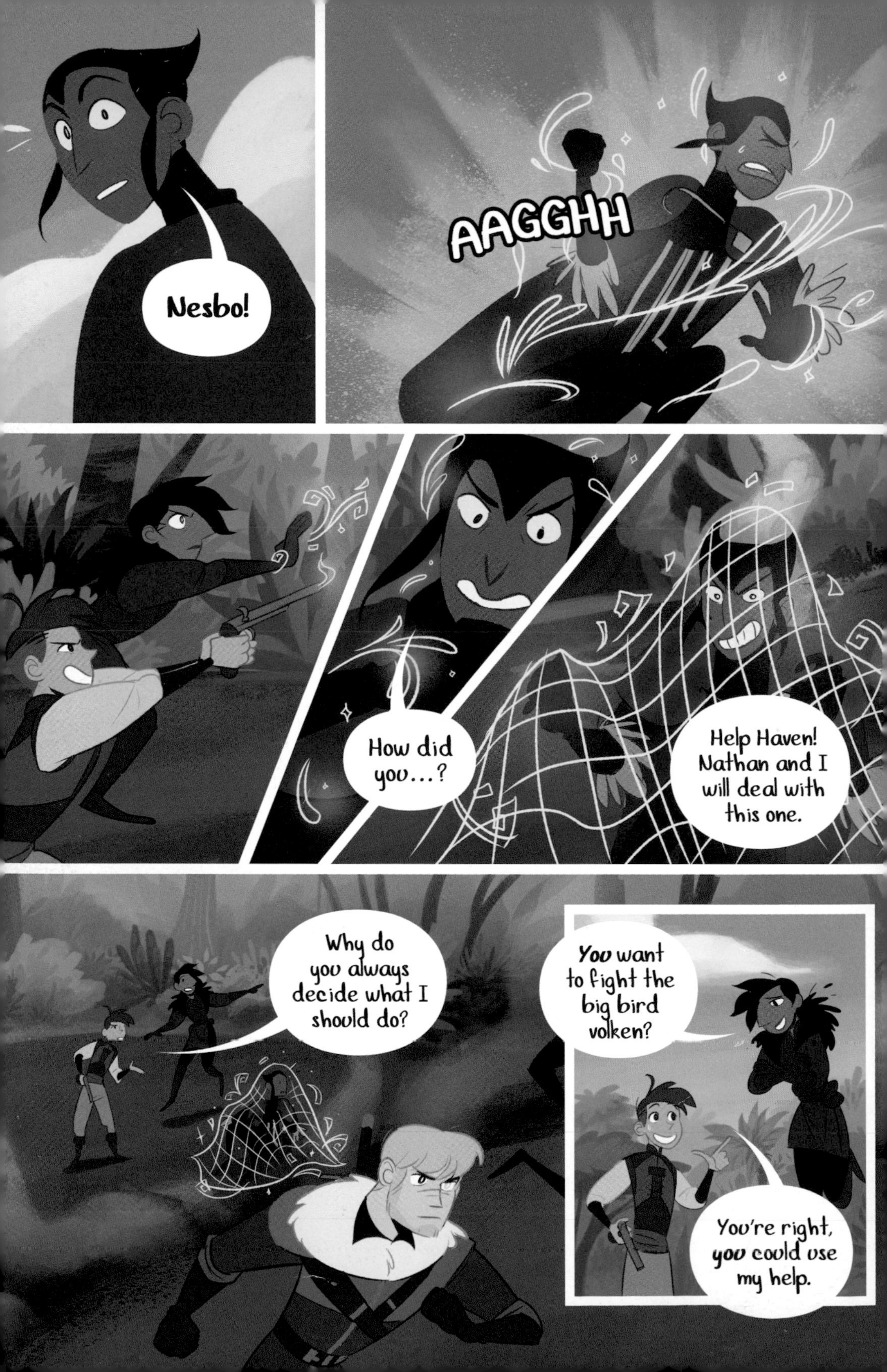
Nesbo!
AAGGHH
How did you...?
Help Haven! Nathan and I will deal with this one.
Why do you always decide what I should do?
You want to fight the big bird volken?
You're right, you could use my help.

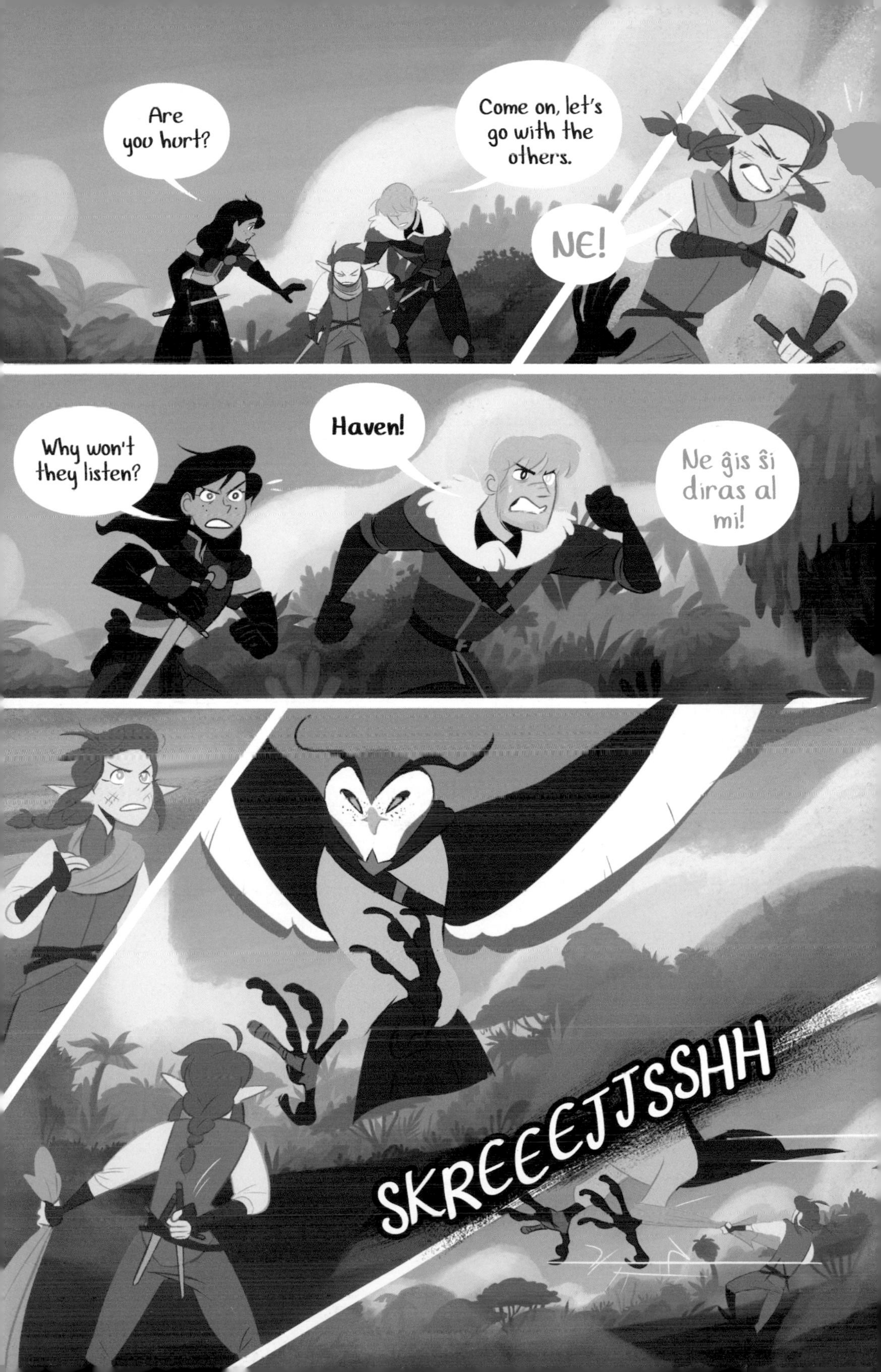

Are you hurt?
Come on, let's go with the others.
NE!
Why won't they listen?
Haven!
Ne ĝis ŝi diras al mi!
SKREEEJJSSHH

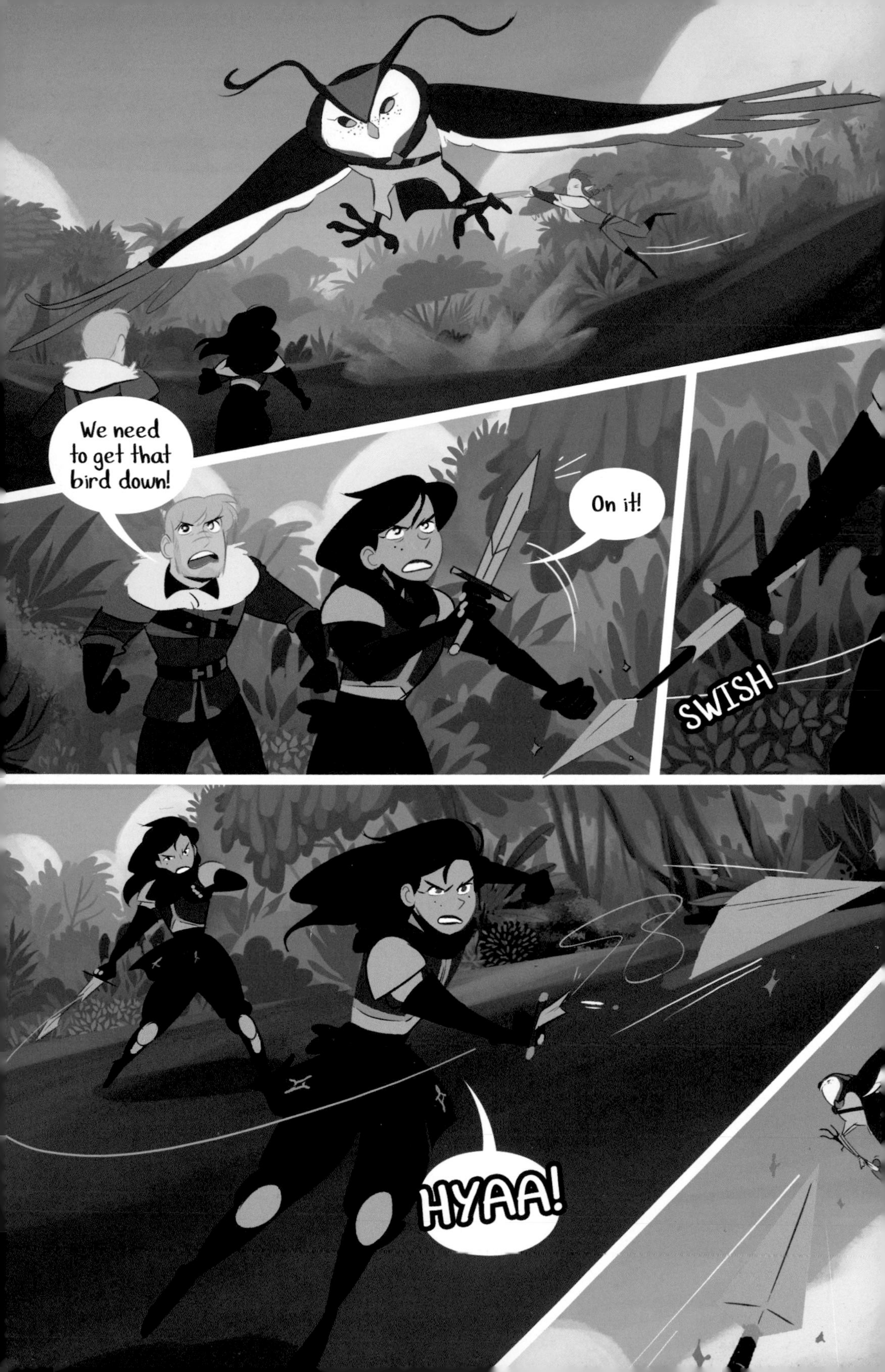
We need to get that bird down!
On it!
SWISH
HYAA!

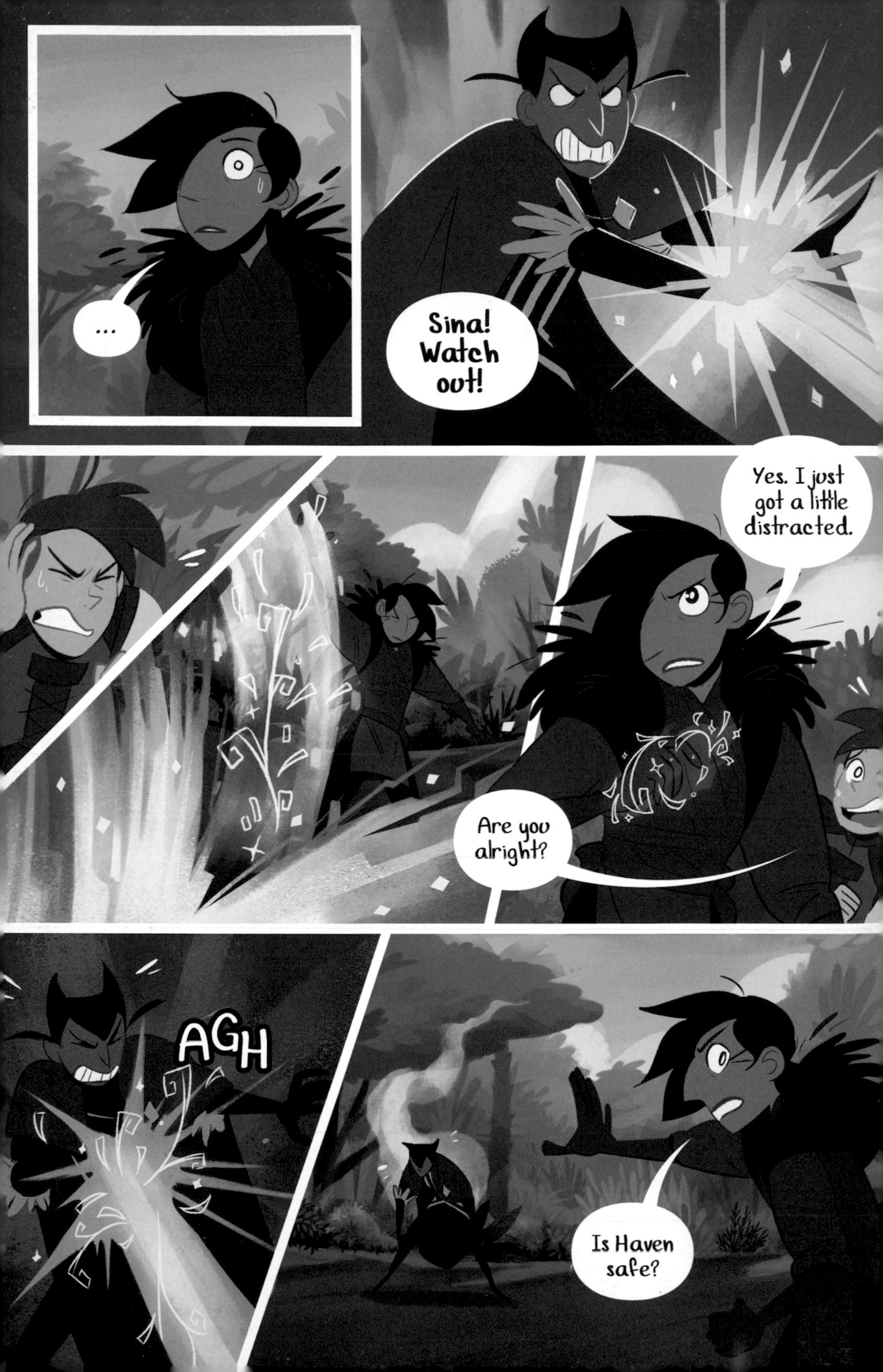
...
Sina! Watch out!
Are you alright?
Yes. I just got a little distracted.
AGH
Is Haven safe?

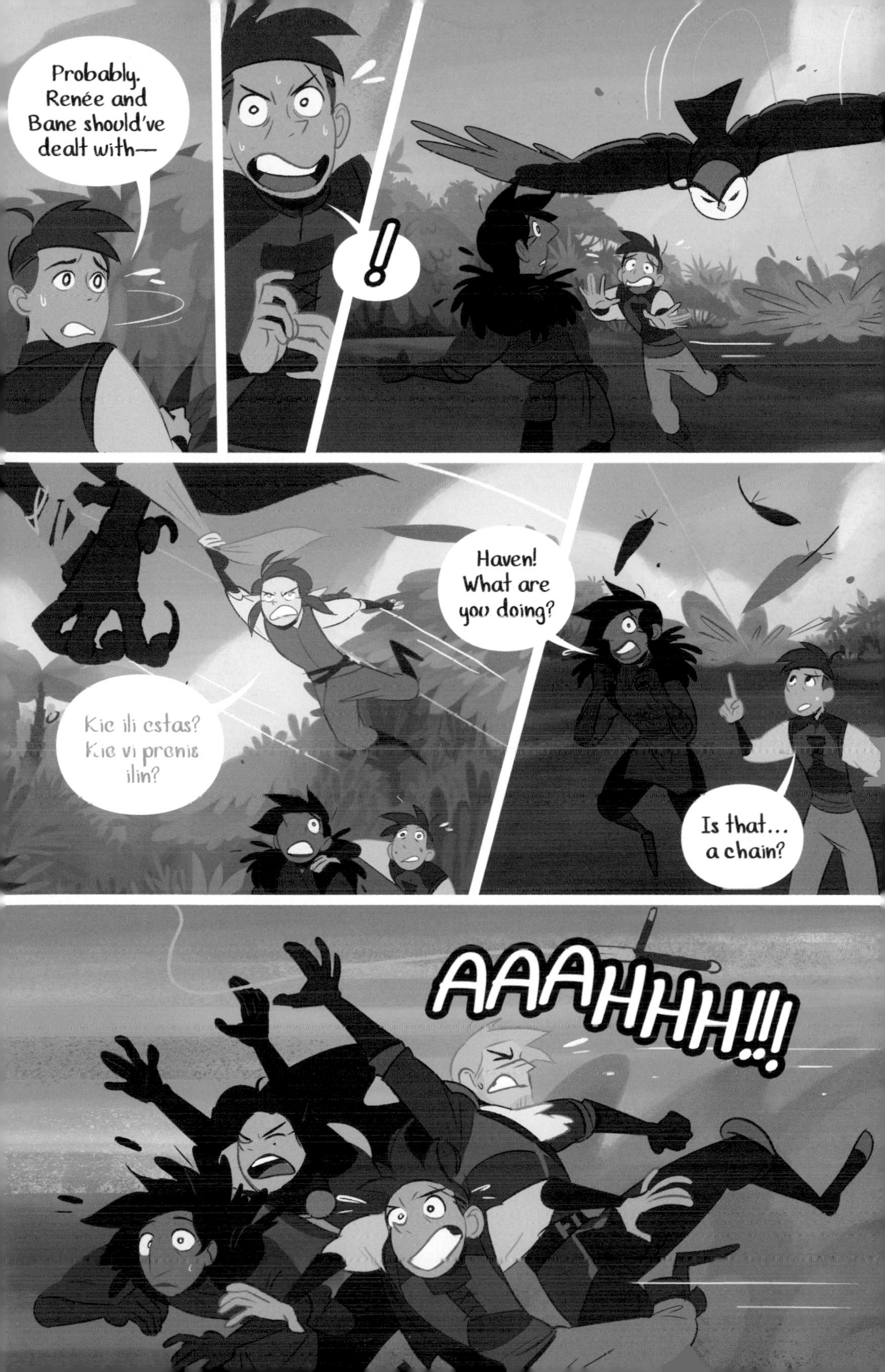
Probably. Renée and Bane should've dealt with—
!
Haven! What are you doing?
Kie ili estas? Kie vi prenis ilin?
Is that… a chain?
AAAHHHH!!!

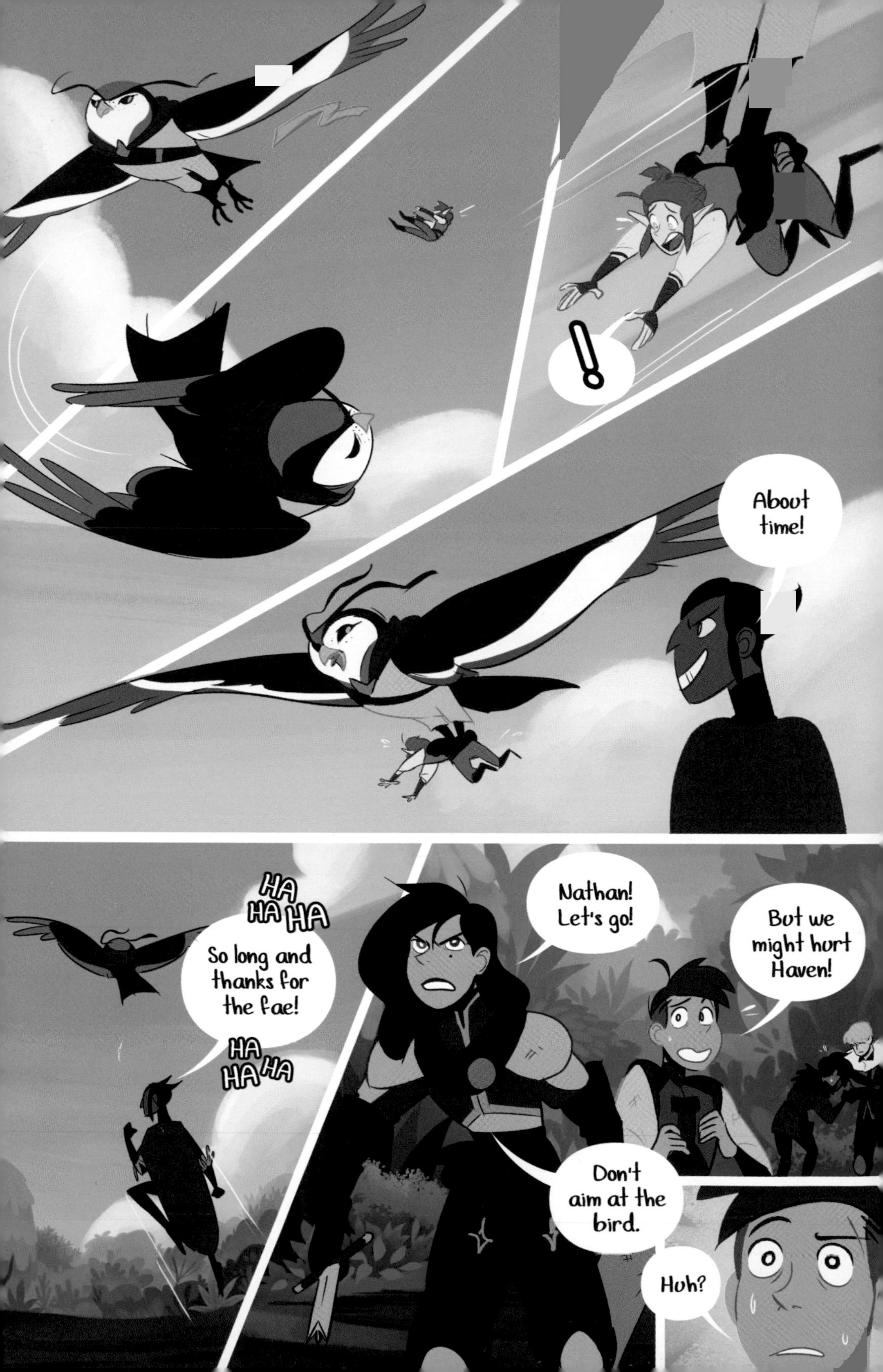
!
About time!
HA HA HA
So long and thanks for the fae!
HA HA HA
Nathan! Let's go!
But we might hurt Haven!
Don't aim at the bird.
Huh?

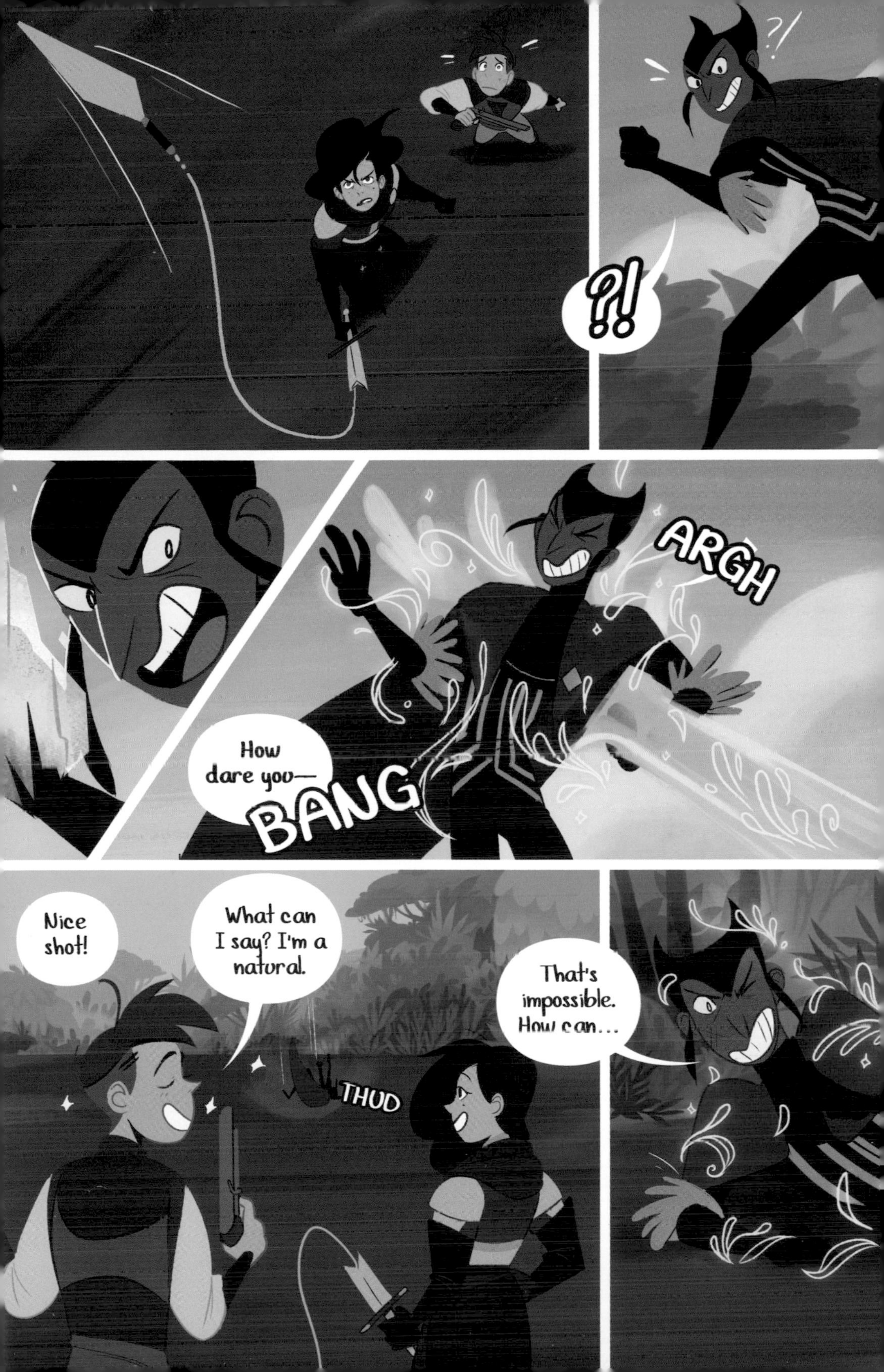
?!
?!
How dare you—
BANG
ARGH
Nice shot!
What can I say? I'm a natural.
THUD
That's impossible. How can...

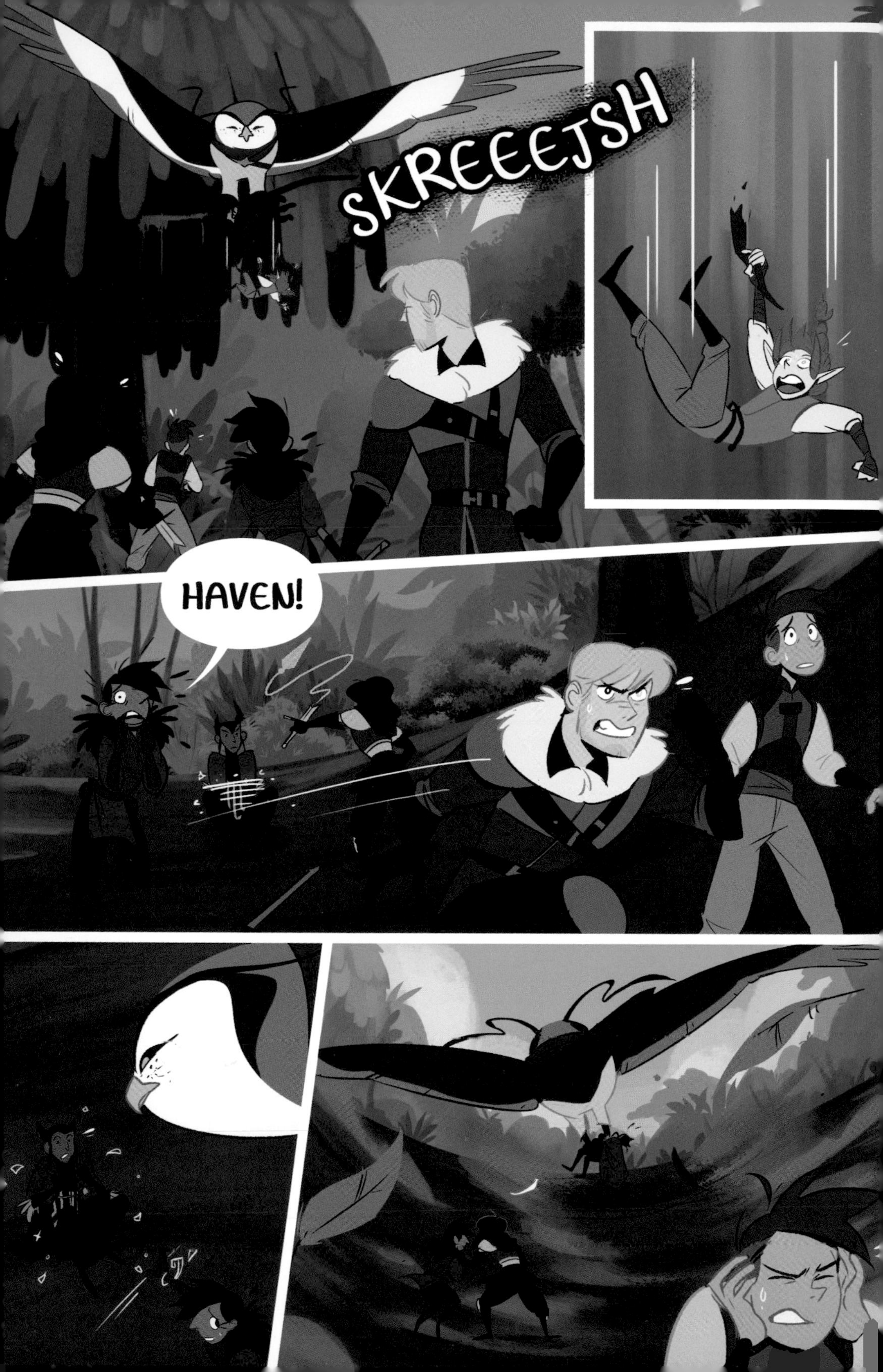
SKREEEJSH
HAVEN!

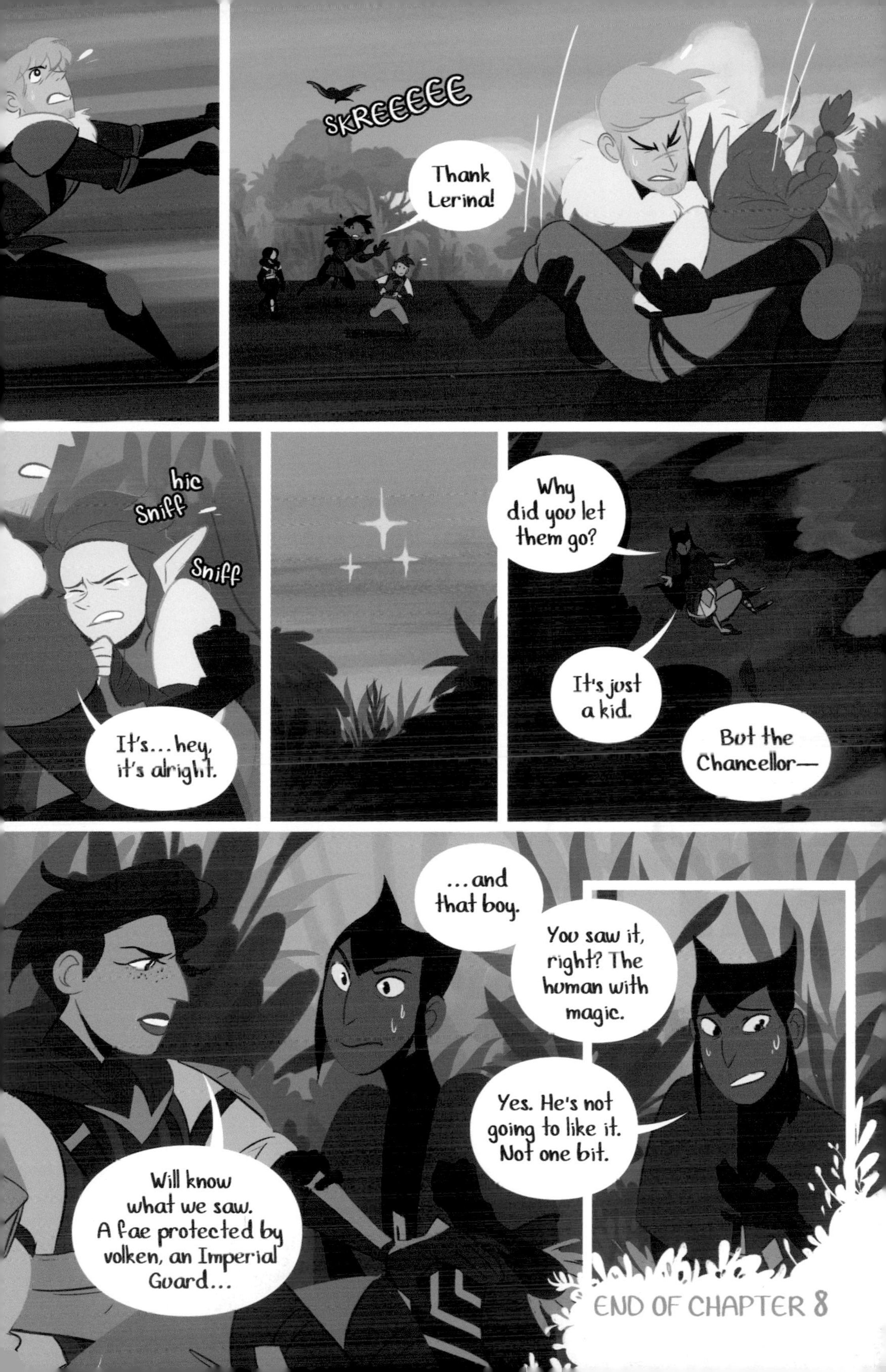
SKREEEEEE
Thank Lerina!
hic
Sniff
Sniff
It's... hey, it's alright.
Why did you let them go?
It's just a kid.
But the Chancellor—
Will know what we saw. A fae protected by volken, an Imperial Guard...
...and that boy.
You saw it, right? The human with magic.
Yes. He's not going to like it. Not one bit.
END OF CHAPTER 8

Chapter 9

Grave of Flowers

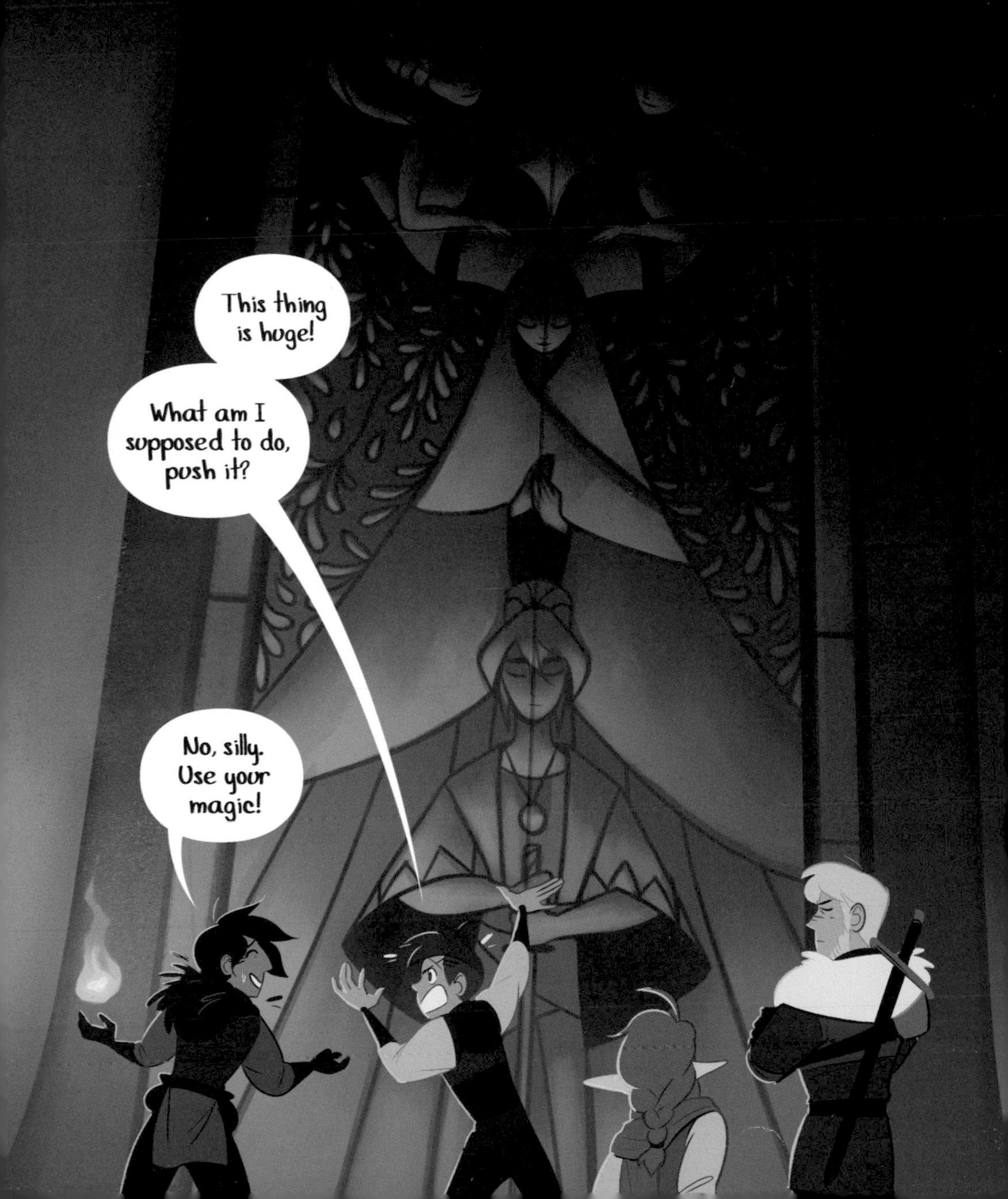
This thing is huge!
What am I supposed to do, push it?
No, silly. Use your magic!

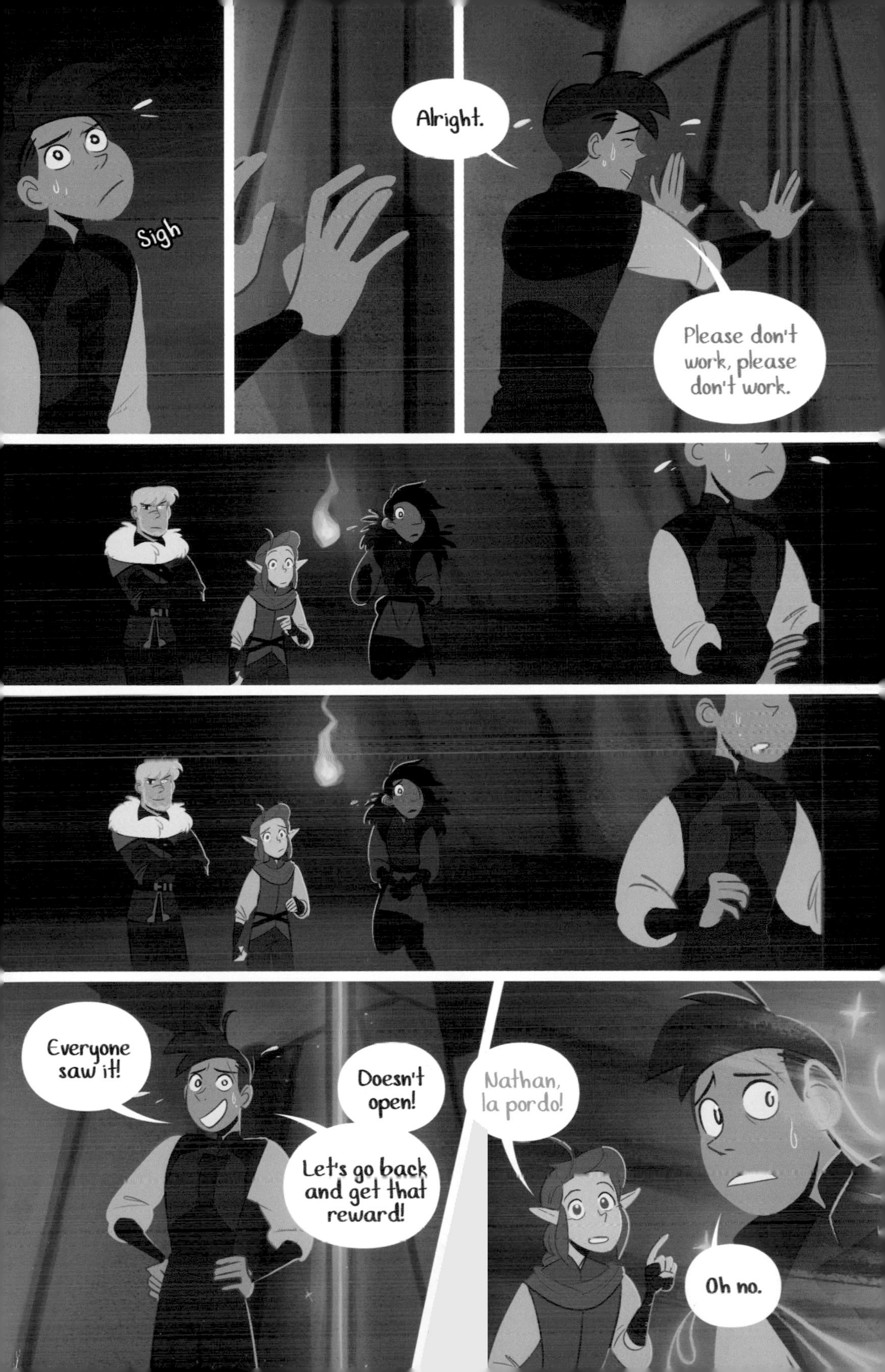
Sigh
Alright.
Please don't work, please don't work.
Everyone saw it!
Doesn't open!
Let's go back and get that reward!
Nathan, la pordo!
Oh no.

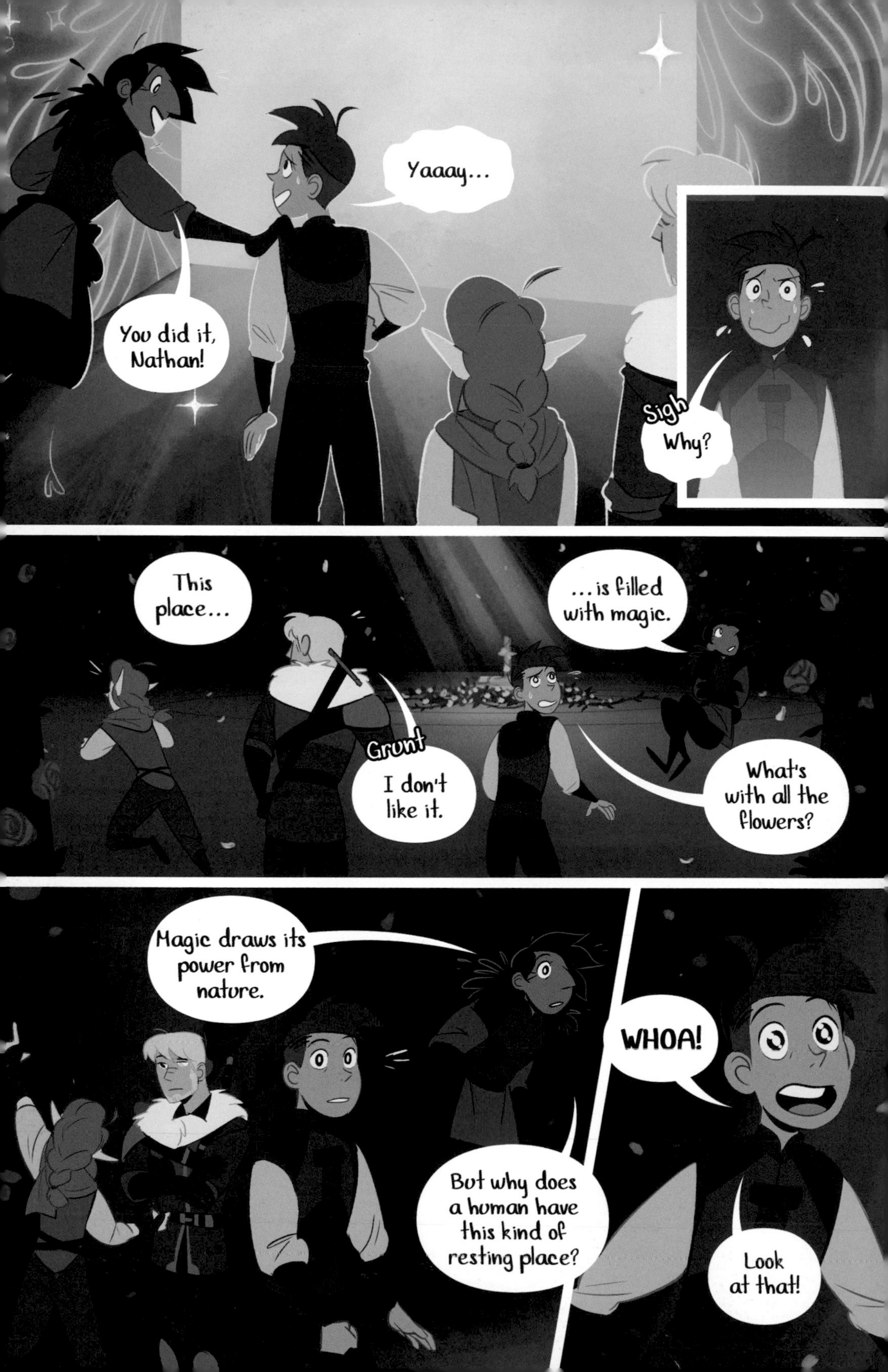
You did it, Nathan!
Yaaay...
Sigh
Why?
This place...
...is filled with magic.
Grunt
I don't like it.
What's with all the flowers?
Magic draws its power from nature.
But why does a human have this kind of resting place?
WHOA!
Look at that!

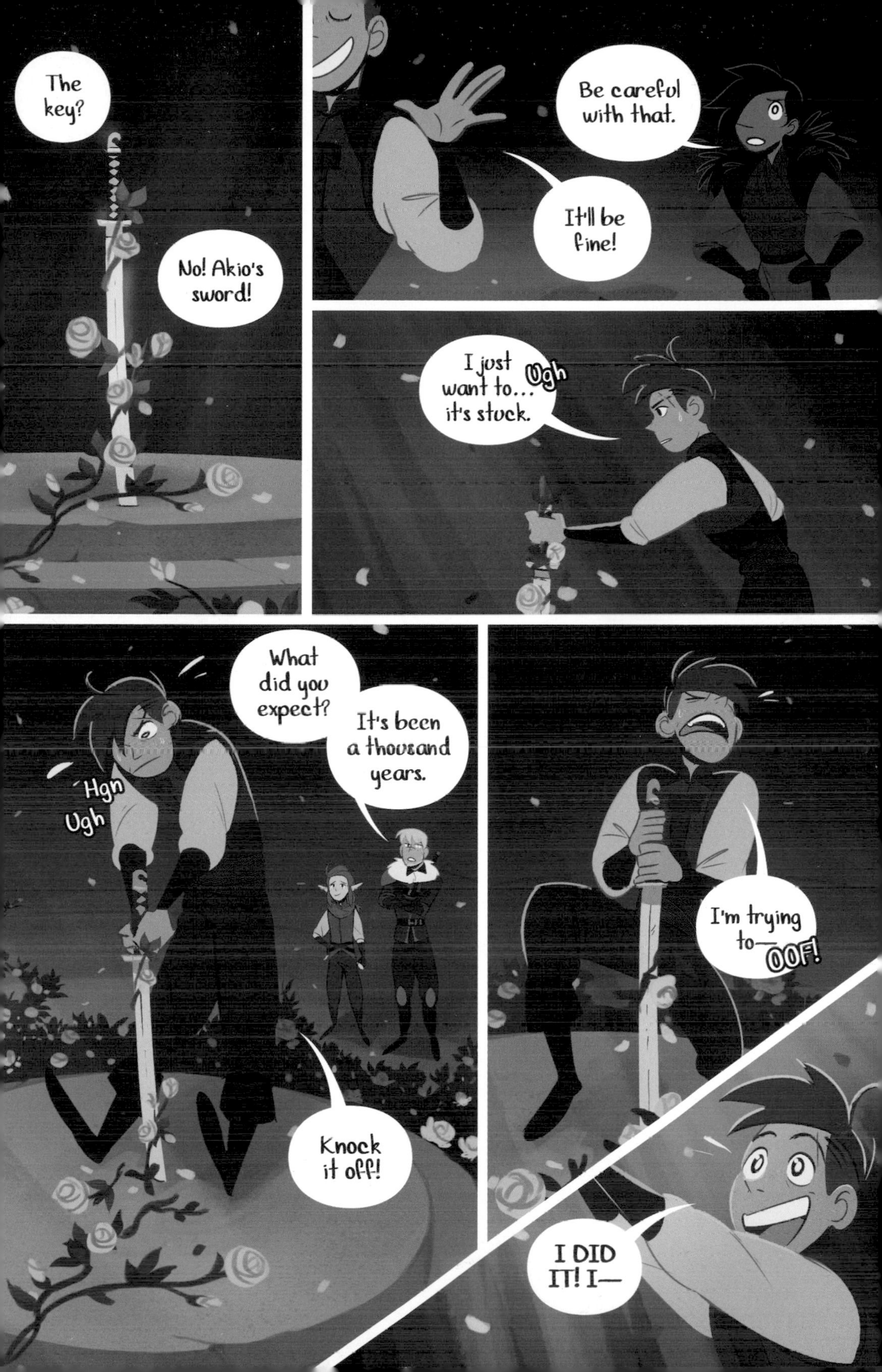

The key?
No! Akio's sword!
Be careful with that.
It'll be fine!
I just want to... it's stuck.
Ugh
What did you expect?
It's been a thousand years.
Hgn
Ugh
Knock it off!
I'm trying to—
OOF!
I DID IT! I—

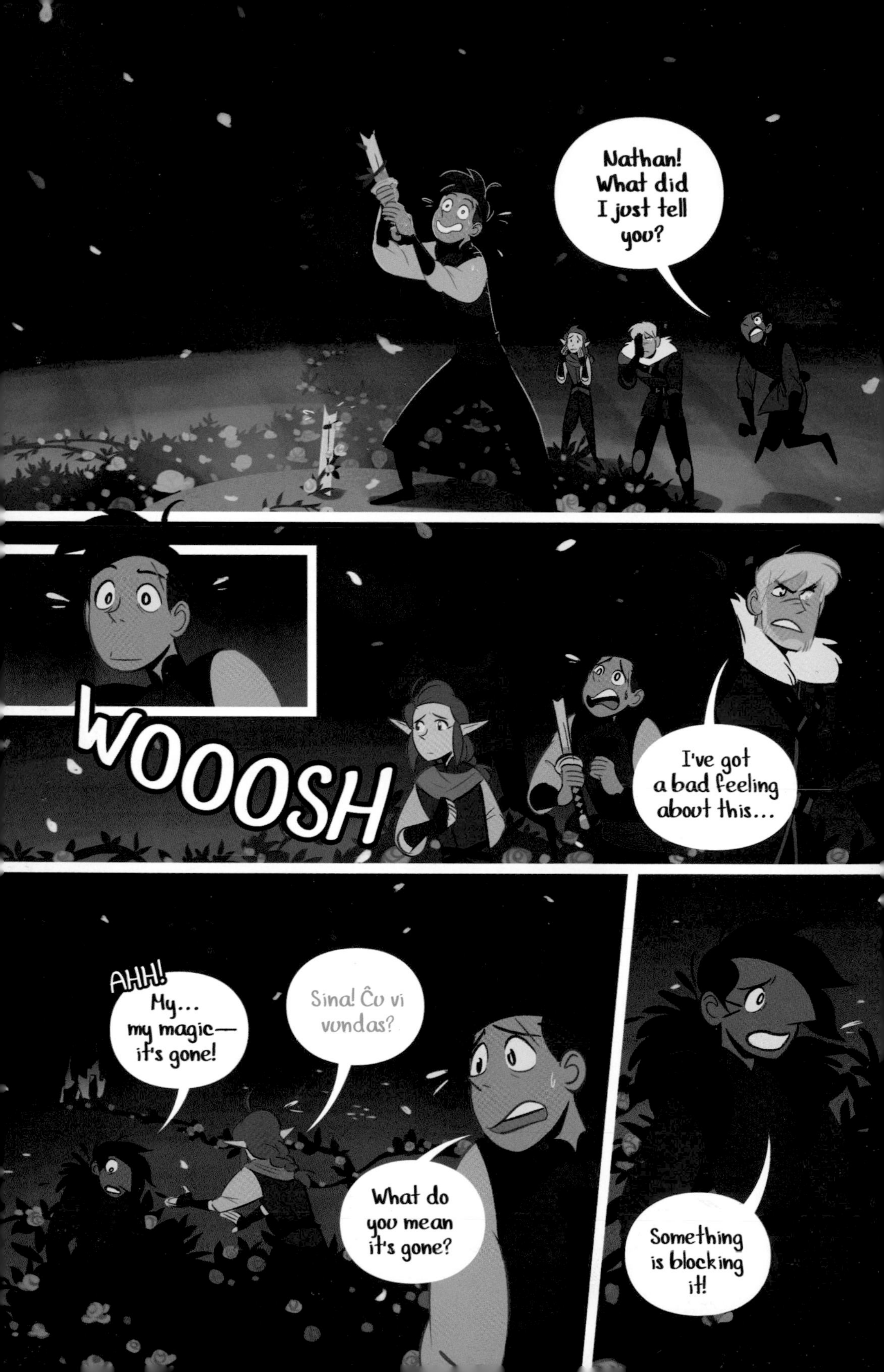
Nathan! What did I just tell you?
WOOOSH
I've got a bad feeling about this...
AHH! My... my magic— it's gone!
Sina! Ĉu vi vundas?
What do you mean it's gone?
Something is blocking it!

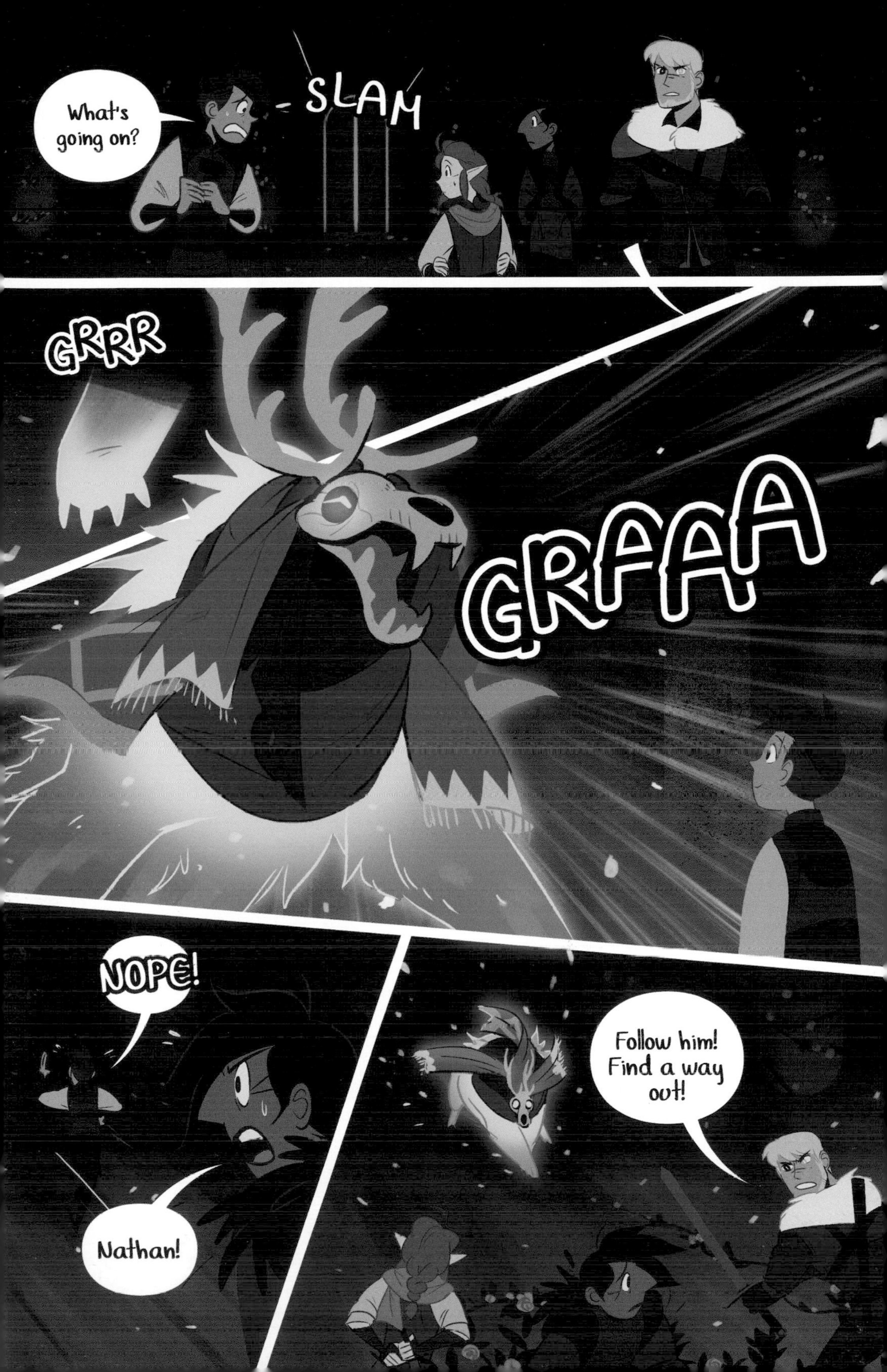
What's going on?
SLAM
GRRR
GRAAA
NOPE!
Nathan!
Follow him! Find a way out!

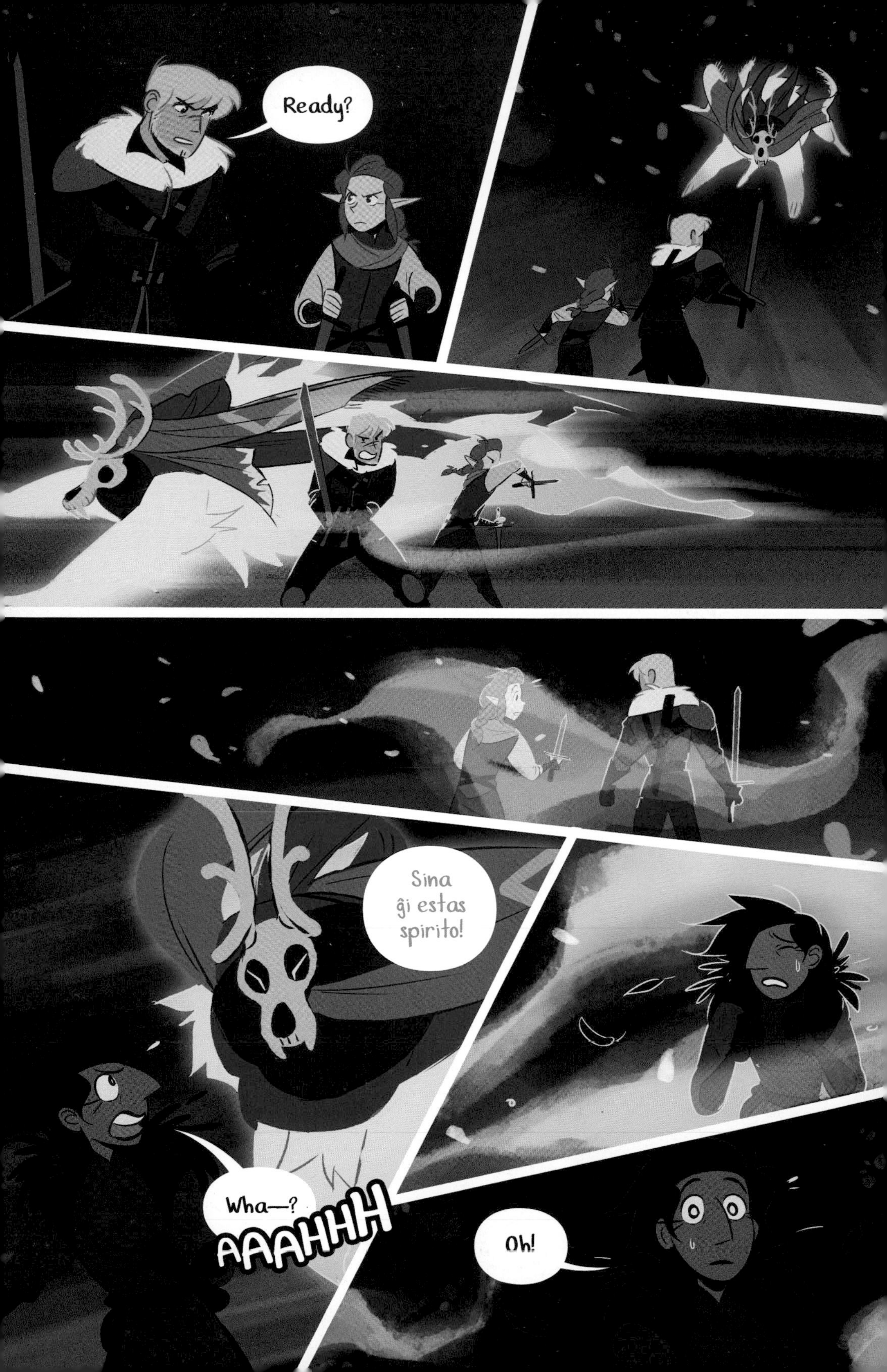
Ready?
Sina ĝi estas spirito!
Wha—?
AAAHHH
Oh!

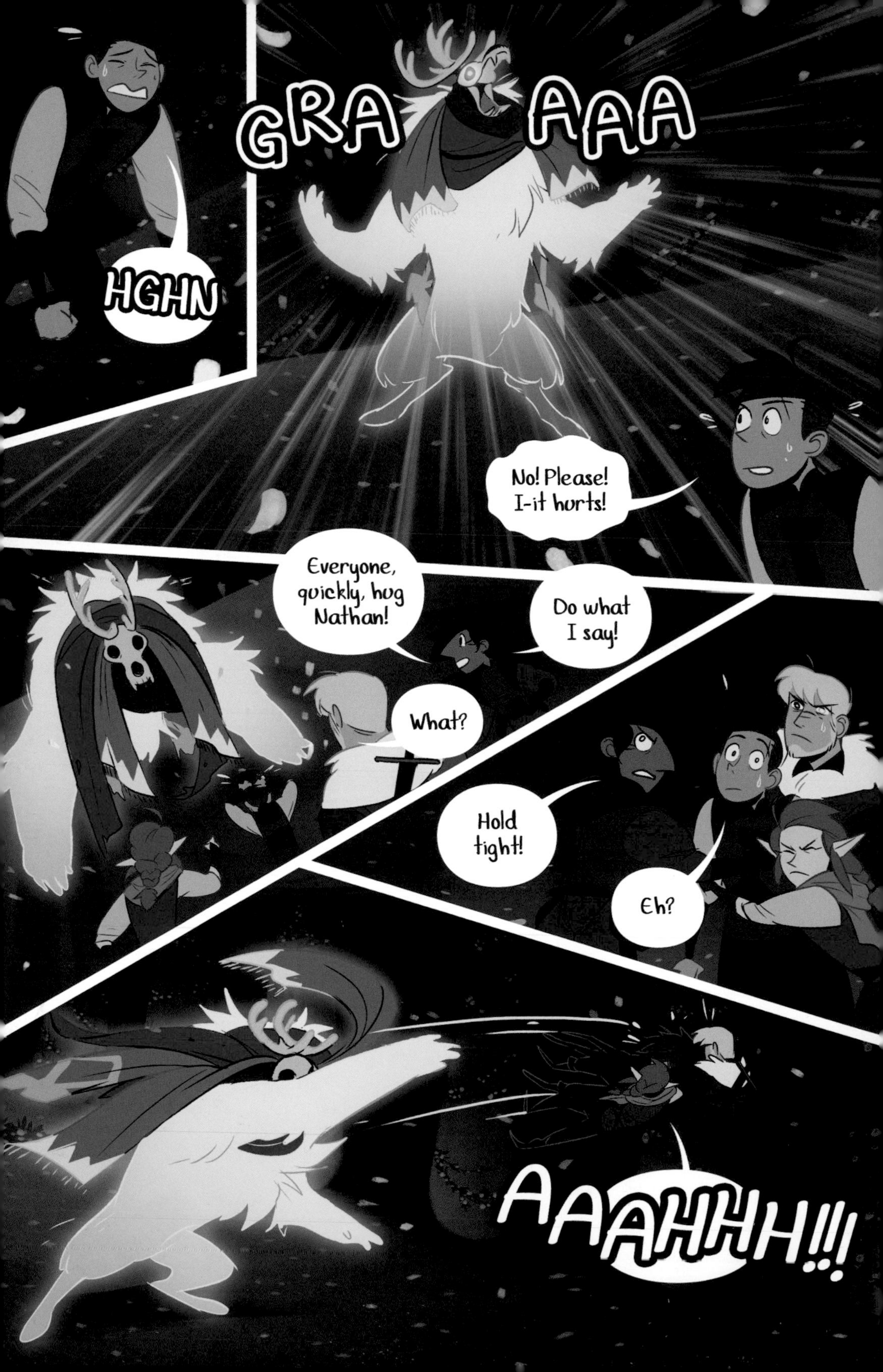
HGHN
GRAAAA
No! Please! I-it hurts!
Everyone, quickly, hug Nathan!
Do what I say!
What?
Hold tight!
Eh?
AAAHHH!!!

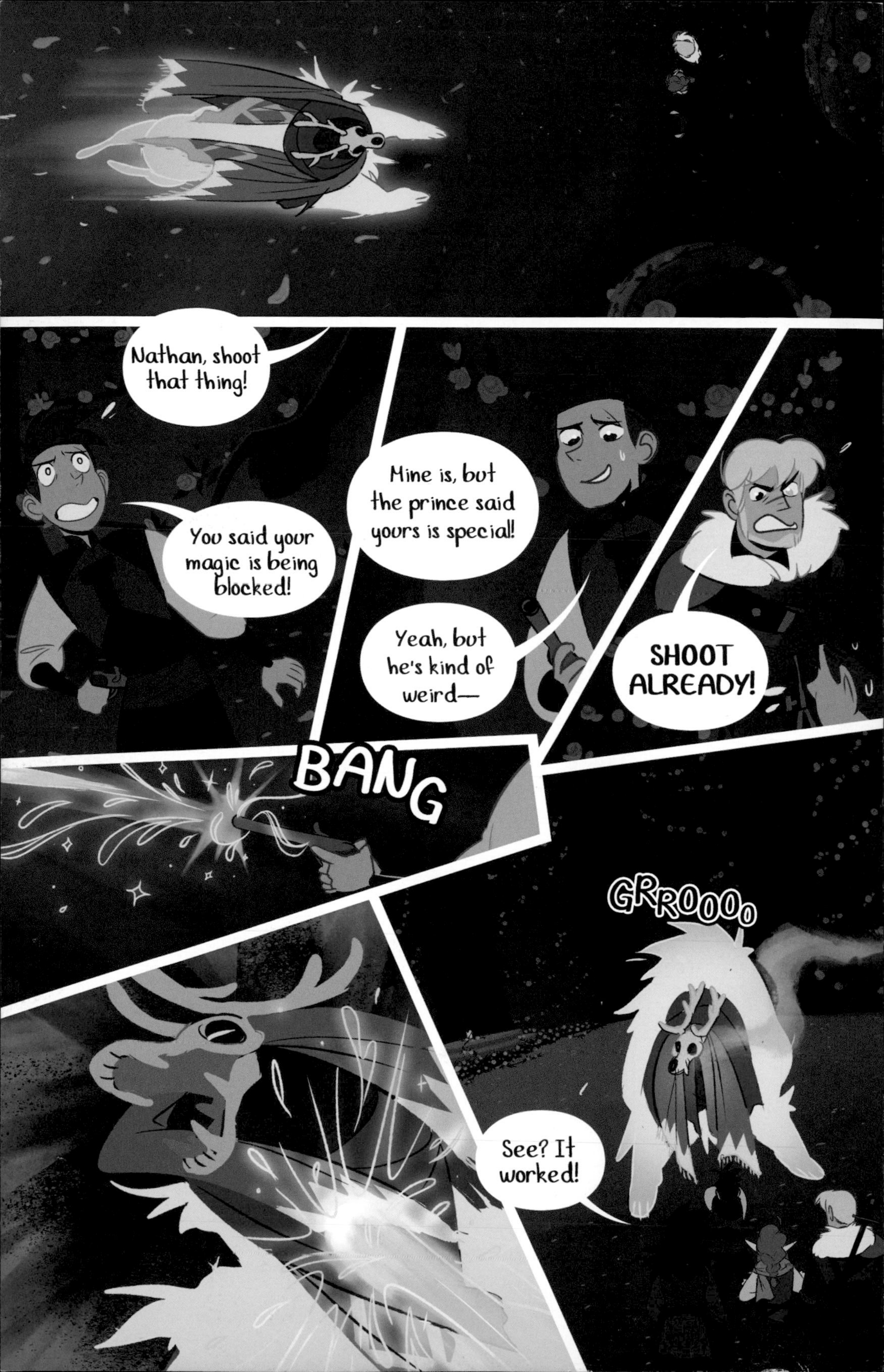
Nathan, shoot that thing!
You said your magic is being blocked!
Mine is, but the prince said yours is special!
Yeah, but he's kind of weird—
SHOOT ALREADY!
BANG
GRROOOO
See? It worked!

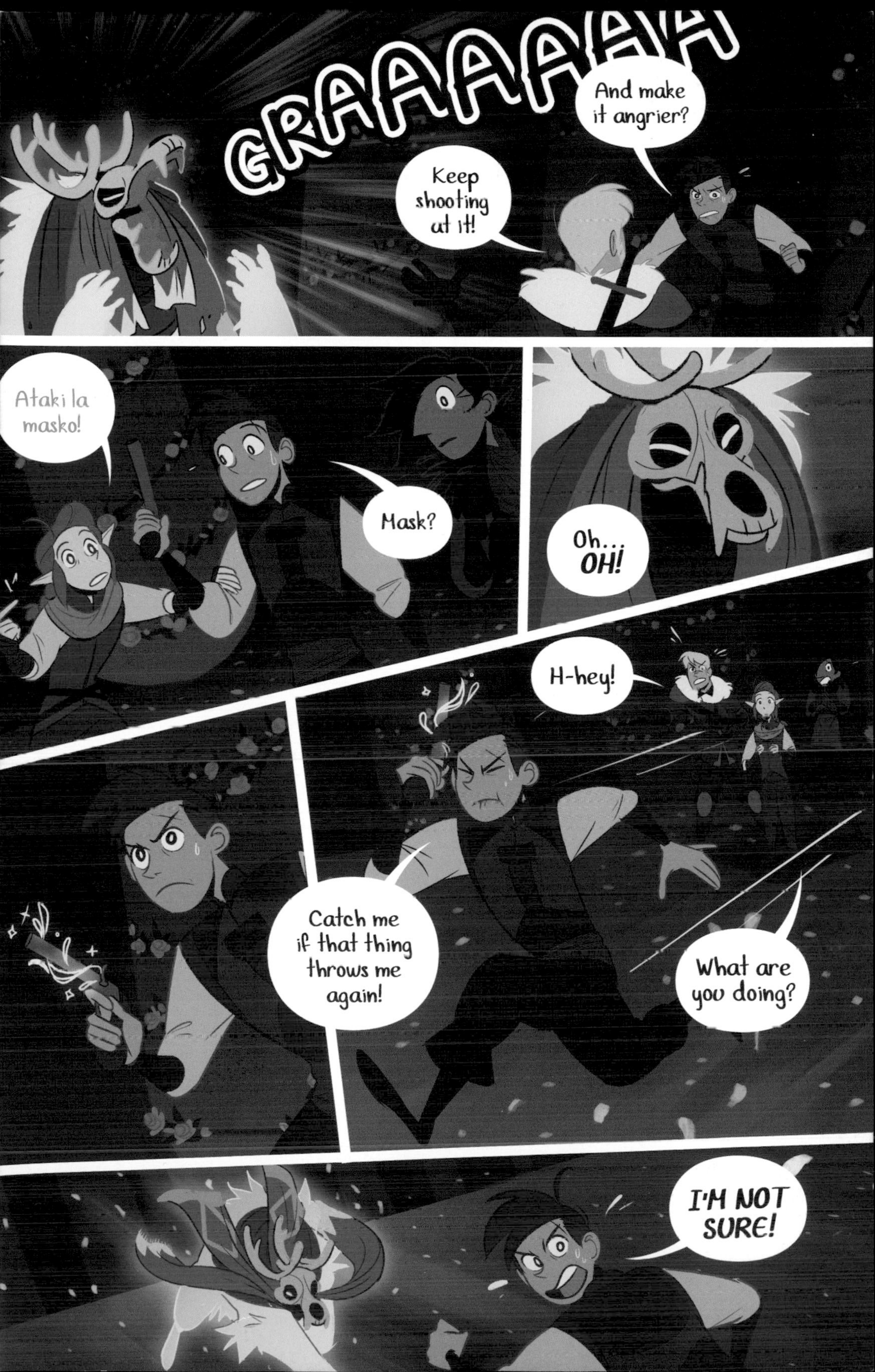
GRAAAAAA
And make it angrier?
Keep shooting at it!
Ataki la masko!
Mask?
Oh... OH!
H-hey!
Catch me if that thing throws me again!
What are you doing?
I'M NOT SURE!

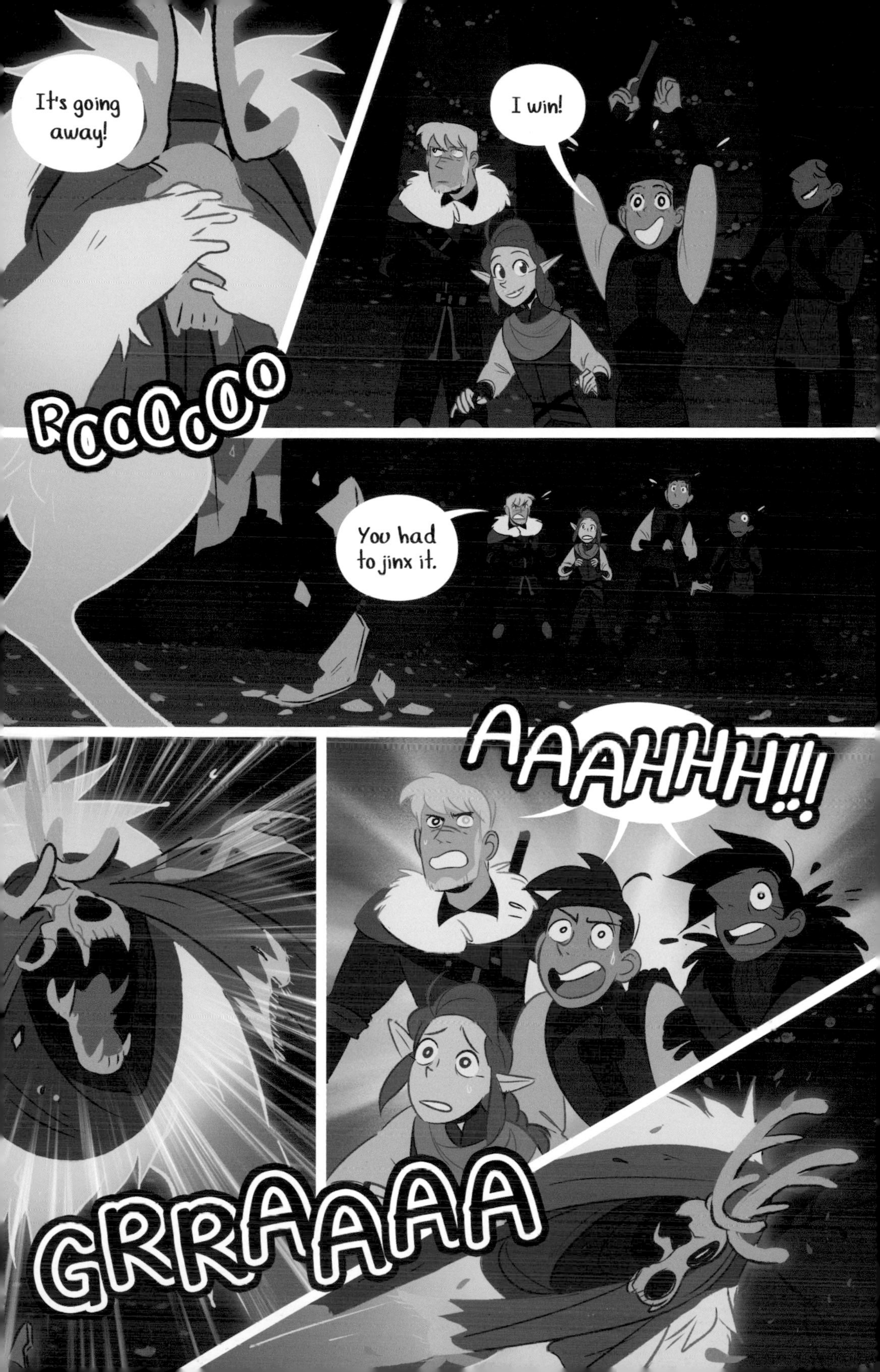
It's going away!
I win!
ROOOOOO
You had to jinx it.
AAAHHH!!!
GRRAAAA

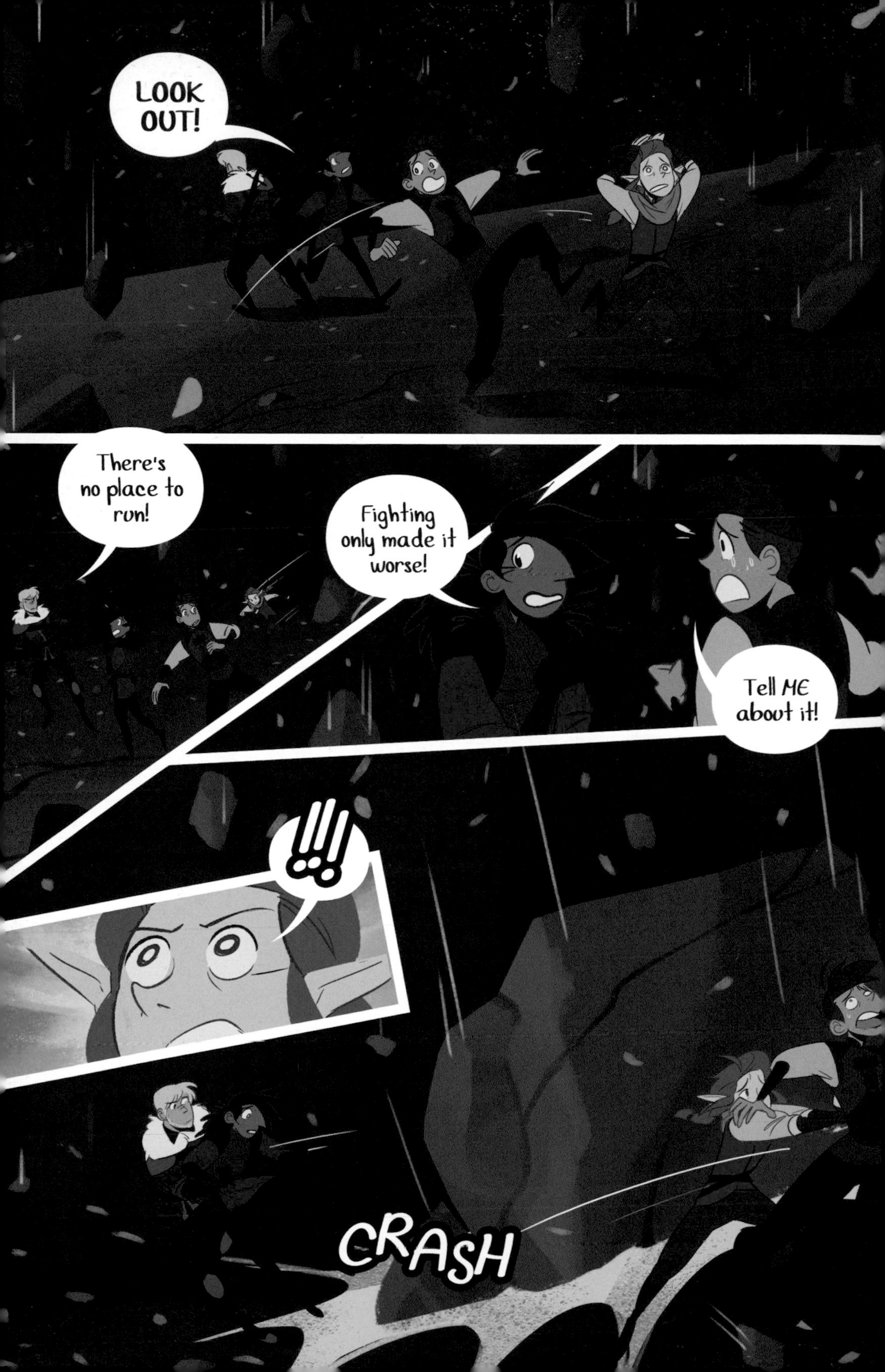
LOOK OUT!
There's no place to run!
Fighting only made it worse!
Tell ME about it!
!!!
CRASH

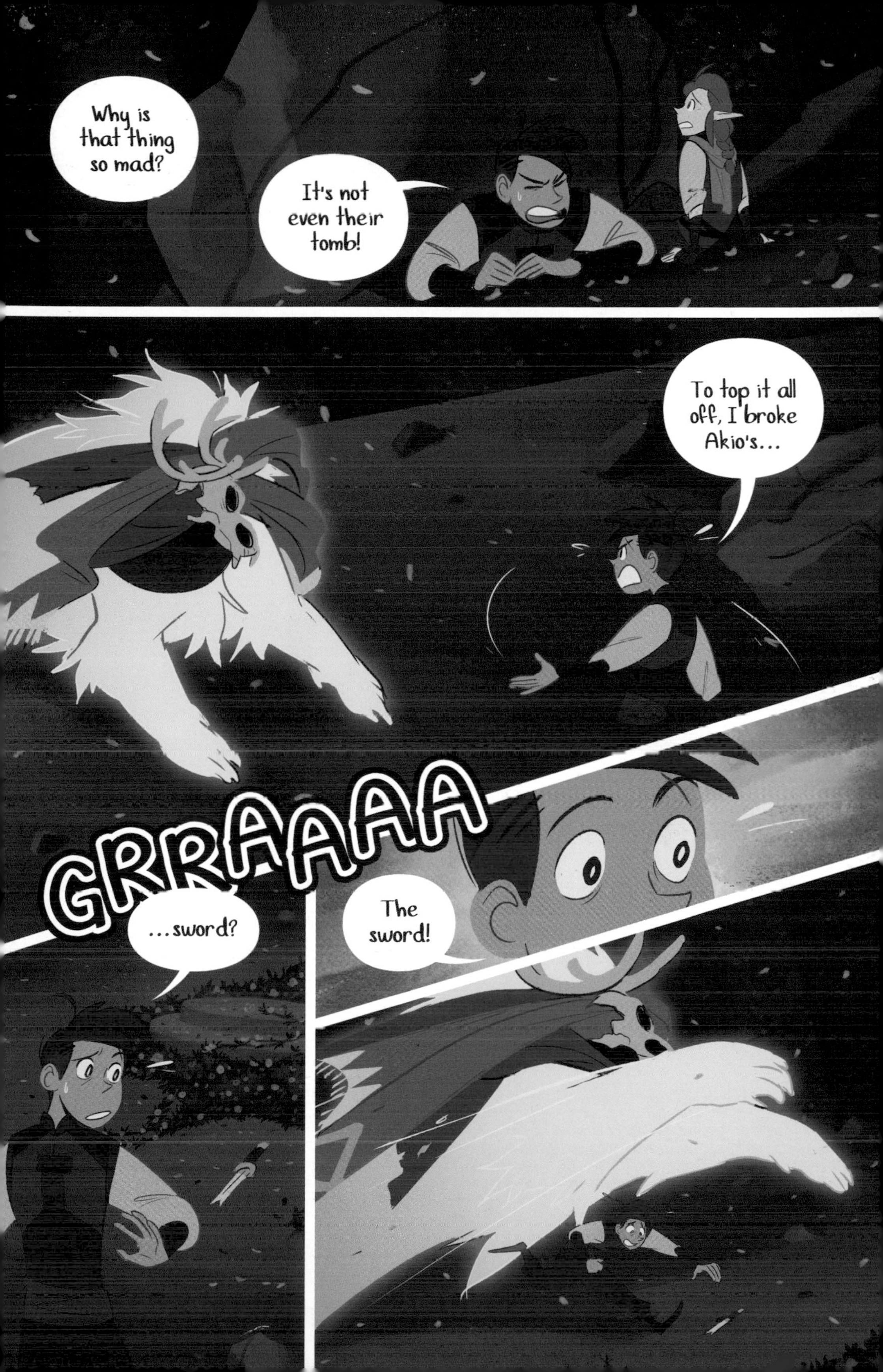
Why is that thing so mad?
It's not even their tomb!
To top it all off, I broke Akio's...
GRRAAAA
...sword?
The sword!

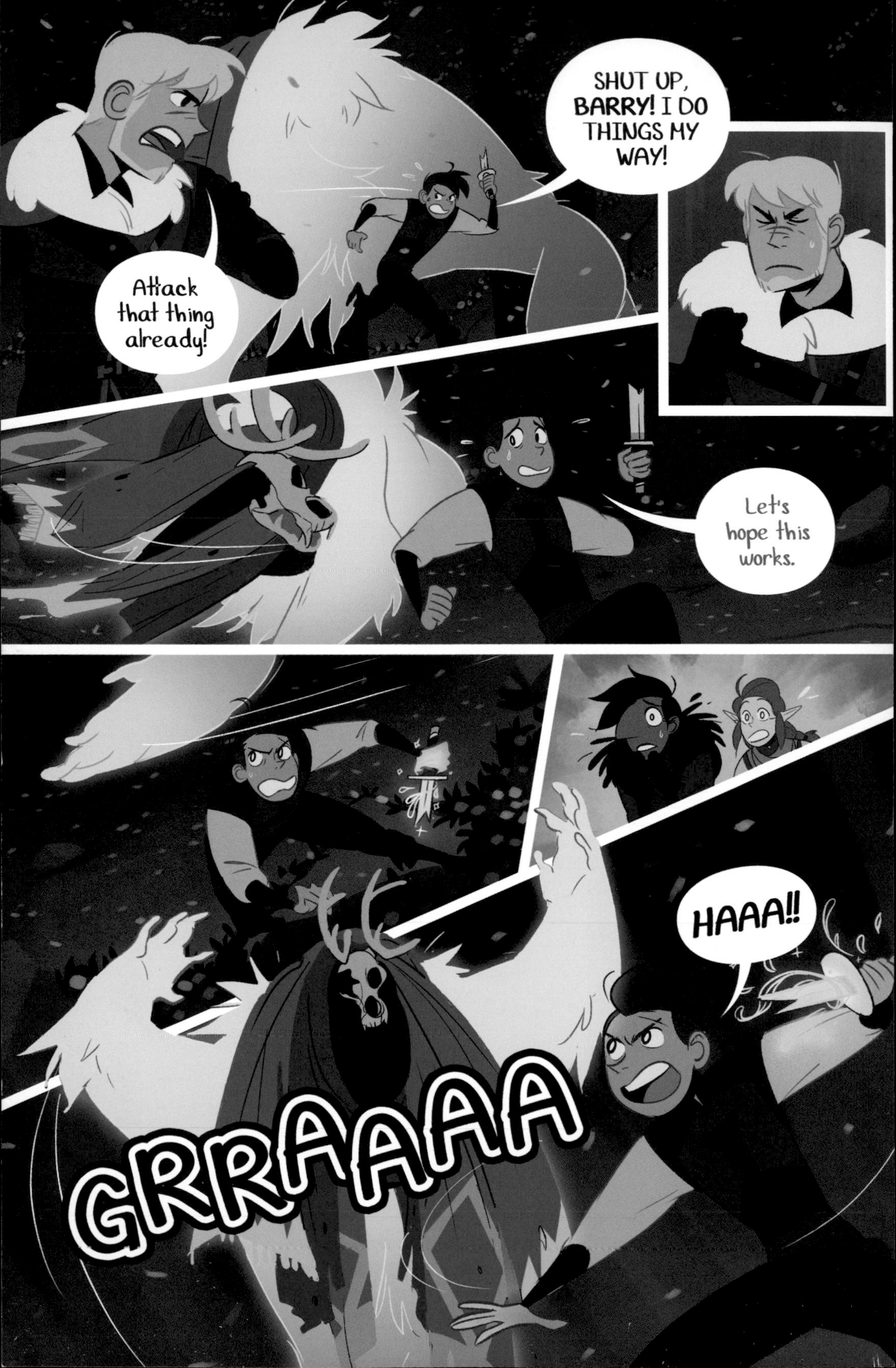
SHUT UP, BARRY! I DO THINGS MY WAY!
Attack that thing already!
Let's hope this works.
HAAA!!
GRRAAAA

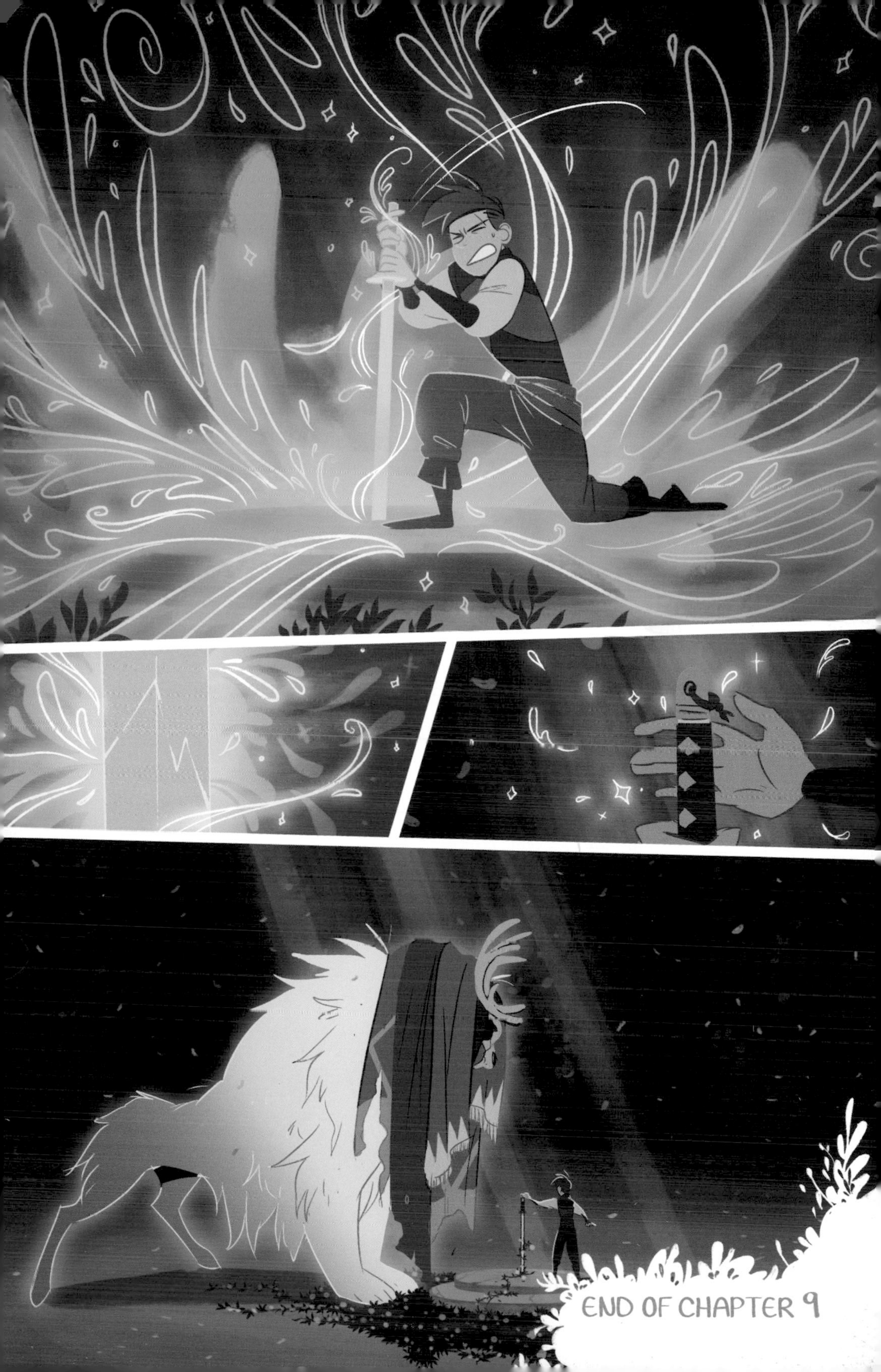
END OF CHAPTER 9

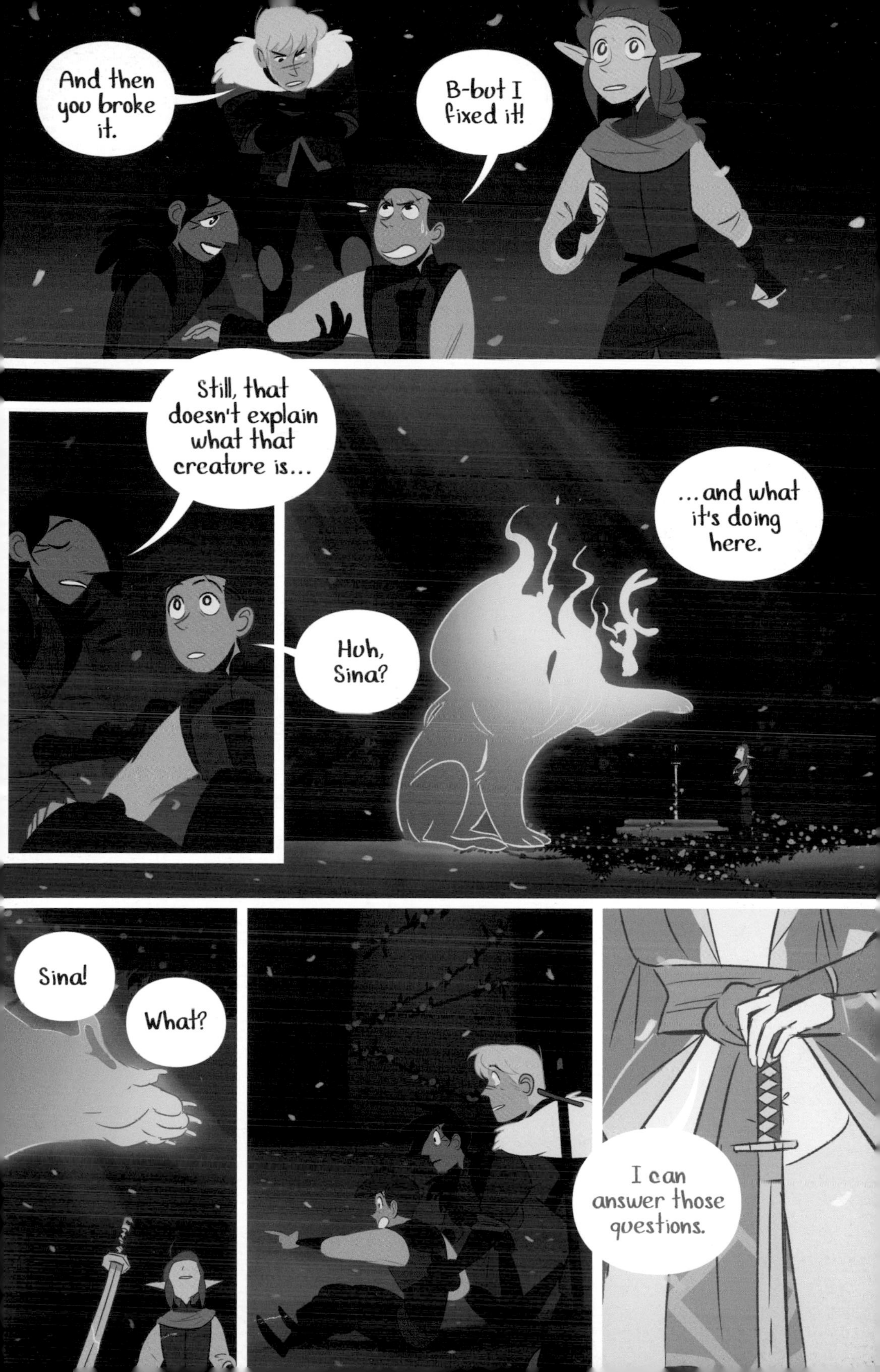
And then you broke it.
B-but I fixed it!
Still, that doesn't explain what that creature is...
...and what it's doing here.
Huh, Sina?
Sina!
What?
I can answer those questions.

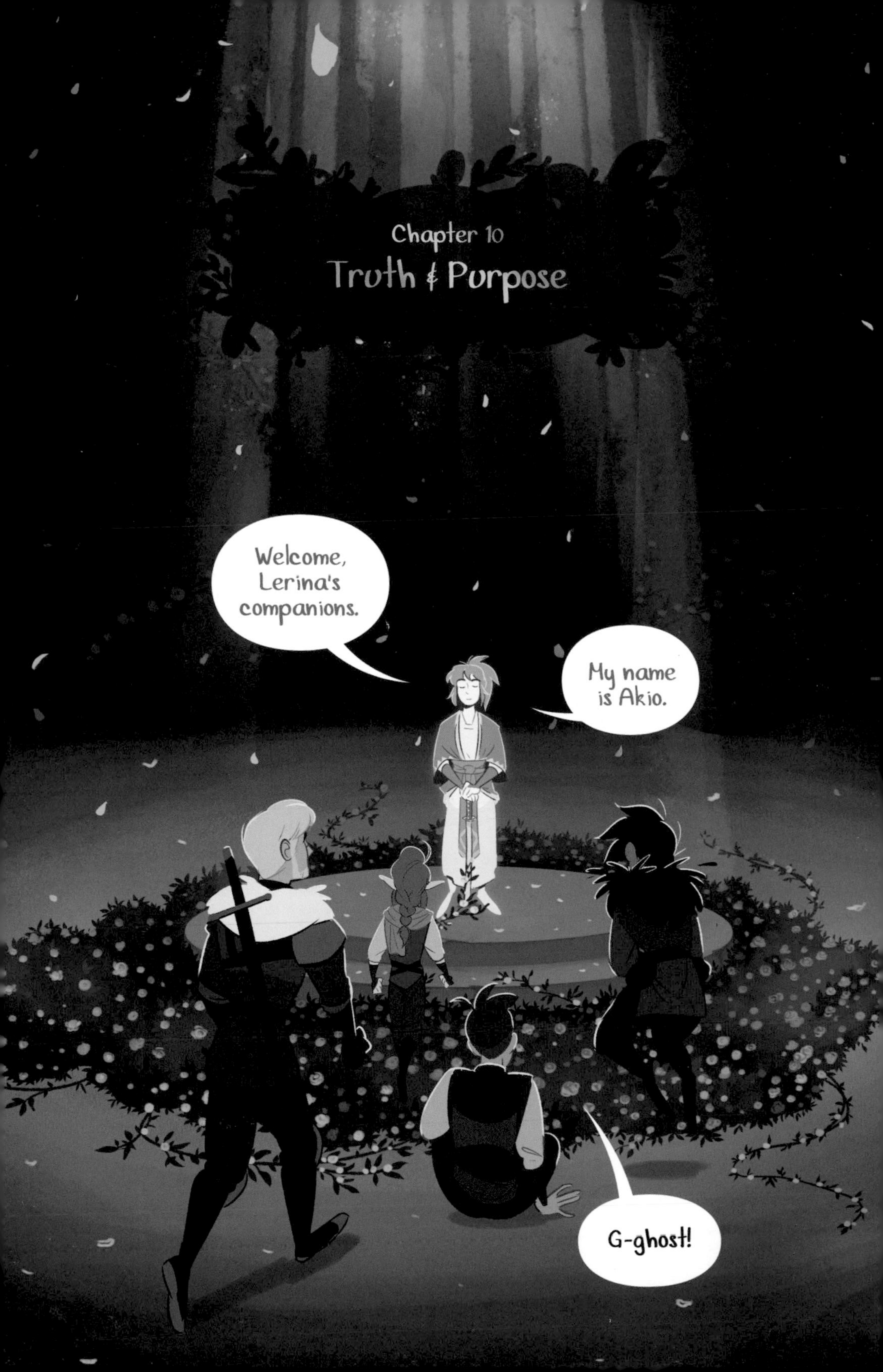

Chapter 10
Truth & Purpose
Welcome, Lerina's companions.
My name is Akio.
G-ghost!

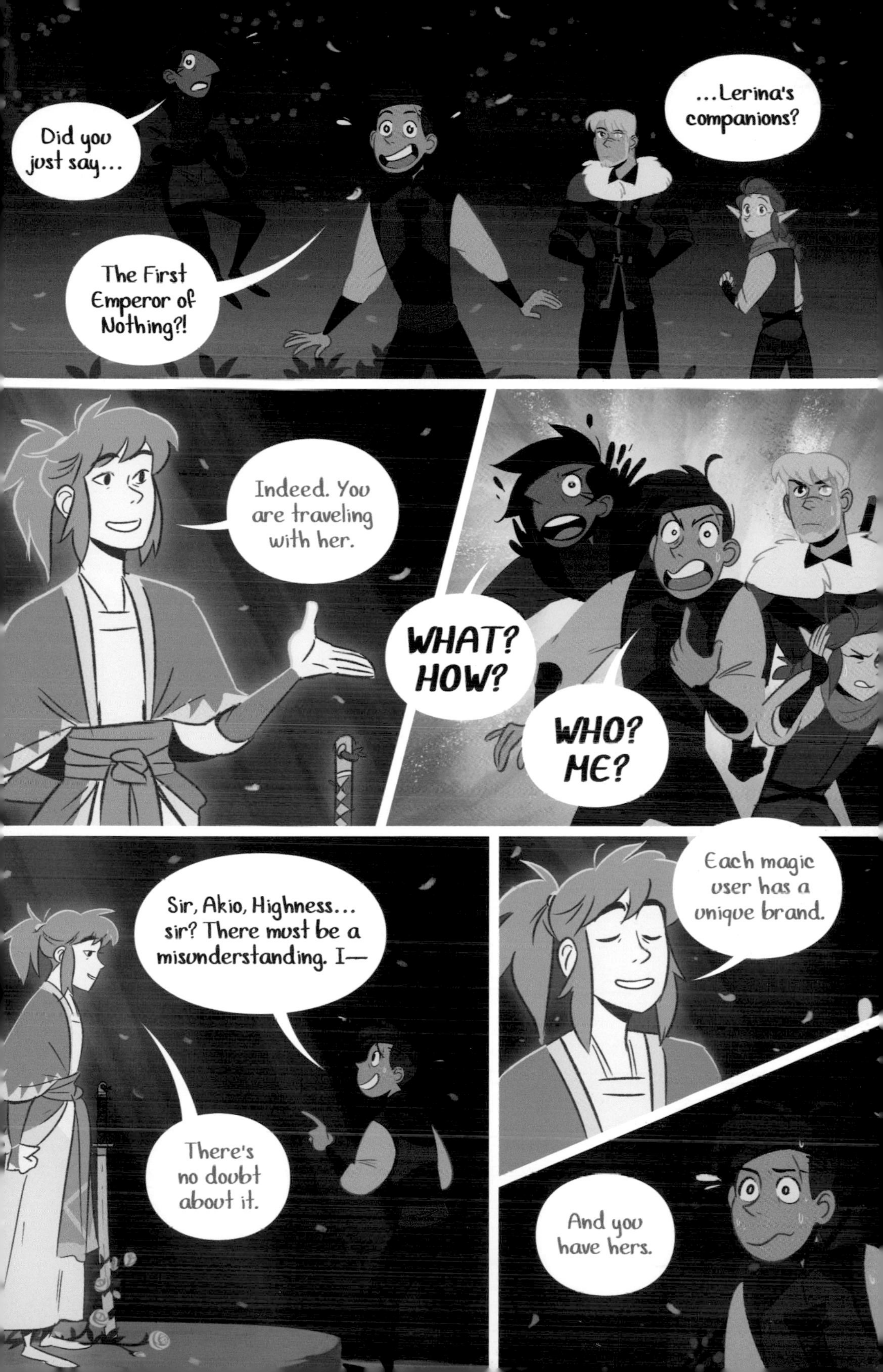
Did you just say...
The First Emperor of Nothing?!
...Lerina's companions?
Indeed. You are traveling with her.
WHAT? HOW?
WHO? ME?
Sir, Akio, Highness... sir? There must be a misunderstanding. I—
There's no doubt about it.
Each magic user has a unique brand.
And you have hers.

I can't believe it's been so long.

What do you mean?

She should've come back sooner.

I've been waiting for so... Sigh

Listen, the "Darkness" the prince told you about.

In our time, his name was Stryx, a wise volken, ruler of That City.

What city?

That City.

Yeah, but which one?

"That" is the name of the city.

Yeees, but—

Stop it.

I was trying to lighten the mood, geez!

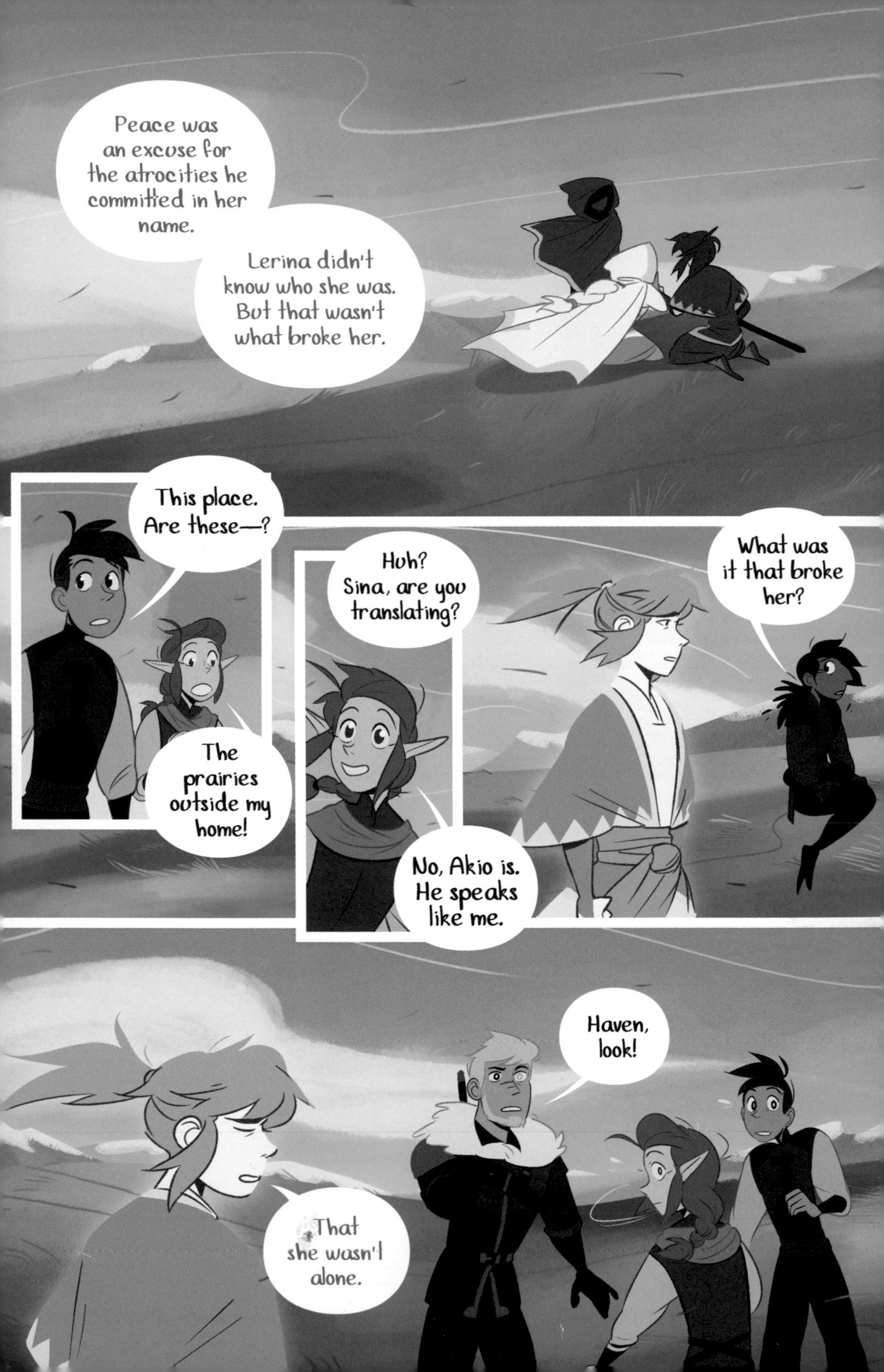
Peace was an excuse for the atrocities he commitfed in her name.
Lerina didn't know who she was. But that wasn't what broke her.
This place. Are these—?
The prairies outside my home!
Huh? Sina, are you translating?
No, Akio is. He speaks like me.
What was it that broke her?
Haven, look!
That she wasn't alone.

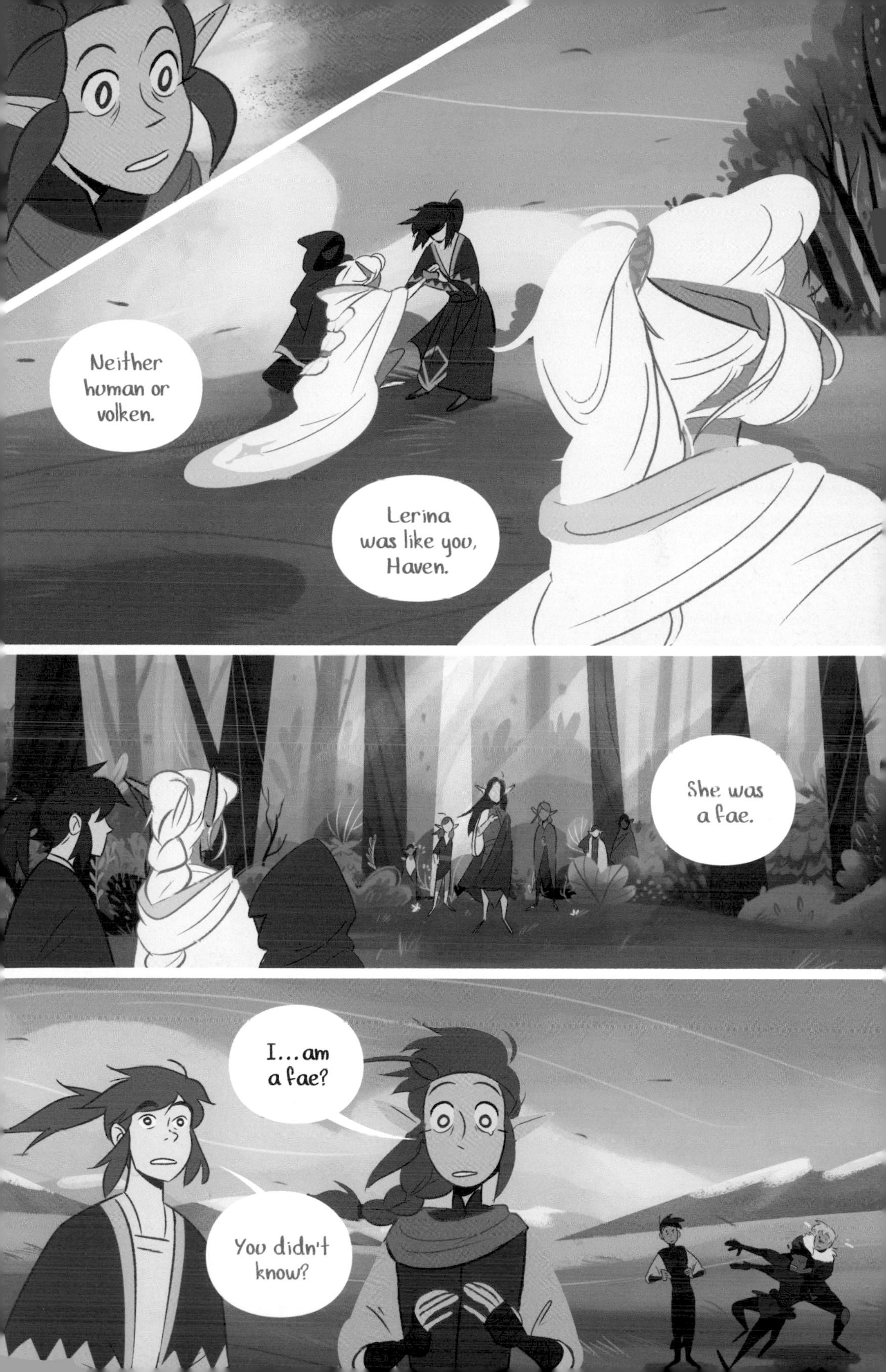
Neither human or volken.
Lerina was like you, Haven.
She was a fae.
I... am a fae?
You didn't know?

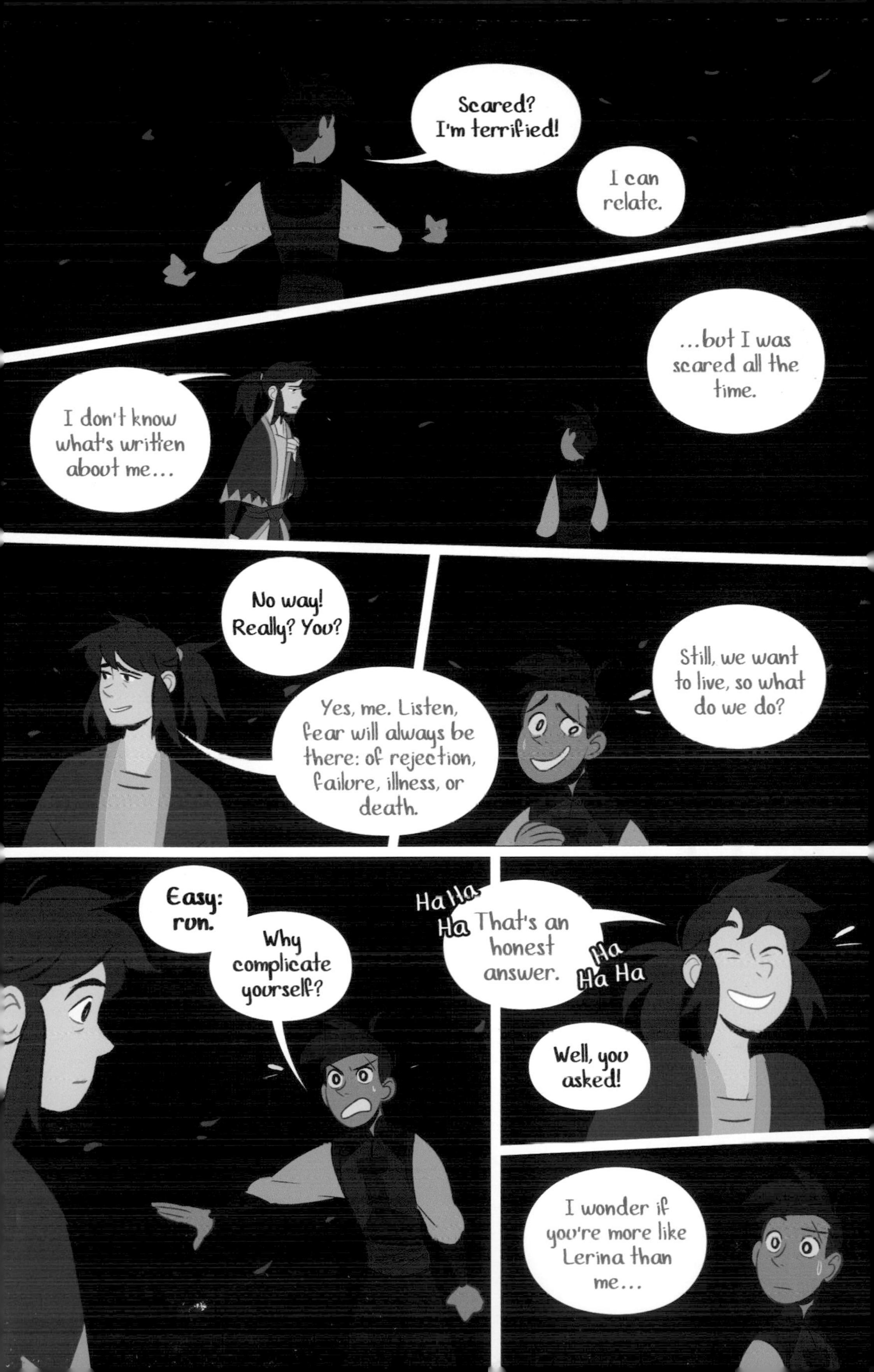
Scared? I'm terrified!
I can relate.
...but I was scared all the time.
I don't know what's written about me...
No way! Really? You?
Yes, me. Listen, fear will always be there: of rejection, failure, illness, or death.
Still, we want to live, so what do we do?
Easy: run.
Why complicate yourself?
Ha Ha Ha
That's an honest answer.
Ha Ha Ha
Well, you asked!
I wonder if you're more like Lerina than me...

END OF CHAPTER 10

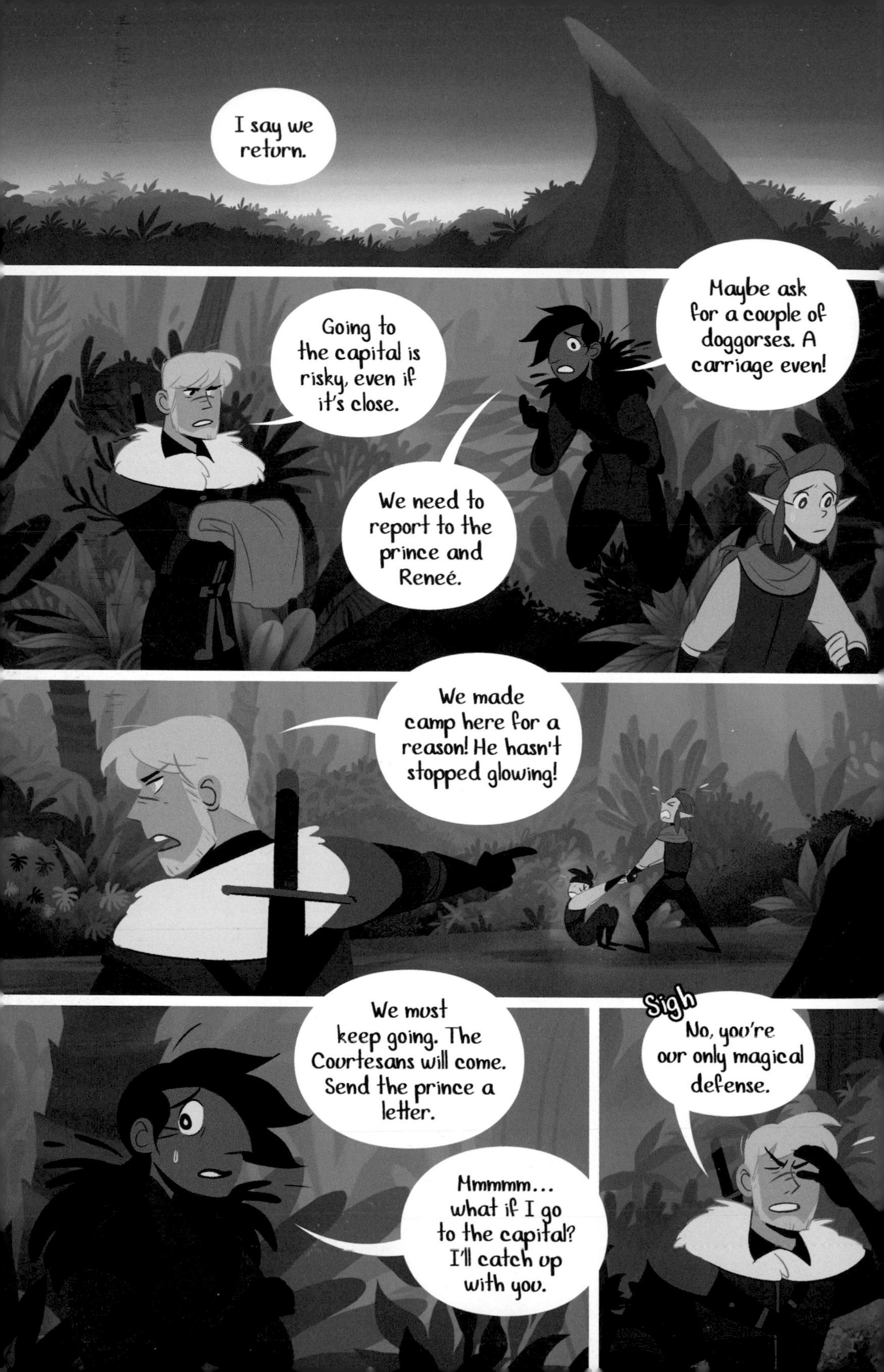
I say we return.
Going to the capital is risky, even if it's close.
Maybe ask for a couple of doggorses. A carriage even!
We need to report to the prince and Reneé.
We made camp here for a reason! He hasn't stopped glowing!
We must keep going. The Courtesans will come. Send the prince a letter.
Mmmmm... what if I go to the capital? I'll catch up with you.
Sigh
No, you're our only magical defense.

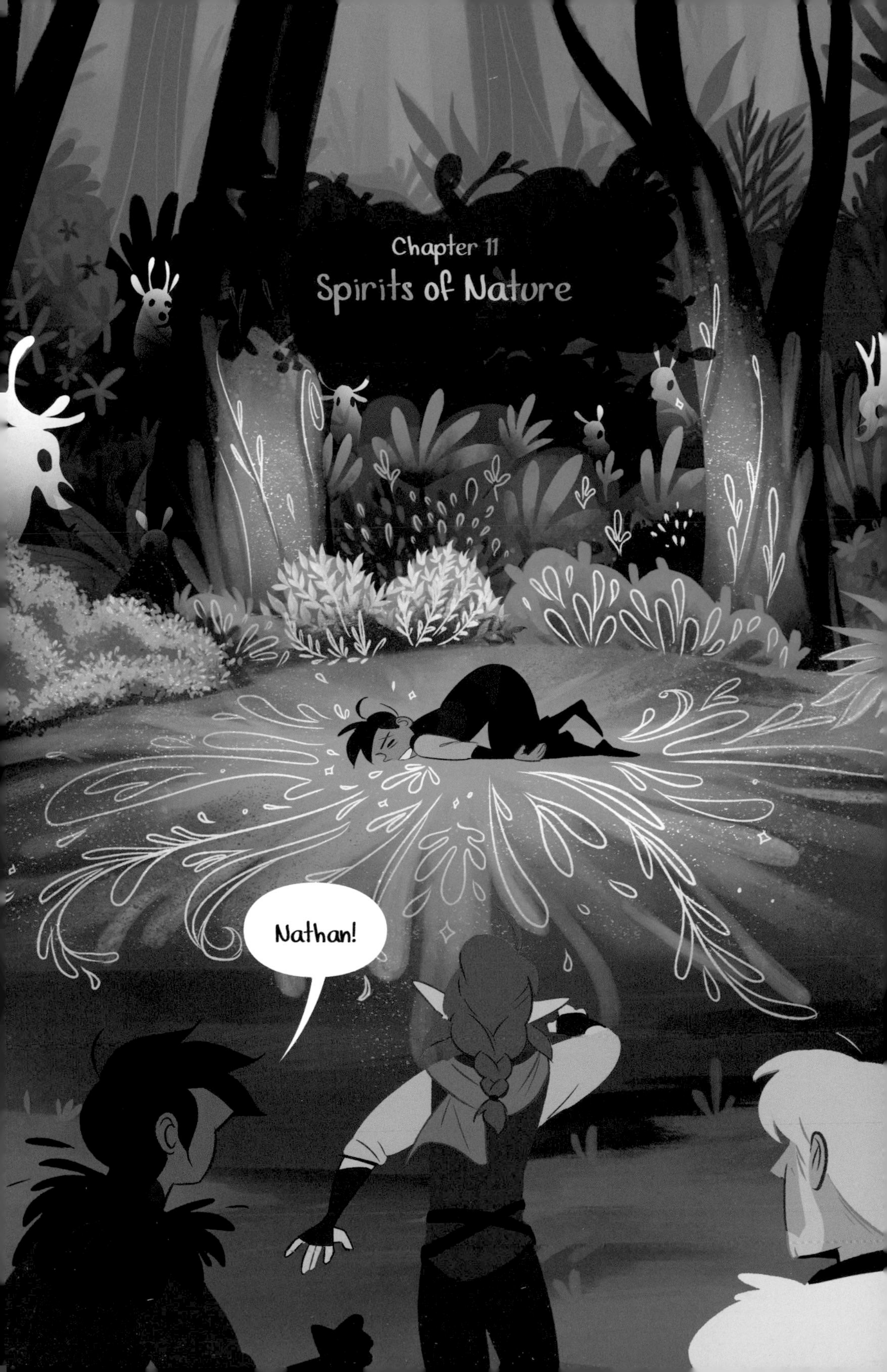
Chapter 11
Spirits of Nature
Nathan!

Ugh... I knew it. Lerina is trying to kill me!

Ill or not, he still has the energy to complain.

Come on, save your energy.

Look at all those stars!

No, that's the light passing through the leaves.

When did you became so good at Common?

Common? You're talking Ancient.

And he does it perfectly.

Not only that. He's changing the surroundings.

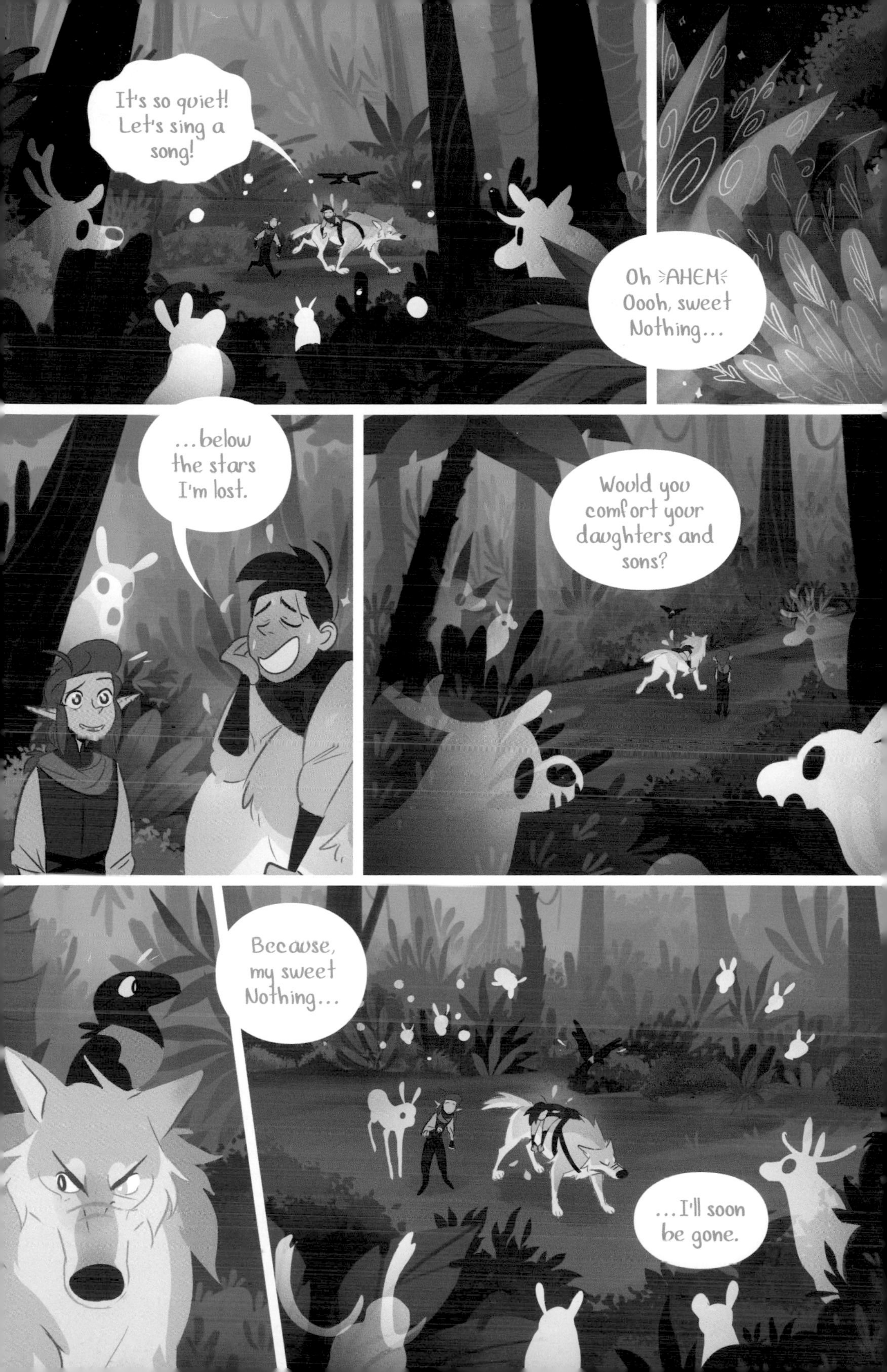
It's so quiet! Let's sing a song!
Oh ≶AHEM≶ Oooh, sweet Nothing...
...below the stars I'm lost.
Would you comfort your daughters and sons?
Because, my sweet Nothing...
...I'll soon be gone.

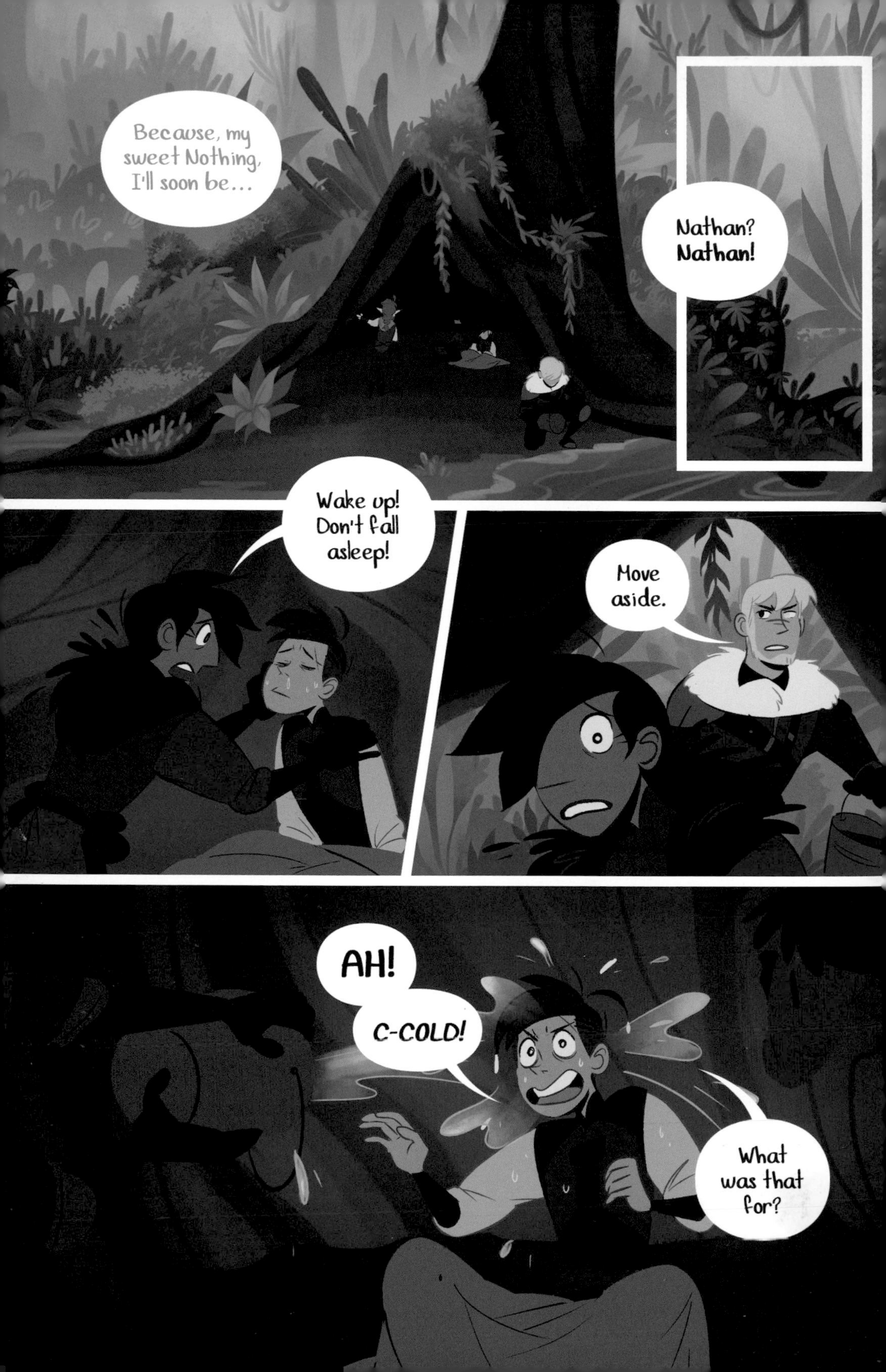
Because, my sweet Nothing, I'll soon be...
Nathan? Nathan!
Wake up! Don't fall asleep!
Move aside.
AH!
C-COLD!
What was that for?

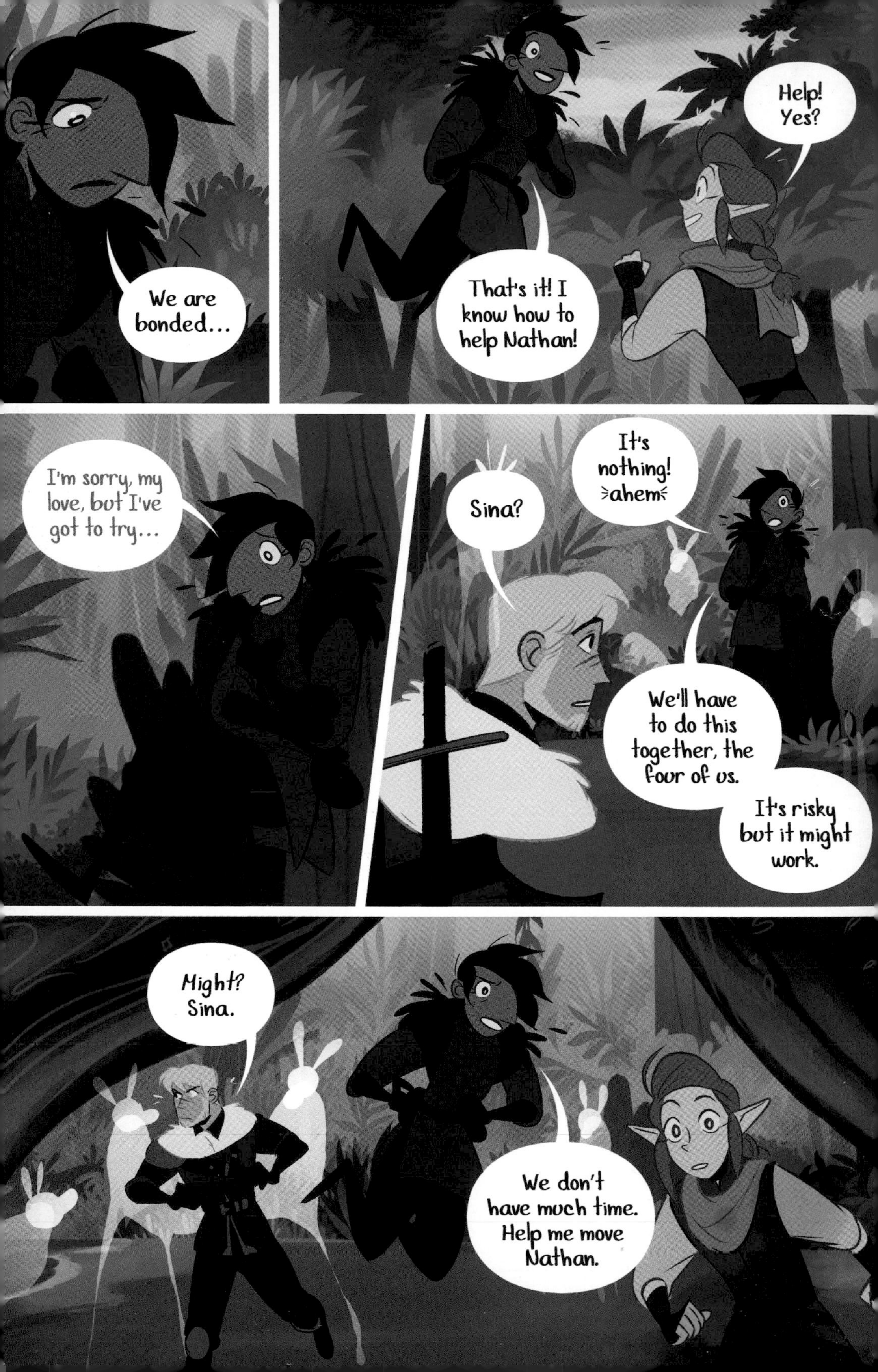
We are bonded...
That's it! I know how to help Nathan!
Help! Yes?
I'm sorry, my love, but I've got to try...
Sina?
It's nothing! ≥ahem≤
We'll have to do this together, the four of us.
It's risky but it might work.
Might? Sina.
We don't have much time. Help me move Nathan.

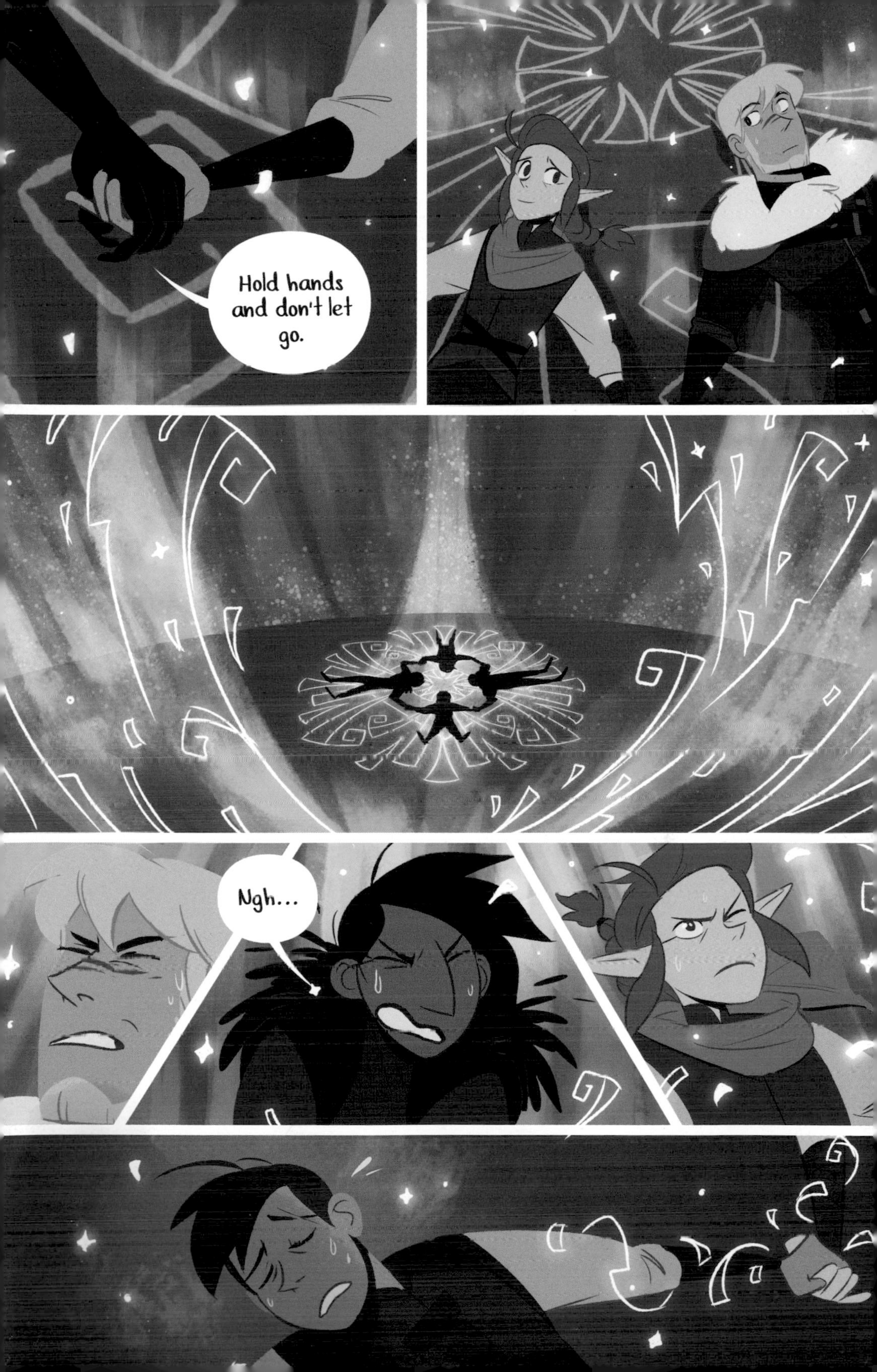
Hold hands and don't let go.
Ngh...

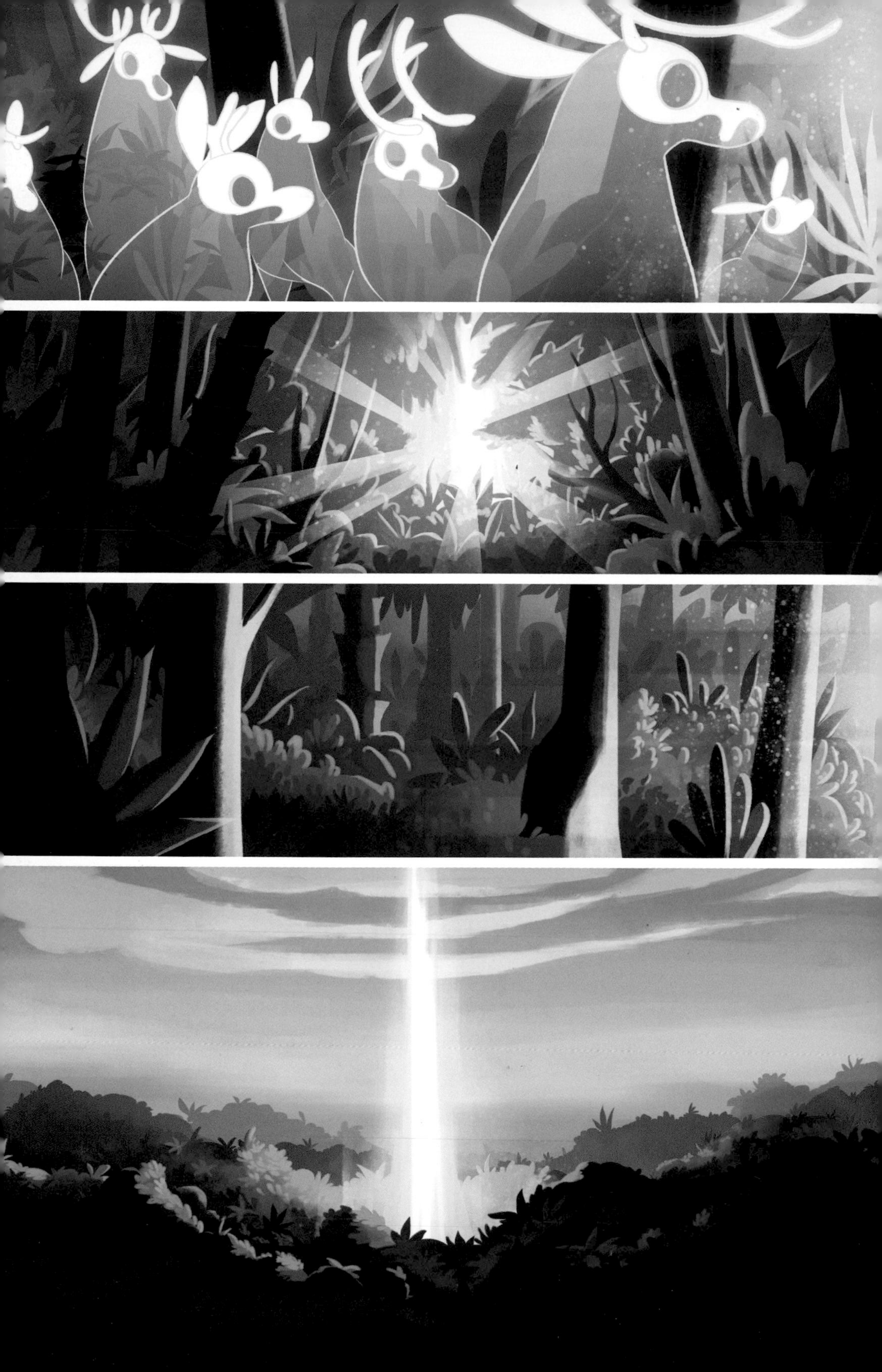

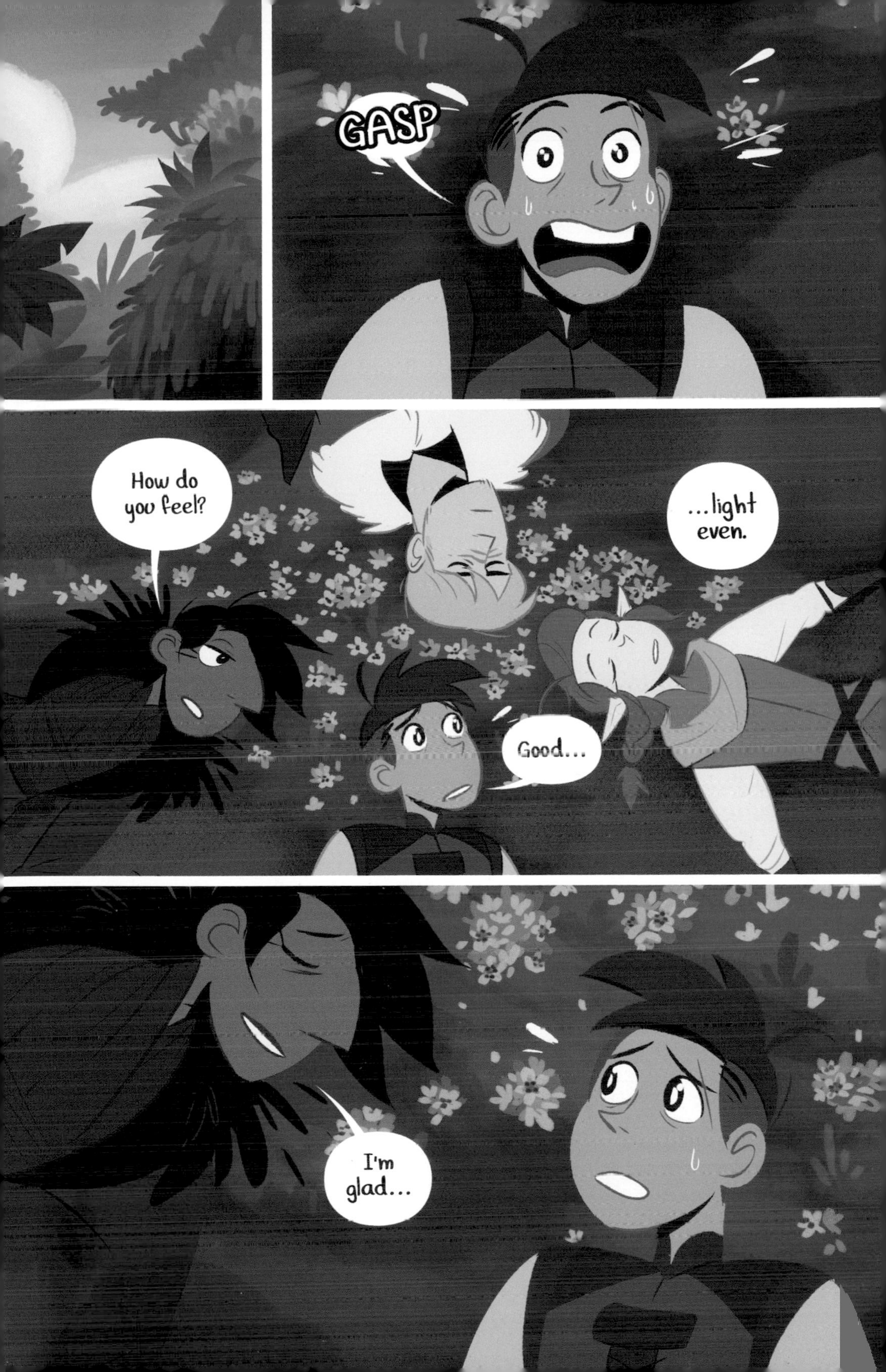
GASP
How do you feel?
...light even.
Good...
I'm glad...

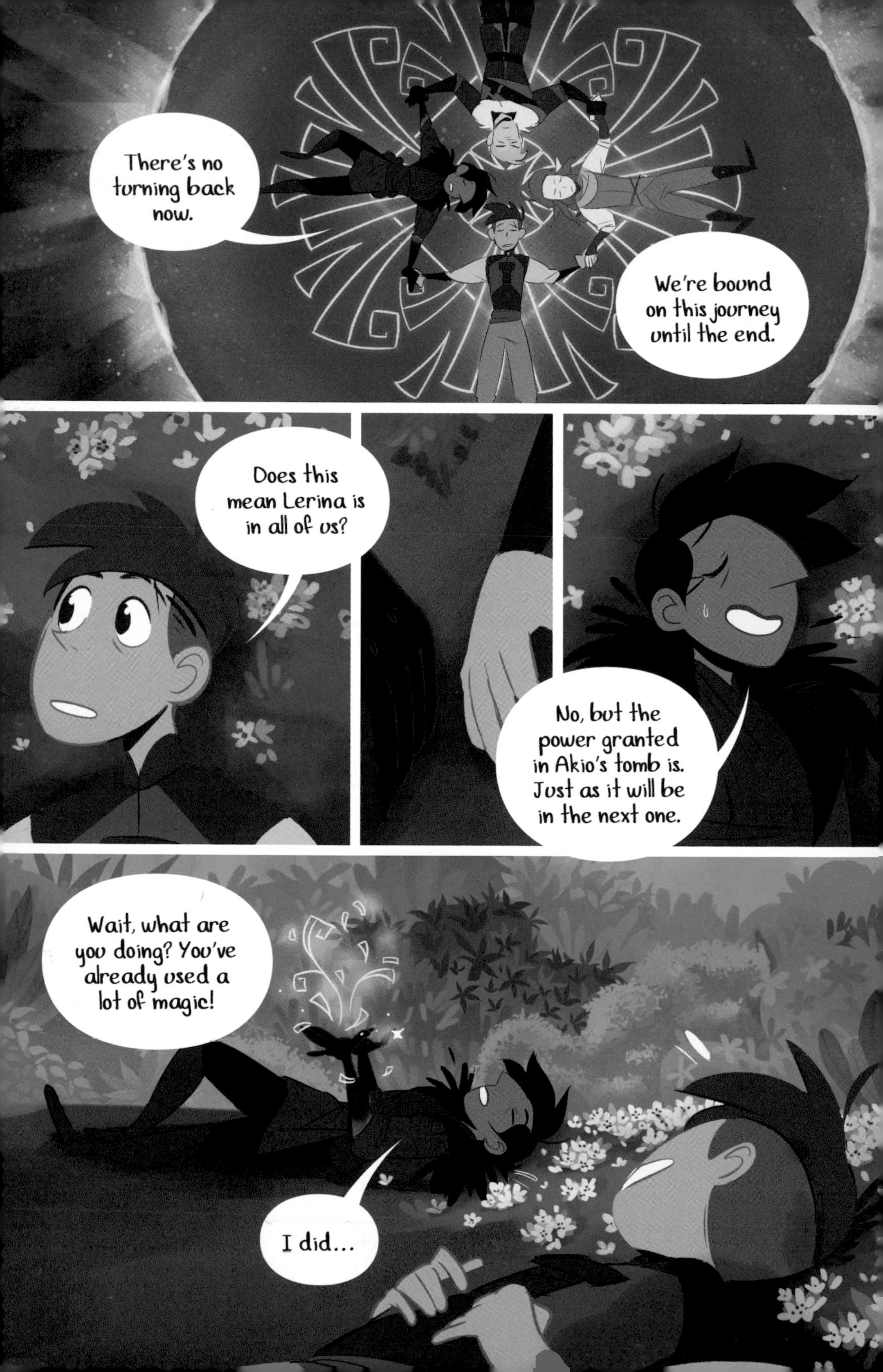
There's no turning back now.
We're bound on this journey until the end.
Does this mean Lerina is in all of us?
No, but the power granted in Akio's tomb is. Just as it will be in the next one.
Wait, what are you doing? You've already used a lot of magic!
I did...

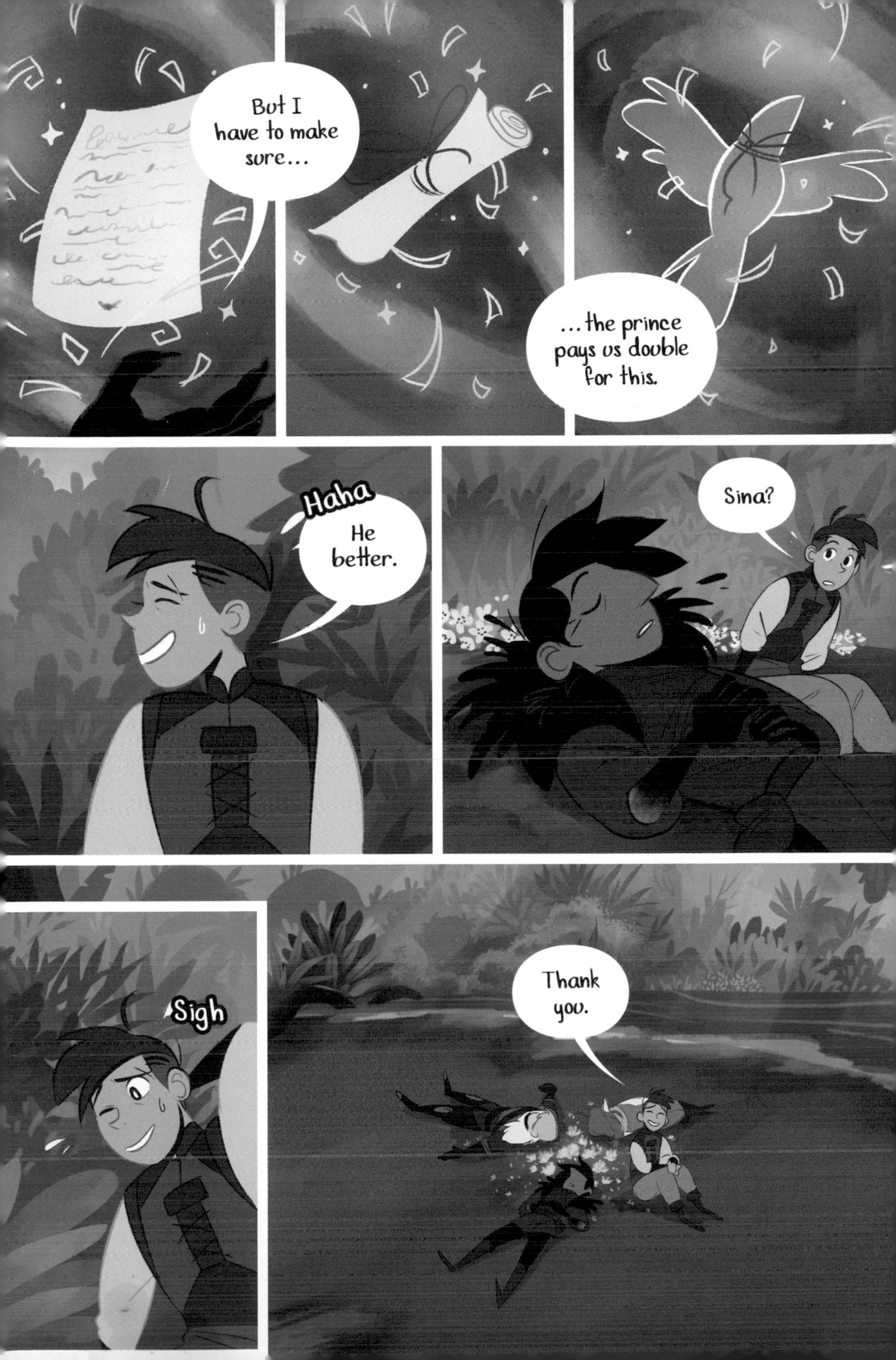
But I have to make sure...
...the prince pays us double for this.
Haha
He better.
Sina?
Sigh
Thank you.

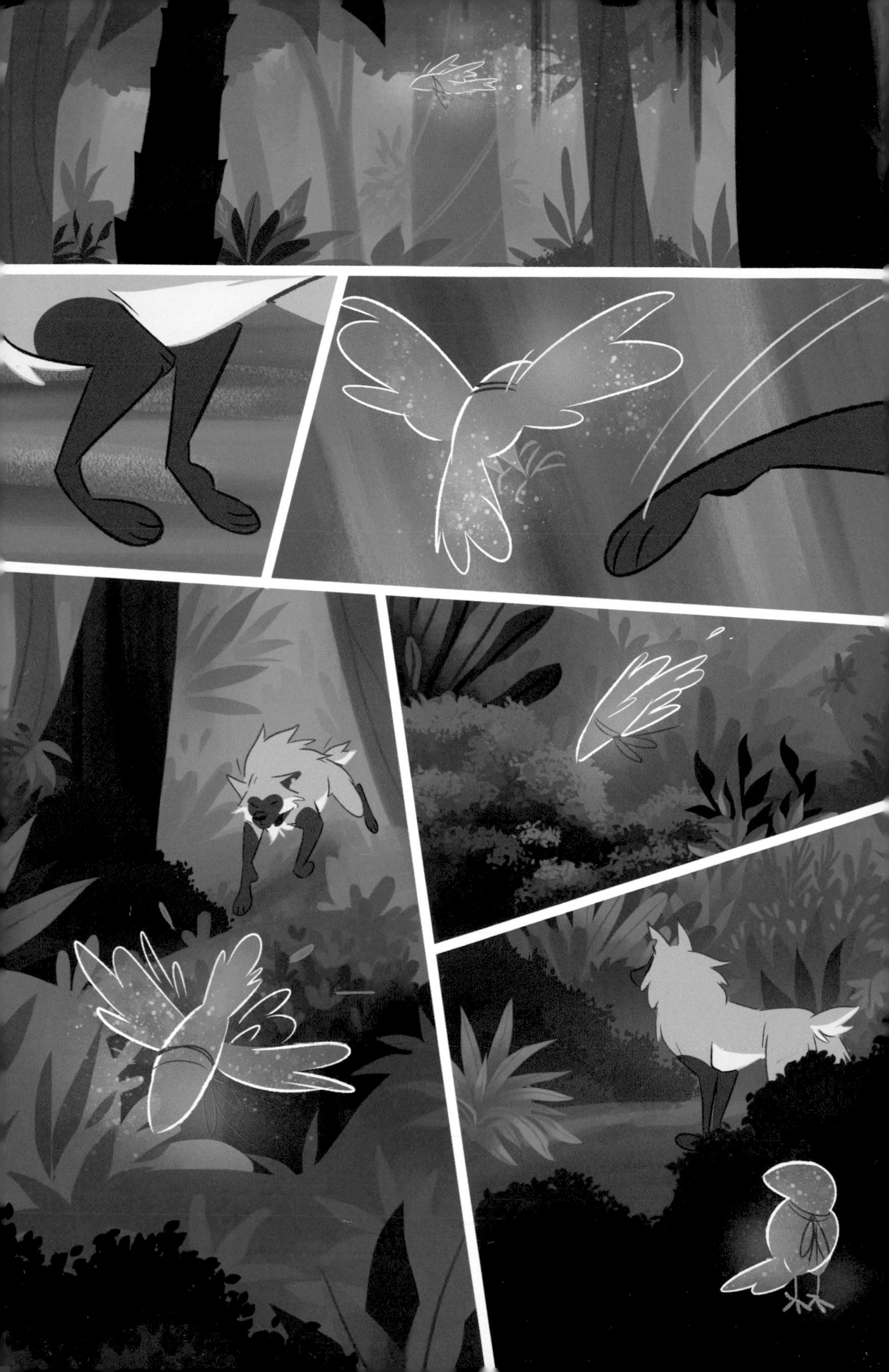

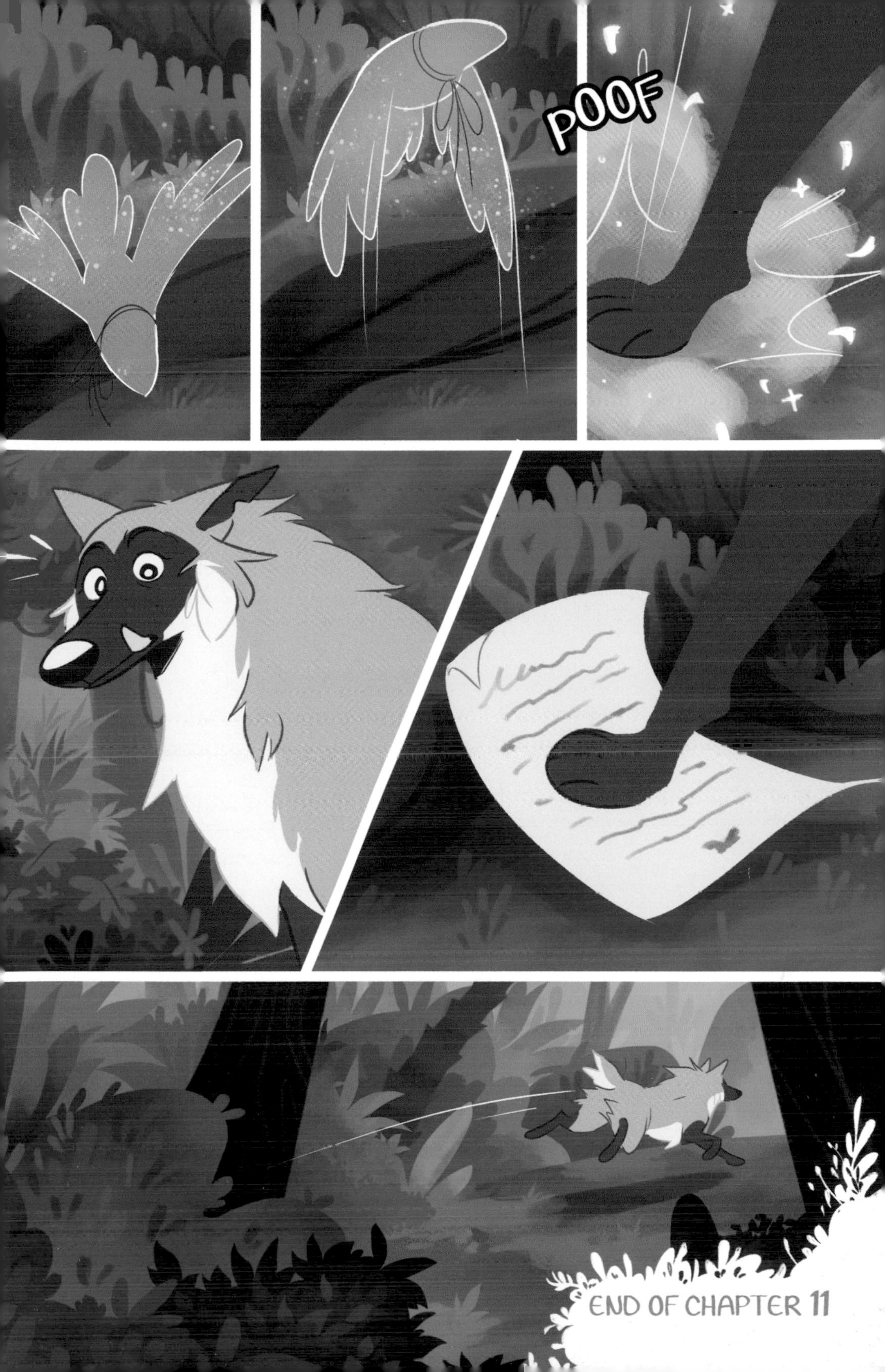
POOF
END OF CHAPTER 11

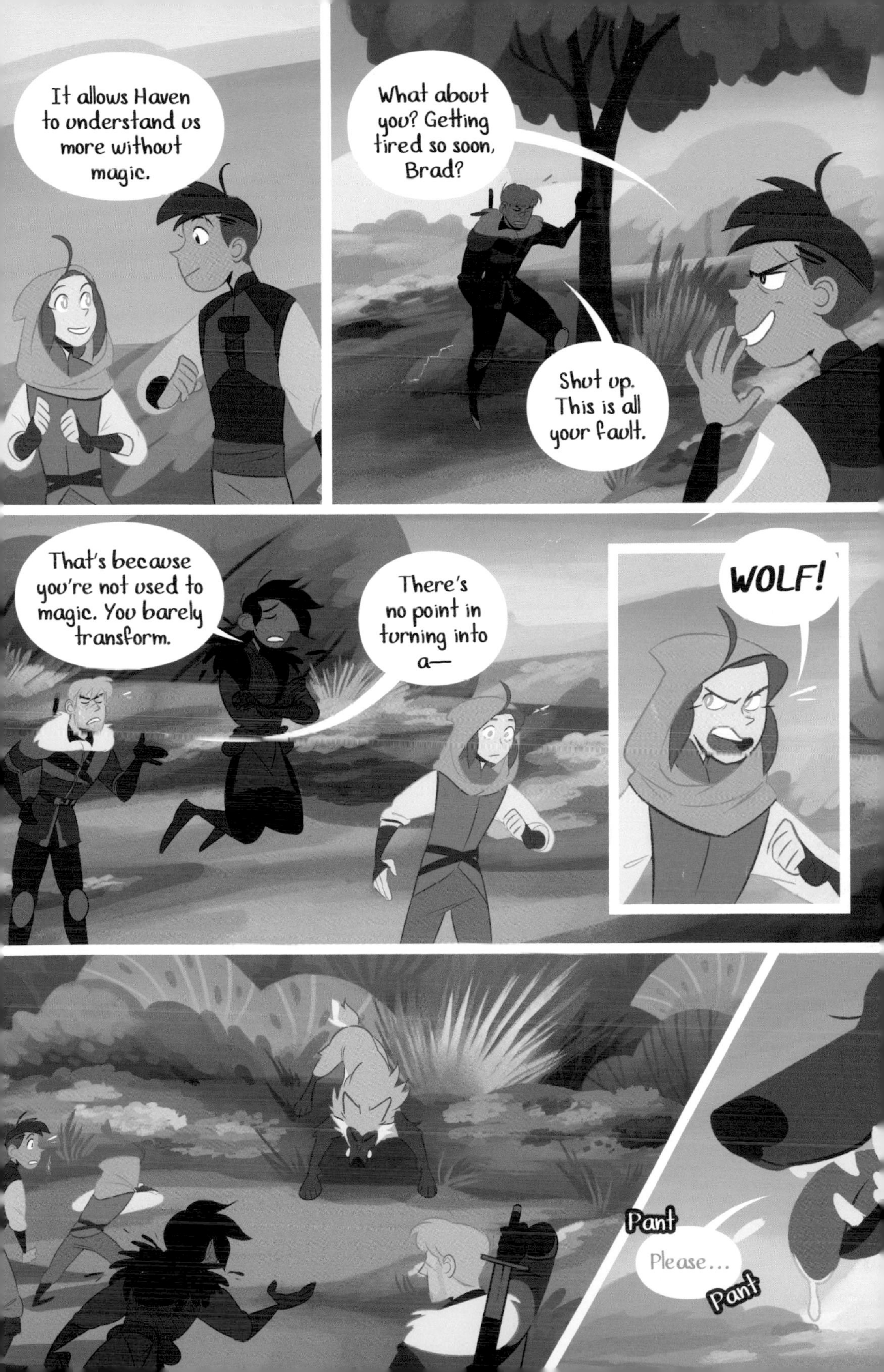
It allows Haven to understand us more without magic.
What about you? Getting tired so soon, Brad?
Shut up. This is all your fault.
That's because you're not used to magic. You barely transform.
There's no point in turning into a—
WOLF!
Pant
Please...
Pant

Chapter 12

Quisling

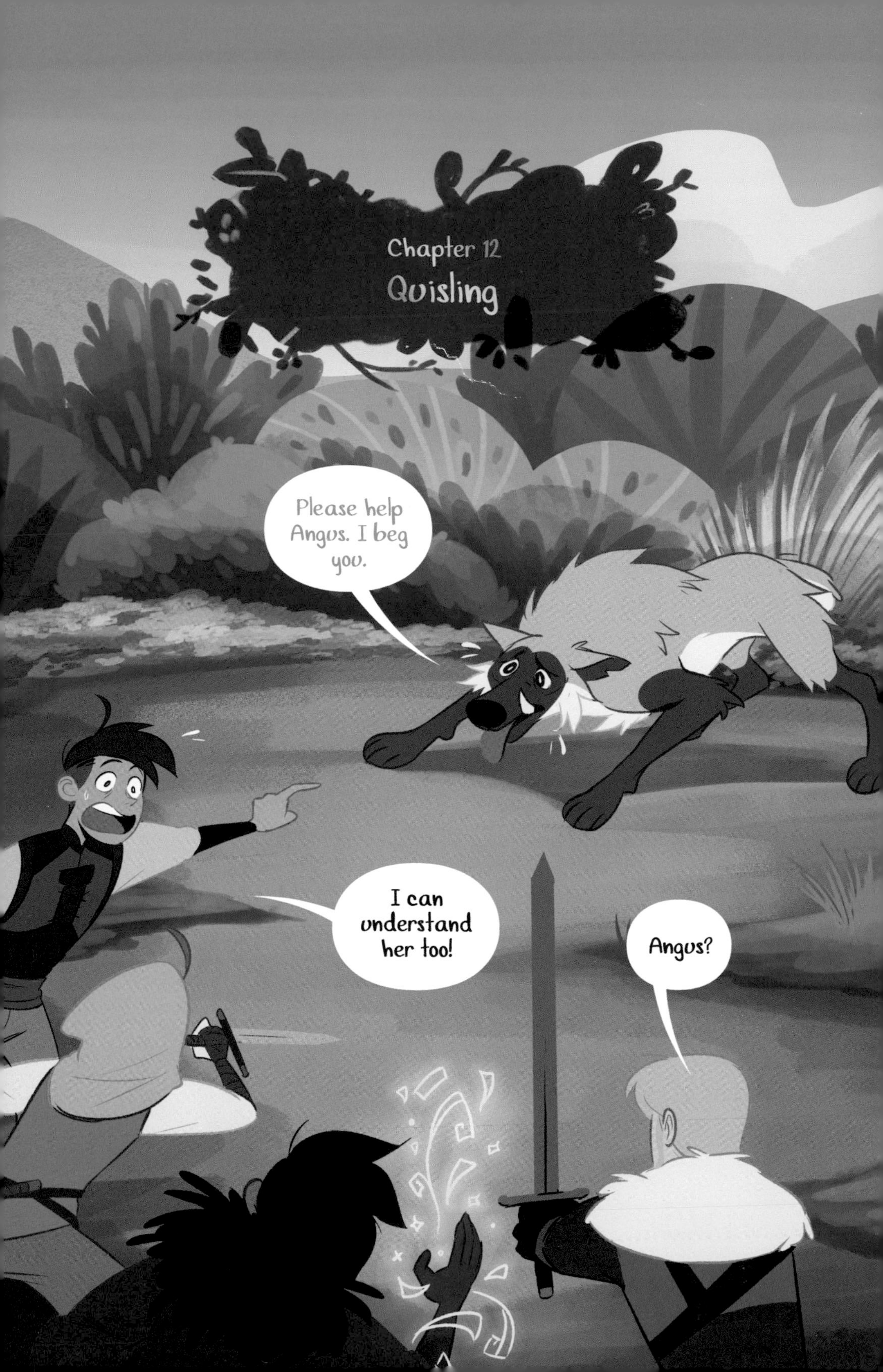

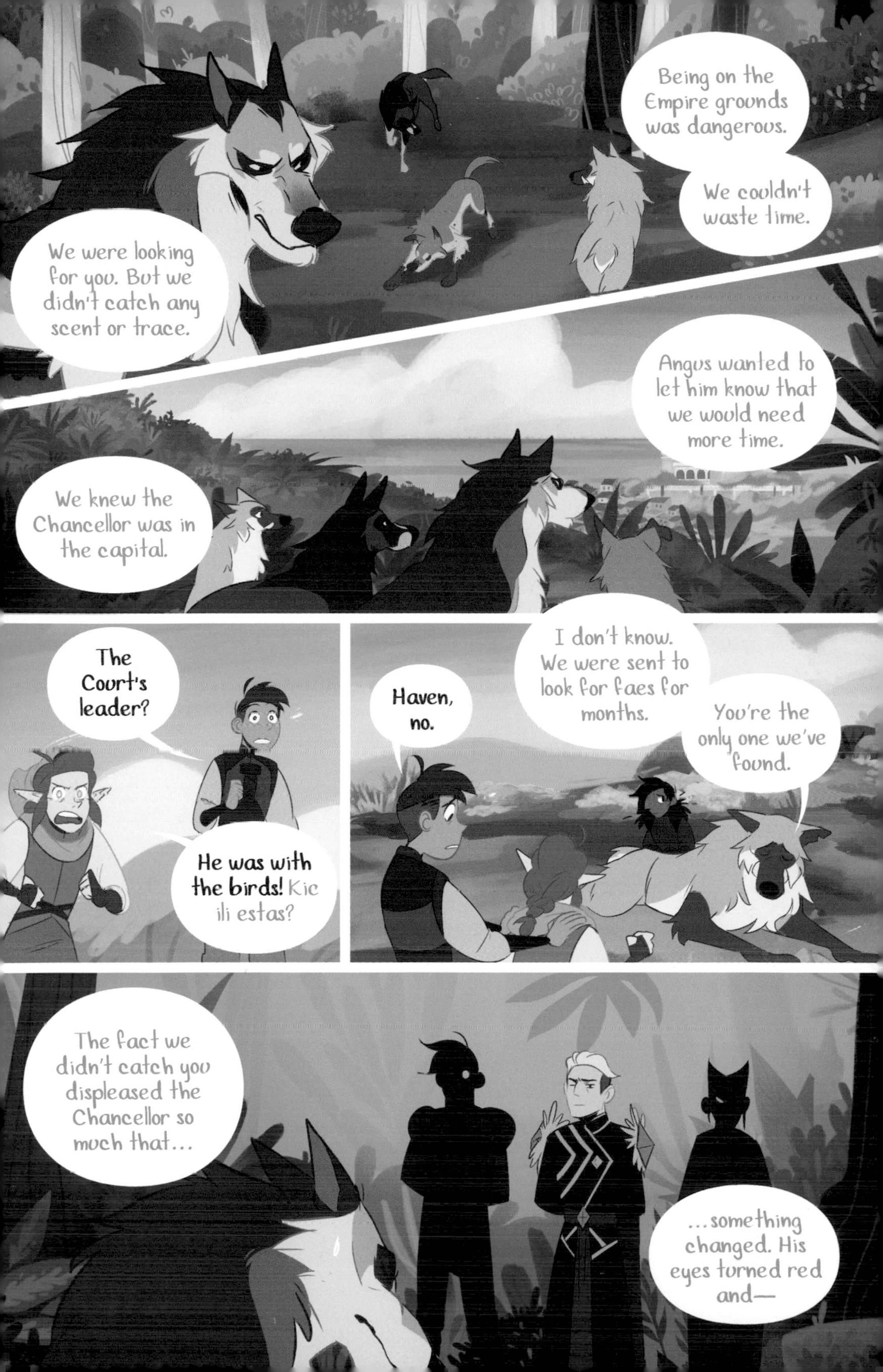

Being on the Empire grounds was dangerous.
We couldn't waste time.
We were looking for you. But we didn't catch any scent or trace.
Angus wanted to let him know that we would need more time.
We knew the Chancellor was in the capital.
The Court's leader?
He was with the birds! Kie ili estas?
Haven, no.
I don't know. We were sent to look for faes for months.
You're the only one we've found.
The fact we didn't catch you displeased the Chancellor so much that...
...something changed. His eyes turned red and—

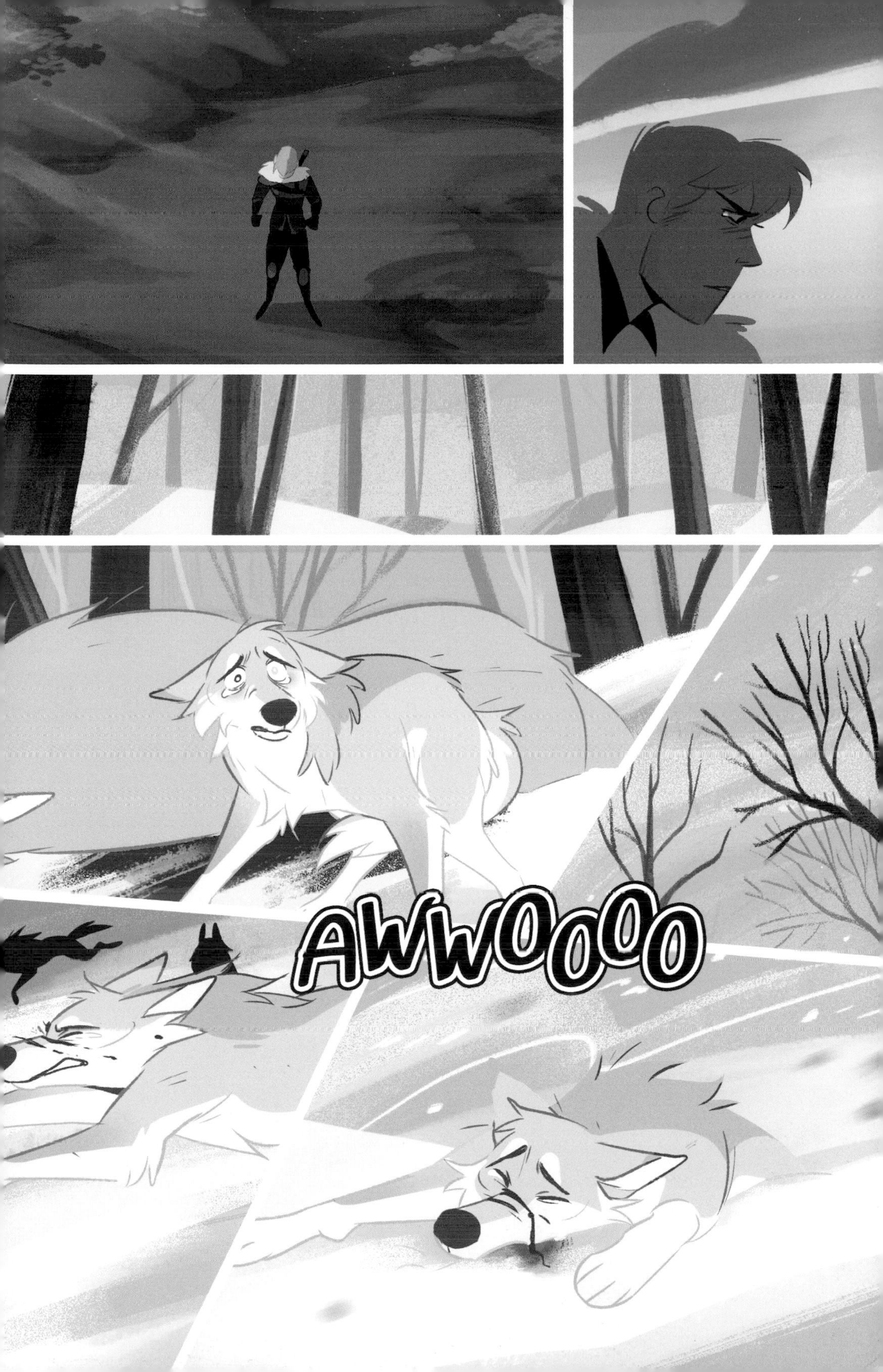
AWWOOOO

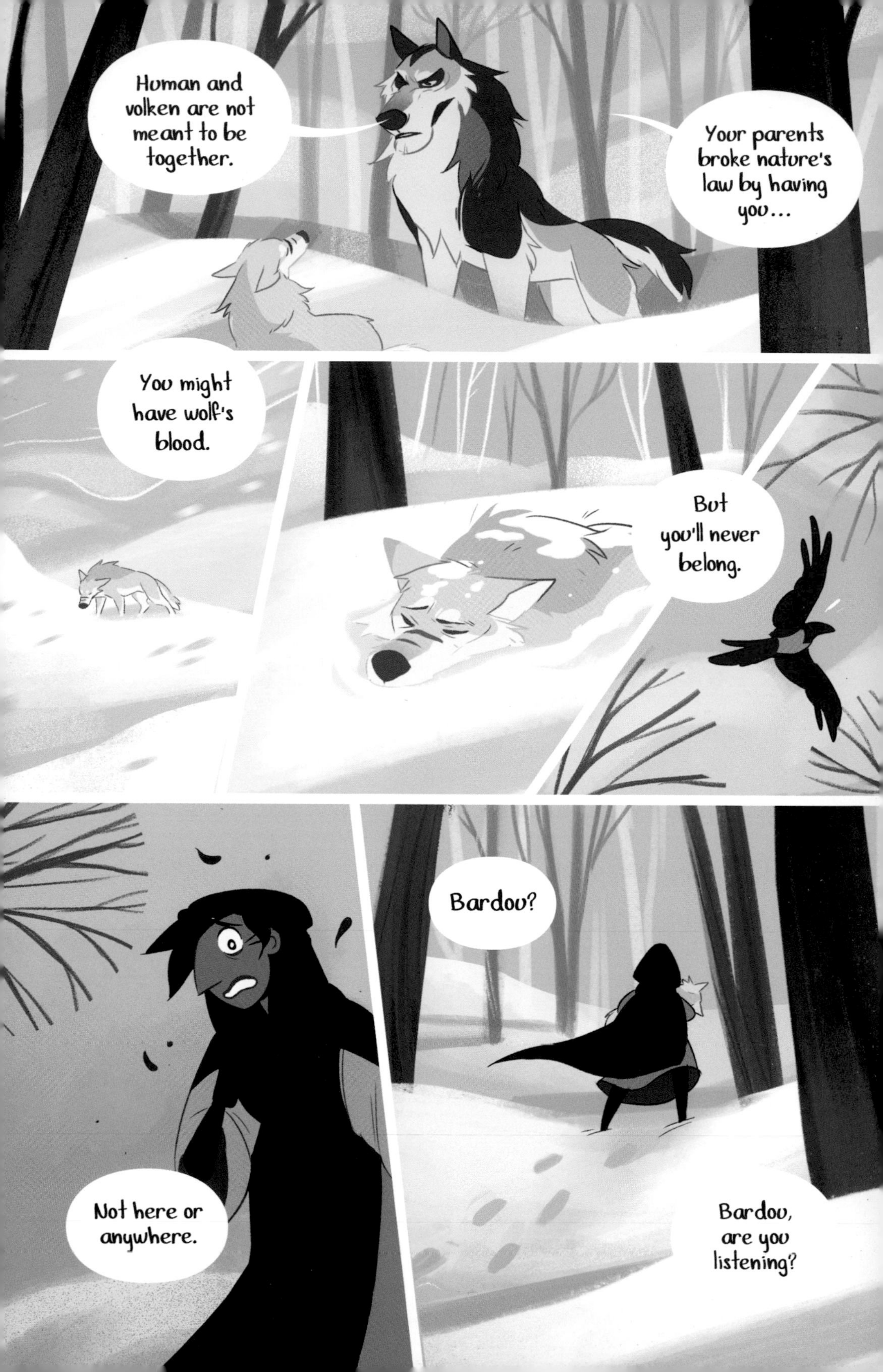
Human and volken are not meant to be together.
Your parents broke nature's law by having you...
You might have wolf's blood.
But you'll never belong.
Not here or anywhere.
Bardou?
Bardou, are you listening?

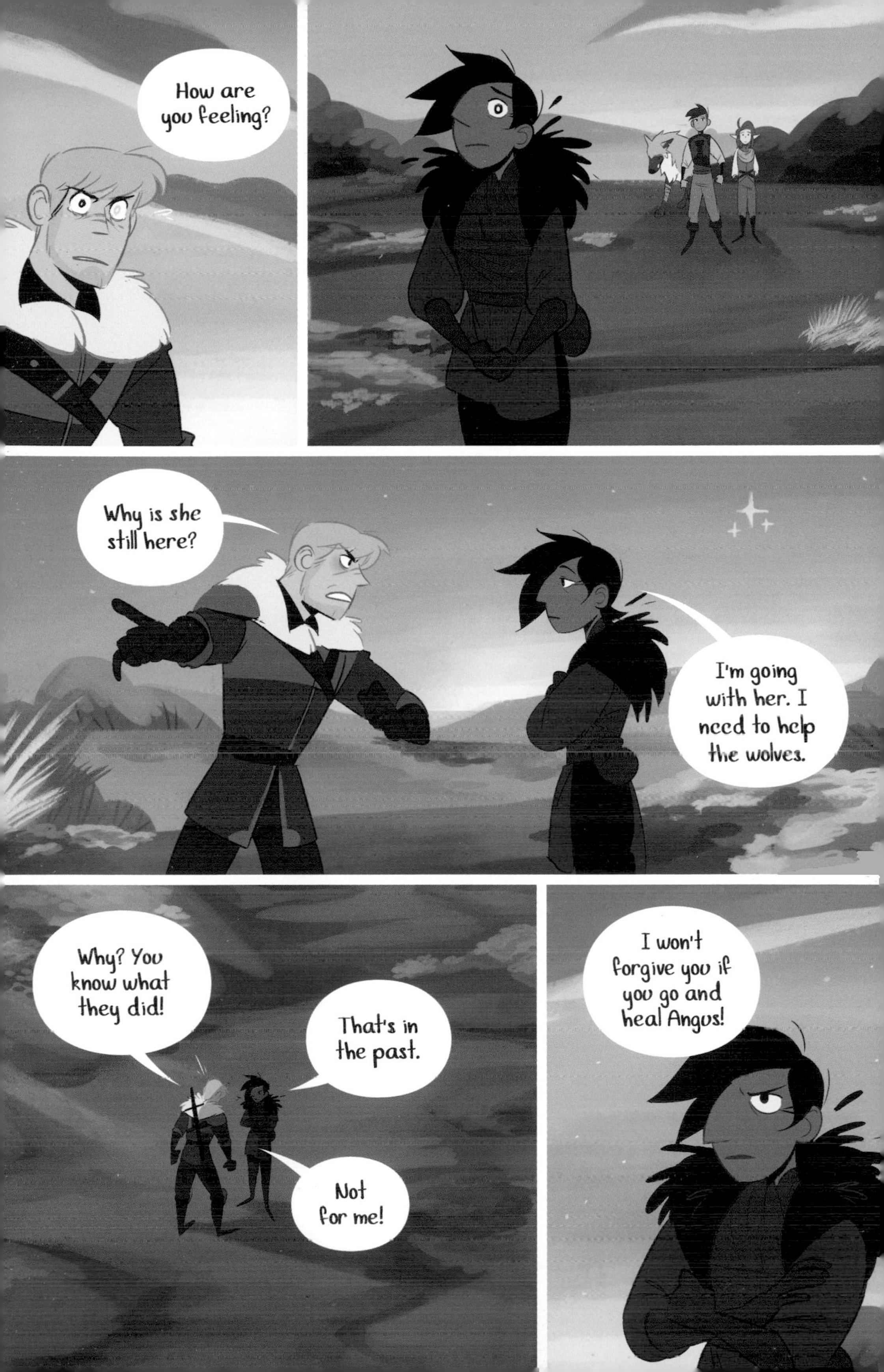
How are you feeling?
Why is she still here?
I'm going with her. I need to help the wolves.
Why? You know what they did!
That's in the past.
Not for me!
I won't forgive you if you go and heal Angus!

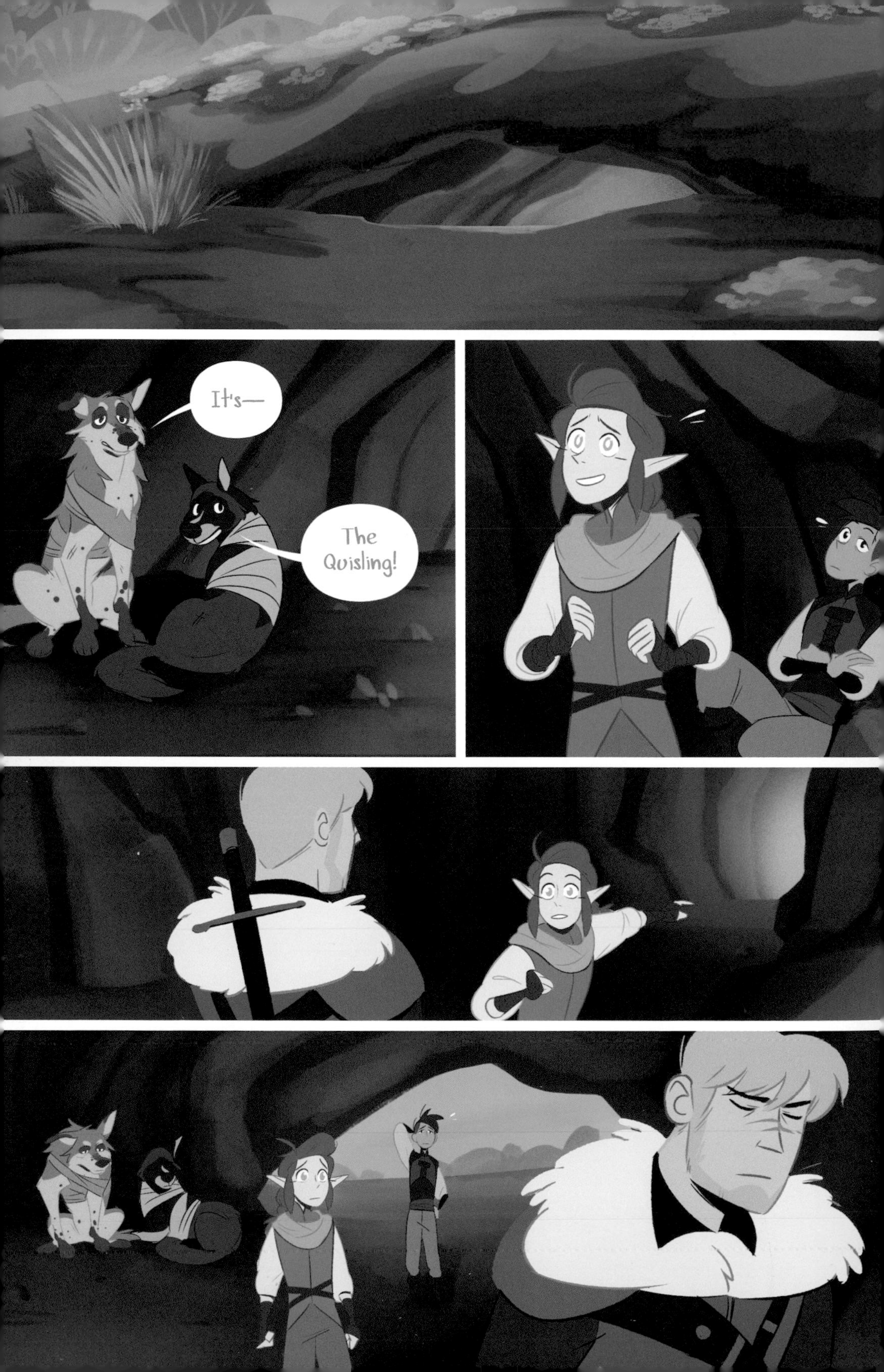
It's—
The Quisling!

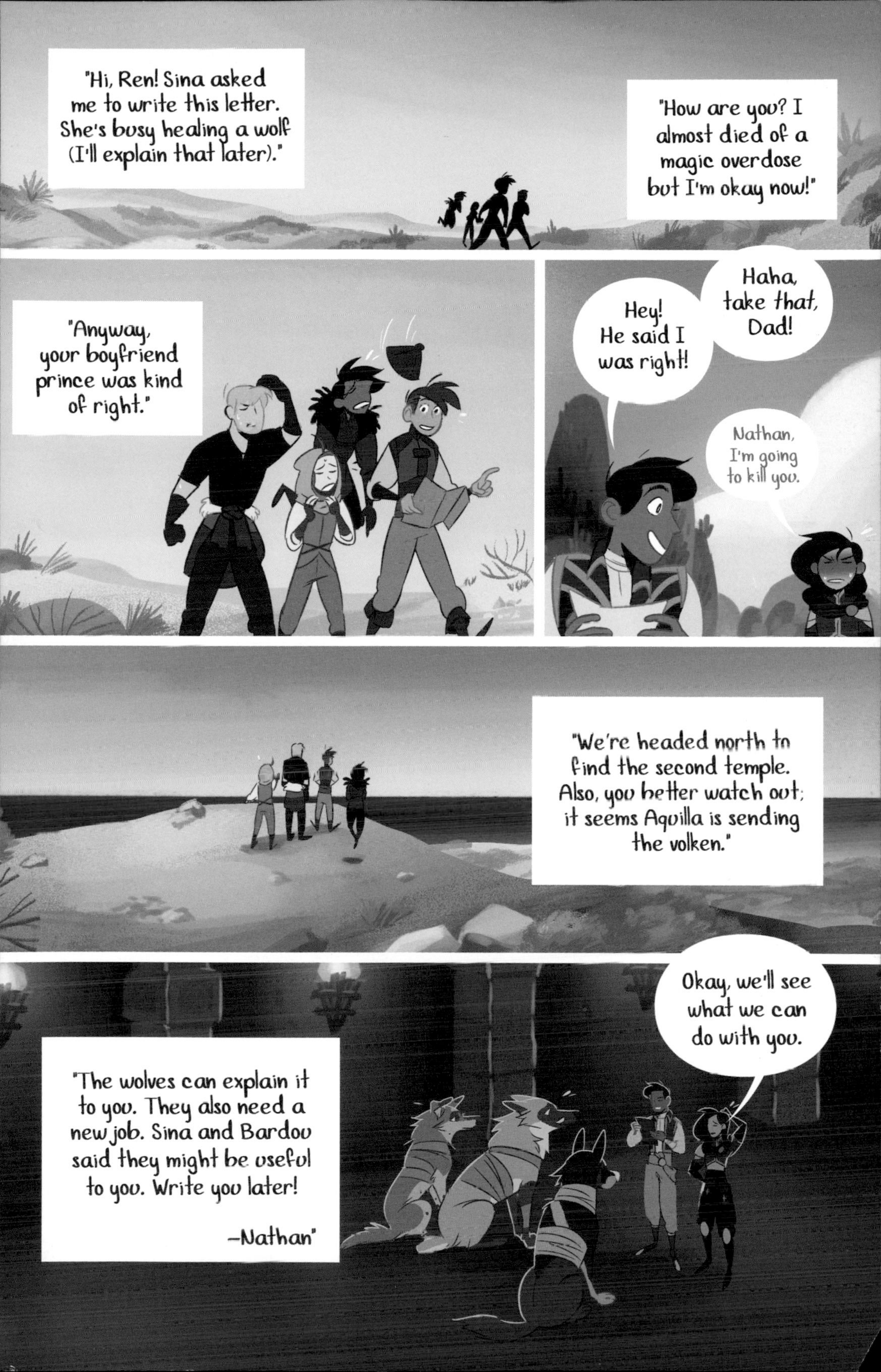
"Hi, Ren! Sina asked me to write this letter. She's busy healing a wolf (I'll explain that later)."
"How are you? I almost died of a magic overdose but I'm okay now!"
"Anyway, your boyfriend prince was kind of right."
Hey! He said I was right!
Haha, take that, Dad!
Nathan, I'm going to kill you.
"We're headed north to find the second temple. Also, you better watch out; it seems Aquilla is sending the volken."
"The wolves can explain it to you. They also need a new job. Sina and Bardou said they might be useful to you. Write you later!
–Nathan"
Okay, we'll see what we can do with you.

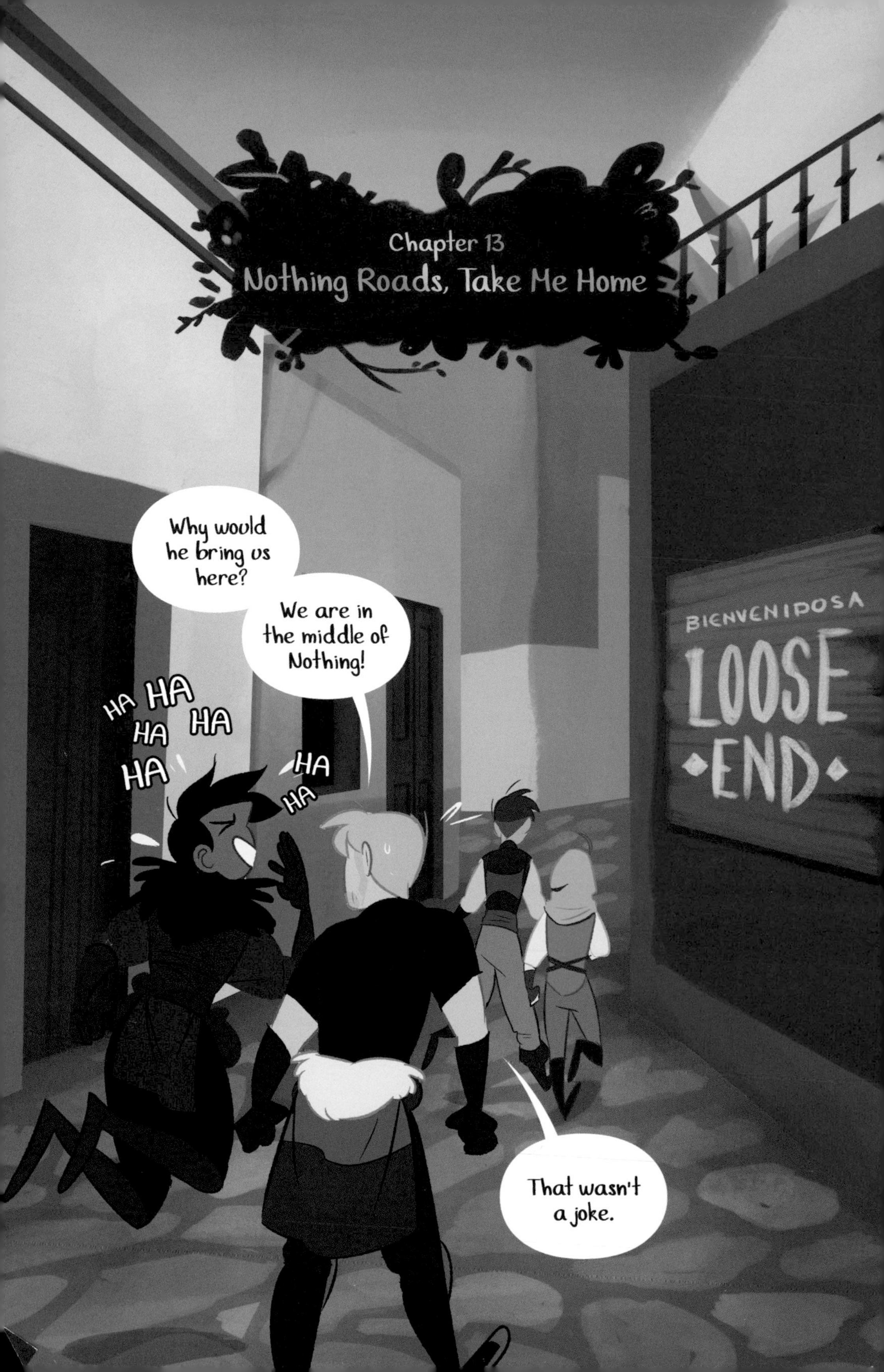

Chapter 13
Nothing Roads, Take Me Home
Why would he bring us here?
We are in the middle of Nothing!
HA HA HA HA HA
HA HA
BIENVENIDOSA
LOOSE END
That wasn't a joke.

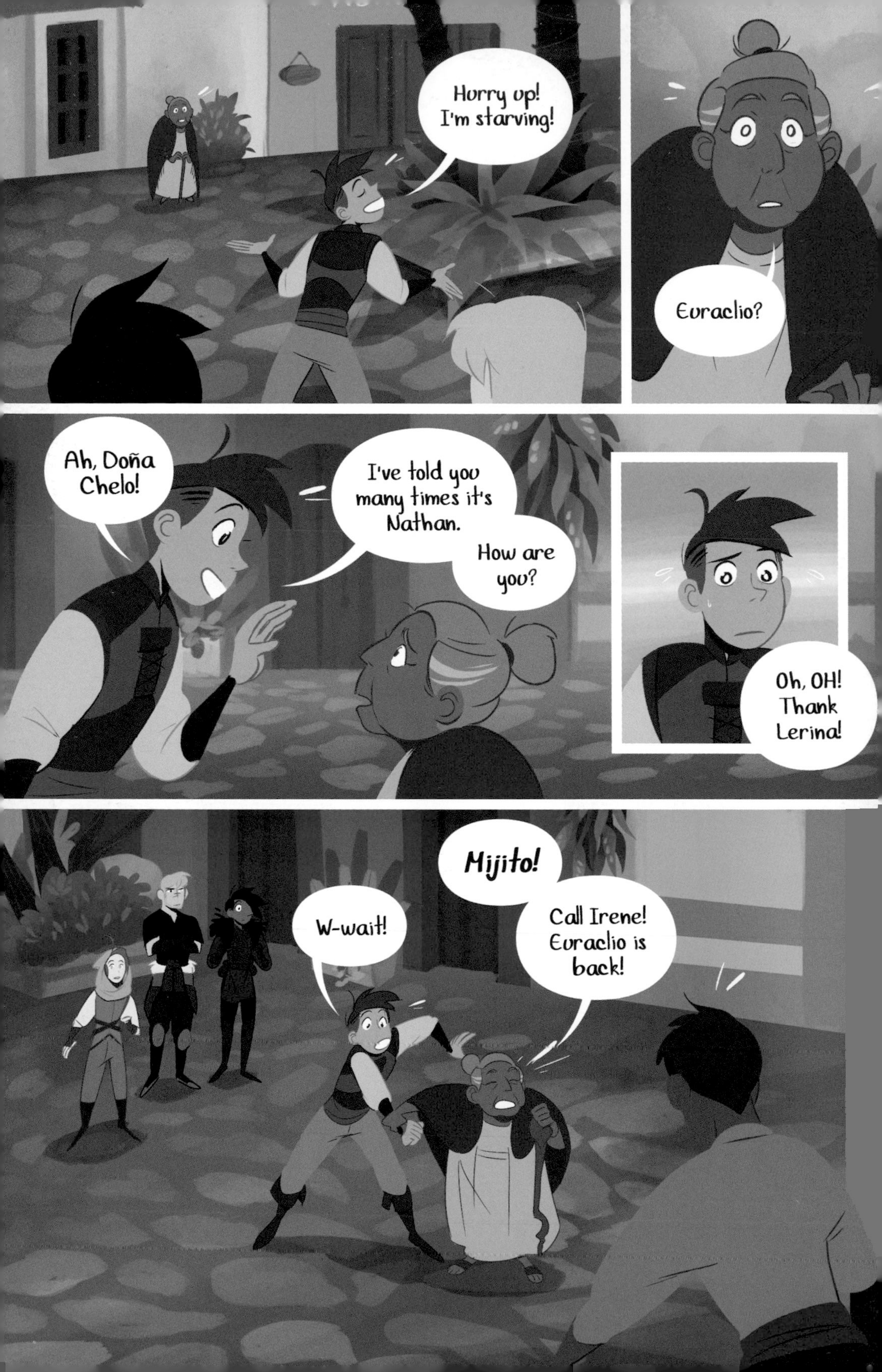
Hurry up!
I'm starving!
Euraclio?
Ah, Doña
Chelo!
I've told you
many times it's
Nathan.
How are
you?
Oh, OH!
Thank
Lerina!
Mijito!
W-wait!
Call Irene!
Euraclio is
back!

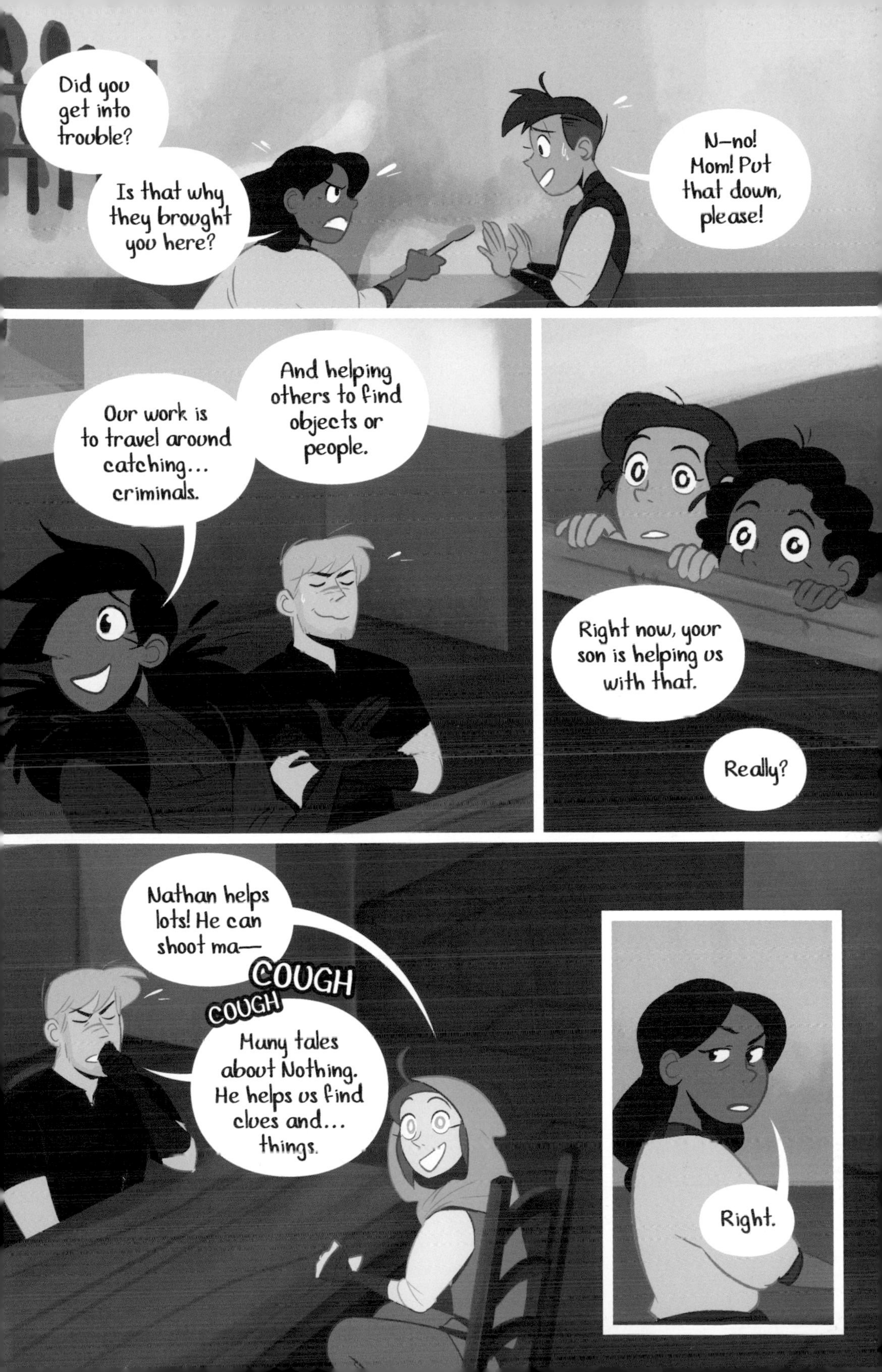
Did you get into trouble?
Is that why they brought you here?
N—no! Mom! Put that down, please!
Our work is to travel around catching... criminals.
And helping others to find objects or people.
Right now, your son is helping us with that.
Really?
Nathan helps lots! He can shoot ma—
COUGH
COUGH
Many tales about Nothing. He helps us find clues and... things.
Right.

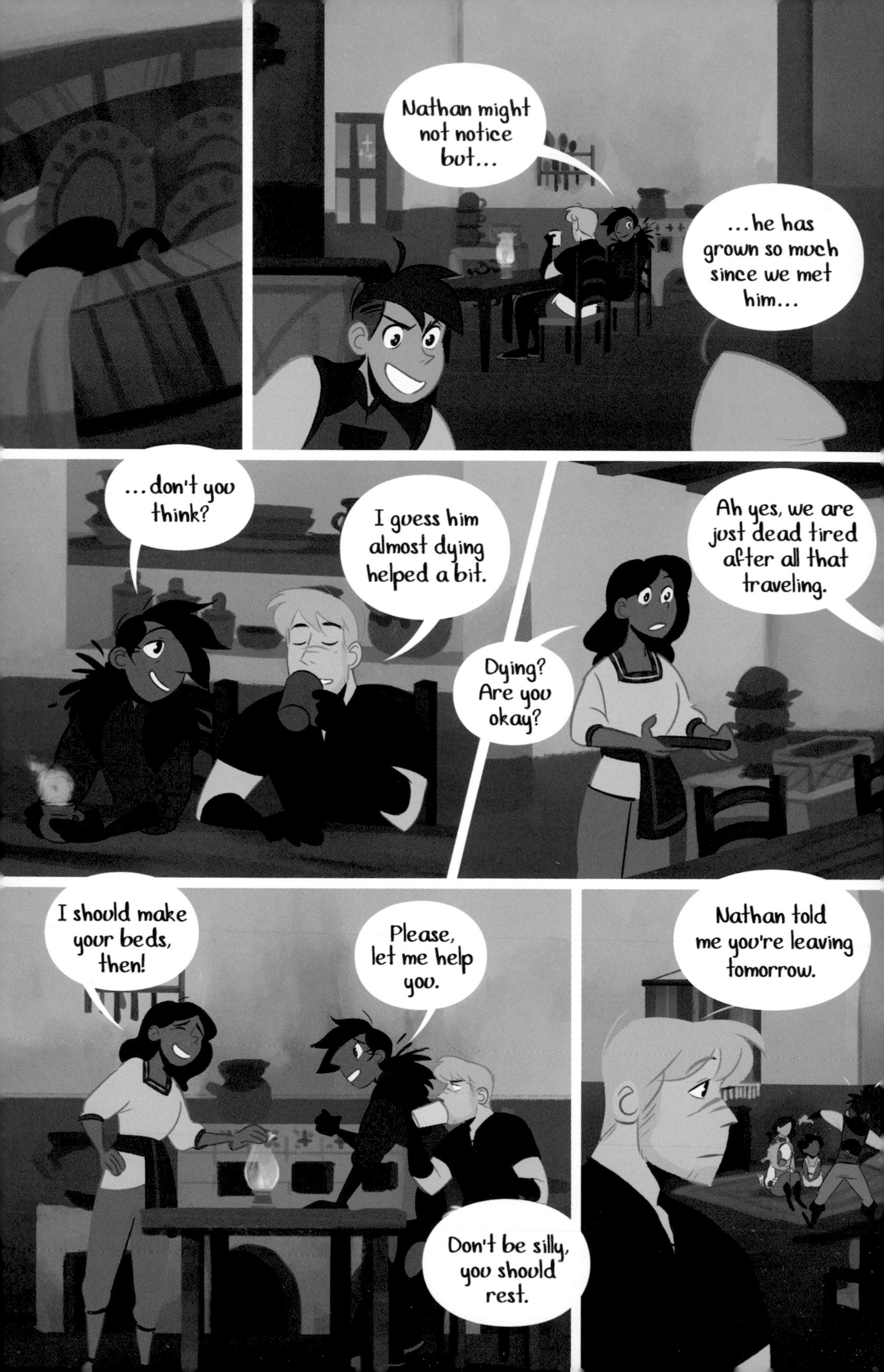
Nathan might not notice but...
...he has grown so much since we met him...
...don't you think?
I guess him almost dying helped a bit.
Dying? Are you okay?
Ah yes, we are just dead tired after all that traveling.
I should make your beds, then!
Please, let me help you.
Don't be silly, you should rest.
Nathan told me you're leaving tomorrow.

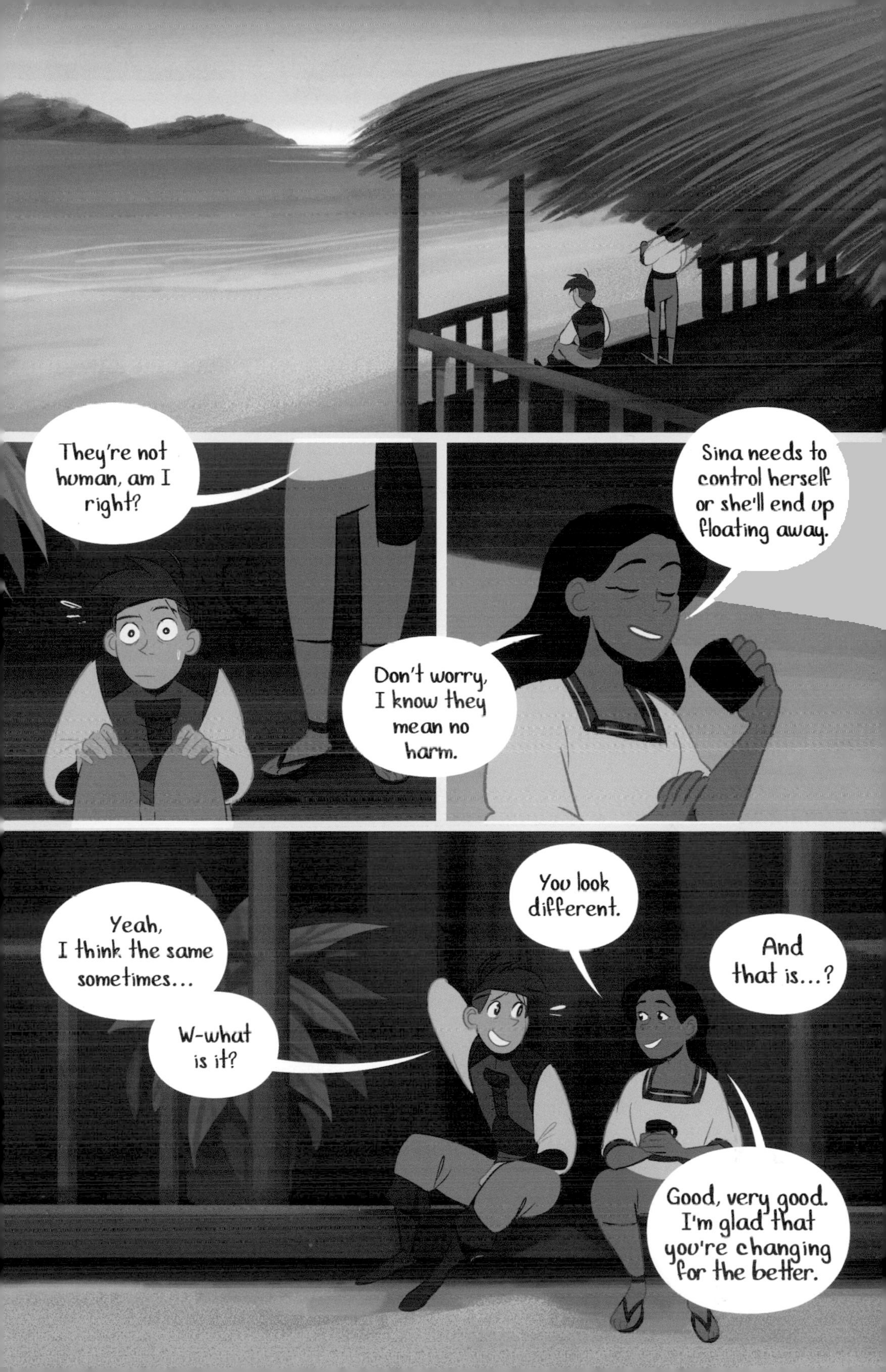
They're not human, am I right?
Sina needs to control herself or she'll end up floating away.
Don't worry, I know they mean no harm.
Yeah, I think the same sometimes...
W-what is it?
You look different.
And that is...?
Good, very good. I'm glad that you're changing for the better.

END OF CHAPTER 13

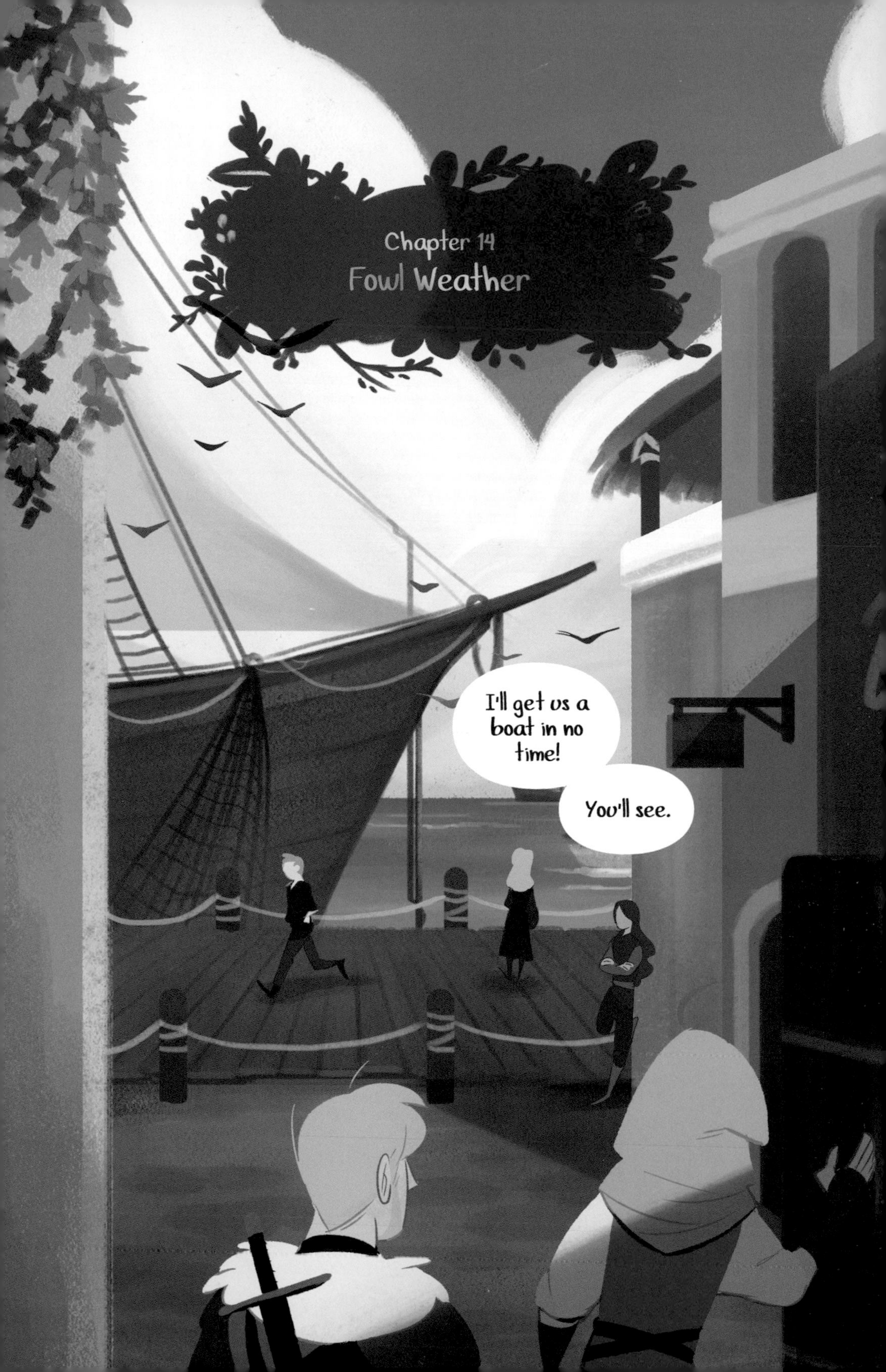
Chapter 14
Fowl Weather
I'll get us a boat in no time!
You'll see.

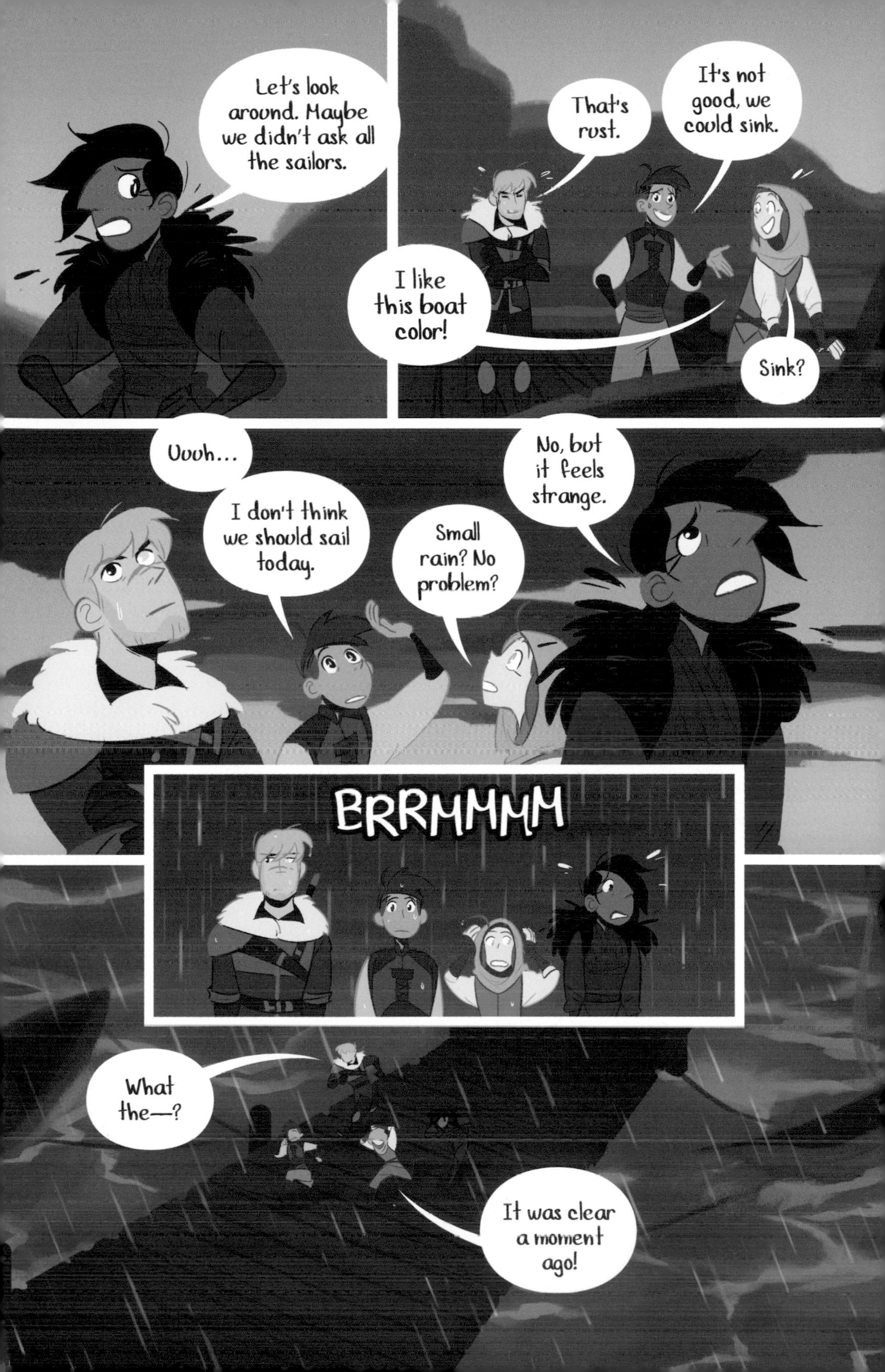
Let's look around. Maybe we didn't ask all the sailors.
That's rust.
It's not good, we could sink.
I like this boat color!
Sink?
Uuuh...
I don't think we should sail today.
Small rain? No problem?
No, but it feels strange.
BRRMMMM
What the—?
It was clear a moment ago!

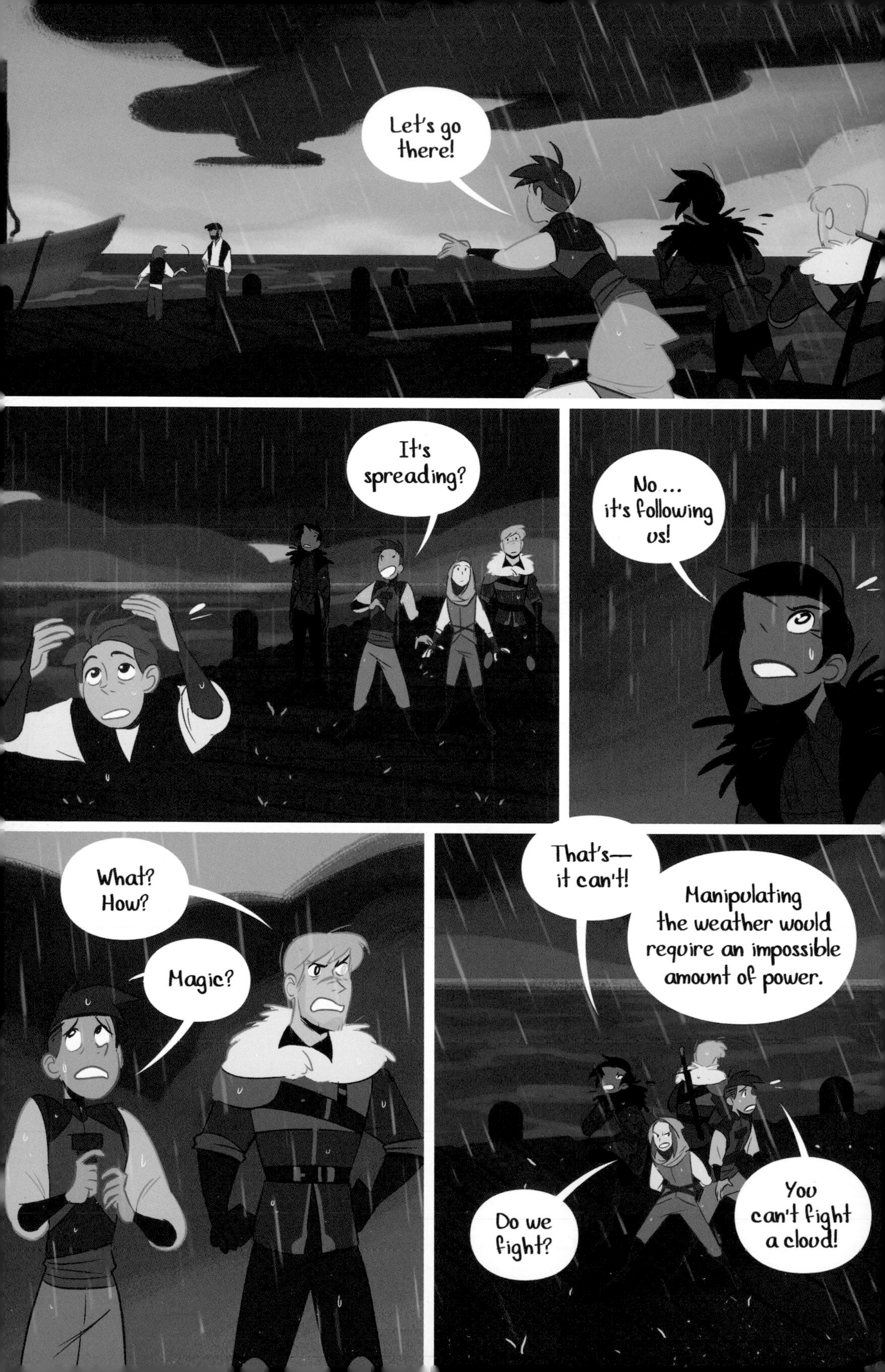

Let's go there!
It's spreading?
No ... it's following us!
What? How?
Magic?
That's— it can't!
Manipulating the weather would require an impossible amount of power.
Do we fight?
You can't fight a cloud!

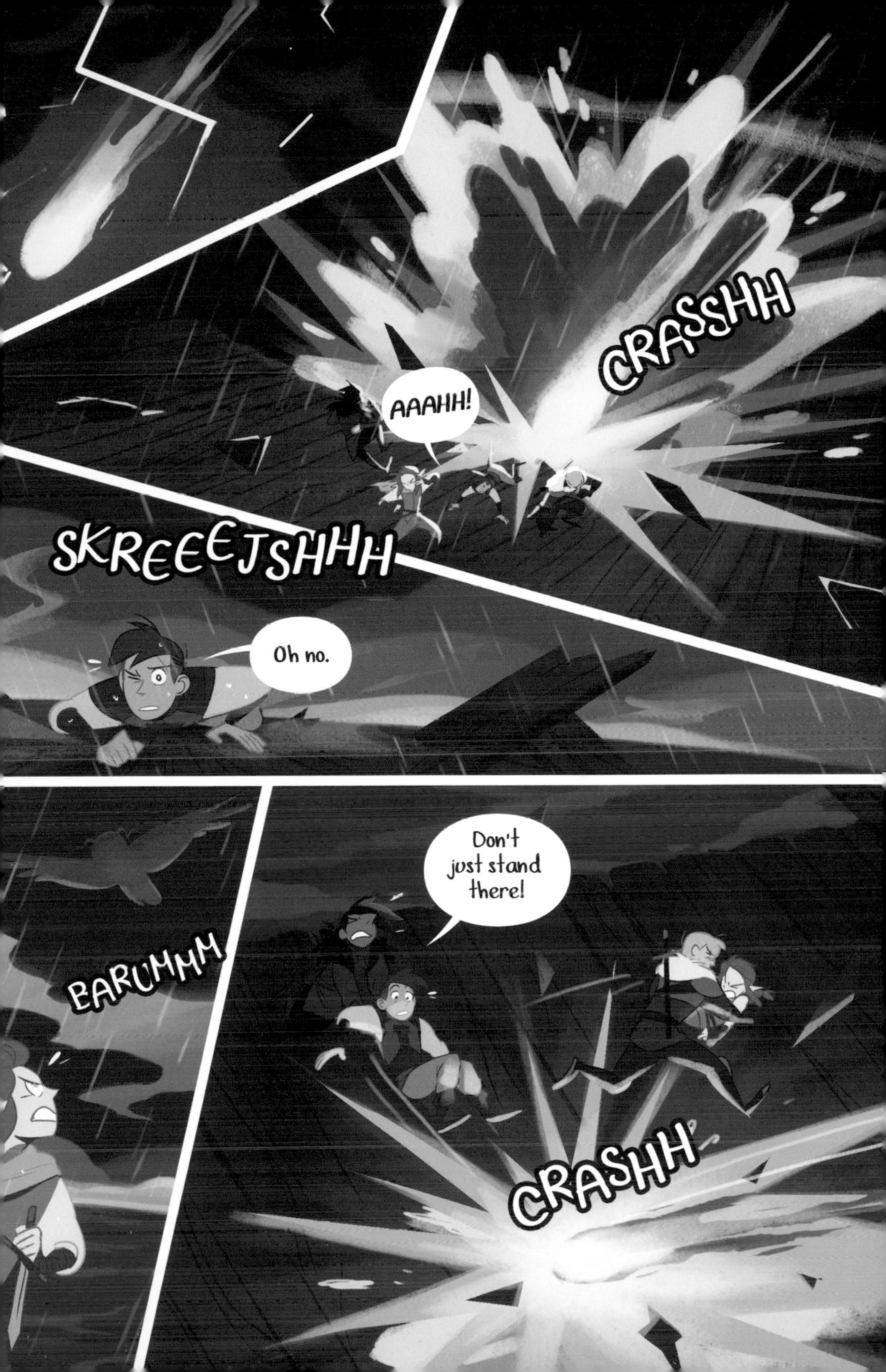
CRASSHH
AAAHH!
SKREEEJSHHH
Oh no.
Don't just stand there!
BARUMMM
CRASHH

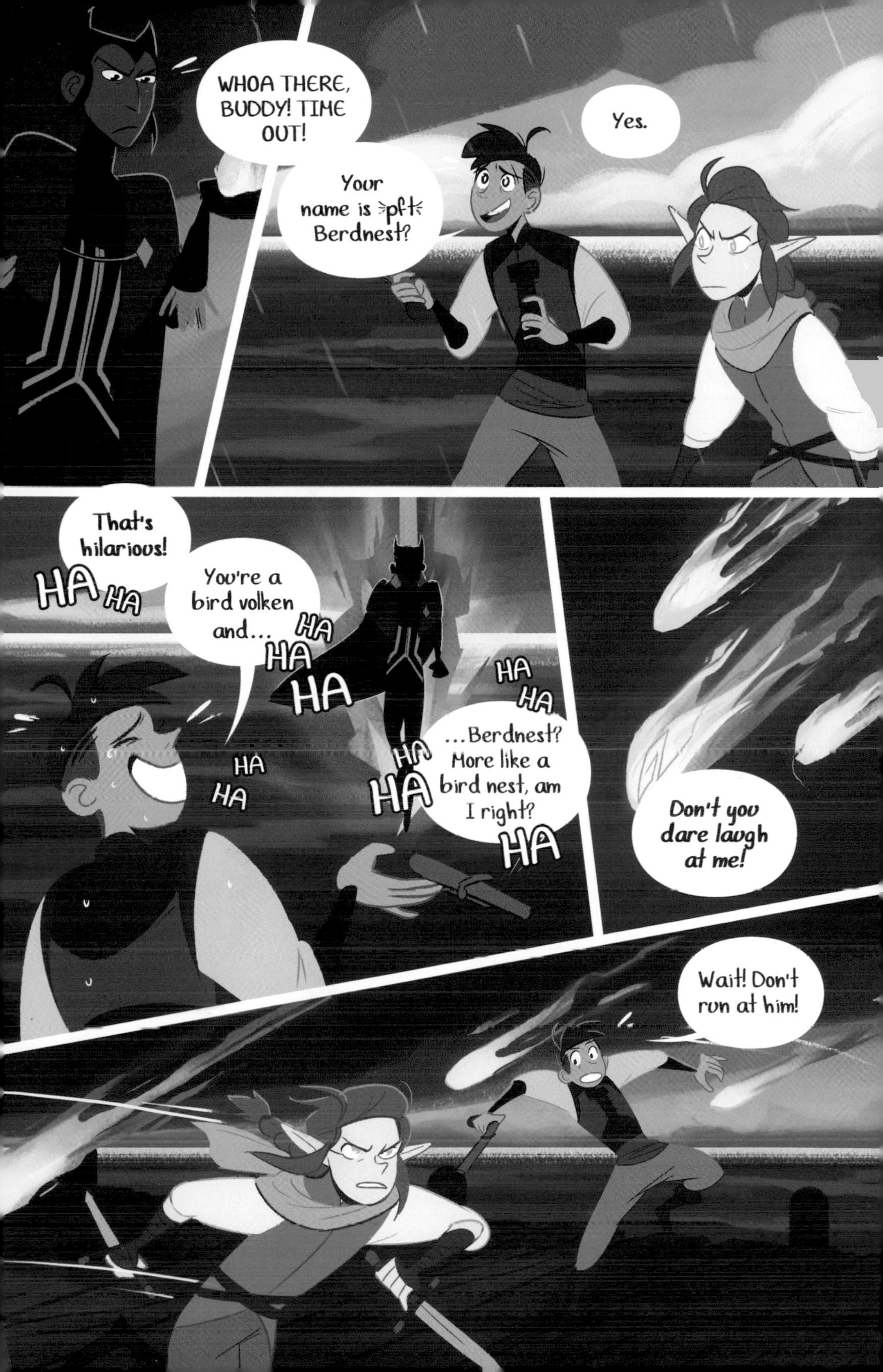
WHOA THERE, BUDDY! TIME OUT!
Yes.
Your name is pft Berdnest?
That's hilarious!
HA HA
You're a bird volken and... HA HA HA
HA HA
HA HA
HA HA
...Berdnest? More like a bird nest, am I right? HA
Don't you dare laugh at me!
Wait! Don't run at him!

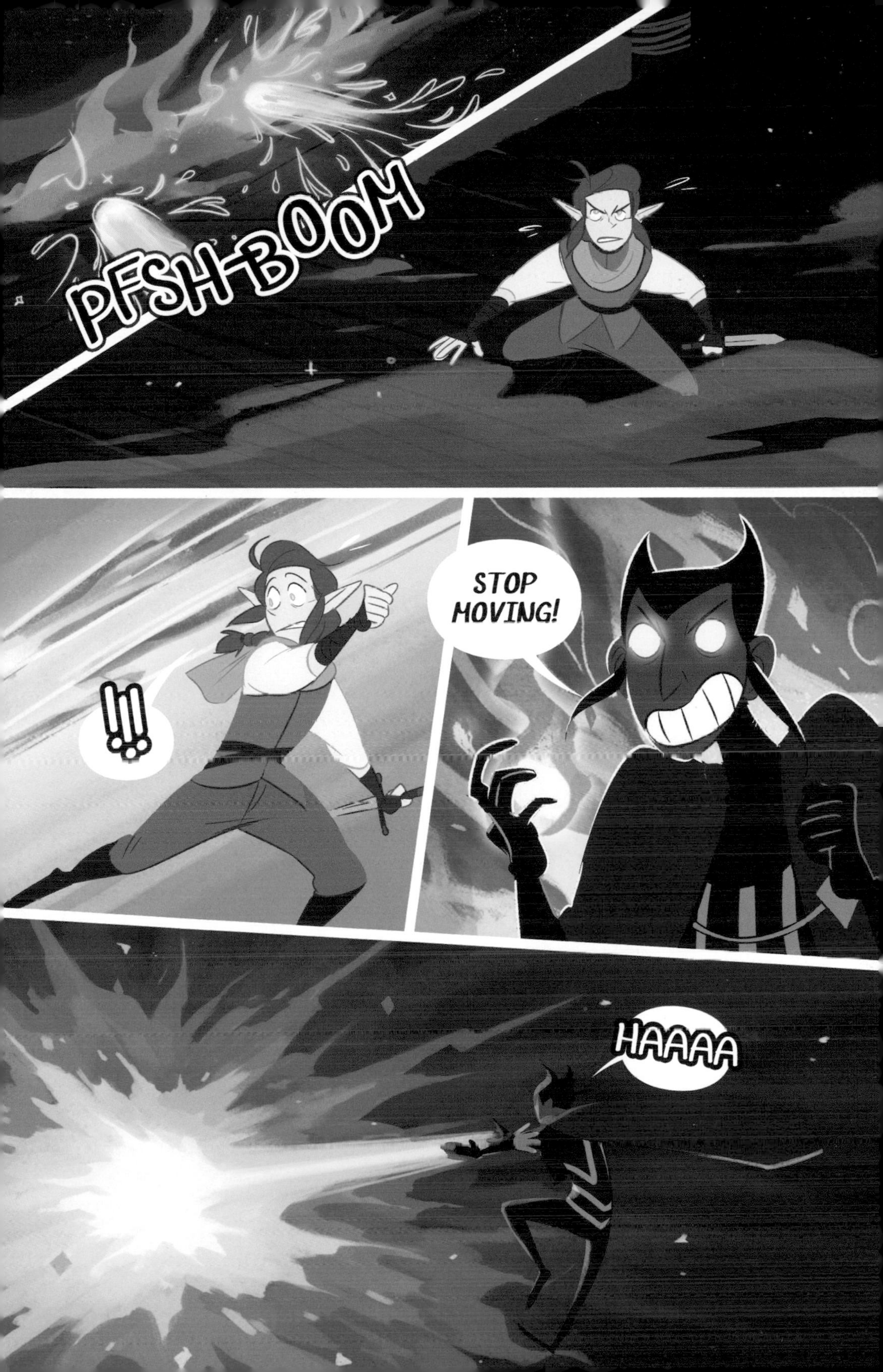
PFSH-BOOM
!!!
STOP MOVING!
HAAAA

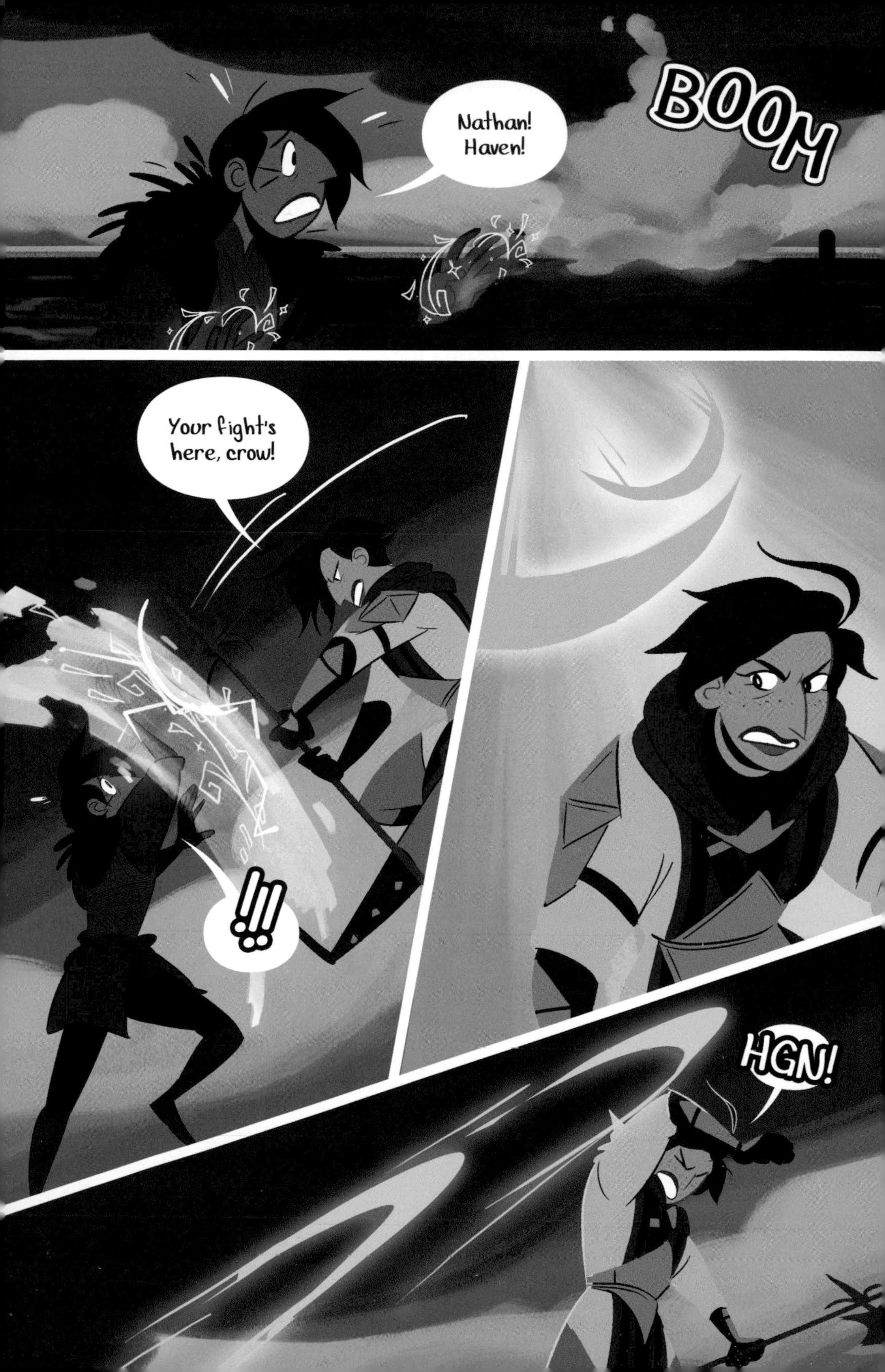
Nathan!
Haven!
BOOM
Your fight's here, crow!
!!!
HGN!

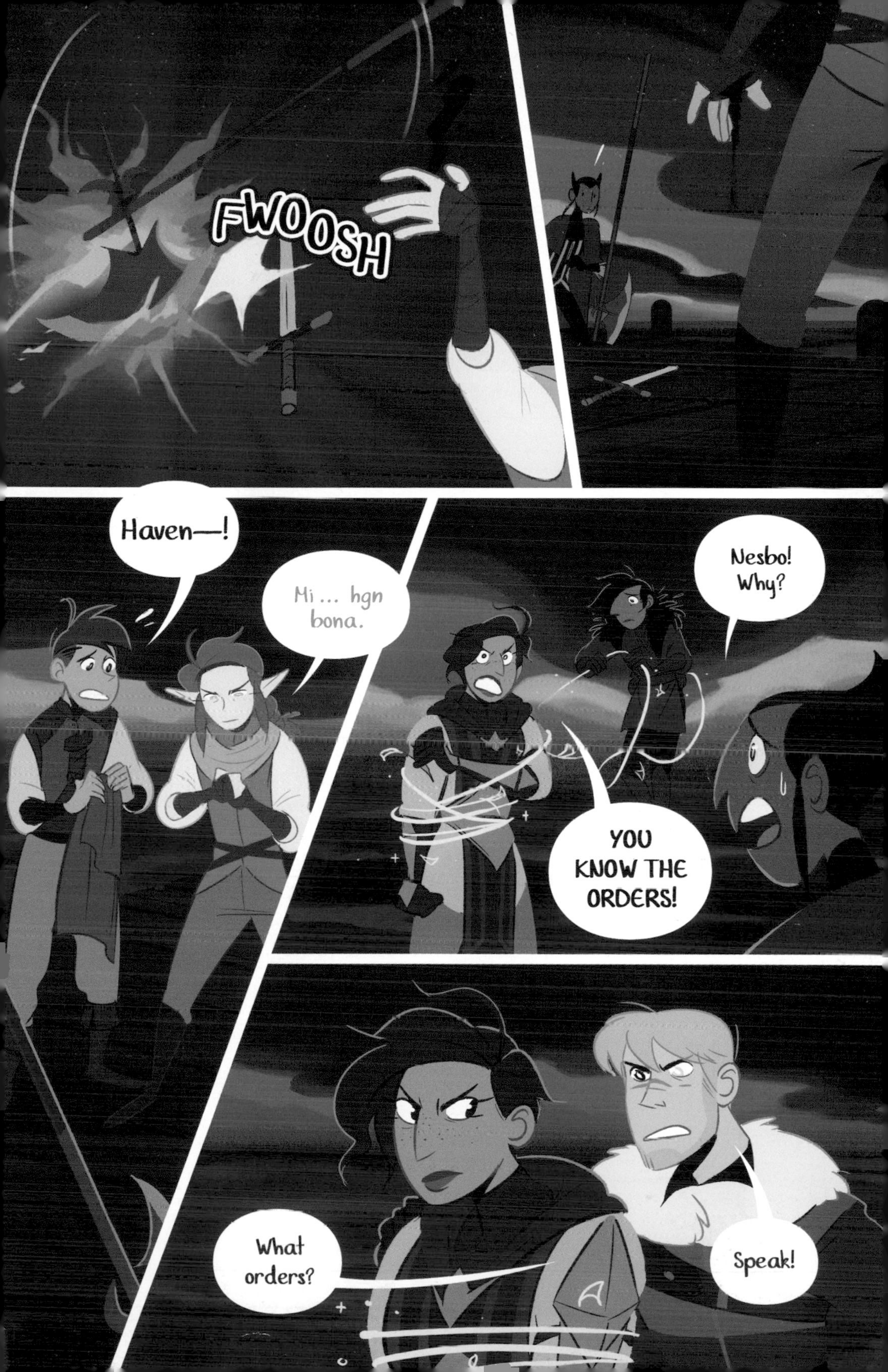
FWOOSH
Haven—!
Mi ... hgn bona.
Nesbo! Why?
YOU KNOW THE ORDERS!
What orders?
Speak!

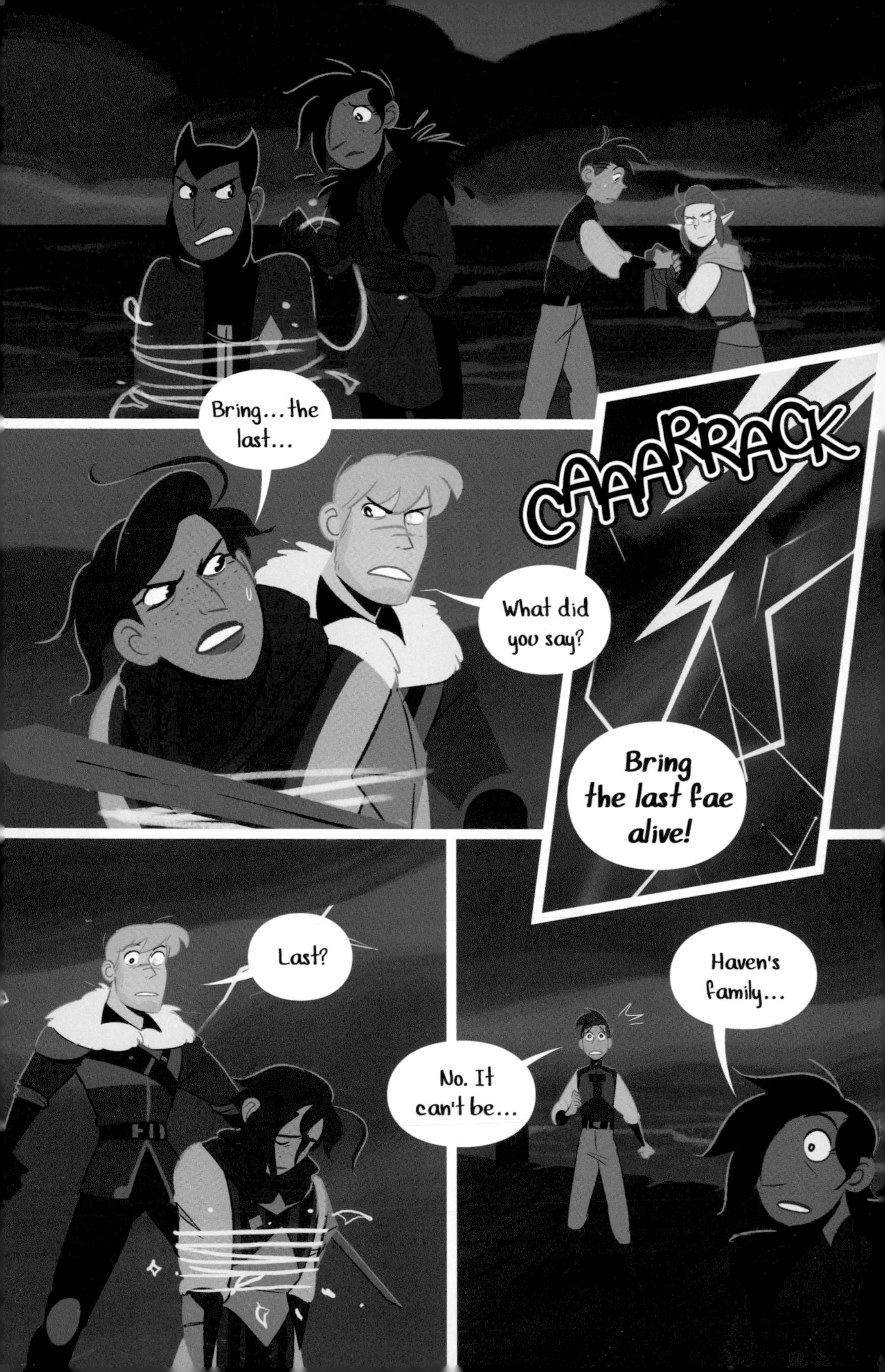
Bring... the last...
What did you say?
CAAARRACK
Bring the last fae alive!
Last?
Haven's family...
No. It can't be...

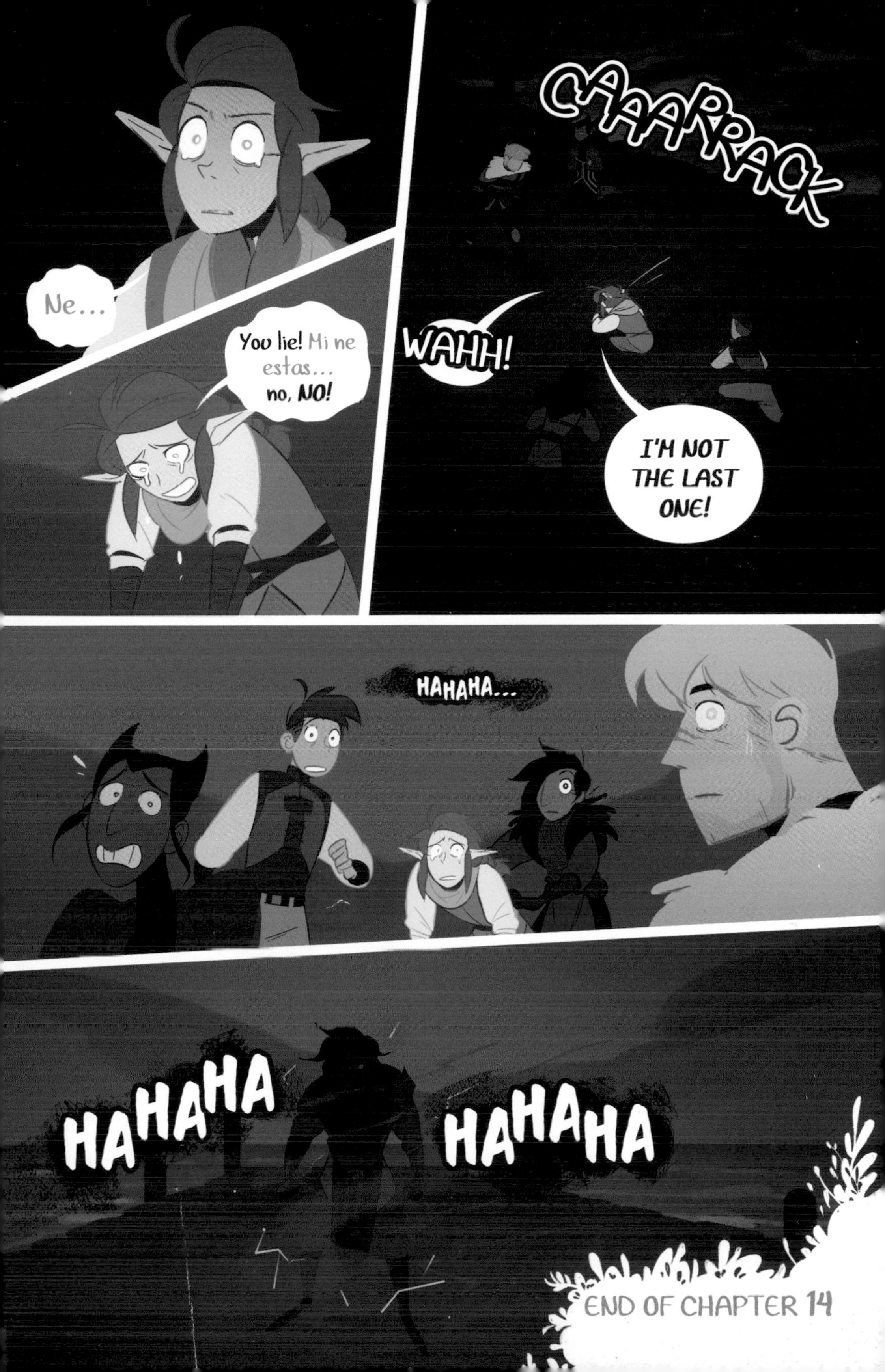
Ne...
You lie! Mi ne estas... no, NO!
CAAARRACK
WAHH!
I'M NOT THE LAST ONE!
HAHAHA...
HAHAHA
HAHAHA
END OF CHAPTER 14

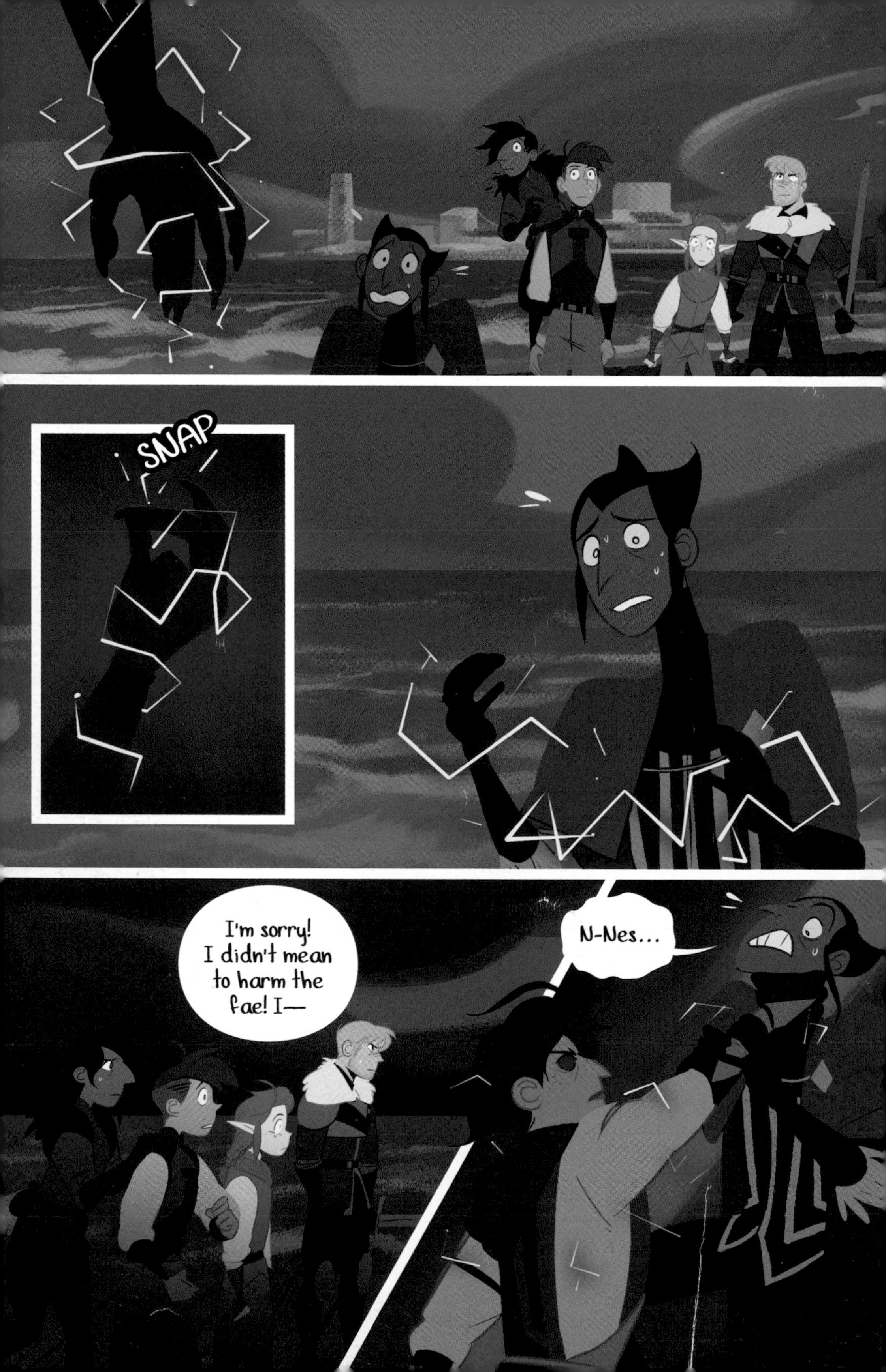
SNAP
I'm sorry! I didn't mean to harm the fae! I—
N-Nes...

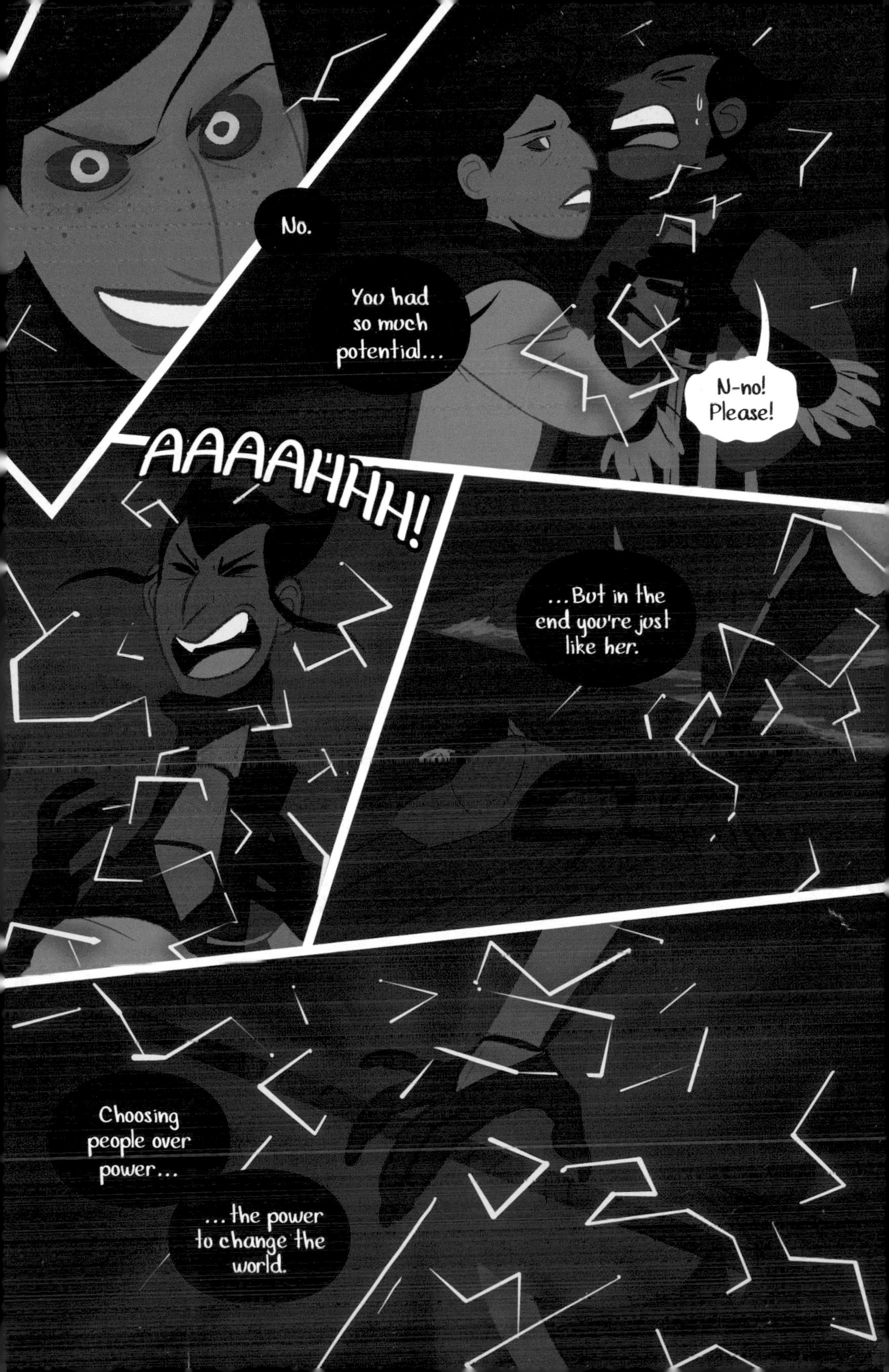
No.
You had so much potential...
N-no! Please!
AAAAAHHHH!
...But in the end you're just like her.
Choosing people over power...
...the power to change the world.

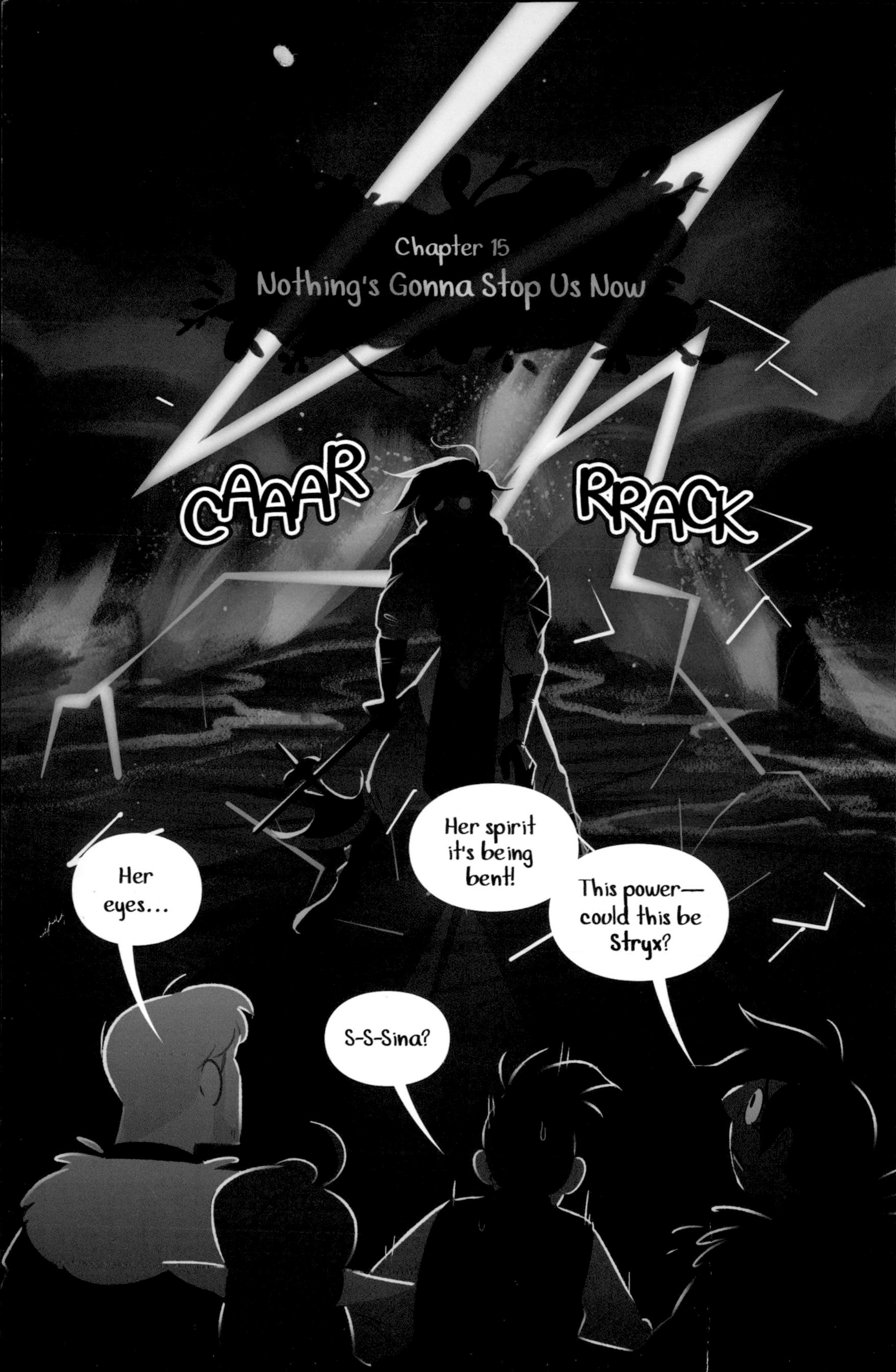
Chapter 15
Nothing's Gonna Stop Us Now
CAAAR
RRACK
Her eyes...
Her spirit it's being bent!
This power—could this be Stryx?
S-S-Sina?

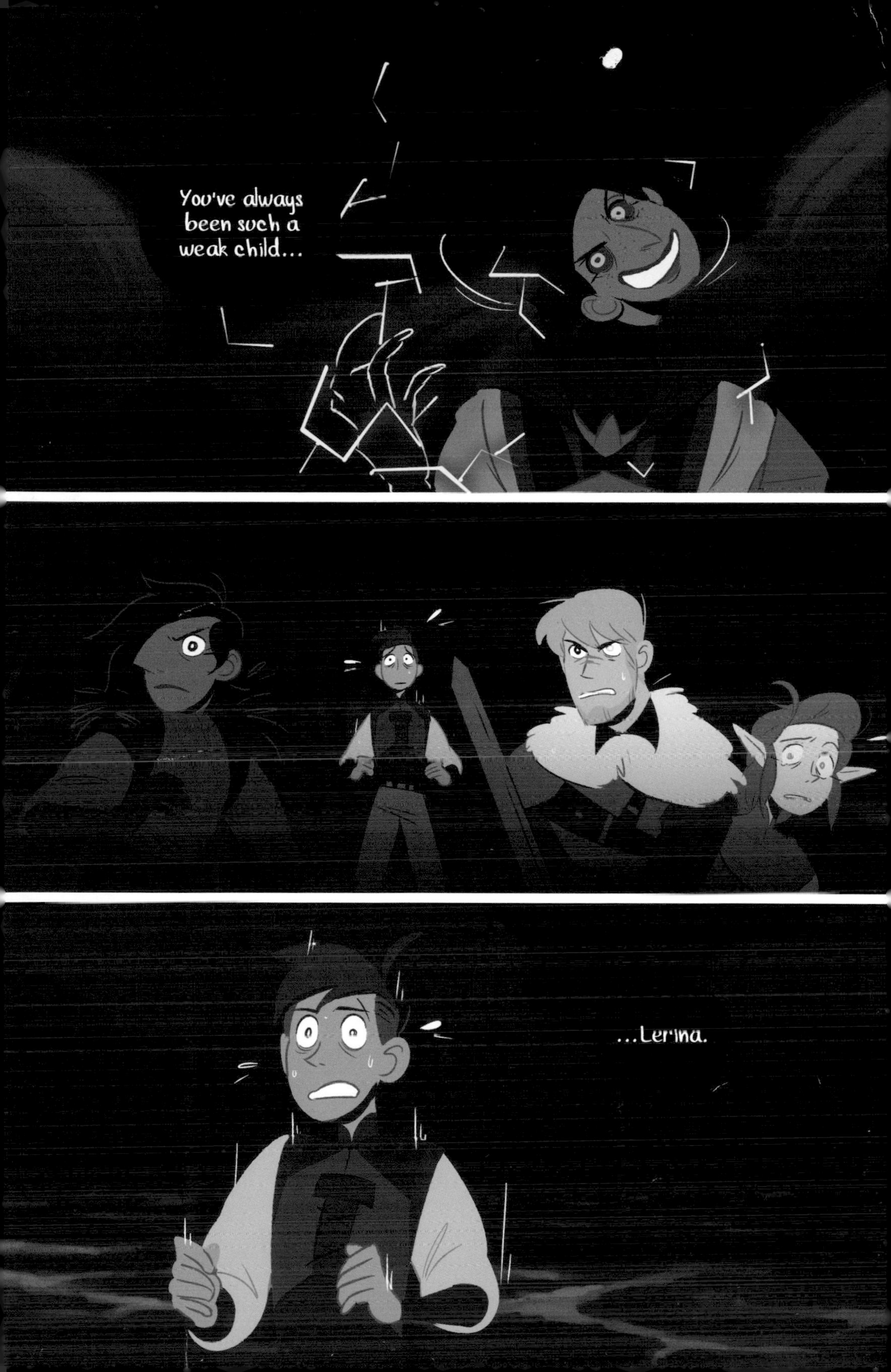
You've always been such a weak child...
...Lerina.

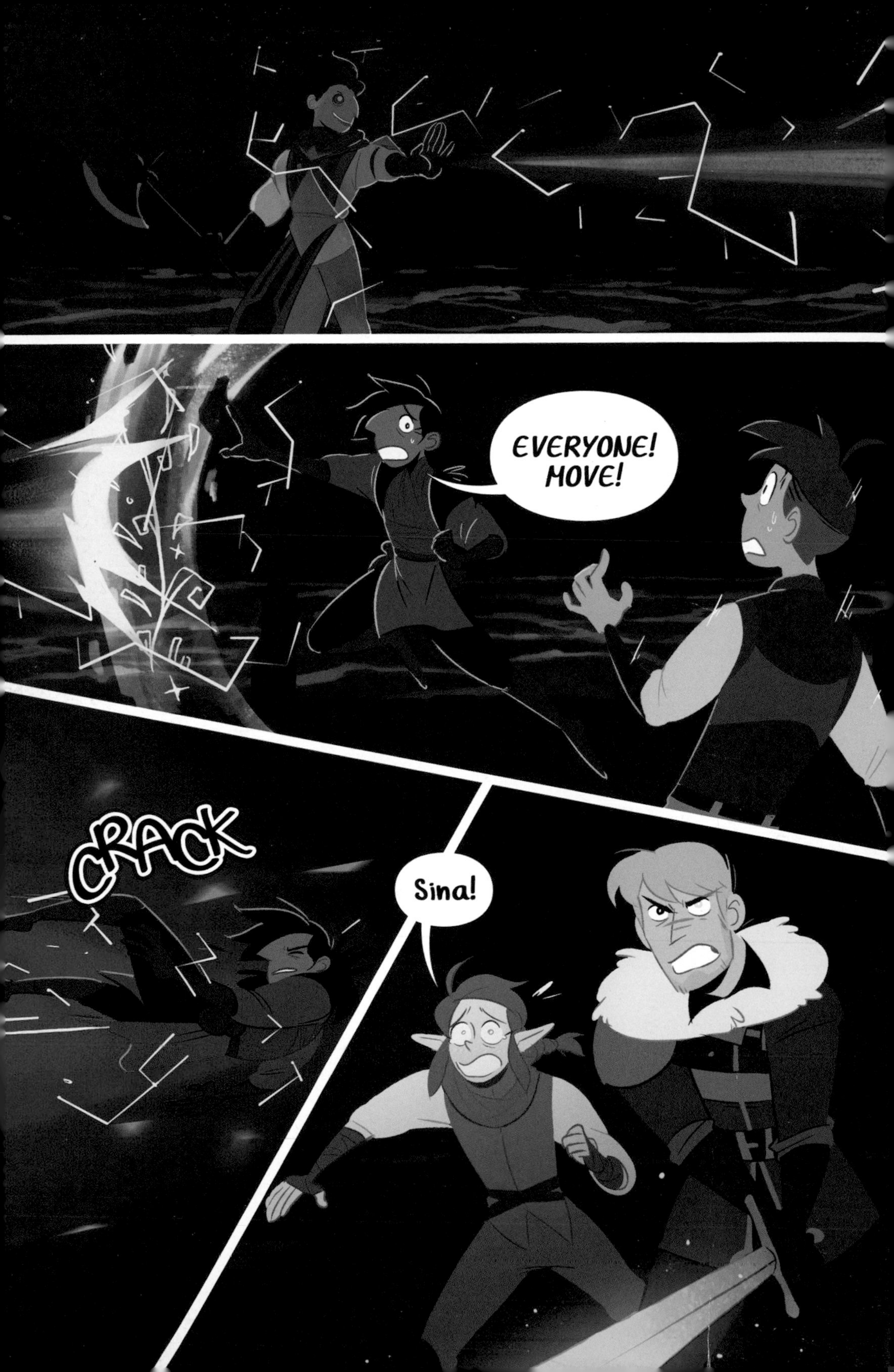
EVERYONE! MOVE!
CRACK
Sina!

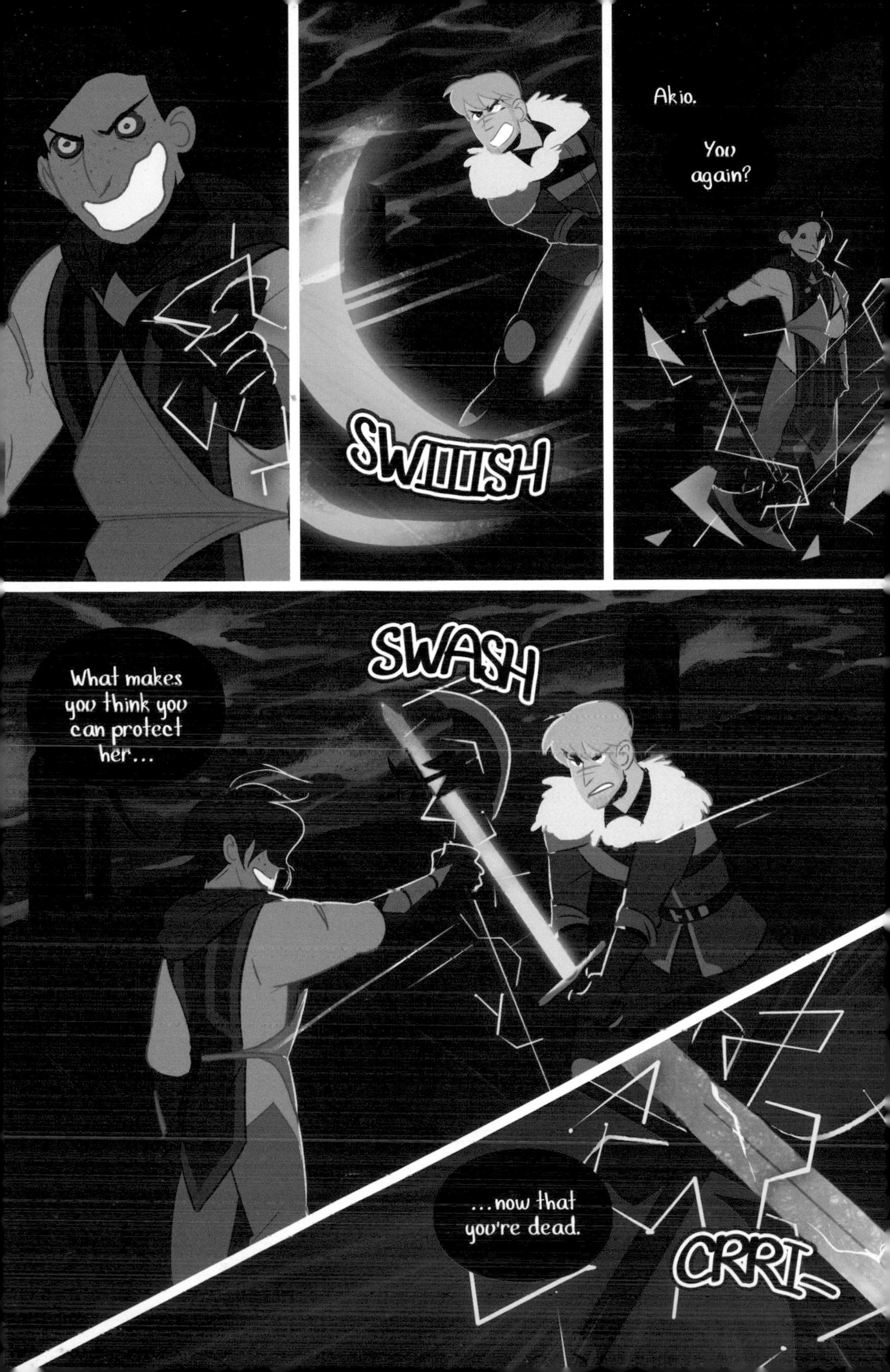
SWIIISH
Akio.
You again?
SWASH
What makes you think you can protect her...
...now that you're dead.
CRRI_

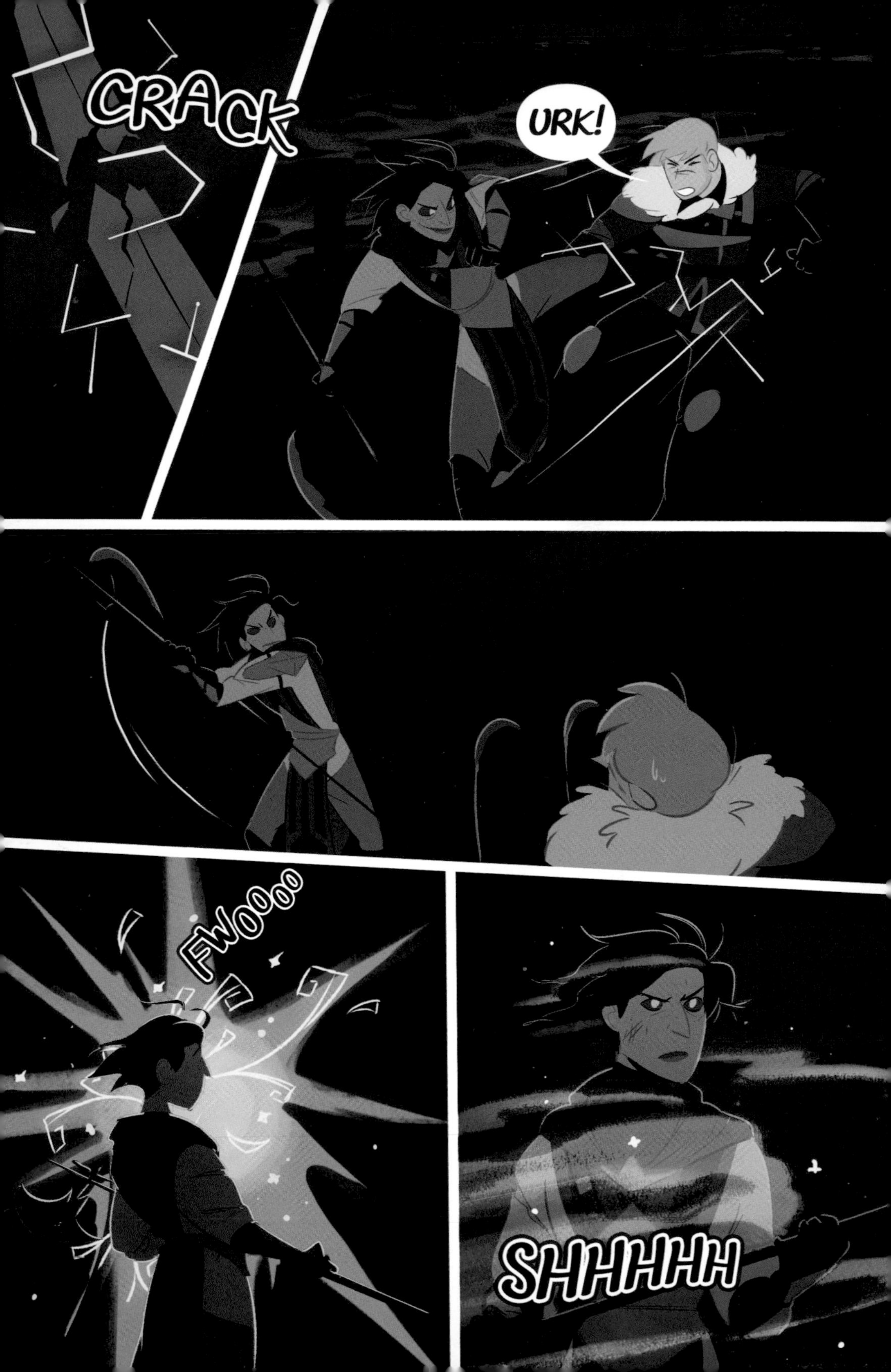
CRACK
URK!
FWOOoo
SHHHHH

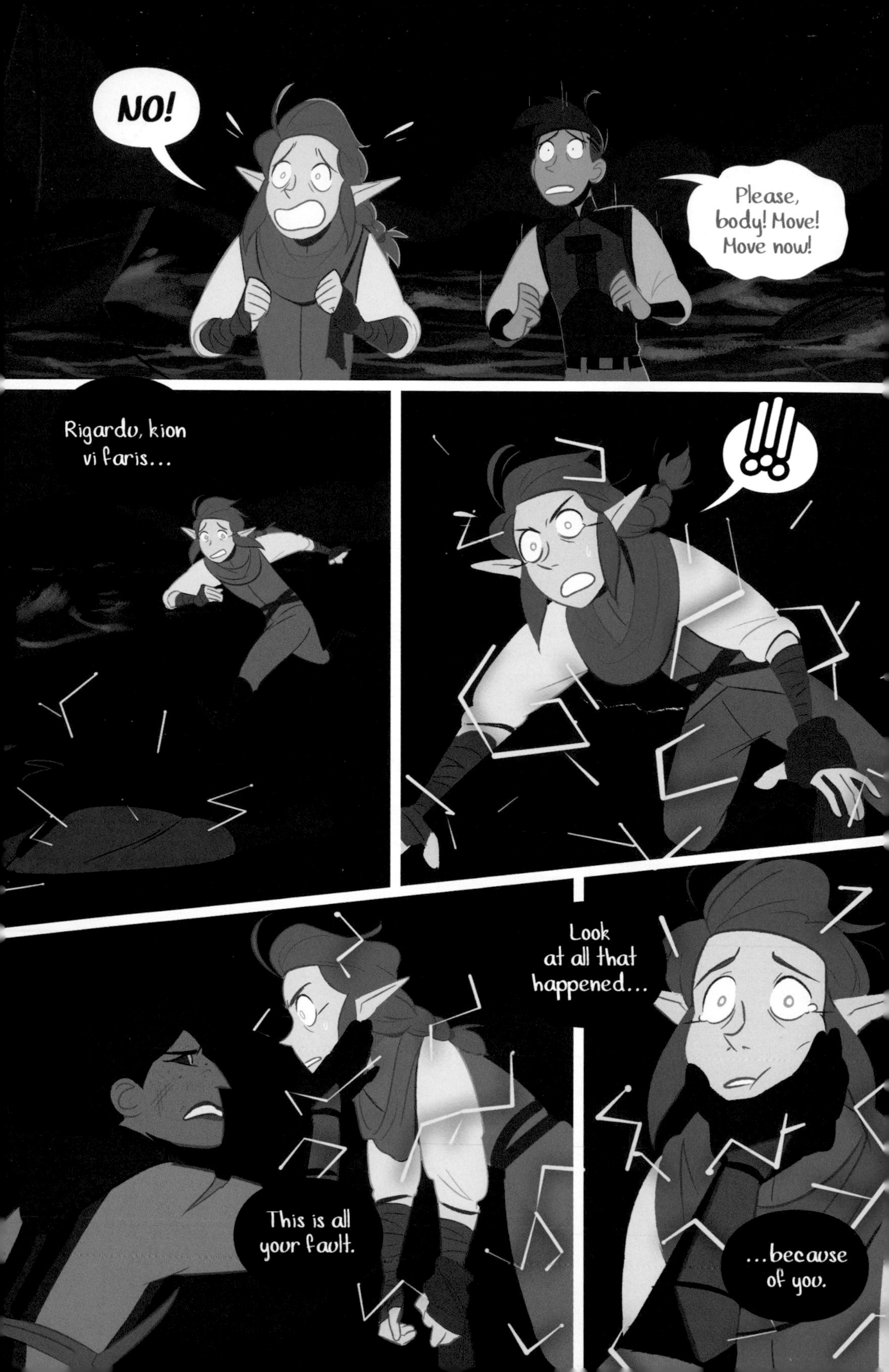
NO!
Please, body! Move! Move now!
Rigardu, kion vi faris...
!!!
Look at all that happened...
This is all your fault.
...because of you.

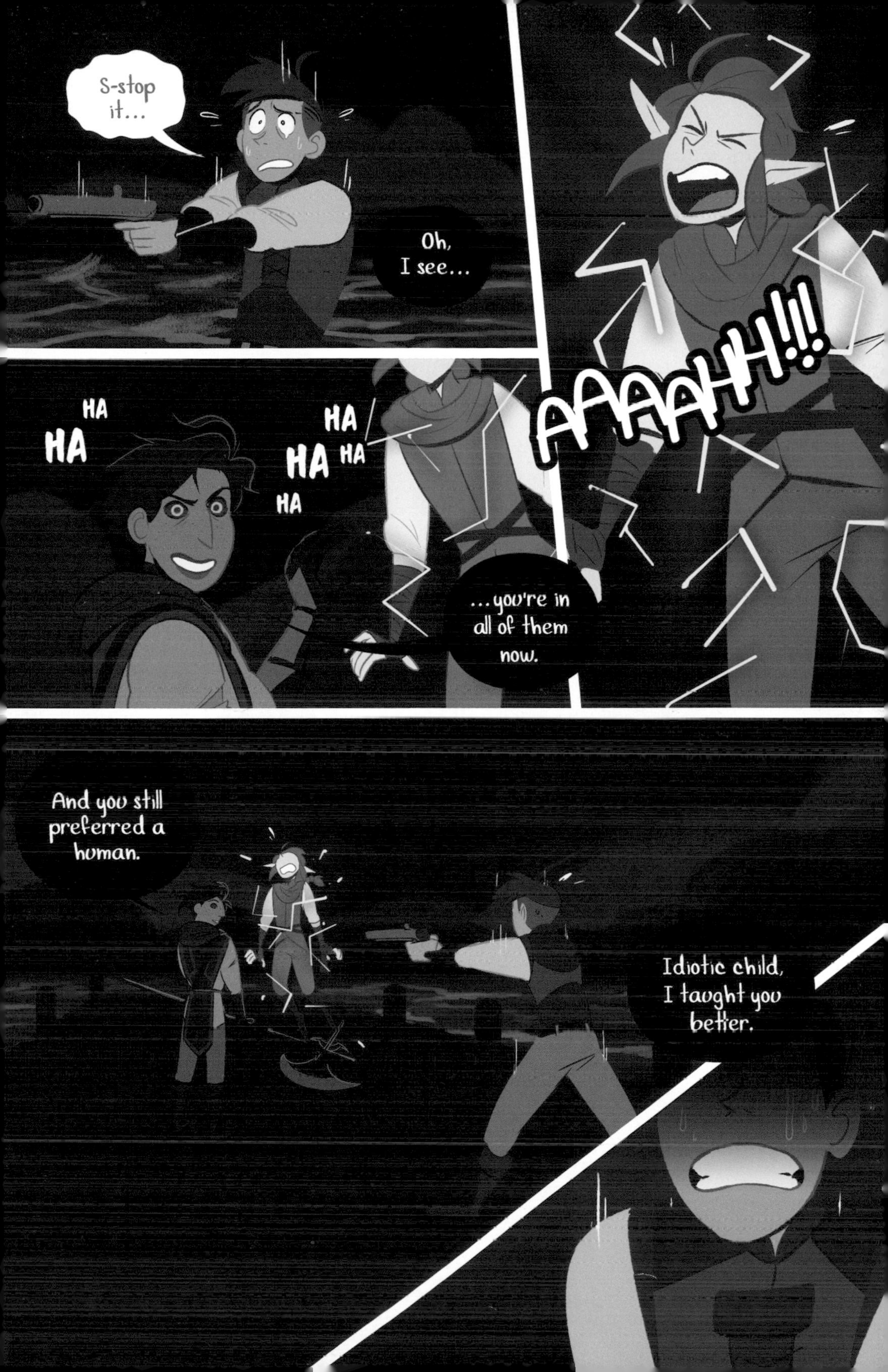
S-stop it...
Oh, I see...
AAAAAHH!!!
HA
HA
HA
HA
HA
HA
...you're in all of them now.
And you still preferred a human.
Idiotic child, I taught you better.

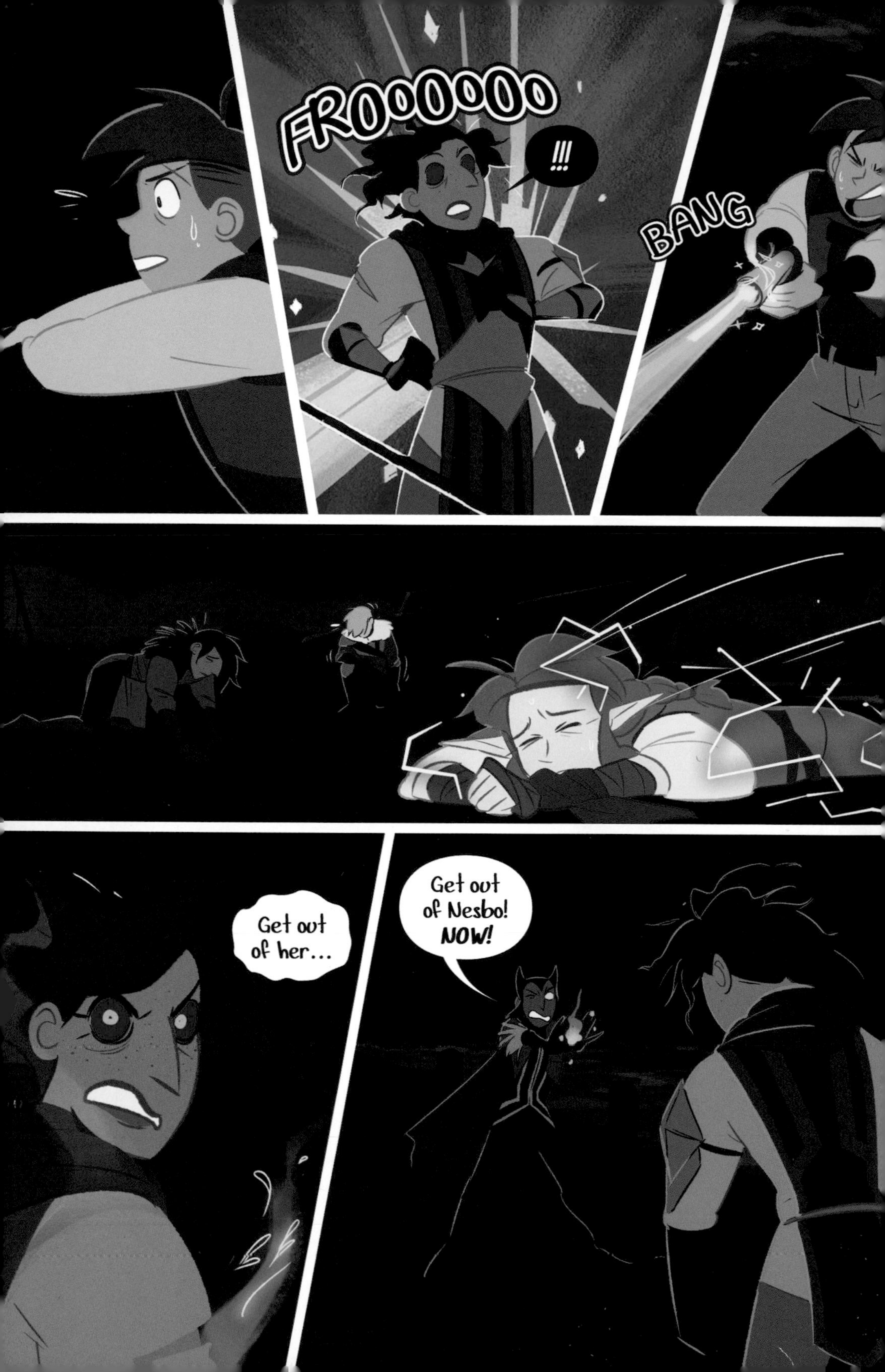
FROOOOOO
!!!
BANG
Get out of her...
Get out of Nesbo! NOW!

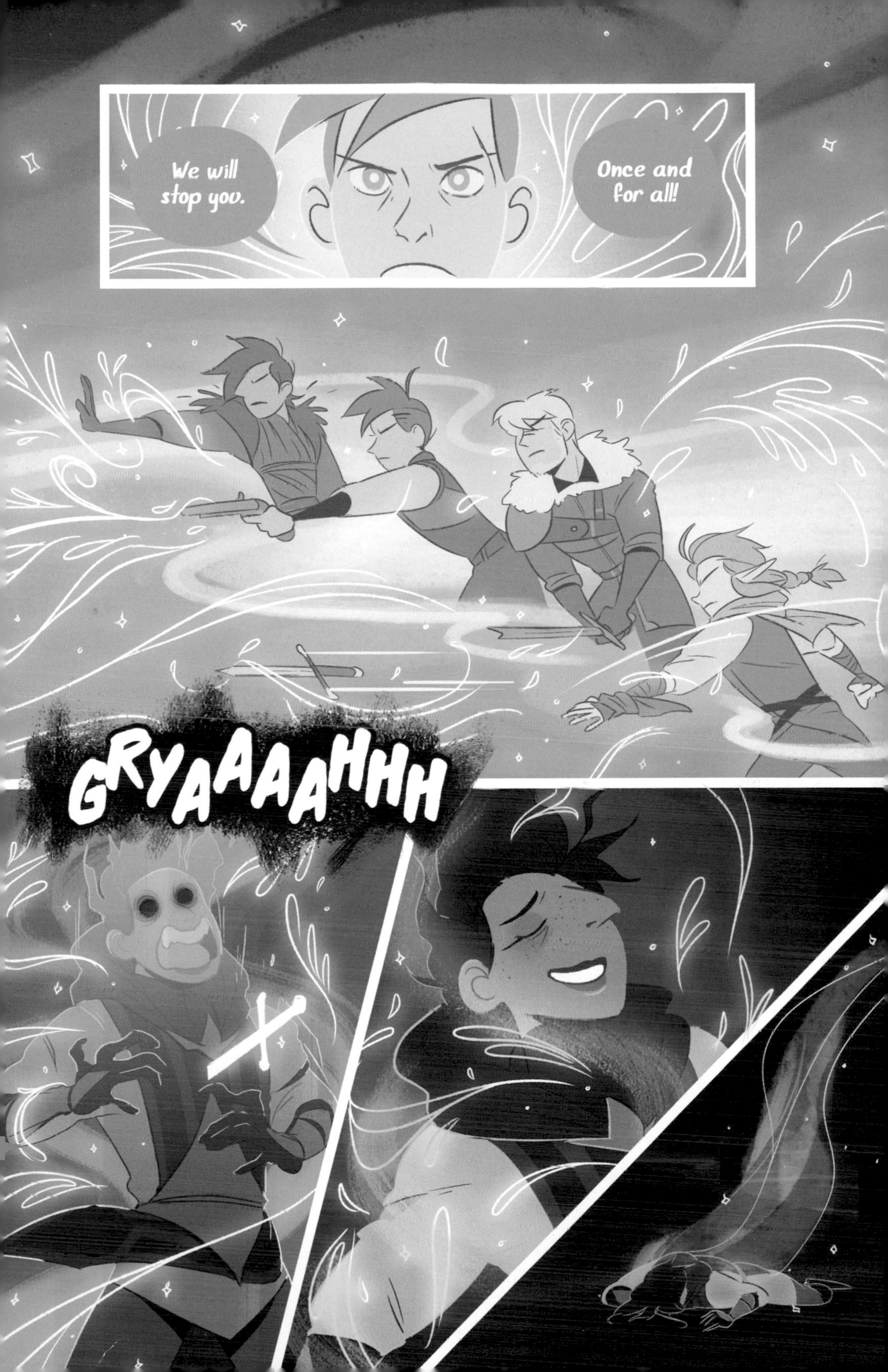
We will stop you.
Once and for all!
GRYAAAAHHH

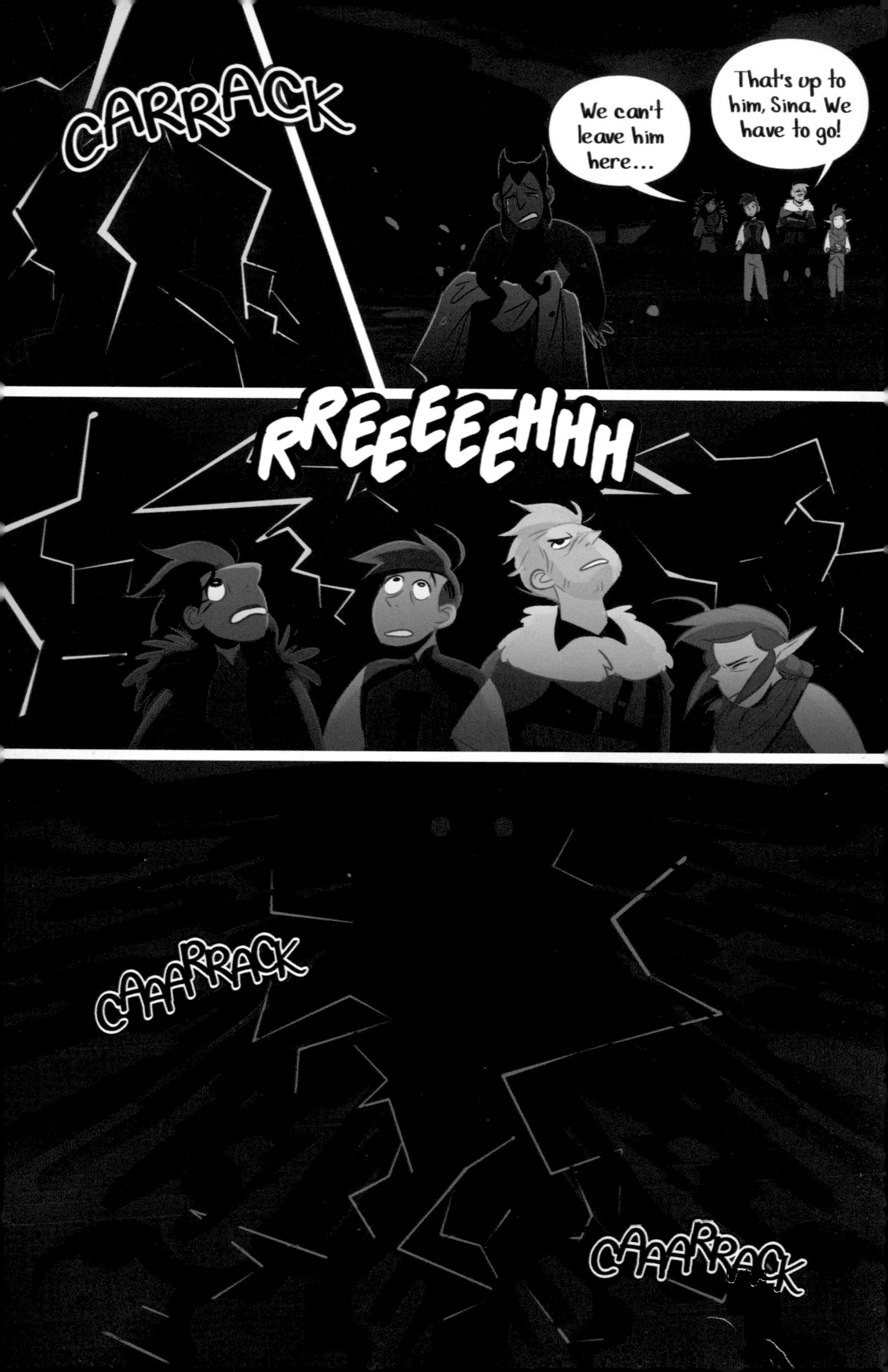

CARRACK
We can't leave him here...
That's up to him, Sina. We have to go!
RREEEEEHHHH
CAAARRACK
CAAARRACK

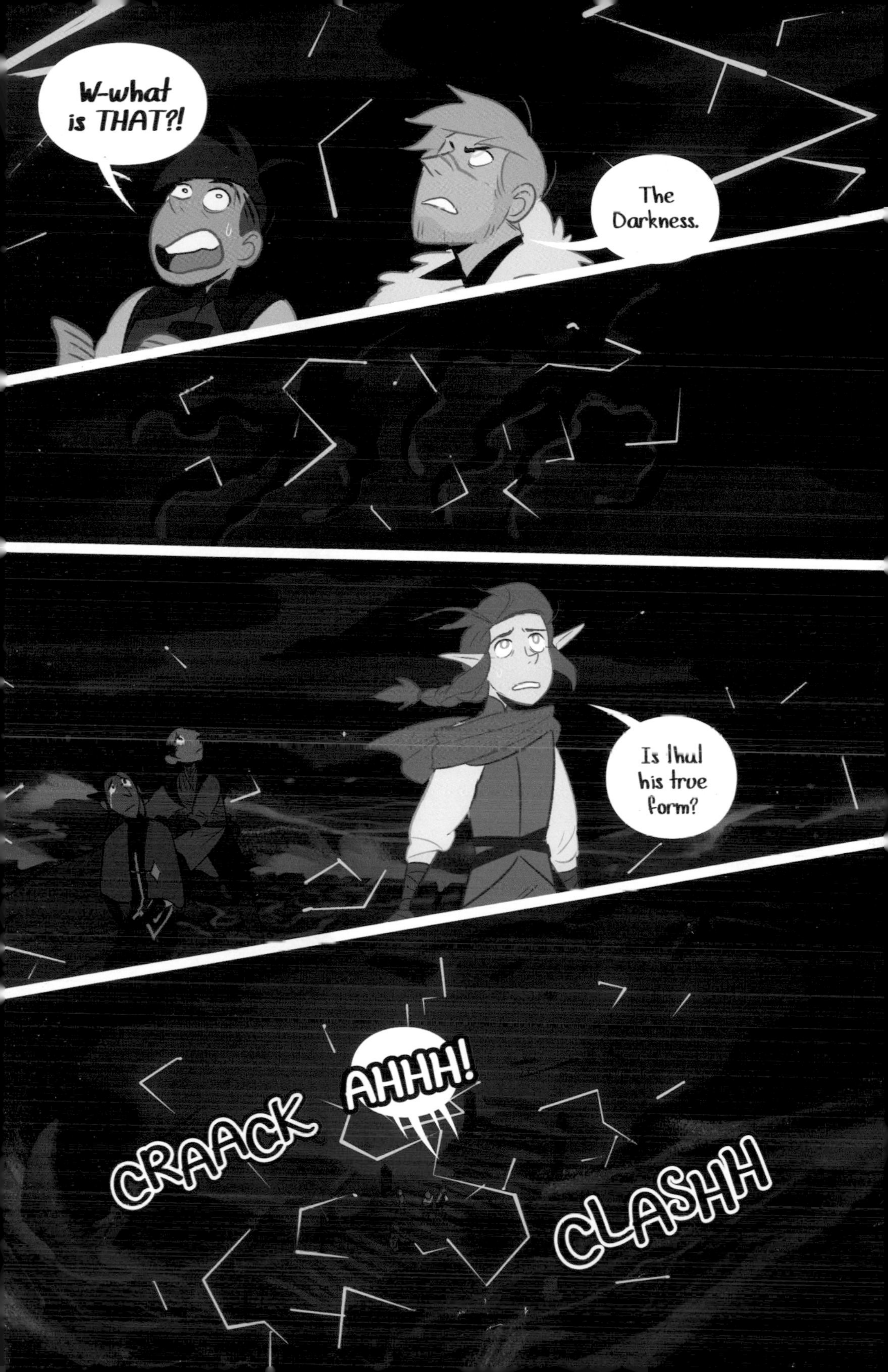
W-what is THAT?!
The Darkness.
Is that his true form?
CRAACK
AHHH!
CLASHH

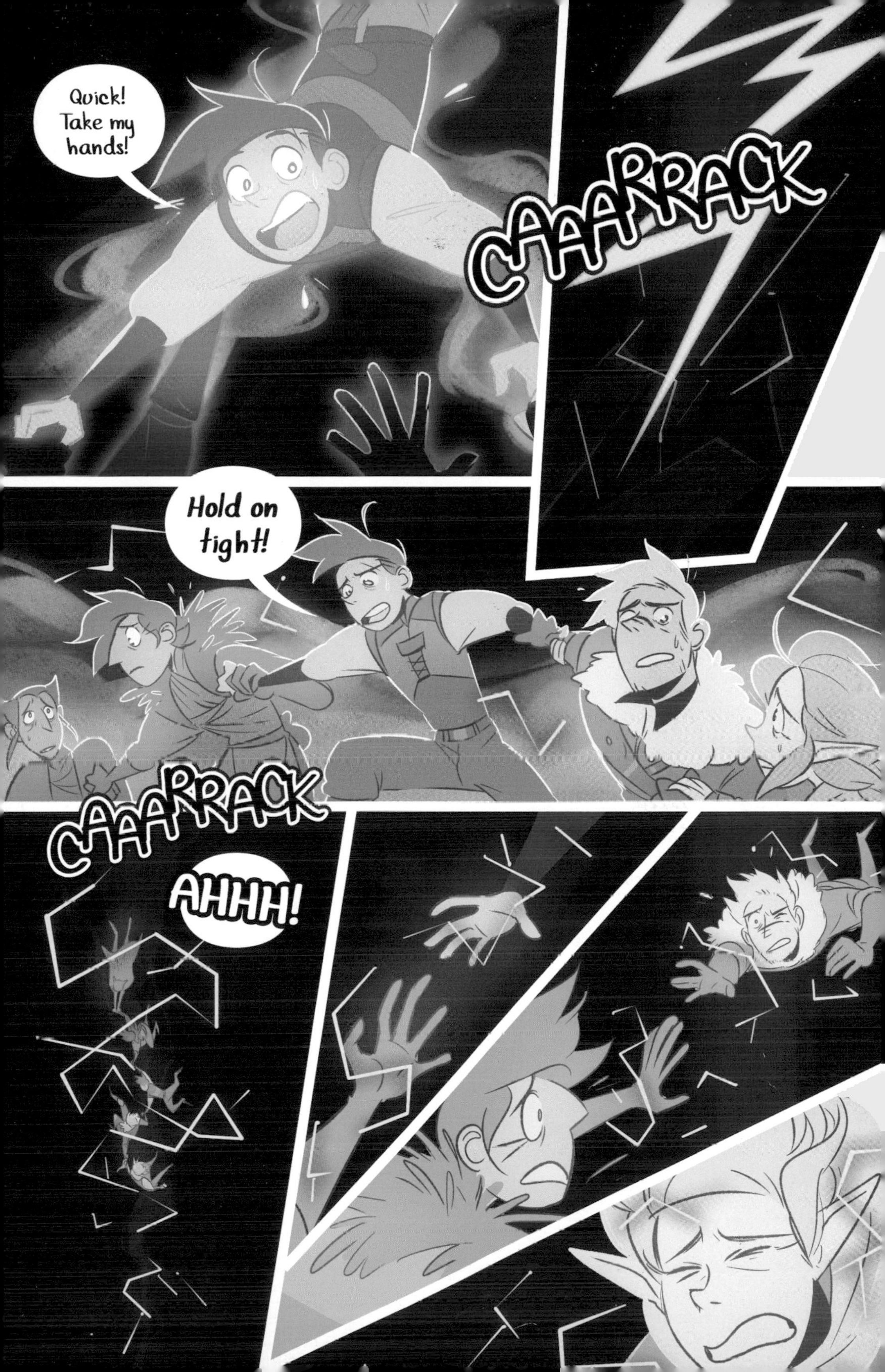
Quick! Take my hands!
CAAARRACK
Hold on tight!
CAAARRACK
AHHH!

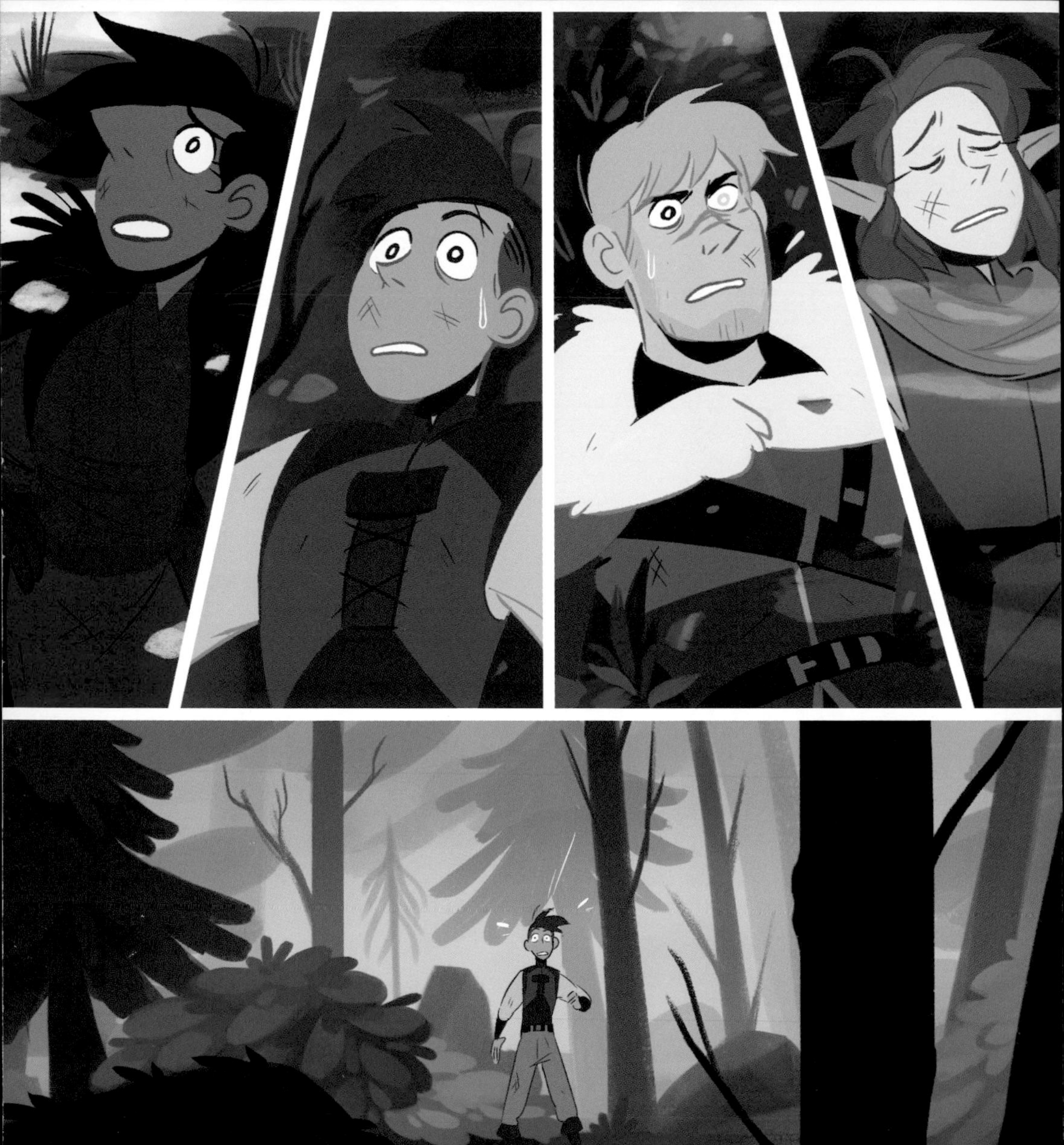

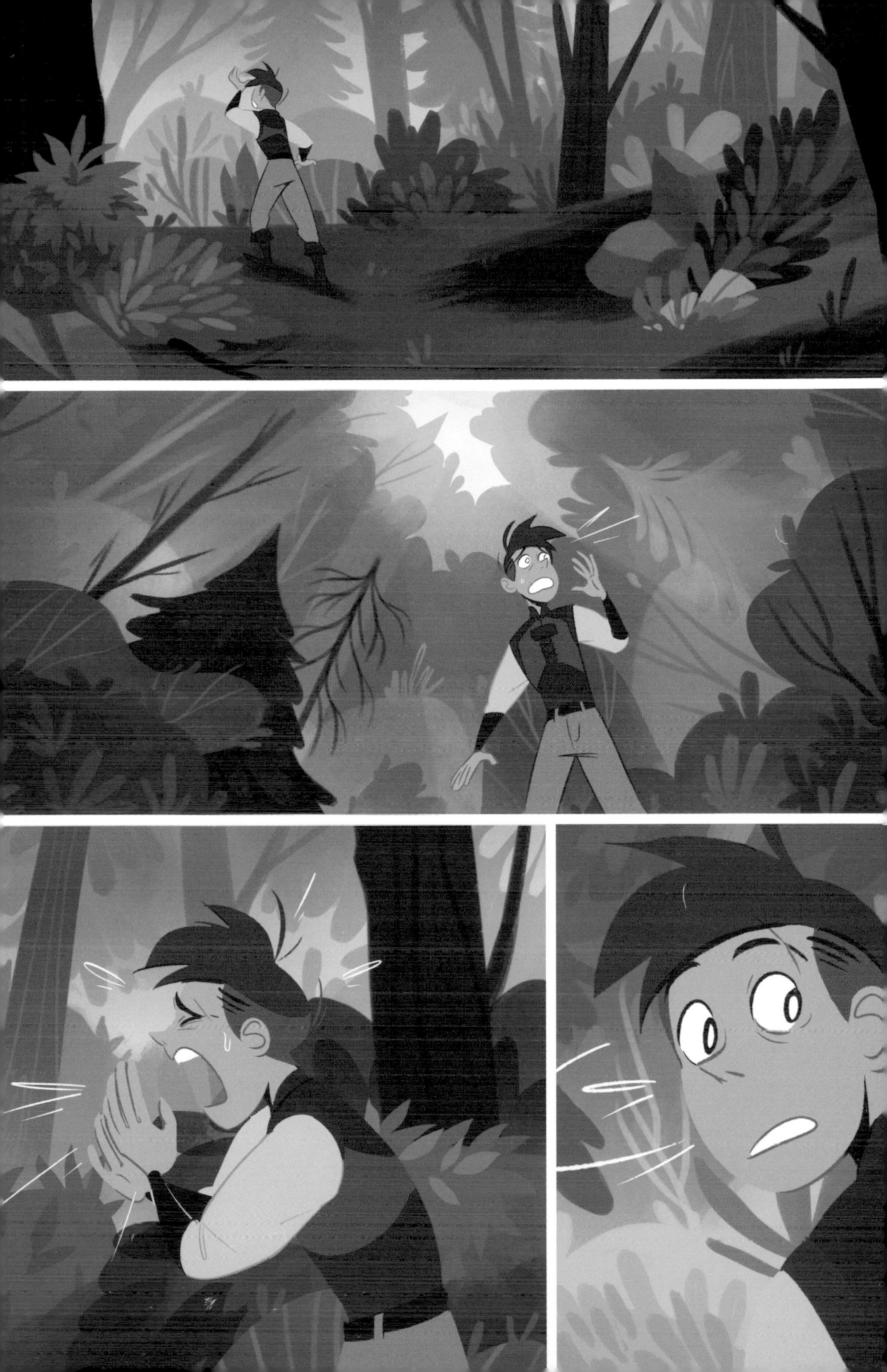

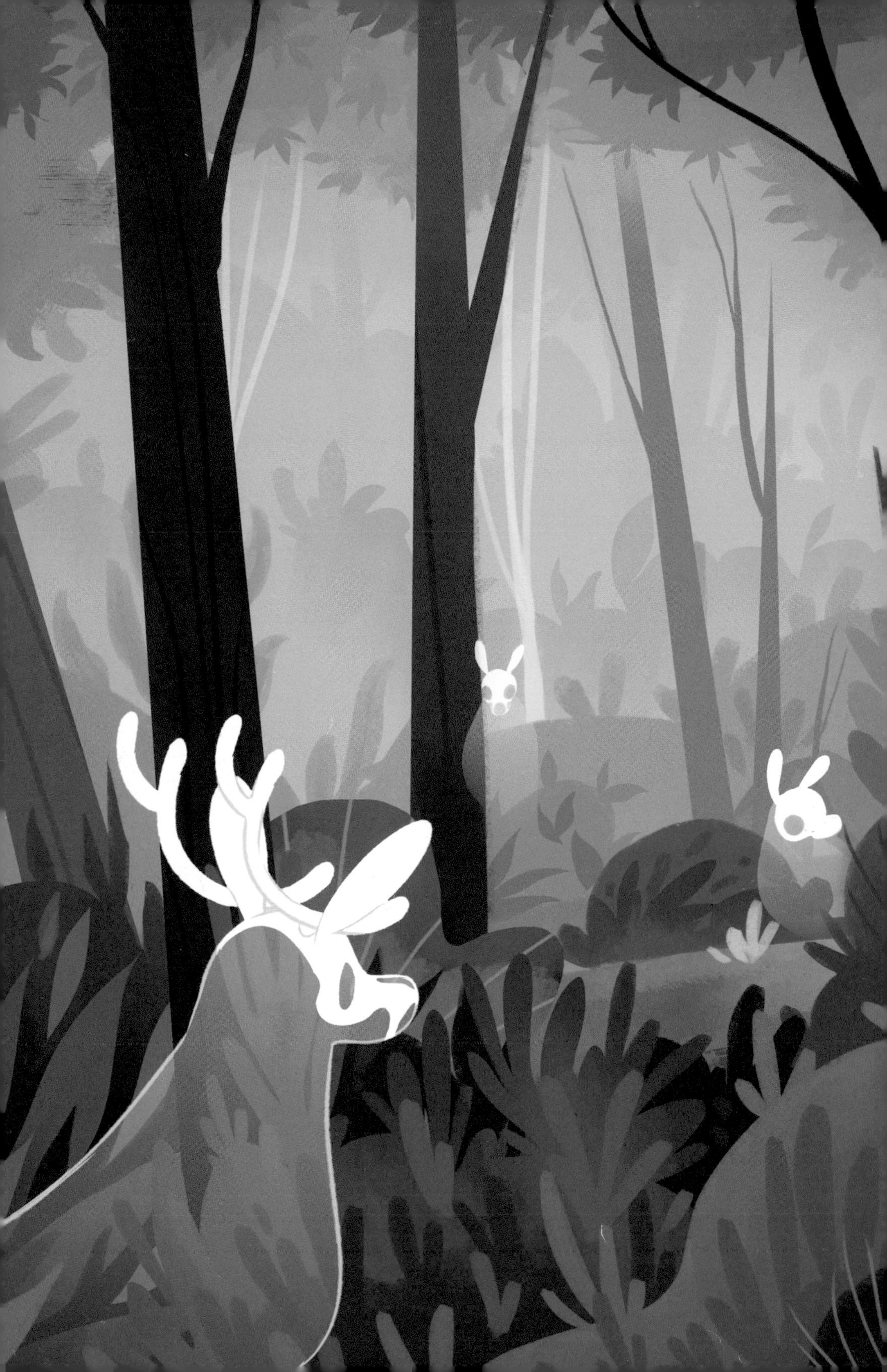

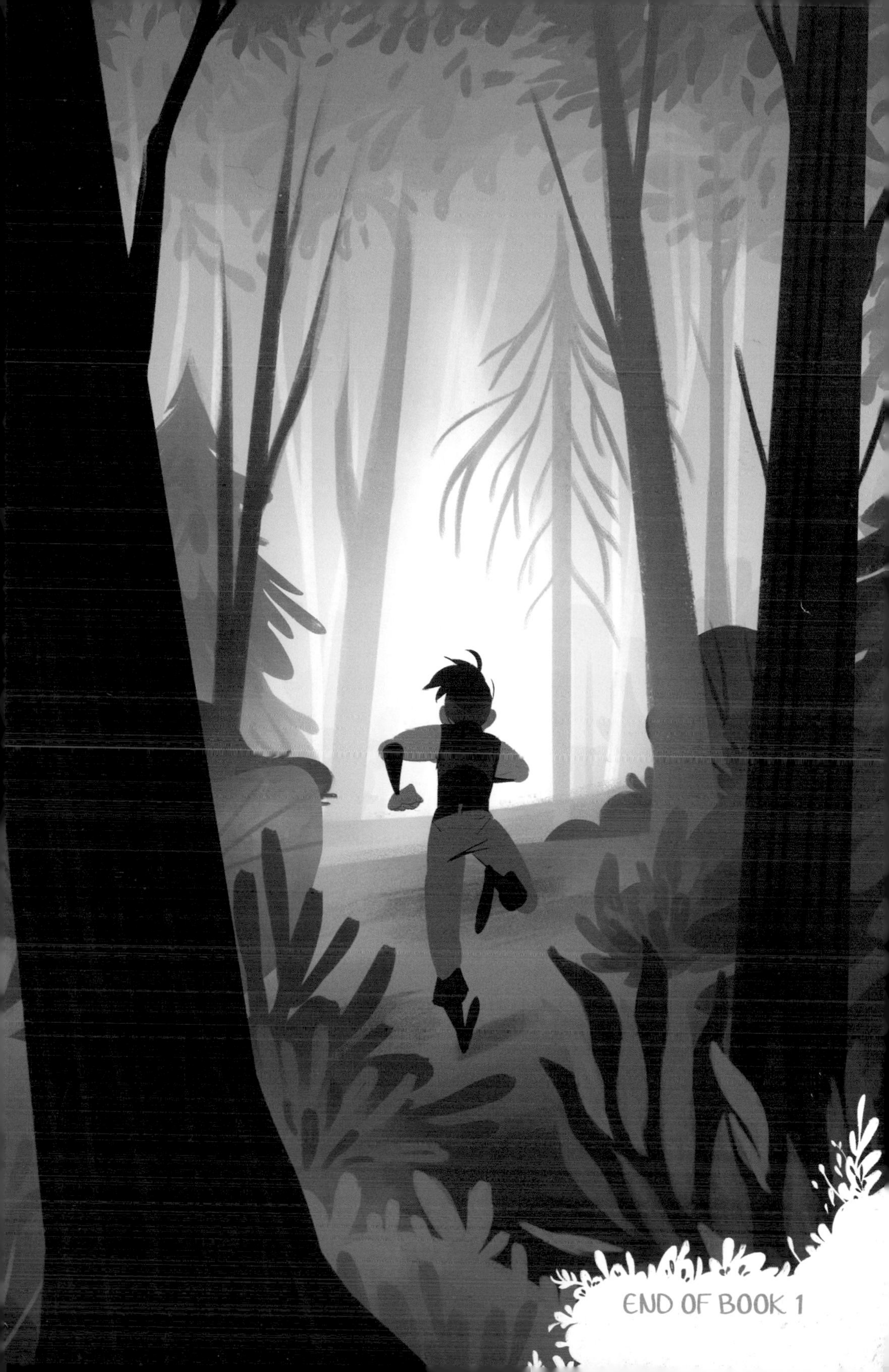
END OF BOOK 1

Acknowledgments

To all the people who were with us these past few years: thank you. Even if you believe you did nothing, those little nothings helped us get here.

Our beloved partners, Sergio and Luis, for your company, love, and understanding.

Our parents, siblings, nephew, and nieces, who maybe at first didn't understand the gist of it all but would still root for us.

Mark, for the comment we believed was spam, then made us believe that our project could be more.

Ben, Tanu, Molly, Amy and the team at Katherine Tegen for your patience and guidance.

To all the readers when this started as a little webcomic on the vast internet, and to our patrons that supported us through this entire process.

To you, reading this. Thank you.

—Ale and Fanny

STARTING NOTHING

This story, back in 2016, with only Nathan and Haven in our heads, was something for us to do for fun while drawing and writing stuff.

Many things changed since then, but some remained the same: Nothing was called "Granda," and Haven was a rebellious heir to the throne; Nathan has always been Nathan, a magnet for trouble.

In 2017, we decided to turn our silly little story into a webcomic, thinking it would be a great way to make a portfolio. We never expected things to happen the way they did.

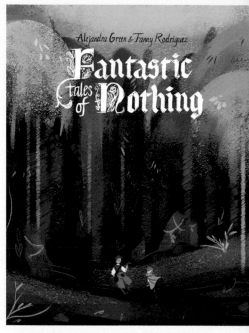

Early concept for creating a webcomic.

Nathan and Haven had a very different dynamic when we first created them.

HOW EVERYTHING WAS DONE

Each page is a labor of love, madness, and teamwork. Here's a quick view of how each page was done after the script was approved.

ough thumbnail from script

Cleaner sketch for review

Line art and flats

olored line art and details

Background painting

Final composition and lettering

Early concepts of Nathan and Haven

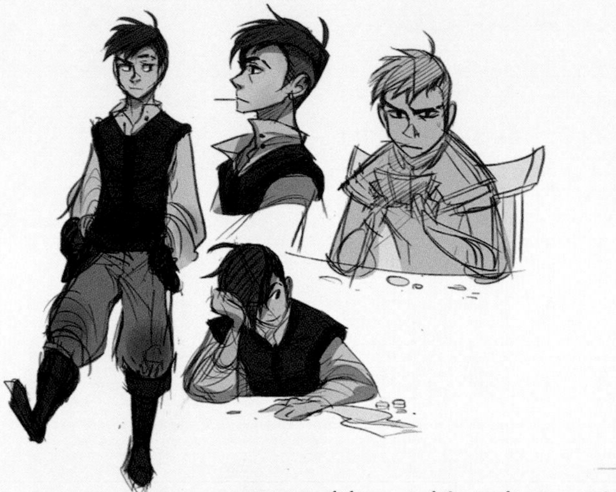

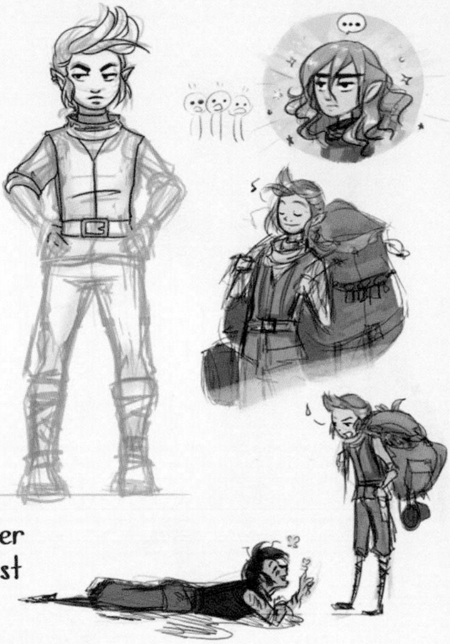

Haven changed the most from their earlier concept. Also, Ale says they're the hardest character for her to draw.

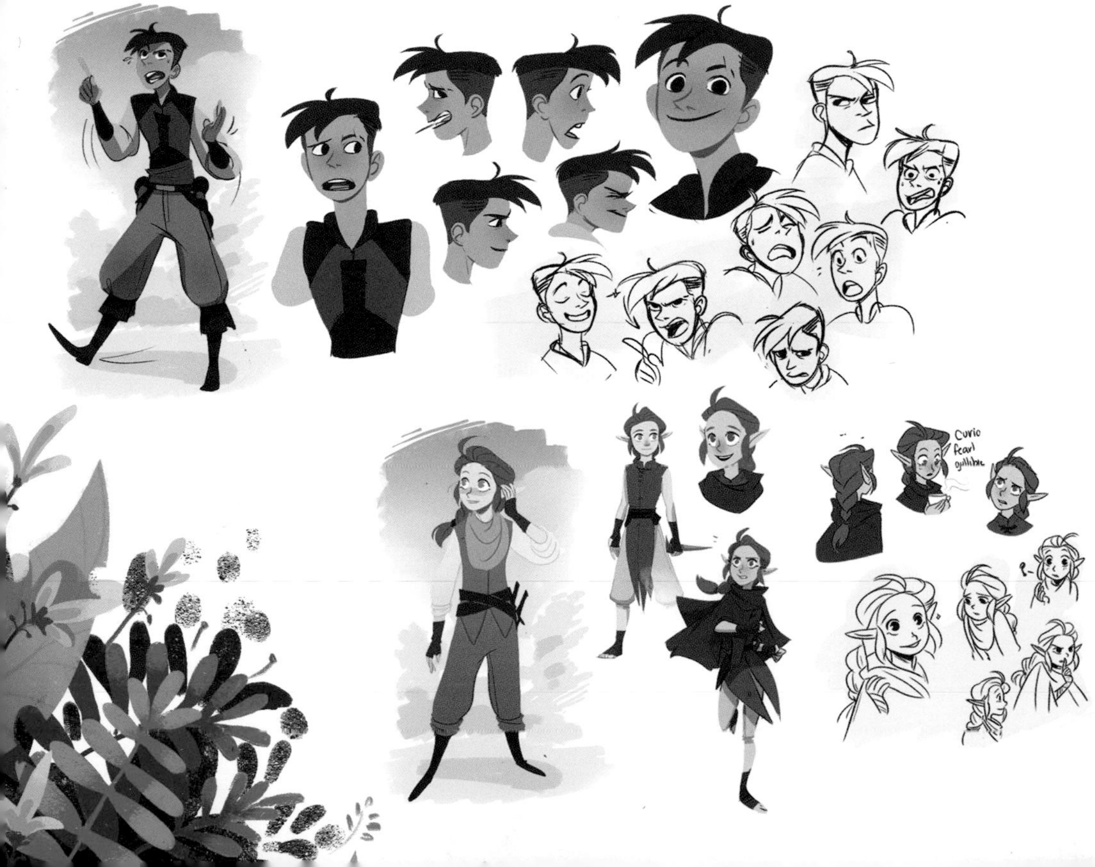
Curio

Early concepts of Sina and Bardou

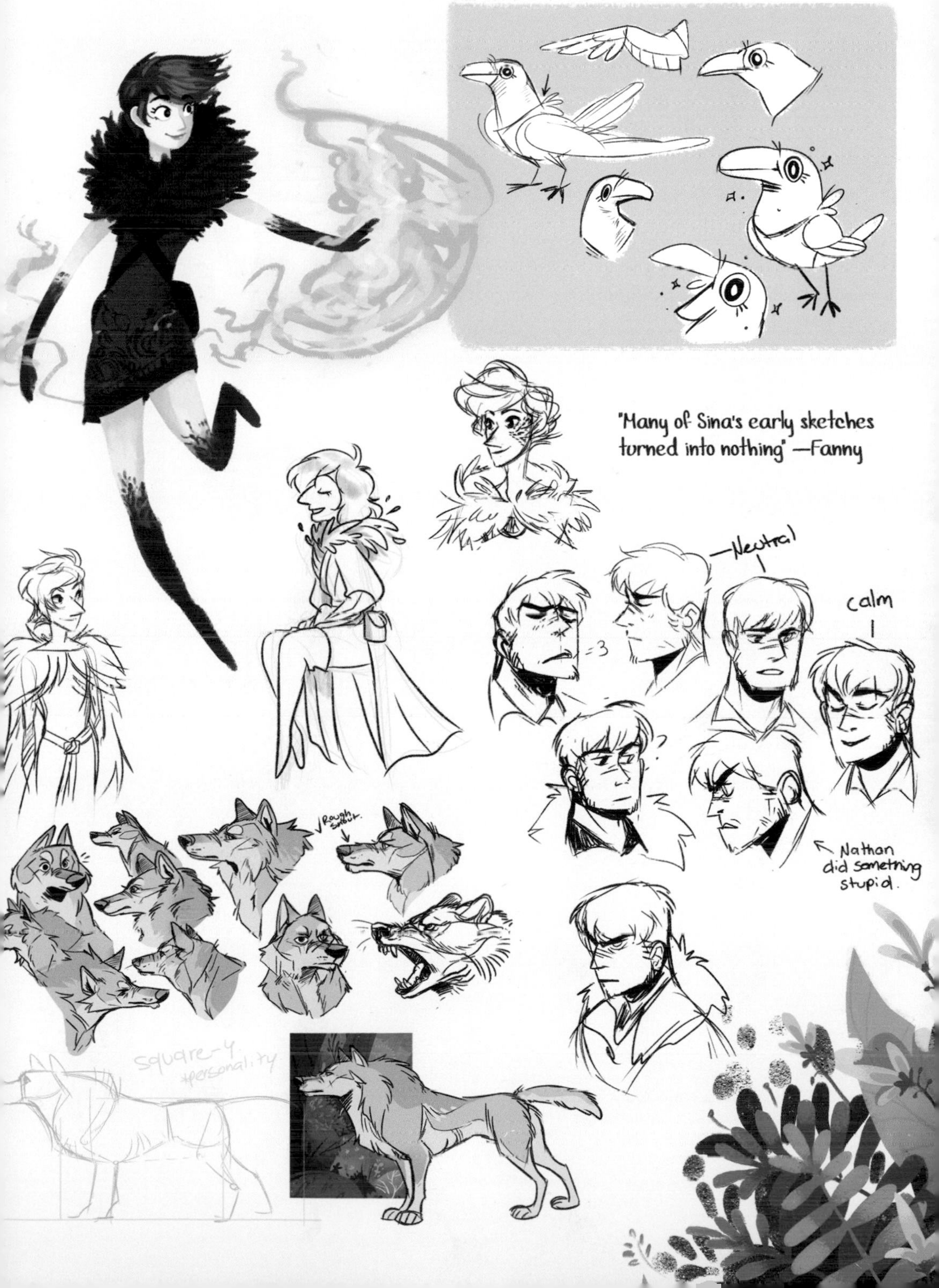

—Neutral
calm
Rough snout.
Nathan did something stupid.
square-4
*personality

"Many of Sina's early sketches turned into nothing" —Fanny

We love Renée and Naoki; they're fun to draw and write. We might simply have a bias and root for them secretly.

Fun fact: Naoki knows this is a book.

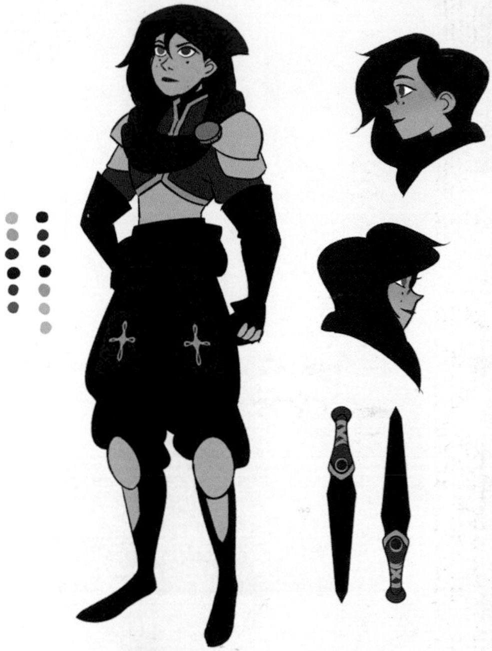

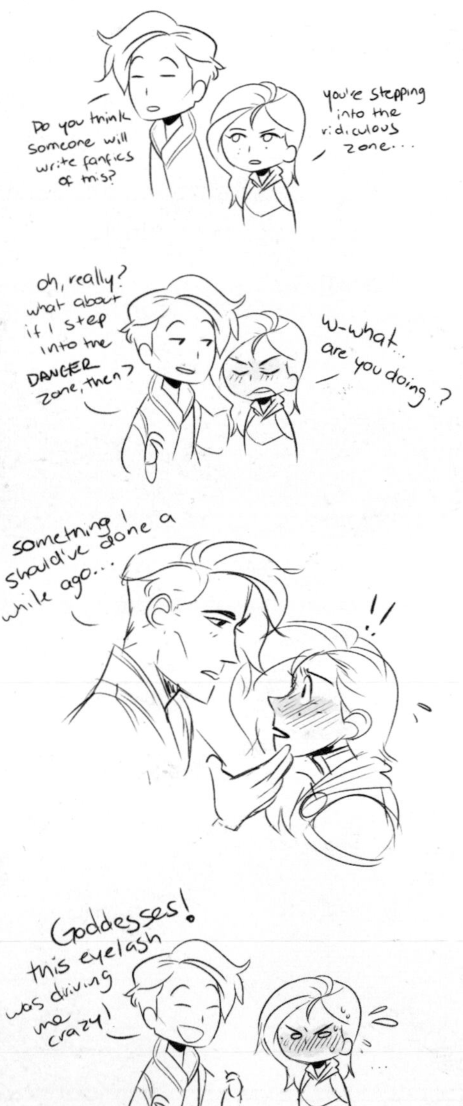
Do you think someone will write fanfics of this?
you're stepping into the ridiculous zone...
oh, really? what about if I step into the DANGER zone, then?
W-what... are you doing?
something I should've done a while ago...
!!
Goddesses! this eyelash was driving me crazy!

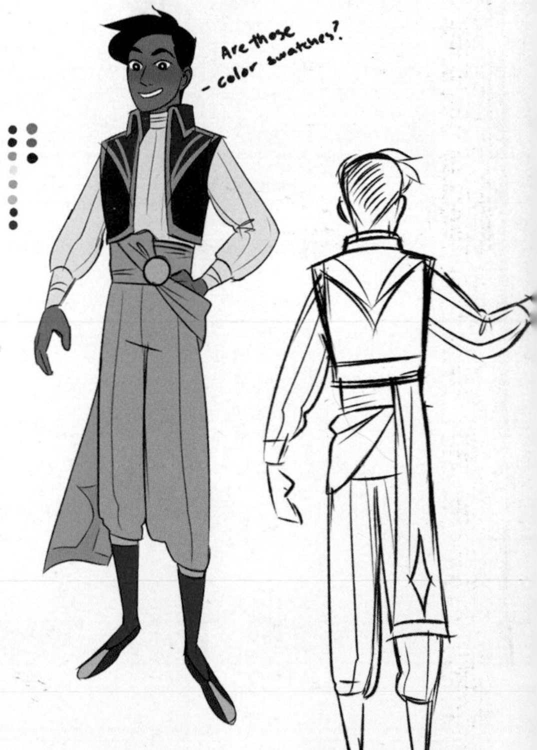
Are these color swatches?

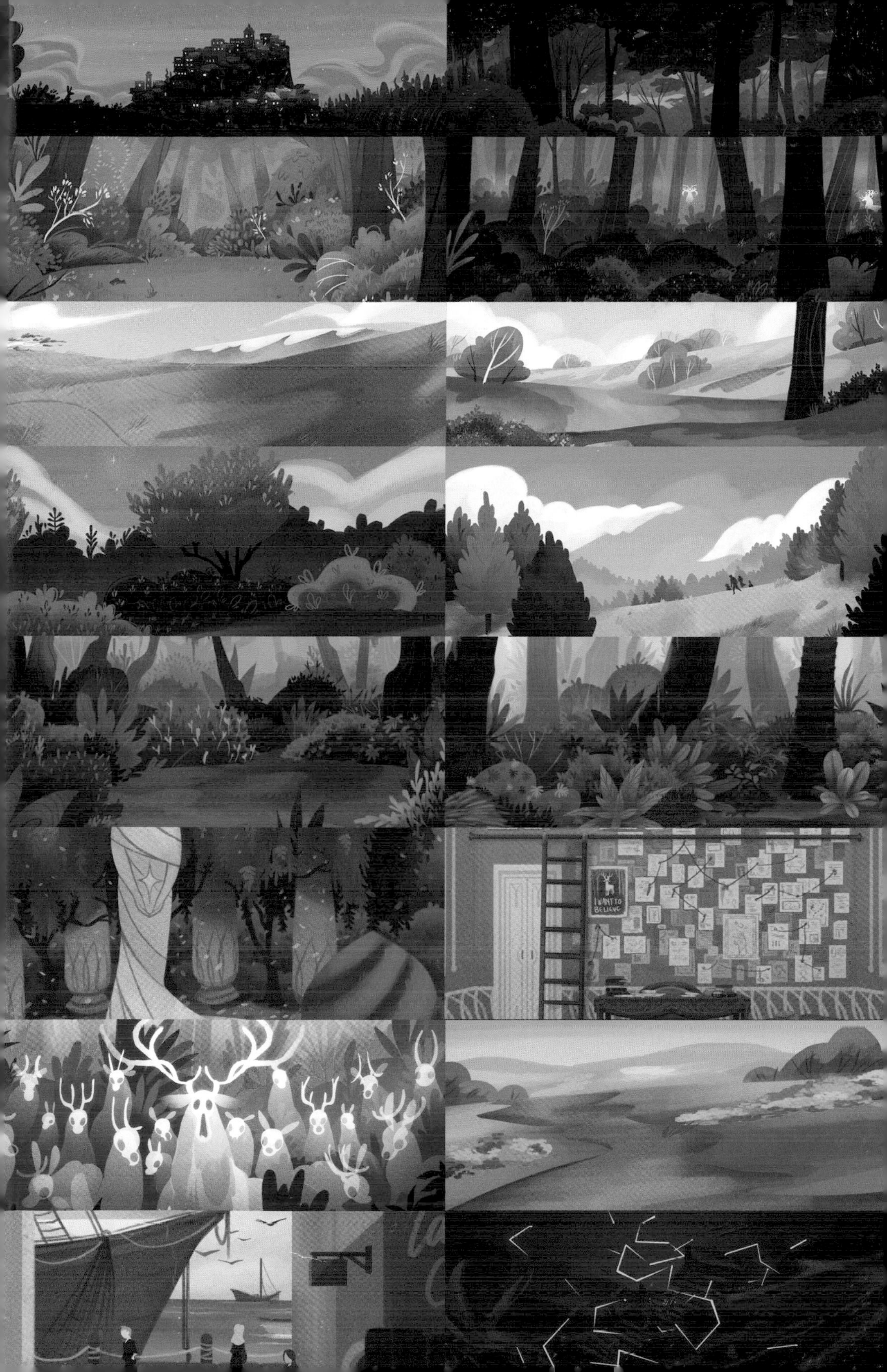
I WANT TO BELIEVE

A not so long time ago, two friends went on an adventure.
One that would change their lives...and ours too.

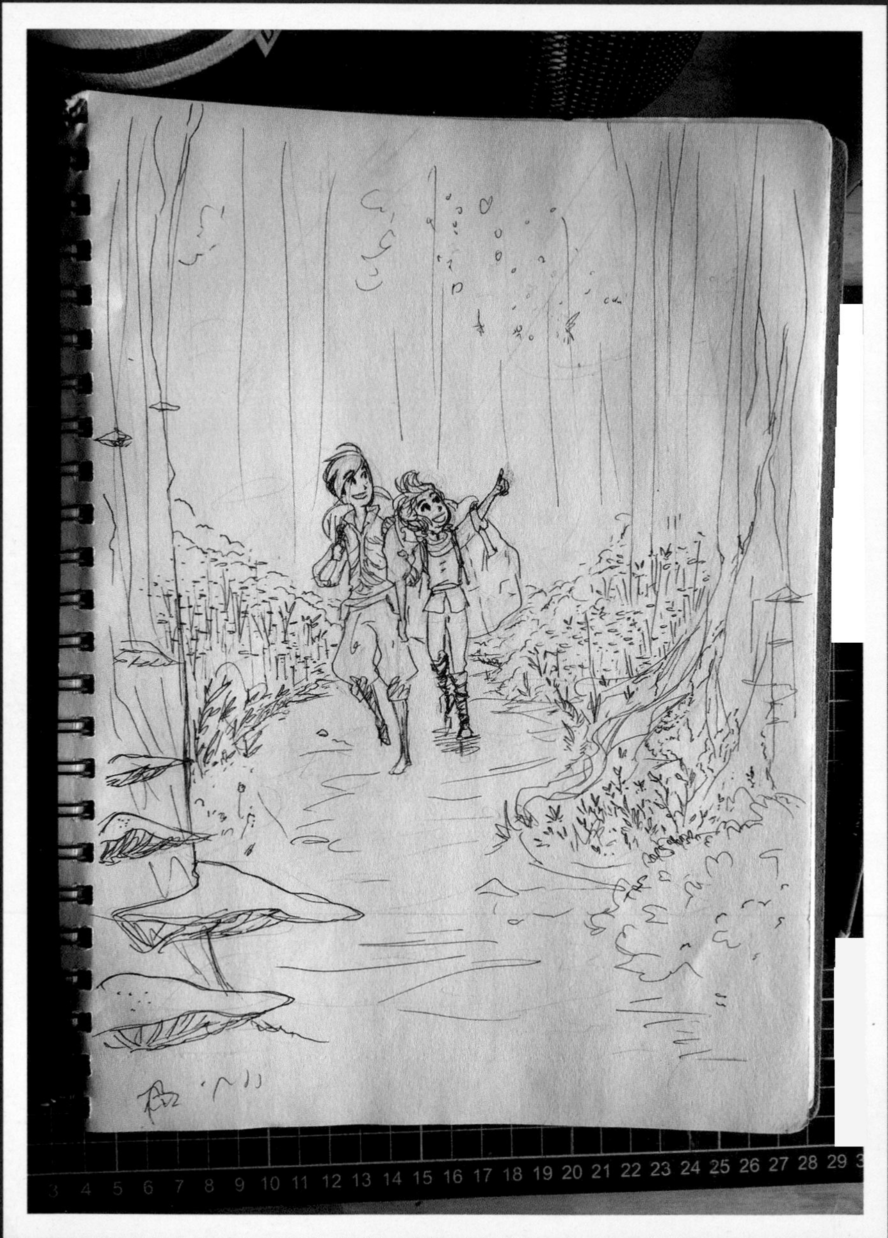
3 4 5 6 7 8 9 10 11 12 13 14 15 16 17 18 19 20 21 22 23 24 25 26 27 28 29

The very first doodle of *Fantastic Tales of Nothing*, back when Ale and I sat across from each other at our old job.